ELIZABETH & DARCY 2000

WHISPERS OF PEMBERLEY
TRILOGY

By FLORENCE GOLD

ELIZABETH AND DARCY 1800

ELIZABETH AND DARCY 1900

MR DARCY'S LEGACY

THE SOLE LOVE

STRUGGLE FOR LOVE

ELIZABETH'S COVENANT

PROMISE OF MARRIAGE

THE UNEXPECTED HEIRESS

MR DARCY'S FIGHT FOR LOVE

AND OTHER

By ANA DAMIAN

SCENARIO FOR LOVE

ELIZABETH & DARCY 2000

WHISPERS OF PEMBERLEY TRILOGY

FLORENCE GOLD

Editor: JO ABBOTT

&

ISBN: 9798879734522
Imprint: Independently published

*To my beloved
Grandparents*

CONTENTS

Foreword to the Trilogy 1

Florence's note 5

Prologue 7

Chapter 1 10

Chapter 2 33

Chapter 3 48

Chapter 4 55

Chapter 5 63

Chapter 6 66

Chapter 7 89

Chapter 8 97

Chapter 9 104

Chapter 10 111

Chapter 11 117

Chapter 12 125

Chapter 13 133

Chapter 14 143

Chapter 15 150

Chapter 16 160

Chapter 17 165

Chapter 18 170

Chapter 19 174

Chapter 20... 186

Chapter 21... 199

Chapter 22... 211

Chapter 23... 216

Chapter 24... 224

Chapter 25... 232

Chapter 26... 244

Chapter 27... 255

Chapter 28... 264

Chapter 29... 270

Chapter 30... 274

Chapter 31... 281

Chapter 32... 291

Chapter 33... 296

Chapter 34... 304

Chapter 35... 316

Chapter 36... 326

Chapter 37... 334

Chapter 38... 340

Chapter 39... 351

Chapter 40... 357

Chapter 41... 362

Chapter 42... 367

Chapter 43... 373

Chapter 44 379

Chapter 45 387

Chapter 46 399

Foreword to the Trilogy

Whispers of Pemberley is a three-volume series that presents a dynamic and original reinterpretation of Jane Austen's seminal work and timeless masterpiece, *Pride and Prejudice*, across three distinct epochs: the 19th, 20th, and 21st centuries.

While in each volume of the series the iconic names *Elizabeth* and *Darcy* are utilised for the main characters, only *E&D 1800* is a variation of *Pride and Prejudice*.

The subsequent two volumes stand as self-contained narratives intricately woven into their respective centuries, utilising coincidences and unique circumstances to maintain the names of the principal characters from the beloved Austen classic.

One need not be a devoted Jane Austen enthusiast to enjoy the plots, as each volume offers a standalone romance that can be savoured independently. Nevertheless, for fervent Austen aficionados, *Whispers of Pemberley* offers a captivating journey through both her personal life and literary realm.

Florence Gold, a profound admirer of Jane Austen, embraces the widely acknowledged notion that Austen played a pivotal role in shaping the modern woman in literature. Characters like Elizabeth Bennet, Elinor

Dashwood, Fanny Price, Catherine Morland, Emma Woodhouse, and Anne Elliot have all, in their distinct ways, contributed to shaping the image of modern women eager to embrace new roles within society and the family.

The three-volume series emerges from the author's wish to honour the life and work of Jane Austen, whose enduring legacy inspired and motivated her successors to play an instrumental role in advancing the cause of women throughout the 20th century. Furthermore, the emergence of a new archetype of man—supportive and appreciative of female achievements—owes much to Austen's portrayal of her male characters.

Elizabeth & Darcy 1800 is a *variation of Pride and Prejudice.*
An unexpected variation, *Elizabeth & Darcy 1800* adheres closely to the canonical plotline, with one notable departure—our beloved Elizabeth Bennet decides to pursue writing not long after rejecting Mr Darcy's proposal.

Defying the norms of the 1800s, much like Austen herself, Elizabeth embarks on a journey to fulfil her aspirations, ultimately finding love along the way.

Elizabeth & Darcy 1900 revolves around Elizabeth Austen, Jane Austen's great-grandniece, and Neville Darcy Lancashire, the future Duke of Lancashire. Set against the backdrop of World War I's final years, their narrative delves into Elizabeth's internal conflict between being a wife and pursuing her calling as a nurse on the European battlefields.

Thankfully, in 1900, much like Elizabeth Bennet, Elizabeth Austen discovers the perfect gentleman who wishes to marry her against all the odds. He ultimately becomes an enlightened partner, supporting her in all her ventures. With the backing of her husband, in 1922, Elizabeth Austen Lancashire chronicles her struggles in a highly successful novel entitled *Elizabeth's Diary*, which is often referenced in the third volume of the series.

While *E&D 1900* pays homage to all the Elizabeths around the world, *E&D 2000*, the third volume, celebrates the Darcys—generous, honest, and forward-thinking gentlemen who dare to change themselves, eager to spend a lifetime with the perpetually intrepid, sarcastic, witty, and wonderful Elizabeths.

Elizabeth & Darcy 2000 is a captivating love story infused with suspense, humour, and passion.

Elizabeth Collister, heiress to a multimedia empire, finds her world upended by her father's death. Along with the daunting task of managing her father's vast company, she is thrust into a quest fuelled by his obsession—to find Darcy Egerton, the enigmatic author whose true identity has eluded everyone ever since his debut novel was rejected by their publishing house.

As Elizabeth navigates the complexities of her inheritance and grapples with her growing affection for a refined earl, her life spirals into a whirlwind of intrigue, passion, heartbreak, and familial machinations. Love threads through this tumultuous journey, ultimately leading Elizabeth to a destination where the unexpected converges with the inevitable, ending in the glorious love that Jane Austen once depicted.

Florence's note

In the novel's conclusion, readers encounter additional information about certain literary characters or events mentioned throughout the narrative. While these details are not critical for comprehending the story's main plotline, the author includes them to cater to those who might have an interest in the historical and literary context surrounding the novel or need an explanation about the connections between this novel and the other two of the Trilogy.

Prologue

"I want to see you as often as possible," Thomas Collister told his daughter Elizabeth. "Because you're the only one who can still look into my eyes and share a meaningful conversation. Not because I love you more, as Kath said last evening."

"It was interesting to hear that she thinks you love me more. All my life, I thought you loved her more."

Thomas smiled. "Did Mr Bennet love Jane more?"

"Come on, Dad, Kath isn't Jane. In fact, she's as far from Jane as she is from any of Jane Austen's characters."

"What about Lydia Bennet?" Mr Collister asked, gazing at her playfully—a rarity these days.

"Maybe. A Lydia with a lot of brains, incredible talents, and a ton of money to do exactly what she wants."

"I love you two differently. Kath's my weakness…while you…you are my assurance that Collister won't die with me."

"That's not a very nice thought for either of us." Elizabeth smiled, surprised by his burst of sincerity. "I don't know what Kath would think, but to me, it sounds like you only need me for the business, and you're manipulating me even now."

"Well, then I'm manipulating you into being an incredible leader and future managing director, who will create a new destiny for Collister, deeply connected to these times. Elizabeth, I love you with all my heart, and I'm grateful for your presence. For talking to me, not mourning."

"With a huge effort," Elizabeth replied. She took a sedative an hour before every meeting with her father—it was the only way. But speaking to him was so important that nothing else mattered, not even an addiction.

"Today is about Darcy Egerton—[1]"

"No—" she interrupted him, but Thomas held up his hand, asking her silently to listen to him. It took a lot of effort for him to speak—not because he was in pain but because he was horribly tired.

"Please, Elizabeth, just today. Then, we'll discuss whatever you want…if there's still time."

Elizabeth nodded, thinking the sedative hadn't been strong enough, feeling the tears ready to fall. She was prepared to discuss even Darcy Egerton if that would please him and make him believe that he was still connected to the world.

"I know you disapprove of my decision to shift our focus for the 2017 celebration from our company's 150th anniversary to a commemoration of Jane Austen 200 years after her death. But life has taken so much from me. At 68, I still have so many ideas to bring to life. My mind's brimming with plans. However, I've got to restrain myself and concentrate on this event. And for me, Jane Austen is of the utmost importance. Not just for me, but also for Collister Publishing."

"I understand, Dad, but Jane Austen's connected to Darcy Egerton for you."

"I won't waste precious time arguing with you. Yes, I have this obsession that he'll write the novel we need to crown our celebration next year."

Elizabeth avoided looking at him, fearing that her eyes would betray her opposition and frustration.

She remained silent for a long while, allowing him to regain his strength. However, as he began speaking again, she noticed the dangerous gleam in his eyes that appeared every time Darcy Egerton was brought up.

"Elizabeth, to cut to the chase, I have come to terms with…with my impending death, but I have one more favour to ask. The last one."

"From whom, Dad?" Elizabeth asked, no longer a grieving daughter but his debating partner—sarcastic, intelligent, and prepared to find flaws in his reasoning.

"From…I don't know, from Zeus and Aton, from Jesus, Allah, or Lord Shiva, the destroyer of worlds—all of them, or simply from a universe that can't be entirely lifeless."

"And what's the favour?" she asked, although she already had suspicions. Nine years ago, in 2007, Collister Publishing had rejected Darcy Egerton's first novel. Since then, the horrible mistake had continued to haunt her father, as Darcy Egerton became one of the most renowned writers of the age.

Thomas Collister fixed her with an intense gaze, as if he wanted to remember every feature of her face and the world surrounding them, knowing it would fade for him all too soon. He coughed, then spoke almost serenely, "To give *you* Darcy Egerton."

Chapter 1

Three months later

"Jane Austen, really? Is *she* going to test us on whether we've read all those novels?" Roland Barkley asked. No one in the large gathering was surprised by his provocative tone; questioning everything was his habit.

"No, *she* is getting married and wants you all to know!" Grace replied, and the entire room burst into laughter.

She was Elizabeth Collister, and they were expecting her in the Grand Hall—the name that room had held since the beginning of Collister Publishing in 1867. Not much had changed in its decor since then. Rarely used, it made sense to convene there when the meeting was about Jane Austen and the upcoming commemoration of the two hundred years since her death.

On the walls, the Collisters who had previously led the company watched them with rather serious looks from different eras. Only Thomas Collister smiled, perhaps to mark the vast changes his company had undergone during his reign.

"Are you daydreaming about marriage, Grace?" Elizabeth's voice resounded, despite the noise in the room. Silence fell, and all eyes turned to the antique bookshelves. Unbelievably, one of them turned out to be a hidden door.

"An old passage." Elizabeth laughed, seeing their astonished expressions. "A team worked all night to make it functional. But it was worth the effort. It makes for a good entrance."

As nobody moved, she laughed again and said, "Come on, guys, I'm not a ghost. This modern world has ripped away everyone's imagination and zest for adventure!" She turned and pushed a book that looked exactly like all the others, and the door opened again to allow Cybil Collister—Elizabeth's mother—to enter.

Only then did the people in the room relax and spontaneously applaud. It was the first time they had seen the lady since her husband had fallen ill.

At sixty, Cybil Collister looked forty. It was not just due to her elegant figure or perfect complexion but also her distinguished and composed demeanour. She looked like a queen among her subjects. The only sign of her grief was in her eyes, which betrayed her profound sadness. She gave a friendly smile and a nod to acknowledge the applause before sitting at Elizabeth's invitation, in Thomas Collister's place at the head of the table.

"Is anybody missing?" Elizabeth asked, and like a bolt of lightning that flashed through the room, they all saw how much she resembled her father. Her stance recalled how they had known their boss, always dominating the room, attentive to everything that happened in his business and interested in the people working for him.

"Almost," Grace replied, looking at the list before her. "Only Kath's missing."

"Kath's coming," Mrs Collister interjected, trying again to shield her youngest daughter from the troubles she continually stirred up.

But Elizabeth was not as tolerant. Not embarrassed—like their mother—she was instead angry. It was one of her sister's many whims and was unacceptable. Not being on time for such an important meeting was too much even for her.

Her incapacity to grow up is like an illness, Elizabeth thought, but she made an effort to recover her composure. That day was about their father, and she wanted to enjoy it with all her heart.

"And Roland—this meeting is about us, as my father wanted. But Collister, in the coming months, is synonymous with Jane Austen. Do I approve of that? Probably not wholeheartedly. Do I adhere to the strategy Thomas Collister devised? Absolutely, because it was our boss's last wish!" Elizabeth replied to the head of Collister Music.

She then turned all her attention to the door, knowing what would happen next.

Thomas Collister's commemoration ritual was about to start.

To everyone's surprise, the room was invaded by waiters pushing trolleys. An enticing smell enveloped the place—a mixture of coffee and hot food emanating from the steaming trays covered with bell-shaped stainless-steel lids.

"We are beginning with breakfast, as Thomas intended for today," Mrs Collister explained. They smiled with nostalgia, as it was typical of Thomas Collister to plan everything in detail.

"The best breakfast in London, from Simpson's Tavern, as my husband used to say," she added, the last words drowned out by the uproar that followed.

Their former boss, who had passed away three months ago, had eaten every morning at Simpson's Tavern, and his first meeting of the day was always in front of a copious breakfast.

"Eggs Benedict, croissants, and coffee. That's what Dad used to have, and we'll also enjoy what Simpson's Tavern offers at breakfast today."

Once again, everybody applauded, but a hint of regret lingered in that joyful atmosphere, as their old boss was no longer with them.

Elizabeth struggled to hold back her tears. So often in the last few years, she had joined him for breakfast, enjoying the meal and preparing for the day to come together. They all shared that memory, as Thomas often invited one or more of them to breakfast, depending on the daily issues he needed to resolve.

It was the natural way to start their meeting; to remember Thomas—the man who had built an empire from the publishing house he'd inherited from his ancestors.

The idea belonged to Kath, as she was spirited and unrestrained, creative and joyful, but never on time, not even for events she herself organised, or for the commemoration of her father, whom she had adored.

"Eat and speak," said Mrs Collister—her husband's famous words that all breakfast guests heard no matter how often they joined Thomas.

And Elizabeth spoke as it fell upon her to open the conversation. "My dear Grace," she said, "I have no intention of getting married!" Those unexpected words had their intended effect. Everyone stared at her, while Grace wondered whether she was angry. But it was impossible to discern what their new boss thought.

"Don't look at me like that. Eat! You heard what my mother said."

Elizabeth wasn't angry, not even with Kath, as all that mattered that morning was her father.

"However, your words are the best opening for a project dedicated by Thomas Collister to Jane Austen."

"It was a joke, Elizabeth," Grace said, trying to understand what was happening.

"Perhaps. But joke or not, it shows that the main question regarding a woman, two hundred years after Jane Austen's death, is still whether she's found a husband."

Marianne smiled. Elizabeth's introduction to the

challenging meeting had been brilliant, and she felt better for the first time in months. Collister was in good hands. She looked at her new boss and asked, "Are you saying that after two hundred years, women haven't changed? Are they still primarily looking to marry, even if they have other rights and opportunities?"

"Yes, that's exactly what I'm suggesting. Deep down, the same inclination persists in many women of our time. If Mrs Bennet were here, at our breakfast, she'd probably look around this table to find out how many of the ladies are married." And she pointed to Jane Austen's portrait on the wall, drawn by her sister Cassandra—the author's only known and verified likeness.

"No," Marianne said. "If Mrs Bennet were here, she would have said, 'have you heard that Netherfield Park is let at last?' Or the modern version, 'We have a new project manager at Collister…Park!'"

Elizabeth nodded with a smile, indicating their new colleague, who had the challenging mission of coordinating the teams for Jane Austen's celebration.

"Marianne's right. However, it wasn't rude on my part. Before introducing our new project manager, I wanted to welcome Jane Austen into our lives," Elizabeth said, looking at the young woman, the only one formally dressed for an official meeting. "Allow me to introduce our Jane Austen project manager, Anna Wilson. You'll find her office on the nineteenth floor of the new building, and I'm sure everyone in this room will collaborate with her in the coming months."

"Is she married?" Andrew asked from across the table.

"Andrew Miller, our CEO." Elizabeth smiled. "And *he* is not married!"

"I hope they aren't scaring you!" Mrs Collister's voice was almost joyful. She had feared the meeting would make her deeply sad and despairing. Yet, she felt at ease among these people who had worked with Thomas, admired him, and brought his incredible ideas to life. Then, unexpectedly, anger besieged her motherly sentiments. She couldn't understand why Kath wasn't there to fulfil her father's last wish. For a moment, nobody spoke, waiting for her to continue, and she finally said, "Welcome to Collister, Miss Wilson!"

"Anna," she said. "Unmarried." Despite her spirited response, she felt uncomfortable. She had prepared for days for that first meeting, only to find a profoundly strange gathering. In her imagination, the top management of Collister were a group of professional executives, like those she had encountered in other companies, but she was wrong. She was the only one who hadn't touched the food, trying hard not to show her shock at the sight of those people eating and speaking while waiters moved around silently.

It was a peculiar atmosphere, and it made her wonder whether these people genuinely managed the company. It bore little resemblance to one of the most prestigious publishing houses in the United Kingdom; it seemed more like a hospital for the mentally ill. The managing director had appeared through a secret passage, they had eaten breakfast, and the CEO had asked her if she was married— a deeply sexist and troubling remark.

She'd felt on top of the world a month ago when she'd landed the job. A Jane Austen project at Collister Publishing was like being knighted. From there, she could choose her position in the publishing world. Collister owned four of the most prestigious magazines in the country, and maybe even globally; the publishing house had one hundred and fifty years of tradition, while some new departments were gaining prominence in the market, like Collister Education, Collister Digital, and Collister Advertising. Dressed in her best suit after studying business fashion trends for a long time, she now found herself in a room full of T-shirts, trainers, and ripped jeans. Only Mrs Collister looked elegant in her haute couture suit, and even Elizabeth Collister was dressed in jeans. Luckily, she was also wearing a stylish white shirt that saved her outfit.

"Eat," a man near her said kindly. "It's the ultimate breakfast. Hard to find anything better!"

He laughed at her stunned expression. "Sorry. Henry— not married. Head of Collister Digital."

Fortunately, they seemed to forget about her quickly, as Andrew Miller spoke. Obviously—even to a stranger like Anna—he wasn't in the best mood that morning.

"From your comments about marriage, Elizabeth, I suspect you're still the fervent feminist from Somerville College."

The table fell silent again. If Andrew intended to be humorous or sarcastic, his question sounded only combative and angry. He was ten years older than Elizabeth. In his heart, he'd dreamt that Thomas would appoint him managing director, the highest position in Collister, and break the one hundred and fifty years of tradition that only a Collister could hold that position. In the past, he'd even envisioned marrying Elizabeth; there'd been a brief and odd relationship between them some years ago.

If his intention was to rile Elizabeth, he failed. She looked at him and replied with a touch of the sarcasm that had been missing in his words, "What an outdated question. I was hoping you knew me better."

"It seems I don't. But I want to know you. We all want to." He gestured broadly towards his colleagues. "Perhaps *you* will also find a way to know us better."

However, Elizabeth was not disturbed in the least by his tone. "What are you saying, Andrew? That I have to continue the tradition of breakfast at Simpson's Tavern?"

"Absolutely not. That was Thomas's way. You need to find your own approach."

Mrs Collister looked from her daughter to Andrew,

unsure what was happening. Was Andrew leading a kind of insurrection against Elizabeth? Her eyes sought help, but everybody stared at the two arguing as if it were a fight.

"Why not? This meeting dedicated to my father is as good a moment as any to establish new rules," Elizabeth said calmly, causing everyone in the room to relax. If some had initially favoured Andrew, Elizabeth's composure won them over. "What do you say to us all having a monthly meeting—with coffee—to discuss any subject related to Collister? An honest and open gathering to present our work and accept opinions and criticism. A brainstorming event for two hours or so?"

"It might be an idea, but we need to know more. Otherwise, it'll be just a good intention," Andrew said with a hint of anger. Though as he looked around the table, he realised that Elizabeth had charmed her colleagues without saying anything substantial, merely a vague promise that she could forget at any time. Her posture, calmness, and absolute confidence in her inner power made her a leader. Andrew felt that vibe, as did all the others in the room. He nodded and continued in a lighter tone, "You didn't answer my question. Are you a feminist?"

"Absolutely not! You're not well-versed in Oxford's history. Somerville College was about the suffragettes' struggle for the right to vote. Their fight ended long ago with a victory—women now vote, end of story. Feminism came later, and I was never part of it."

"Why not?" Vanessa asked.

"Why not? Isn't it obvious?" Elizabeth laughed. "I'm a woman, and I'm head of Collister. I don't need a cause to fight for."

"You're the head of Collister because you're a Collister," Andrew said, and again, his words and tone didn't have the effect he intended.

Marianne, from the other end of the table, observed the scene. Even though Elizabeth didn't need help, Marianne wanted to cool Andrew down—for his own sake.

"Dear Andrew," Marianne said condescendingly, knowing how much he disliked that attitude. "Thomas loved his family and Collister with a passion, but he never mixed them. And I'm so glad we can discuss any problem this openly and in front of everybody." Unofficially, as the head of publishing, she was as high in rank as Andrew, while her prestige in the company was immense.

All heads turned to Elizabeth, as if it were a tennis match, waiting for her response. She smiled, and once again, they admired her self-assurance. Looking at Andrew, she replied, "You can openly question my *ability* to run Collister but never my *authority*, which puts an end to this subject."

Her tone was as sharp as a razor blade, and Cybil Collister was surprised to see how Elizabeth's words completely defused the atmosphere. In just one sentence, Elizabeth showed that she was prepared to lead and manage Collister while being open to accepting criticism and ideas.

Looking entirely at ease, Elizabeth continued the conversation as if nothing had happened. "If Andrew is right and Thomas Collister appointed me as his successor only because I'm family, then that also explains why I'm not a feminist. In 2016, it no longer matters whether you're a man or a woman in terms of inheritance. The entail that tormented Mr Bennet's life is finally resolved, as it should be—property is inherited by family, and the heir's gender isn't important. Nowadays, feminism is a doctrine—an ideology without clear aims and targets."

"And what about abused women?" Emily Robertson, the head of Collister Magazines, asked.

"They have instruments to condemn abuse and defend themselves from their abuser."

"Are we talking about women beaten by their husbands—do they have those rights?" Andrew just couldn't let it go.

Everyone enjoyed the conversation; some even had

more food to prolong the discussion.

"Andrew wanted to know me better. Well, some eight years ago, I dated Kaiden Cole."

A huge sigh accompanied her words. All the women in the room looked at her with envy; Kaiden was a well-known musician in the UK.

"I was naive, and I thought he was the one, while he thought that Collister had something to do with music."

"You're being mean because he left you," Anisha from *The Ladies' Magazine* cried with feigned reproach.

"Actually, he didn't leave her," Mrs Collister replied, and a smile floated on her face while Elizabeth nodded.

"He didn't. One evening, we went to his place—not the huge mansion he probably owns now but a small and comfortable apartment, the first he ever bought. I was completely enchanted by this guy who didn't drink or do drugs and had bought a house with his first pay packet. It was empty, as the furniture hadn't arrived yet, so I suggested we go to my place. It was a harmless request. I was in love with him and wanted a nice evening. Even today, I don't understand what happened. We ended up quarrelling over it, and he punched me in the face."

Many of the people at the table put down their cutlery. It was an intimate confession that held even more weight coming from Elizabeth Collister.

"In half an hour, we were at the hospital. I drove because the poor idiot couldn't—nobody warned him not to punch a lady with a black belt in martial arts. That night at the hospital was the last time I stood in the same room as him."

"So—are you saying we shouldn't try to change men but take judo lessons instead?" Vanessa asked.

"I am saying that we can't change the people around us. It's an illusion shared by millions of women…and men. But I've got all the legal instruments to protect myself from a man like him."

"Because you've got a black belt!"

"No, Vanessa, because there are laws, policemen, lawyers, and a whole array of methods to fight those violent men."

"Tell that to the next woman brutally beaten," Andrew said.

"That's precisely what I am telling her. I'm part of an association that fights domestic violence, and thank you, Andrew, I accept your generous donation!" she replied, laughing, then took a sip of her coffee.

"Then, what's changed in the last two hundred years?" Marianne asked.

"Really? Marianne Beaumont's asking me what's changed? You've got hundreds of people under your control across five continents. And I see some other ladies at this table in similar positions. We've got laws and rights, and if we're still being beaten, it's not just because they— the men—think like they did in the 1800s but because we, the women, have the same mentality. We accept that role and that fate. Do you know how many women actually take action? Less than thirty per cent. Jane Austen had to sign her novels as 'A Lady', while I could have destroyed Kaiden's career if I'd wanted to. It's no longer just about the fight of *women*. It is about *each woman*'s fight. We've gained our rights but don't know how to use them. That's the problem! It's a personal issue now and an individual fight to see the laws applied."

"Tell that to the assistant harassed by her boss or even assaulted. I've been there," Anisha murmured, and everyone heard her.

"You fought for your rights, Anisha. You're the best example," Emily Robertson, her boss, responded.

"I was lucky. I didn't have a family to support, and I lived at my parents' house for a year before I found a new job. That scoundrel promised me I'd never find another job in the UK, and the police did nothing."

"But he's under investigation—you're not the only one

who complained. I didn't say it was easy. I'm only saying there are means to fight, which didn't exist in Jane Austen's time. She's our legacy because she's one of those brilliant and courageous women who opposed the system in their own way," Elizabeth said.

Anna had mixed feelings about the atmosphere in that old room. When she finally decided to taste the food, the secret door opened again, causing her to put her fork down for good. A girl her age, in her late twenties, entered, dressed like a disturbed model on a Parisian catwalk.

"Harajuku Gothic," Henry whispered in Anna's ear. She didn't seem to understand, so he continued, "Kath's outfit is Harajuku Gothic."

All eyes were on her, but Katherine Collister didn't care. She'd lived in the spotlight all her life.

She wore a masculine, oversized black shirt with braces over her bare shoulders. A black gauze skirt and platform boots completed her look. It was shocking, but all the pieces came together harmoniously on her.

"Sorry I'm late!" she said nonchalantly, sitting next to her mother and starting to eat as if it were her first meal in days.

Anna couldn't take her eyes off her, and once again, Henry whispered some information to help her recover from the shock. "Katherine Collister, Elizabeth's younger sister. You'll have to get used to her. You'll collaborate with her. But first, eat. You'll feel better afterwards."

But Anna couldn't touch the food. However, it wasn't the eggs Benedict that made her feel nauseous; it was the place, the strange people, and the fear of not fitting into such a team.

The waiters quickly cleared the table, and the remnants of the copious breakfast disappeared as if nothing had happened.

"A quick cigarette break," Katherine Collister said, taking over the role of announcing the programme from her mother.

Ten minutes later, back in the room, they found a box in front of each chair. Was this still related to Jane Austen? That was the question on everybody's lips, yet as the meeting had no specific schedule, anything—like the recreation of Thomas's breakfast—was possible.

"We now have a message from Dad," Kath murmured. She still couldn't talk about her father. "A recording—if it can be called a recording."

"It can. It's nothing but a recording in VR—virtual reality," Henry Marshall said. He was the master of that game as the head of Collister Digital. "We tested it with Marianne yesterday. It's simple if you follow the instructions."

"It is simple," Marianne agreed, "but it's so powerful that you need a strong heart and handkerchiefs. But I was…glad to see him in the end. It's not easy, but it is pleasant. I constantly had the yearning to touch him. Luckily, Henry was near me and wouldn't let me stand up or do anything else crazy."

Henry nodded and continued. "Please sit, don't stand or make any sudden movements. Three of my colleagues will keep an eye on you. Each of you has got a VR headset in front of you. Please put it on. It's got glasses with a screen and headphones. The on/off button is on the right, so please press it before you put it on. You'll know you're connected when you're in Thomas's office."

And fifty people sighed in reality, almost fearing to find themselves in Thomas's virtual office. It was so real and overwhelming that some struggled to even put the headset on. Henry patiently waited for them to overcome their emotions, and only then did Thomas appear at his desk. Real, just as they had seen him so many times.

Kath exclaimed, "Dad!" She was the only one standing. But beside her, a young man gently pushed her back into her chair. She continued talking, as for a few moments, she forgot that he was dead and that she was only in a virtual room.

"My dears," Thomas said with his familiar sarcastic smile. "I know it's bad taste to say, 'If you see this recording, it means I'm no longer with you,' but I couldn't think of anything better. It is indeed a fact. I'm rather furious that I had to go, but you can't refuse this final journey."

He smiled again, his expression so sad that most people had tears in their eyes. He was the same old boss they'd liked and probably feared occasionally.

"It's rather infuriating that I can't take part in Jane Austen's celebration next year—the one I dreamt of for so long and prepared for. I spent my last few months sketching out a plan, but I expect you to make it even more grandiose—something which will be remembered for the next hundred years.

"You're used to working with profit and loss statements—P&L, as you call them—for each project to declare how much your work makes compared with what was expected. Instead, I want you to invent another template, with lines and columns that reflect the happiness, joy, and fulfilment that my project will produce. Please do that for me. I want each of you to record this project's profit in terms of personal achievement by the end of July 2017. I'm sure some of you are wondering what an outdated, old, antiquated writer from two hundred years ago could give us. Well, I'll let you discover that. The project will involve all departments. Elizabeth will hire a project manager, and I hope she or he is already in the virtual room with us. The artistic director will be Katherine, and I asked Henry to wait to show this presentation until she joins you. Yes, my love, I knew you would be late. You are for ninety percent of our meetings.

"But let's stick to my beloved Jane Austen. We'll have a complete collection of her works, which the *Austen Integral* could not have had in 1917. Marianne, it's on you to make something unforgettable. Then Henry, guided by Marianne, will prepare the most comprehensive Jane Austen digital collection. We have the rights to almost all the films ever made on her work. Even *Bridget Jones's Diary*. We'll remember the *Pride and Prejudice* variations—the fan fiction literature unique for a classic writer. The digital department will develop an educational application to be distributed free in schools. Our magazines also have some tasks. Everything will culminate in July 2017 at the Warminster estate in Wiltshire—my Pemberley—with a programme I'm sure you'll plan, to show Miss Austen's perpetuity and Collister's incredible capacity to adapt to the new digital age while preserving its traditions!

"Elizabeth has been by my side for the last eight years, and she's managed Collister by herself during the last year. There'll be no need for a transition, as she's already the boss. You'll find in her the leader you need for this century. I hope she'll accept this huge responsibility but also immense honour. I have complete confidence in you, my princess."

He paused and drank a glass of water, obviously tired. They understood that the recording had been made during the last days of his life. He continued looking ahead as if speaking to each of them individually. "We have an important anniversary at Collister next year. I haven't forgotten that in the preparations for Jane Austen's celebration. Far from it. Kath came up with a brilliant idea, and I completely embraced it. We won't talk about ourselves, boasting about our achievements. Instead, we'll let our achievements speak for us. You'll prepare such a celebration for Jane Austen that the world will exclaim, 'Only Collister could do it!' at the end. The *Jane Austen Project* is our celebration. Be innovative and celebrate each day, showing how a company has interwoven its destiny with Jane Austen's work for a hundred and fifty years. And in the end, enjoy yourselves, and allow your hearts to feel the beauty of such a project."

One by one, they took off their headsets. It had been such a remarkable experience that most of them found it hard to return to the real world.

"All my headsets are damp," Henry joked. Though he was also deeply moved, even though he'd seen the recording more than once.

"You scoundrel," Kath suddenly said and ran to Henry, who caught her in his arms, trying to wipe the mess from her face; her heavy makeup was all over her cheeks.

"You should use waterproof makeup, dear!" he said. Everybody laughed at his words in a vast emotional release. They all knew that Henry was Elizabeth and Kath's friend from their childhood. Thomas didn't avoid hiring friends or family but never discussed their private lives or relationships at Collister HQ. And—Thomas's rule—everybody was hired after an incredibly tough interview that seemed more like a police interrogation than a job interview.

"I want to see him again," Kath spoke, still crying.

Her mother took her from Henry's arms and gently said, "Dad gave strict instructions that this recording could be seen only once!"

"No!" Kath shouted and looked to Elizabeth for help.

But Elizabeth shook her head, trying to stop her own tears. "Sorry, Katherine, even from heaven, Dad's still the boss today."

"We've prepared another recording, as we thought it was only fair for him to open the celebration in Wiltshire."

As if the breakfast and the whole atmosphere were not enough, that strange presentation made Anna question her place among them once again. She was unsure whether she could work with those people, eating together and then crying in the real world after a virtual presentation. She recognised Kath from glossy magazines as part of the jet-set, flying to New York or Paris. And for sure, her outfit was not from Brick Lane but from Milan or Tokyo. She was still crying, and everybody was around her. Her assistant brought cleansing wipes, and in a few minutes, she was hardly recognisable. Without makeup, she became just another oddly dressed girl.

"We've definitely scared you, Anna," Vanessa said. "They're not like this every day!" And she gestured to the people around the table. "Thomas left us so unexpectedly that we're still very emotional. We want to fulfil his last wish—this Jane Austen Project you'll manage."

"We know it'll be quite a challenge without my father," Elizabeth said, finally composed. She was only wearing light makeup, and Anna understood why. She had probably known what was coming.

"You'll receive all the information you need, but now I want to introduce you to some of our key people and their departments. You've met Henry Marshall—the boss at Collister Digital, guilty of all this commotion, as I'm sure he suggested this drama to Dad. But it's a good beginning as we'll use the same technology to present our products. What do you say, Henry?"

Henry looked like a teenager, but he was much more than just a geek; he was the only one in the room with a computer. That was another peculiarity. In the companies where Anna had previously worked, a laptop was a must in any circumstance, but mostly at meetings. But then, what kind of meeting was this with croissants and tears?

"Andrew Miller is the CEO of Collister, Marianne Beaumont is the big boss of the publishing house, or *Books* as her department's known. Emily Robertson is the manager of Collister Magazines. Each magazine has a manager you'll meet in time. The advertising man is Roger Chapman, and Vanessa Steward is from Collister Educational. Anyway, it's hard to remember it all today. Collister Music and Film—you already heard Roland Barkley complaining about this dull meeting about Jane

Austen—he's the boss of that department. Grace is the Human Resources' manager. On your right is my personal assistant and the coordinator of assistants at Collister, Clarice White. Then our sacrosanct Arthur Johnson, finance manager. You must know he's also my uncle, my mother's brother. Still, as Marianne said, we're colleagues, not relatives at Collister. You'll see that any conversation with him is a battle, and he doesn't lose any. Fabien Griffiths is our legal manager who solves all the crazy problems the others create occasionally."

"We're not a happy family," Andrew Miller said, "if that's what you thought after this morning. The departments are in constant competition. We work much more than the norm, and we use a management method that's usually seen in IT companies, but it works for us too."

"It all seems so different and difficult," Anna said, and she couldn't hide her worries.

"It is," Marianne Beaumont said. "Especially when you collaborate with artists like our writers or musicians. But you'd be surprised how eager they are to adapt to this kind of work. It's also a matter of adjustment for all our employees."

"And I'm sure Anna will adapt. She's a Somerville College alumna," Mrs Collister said.

Their gazes—all fixed on her—made Anna even more uncomfortable.

"Wow, am I detecting nepotism?" Andrew Miller said. But he was joking this time; his previous acts of rebellion were forgotten.

"Absolutely!" Elizabeth replied. "When the principal of Somerville, Dr Alice Prochaska, tells you someone is the best alumna in years in an interesting field, you hire her. That's exactly what I did."

"Darcy Egerton syndrome?" Marianne Beaumont asked, and a burst of laughter exploded in the room, leaving Anna feeling dismayed.

"Sorry, Anna," Henry said. "We're only laughing because Thomas isn't here. And sorry, Thomas, wherever you are. It's the first time we've ever laughed about that subject. It's a kind of release. Nine years ago, in 2007, Darcy Egerton sent his first novel to Collister Publishing House…and his manuscript was rejected."

"I know the story," Anna admitted.

Rejecting Darcy Egerton was a mistake that could kill a man like Thomas Collister. Literally, kill the man and then destroy the publishing house. She looked at Marianne, who fought back hastily. "Don't look at me. Since then, *Books* has been completely changed. When Thomas understood what they'd lost, he became obsessed with never losing a writer like that again, and with getting Darcy Egerton back."

"But nobody knows who he is!"

"Exactly, so Thomas concentrated on *Books*. In 2009, he fired the entire department, never seen such a thing before, but he did it."

"And then he hired Marianne," Elizabeth continued, "and for a whole year, they reorganised *Books*. Unfortunately, Darcy Egerton became an obsession, creating uproar every time the name was mentioned. It was suicide to say 'Darcy Egerton' anywhere near my father."

They spoke one after the other, taking over where one left off and continuing each other's sentences.

"We tried to remove all traces of Darcy from Thomas's presence, but it was impossible when that guy wrote a book every year. Luckily, he was like clockwork—a novel every June—so we knew in advance when a new book was about to be launched, and we fought to book our holidays that week," Marianne said.

"Nothing worked," Roland offered. "Thomas was an engaging boss, but he had one obsession."

"Darcy Egerton never came back to you?" Anna asked.

Nine years later, Darcy Egerton was the most appreciated writer in the UK, US, and worldwide. A considerable loss of money and prestige for Collister that Thomas never overcame. *A horrible catastrophe* as he named the event that stained his publishing house's honourable name that had been forged over a hundred and fifty years.

"A few years ago, a magazine found out which publishing houses had rejected that first manuscript. We're on a list of shame, my dad used to say in agony," Elizabeth explained.

"But how is it possible that no one knows who Egerton is?" Anna asked.

"I'm sure he's a geek," Henry answered. "People in the industry are saying his emails come from the deep web."

"Yes, and some people think he's Michael Jackson, who's not dead," Marianne joked. "He's created a legend around himself—a myth. He could be someone we know, a public figure. I don't see why a completely unknown person would hide for years."

"And the way he chose his pen name," Anna said, finally regaining some of her confidence. "Darcy—like Fitzwilliam Darcy from Pride and Prejudice, and Egerton like Austen's first editor who published her book with her family's money. It's said that he did the same—he financed his first book, but that could just be a legend." She stopped as she suspected those stories were already well known at Collister.

"I wonder what Thomas did to try to find him," Roger Chapman mused, imagining the explosion of interest Collister would have if Egerton gave them his tenth novel. He could already visualise his campaign.

You don't want to know, I assure you, Elizabeth and Marianne thought in unison. Only they knew, and very few others in Collister, that Thomas never stopped in his obsessive search for Darcy Egerton.

Elizabeth remembered one evening when she'd gone to her father's office. He'd been speaking on the phone but also eating, and speakerphone was on when a voice said, *"Mr Collister, I can look for Darcy Egerton, but it would be a waste of your money. Every agency in England has been trying for the last five years. I'm sure you've been trying too."*

"He tried in every possible way," Elizabeth finally said, "but he didn't succeed in finding Darcy Egerton."

"At least the pressure to find him is gone." Mrs Collister was smiling with that sad expression they were already used to seeing on her face.

"And we can talk about him," Marianne continued.

"I suggest you all forget Darcy Egerton for good and turn again to Collister," Elizabeth said.

Anna looked around at those in the room. Elizabeth could say only a few words and be listened to. She was a leader, and that couldn't be denied. Her words were unimportant; they were few and familiar, but she electrified her audience with her energy and determination.

Mrs Collister cleared her throat. "As you probably know, Thomas appointed Elizabeth as his successor. Elizabeth agreed to be the managing director of Collister yesterday, in the presence of our lawyers. This morning, as has always been the tradition, she'll accept in front of all of you, her staff."

It was not precisely breaking news, but still, it was an exciting moment for all of them. Except for Mrs Collister and Mr Johnson, all those in the room had known only one boss.

"My father-in-law, Arnold Collister, died eight years ago, but Thomas had been running the place since he was thirty. For thirty-eight years," Mrs Collister said, and the tears she had kept from falling since the beginning of the meeting defeated her.

Arthur Johnson, her brother, continued on her behalf. "Thomas became managing director long before his father's death, as Arnold Collister had only one wish—to be just a simple editor in his own publishing house."

It had never been explicitly stated, but Thomas had always blamed his father for not catching Darcy Egerton.

His father had run *Books* as it had always been run, incapable of seeing the changes in the industry and the new wave of writers who invaded the market. Until his death, nothing was done in *Books* no matter how the company progressed in all other directions. He was, after all, the boss, even though he let his son run the company. However, after Arnold Collister's death, the changes in *Books* were finally possible.

"Under Thomas Collister's management, the company progressed from an important publishing house to a media giant. And now, here we are welcoming Elizabeth to this chair that has seen seven generations of Collisters. Elizabeth—"

Elizabeth hesitated for a few moments. It was not too late to say no to the question that had tormented her since her father's death, yet she was prepared to take his place. For the last few years, she had been his right hand; in many ways, her father had enabled her to make decisions and run Collister in her own style. He trusted her and her fresh look on the market, yet to do the job forever was scary. A colossal task that would engulf her private life, which didn't amount to very much even at the moment.

"It's not easy to stand in this room," Elizabeth said, throwing her arms wide to indicate that place that had seen one hundred and fifty years of history. "Thomas Collister led his company in the spirit of his heritage, that consisted mostly of the respect and admiration we've gained over the years. But he was a genius who made this company the way it is today. We always had confidence in him, and his decisions never failed. Dad's last words to me were, 'You can do it, Elizabeth Collister!' I was his last decision. I ask you to have confidence in him one last time."

Kath was the first to congratulate her, although the sisters shared an odd relationship. Only two years younger, Kath saw Elizabeth as their father's ally, and whilst she adored her father in their private life, she feared him at work. Consequently, she didn't much like her sister, who had always been the excellent example she had never followed.

"I'll try to do better," Kath said in her sister's ear.

Elizabeth looked at her with their father's indulgent smile and shook her head. "I doubt it," she murmured, while her voice full of love stunned Kath. As if it was not Elizabeth speaking but her father, and that was confusing.

Elizabeth didn't let the others come up to congratulate her. "Send money to my association against domestic violence." She smiled. "Let's get to work now."

And for the first time that morning, Anna could say that she understood what was happening as each department manager described their roles, speaking mostly to her.

Chapter 2

"Please, have a seat." Elizabeth invited Marianne to join her in the comfortable armchairs that faced the library in Thomas Collister's office. Impressive and strange at the same time, the office was located in the newest part of Collister, a nineteen-floor building, yet the decor was one hundred and fifty years old. Every book or magazine ever published by Collister was displayed on mahogany shelves, making the room resemble a museum.

"I won't be using this office. I could hardly sit at his desk and feel at ease, expecting him to come in any minute," Elizabeth said.

Marianne nodded; she felt the same.

When Collister had hired her, she'd just got married. At thirty-five, life had given her all that anyone could ask for. She was very much in love with her husband. Directly from their honeymoon, she entered that office to find Thomas at his desk, and her world crumbled—for all those years, she'd been in love with two men. Fortunately, Thomas was a rare gentleman and a considerate boss. He valued his family and his standing in society, and his family's reputation was far more important than any extramarital affair. More than once, Marianne had felt that Thomas harboured stronger feelings for her, but then he passed away, and she never discovered the truth. Looking around the office, she remembered their discussions, arguments, and the occasional silences, which both had cherished.

"You have half an hour," Elizabeth said, observing Marianne's sad expression, still stunned by the void her father had left in so many lives at Collister.

"Darcy Egerton," Marianne mentioned, watching Elizabeth filling two glasses with whisky from Thomas's collection, which came from a distillery in Campbeltown in Scotland. Few knew that the distillery had been in the Collister family since 1923 and was Thomas's secret pride.

"Do you know that we own this distillery?" Elizabeth revealed, showing the bottle.

Astonished, Marianne almost dropped her glass. They'd drunk that whisky many times, but Thomas had never revealed this simple truth.

"I thought you didn't know," Elizabeth remarked, observing Marianne's reaction.

Marianne tried to hide her feelings and then hastily spoke, concealing her true emotions, fearing that Elizabeth knew her too well. "I need to know what I can tell Anna Wilson about Darcy Egerton."

Suddenly it was cold in Thomas's office. Elizabeth stopped her with a gesture and a sharp voice. "Marianne, please stop this. Dad was an exceptional man, but when it came to Darcy Egerton, he was obsessed and absurd, and I want that madness to end now!"

"Elizabeth, please let me finish. There are things that you don't know."

Reluctantly, Elizabeth took a large sip of whisky. That day was dedicated to her father's memory. She would let everyone believe he was still present at Collister. But it would be for the last time. The next day would see another managing director take charge, someone who would impose her own style and methods. Her staff, even Marianne, needed to understand that decisions would come from her office, not from her father's lingering presence beyond the grave.

"Thomas was close to knowing Darcy Egerton's true identity," Marianne disclosed, and Elizabeth made an effort to appear calm, but it was difficult. She had heard that same claim at least ten times over the past few years.

"I know you're cautious, but he might be right."

"Please don't tell me about Professor Markson from Oxford."

"It's also about Professor Markson. His initial study on Darcy Egerton was completed more than a year ago, and we drew some interesting conclusions." Marianne defended his position, remaining loyal to Thomas no matter what.

"Yes, and in the meantime, he wrote another thesis on Dad's idea—he became a profiler on writers. They're not treated very differently from serial killers."

"You're being harsh."

"No, I'm well-informed. It wasn't hard when I dined with Dad every night during his last months of life. Using traditional investigative methods and adding others specific to the *noble* profession of profiler, one can learn a lot about a writer just by reading their work—their main influences, obsessions, problems with parents, spouses, and children—and even predict general ideas for future novels. All for the eternal glory of publishing houses."

"That idea proved clever in the case of Darcy Egerton."

"Perhaps, but this idea could ruin English literature forever by castrating its writers, both men and women. Please, Marianne, let us do our job while the writers do theirs."

"You might be surprised by the profiler's results in Darcy Egerton's case—"

"I'll tell you what surprises me even more," Elizabeth interrupted Marianne. But since they were good friends beyond their professional relationship, the conversation became informal. "I'm surprised this obsession didn't die with my father. That man…or woman, was rejected by six influential publishers in the UK."

"*He*, definitely *he*. Darcy Egerton's a man."

"Fine. Afterwards, *he* had his revenge by raising Heathcliff Publishing from a second-rate house into an important player in the market."

"In terms of money, you mean. For three years, and then he chose another publisher. He turned three publishing houses into success stories. Now it's time for the fourth, and the industry is in turmoil, waiting for his decision for 2017."

"OK, let me try a profile. Let's suppose—as you say—he's a man, even though there were moments when we thought Darcy Egerton was a woman. What if that man isn't the mastermind you imagine? On the contrary, I see him as an artist who wanted to keep his creative space untouched by what we consider important—marketing and publicity…and paparazzi. He wanted to avoid running from town-to-town meeting ardent readers and obsessed fans looking for something more than his novels. Maybe there was no initial plan to remain unknown, as Dad imagined. Sonia Richter worked at Heathcliff Publishing ten years ago. She wasn't in charge of his novel, but the information about the new writer was initially shared with a larger group."

"What could she know that we don't already? Your father had dozens of conversations with her until the poor woman ran off to work in France," Marianne said.

"Dad told me that she remembered a conversation she overheard. When his novel was accepted, he was using a different name."

Marianne nodded, considering the outdated information that had no relevance now. "We supposed for a while that he'd used his real name."

"No, he hadn't, and when the book was published, he was Darcy Egerton. After his first novel was finally accepted after six rejections, he decided on this name, and it seemed like he found it amusing. We didn't need a five-year analysis to determine that he read Jane Austen and knew more about her than a simple reader. Dad went nuts about this Jane Austen commemoration thing, mainly because of Darcy Egerton. Because of that profile, which suggested he was a scholar and well-acquainted with Austen's work professionally." Elizabeth spoke in a slightly aggressive tone, a rarity for her.

"You disapprove of your father's decision to celebrate Collister by commemorating her?"

"Yes. Anyway, he never asked for our permission or opinion. It was his decision, and by the time we learned about the plan, he'd already given that famous interview, announcing the extent of the celebrations.

"Austen *is* a great idea, although he went a bit overboard with it. And let's face it—he didn't do it for his favourite author's eternal glory but because he hoped that Darcy Egerton would come out of hiding, tempted by a subject that seemed dear to him too. Am I right?"

Marianne didn't respond. Elizabeth knew her father better than anyone. She'd been his right hand in his last years and managed Collister alone the previous year, except in Darcy Egerton and Jane Austen matters.

"I think it was his way of ending his obsession," Marianne explained, but Elizabeth shook her head.

"That might be true if, and only if, Darcy Egerton materialises in the next few weeks in Collister's reception hall with a novel about Jane Austen. Otherwise, this celebration is just another stunt in Dad's search. So, to conclude, you can say anything to Anna. There are no more secrets or mysteries, and she needs to understand the full extent of this madness. We tend to believe that everyone knows the details, when in fact, it's a nine-year-old story that's no longer interesting—"

"I disagree. The madness revives every year before Darcy Egerton launches his new novel."

"Yes, for a week or so, and mainly among literature enthusiasts and industry professionals."

"Still, his sales grow impressively each year." Marianne tried to make her point.

Elizabeth glanced at her watch and said, "The half an hour is almost up."

"Yes, I wanted to tell you something important, but as always, when it's about that man, the conversation tends to go crazy."

"Exactly. Even between us, with Dad buried for almost three months, we still can't escape the subject. That's why I want to bring it into the light and end this obsession."

"It's not that simple. Thomas initiated many—"

Elizabeth sighed, exasperated by the topic. She felt like she was getting tangled in a maze. "Please, just be brief!" she requested.

"Thomas launched our novel contest for 2017 at the beginning of this year, as always happens. For the first time in a century, we asked for a specific subject: Jane Austen's life, work, or legacy."

Elizabeth nodded and smiled. "Did Dad think that a man in hiding like Darcy Egerton would fall into such a simple trap as to participate in some contest, given that he's the best-selling author in the UK and USA?"

"It's not *just any* contest. The Collister Fiction Prize has seen big names participating for over a hundred years. Our contest is even more prestigious than the Goncourt Prize in France."

"Alright, so Dad thought that Darcy Egerton might decide to come forward and participate in our contest," Elizabeth said, amused, but Marianne didn't seem discouraged.

"Yes, based on some analysis, it appears that Darcy Egerton might come out of hiding next year at the same time as his tenth novel."

Elizabeth gazed at her friend, fearing that the madness

hadn't ceased. Somehow, her father was continuing to manipulate his followers from beyond the grave with cunning tactics.

"Is it a supposition or a dream?" Elizabeth asked.

Marianne smiled. "Just a little bit of confidence, please?"

"It's difficult. Over the years, I've heard hundreds of ideas and witnessed the craziest plans."

"This is the last time, I swear."

"Alright, I'm listening."

"We have three significant findings about him that are likely to be true—"

"He received a classical education—whatever that means—has some hacking skills and is a man."

"Yes, those are still important, but now we have new ones."

"I'm listening."

"He closely monitors the betting on the plot of his next novel, and it's not just for marketing or publicity—"

"Explain!"

"As you know, he hints about his next book in his latest novel's epilogue. Since his second book, people have been able to place bets regarding the plot—town, country, era, leading characters, and so on. Initially, the bets skyrocketed, and some enthusiasts even won significant money."

"Oh my God, how do you know that? Did Dad hack the bookmakers?" Elizabeth cried.

Marianne shook her head, smiling again. "You really think the worst of Thomas."

"When it comes to Darcy Egerton, I do. I'm sure he would have done anything—legally or illegally—to find out who that man was."

"You have too dramatic a view of his obsession. Thomas was a gambler, and Darcy Egerton was a game, not a vile addiction. It was like treasure hunting for him. However, our analysis suggests that Darcy Egerton is also a gambler, and he was playing some kind of 'catch me if you can' game with your father."

"Are you serious?"

"Yes."

"Darcy Egerton was toying with my father. Is that one of the grand conclusions from that study, paid for by a sizeable chunk of Dad's personal wealth?"

"Yes."

"So this guy was overseeing the betting, playing with Dad, and—?"

"And he decided to reveal his identity with the next novel and participate in the Collister Fiction Prize."

Elizabeth laughed, but it wasn't a joyful laugh.

"Poor Dad was definitely crazy, as I've always suspected. A mad genius, like John Nash—but you, Marianne? How can you believe such nonsense?"

"It's not nonsense, believe me. It's as well-documented as the other conclusions. Will you let me tell you everything?"

Elizabeth, hardly interested, nodded stiffly, signalling Marianne to continue.

"Even though Egerton's books still sell well, betting has declined dramatically in the last two years. And that could mean his readers are growing tired of not knowing who he is. We think Darcy Egerton initiated those bets to gauge whether his readers still prefer him to hide his identity."

For the first time in the conversation, Elizabeth seemed intrigued. "My father never told me this."

"Your father had secrets. He was obsessed and rational at the same time. As I told you, for Thomas, it was a game."

"Tell that to the addicted gamblers."

"Exactly. He was addicted, obsessed, but he highly respected Darcy Egerton. If he wanted to find him, it wasn't just for money or public glory, but mainly to satisfy his ego that he'd ultimately won *The Game*."

"Even more frightening."

"Based on the betting results, we believe that Egerton

understood the message and decided to reveal his identity with his tenth novel."

Elizabeth sighed heavily, processing the revelation that seemed interesting but not documented enough.

"And this alone gave Dad the certainty that Darcy Egerton would reveal his identity?"

"Yes, because Egerton is brilliant. He's managed his entire advertising campaign impeccably over the years. The odds of the bets from the last two years indicated that people were no longer interested in his mysterious identity. If he wanted the same impact, he had to change his promotional method."

"And come forward this year. Maybe the publishing house supported the campaign ideas."

"Correct, but the same analysis revealed that Egerton managed his campaigns by himself and initiated the odd betting thing."

"A rather weak deduction, if you ask me." Elizabeth recalled the dossier she'd never read. For once, she regretted not listening to her father. "I agree that the betting matter is interesting, but the other conclusions are quite weak."

"I assure you, the study's well-documented, and the analysis is as scientific as possible. Darcy Egerton was also playing a game with your father. There's a clear hint in the single interview he *ever* gave at the end of last year. He revealed the name of the novel he intended to publish in June 2016. When asked about his plans for the 2017 novel, he said it would be centred around a biblical sceptic who refuses to believe without direct personal experience."

"Doubting Thomas," Elizabeth murmured, stunned.

"Yes."

"I agree it makes sense now, but why use our contest to come forward?"

"Because Collister was the first publishing house that rejected his novel. He wanted to close the circle—*ten years ago, they rejected me. Are they any better now? Can they recognise me among the contestants?"*

Elizabeth didn't say a word for a long time.

"Your father made a plan to find him among the contestants."

"My God! Dad made a plan to find him, and now Dad's dead. We can shut down Collister Publishing for good if we don't find Darcy Egerton among the contestants. On my watch!"

"Thomas didn't want to die."

"No, but he also didn't end this madness to protect us from failure."

"We have a plan," Marianne said.

"And who did Dad involve in this ultimate plan?"

Marianne's silence filled Elizabeth with concern. Her father had devised a new way to torment her with Darcy Egerton even after his death. Clearly Marianne didn't know how to break the news to her.

"No, no, no!" Elizabeth cried, vigorously shaking her head. "He wanted something from me!"

"Elizabeth—"

"No, Marianne, no!"

"Just listen to this, and then you can decide."

"No! It's his way of ensuring this problem never ends, even after his death. Besides, he didn't say a single word about these new developments, not to me, not in his will!"

"Maybe he was afraid to tell you—" Marianne looked intently at her, trying to convey something.

"Yes, because it's so wrong to carry on like this. It was his game, his obsession; he had no right to burden me with it. He's got no right to ask something from beyond the grave when he dared not ask me while he was alive."

"It's not about courage. He was desperate to ensure you'd follow our plan."

"Our plan, Marianne?" Elizabeth cried, outraged.

"Yes, it's my plan as well because it's what he wanted

from me—his final wish from me. How can you think I wouldn't do anything for him?"

Marianne's face became a mask of suffering. She couldn't remain composed when faced with that memory— the last with him, in a hospital bed, glasses perched on the bridge of his nose, thin as a skeleton yet still interested in life. Elizabeth embraced her to comfort her, trying not to succumb to the treacherous path of mourning.

"I'll listen to you, but that's all I can promise."

Devastated, Marianne took some time to regain a semblance of serenity.

"I'm overwhelmed with work, Marianne." Elizabeth attempted to guide her friend back to the present and away from her pain.

"I know!" Marianne replied.

"Please assure me, at the very least, that you're not manipulating our honourable competition in any dishonest way."

"No, of course not! Wait, please, wait to hear the whole story. We're not tampering with the contest's commission or its outcome. The competition will proceed as it has for the past hundred years. The only alteration in the rules— and only for this year—was that on the 3rd of January, we announced a theme for the novel—*Jane Austen's life, work, or legacy.*"

"The 3rd of January, a few days after Egerton's interview," Elizabeth mused.

"Exactly. Thomas responded to the interview, and our competition ultimately followed the plan he proposed to Darcy Egerton. There were 980 applications to write that novel. Contestants sent in five chapters or fifty pages of the novel in April. Sent by mail, not email!"

Elizabeth nodded. Typically, entrants submitted the completed work in September, and the winner was determined the following February. Collister announced the winner in March, with the novel hitting bookshops the same day. But because this time they'd also specified the subject, the books were to be written in 2016.

"The Collister Commission selected twenty-five finalists who were then asked to submit half of the novel. We shortlisted five contestants just before Thomas passed away, maybe ten days before."

"You and Dad?"

"Yes, and Olivia."

Olivia was her aunt, her uncle Arthur's wife, and the only person in the world Elizabeth wholly trusted.

She allowed herself to sink into the armchair cushions and closed her eyes in despair. "You involved Olivia in this. You might be secure in your job, but Olivia has a reputation to uphold."

"She's not doing anything wrong."

"She's a member of the Collister Commission."

"Not this year. Meanwhile, we sent the twenty-five texts to Professor Markson and his study group. They also selected five finalists, and the Collister Commission chose five."

"So, there were three separate panels—you, Professor Markson, and Collister—"

"Yes, each had five finalists. And here's the most exciting part—out of those five, we had three finalists selected by every panel. All males!"

"Wow!" Elizabeth exclaimed, genuinely astonished.

"Yes, wow. An incredible outcome." Then Marianne sputtered as if fearing her own words. "Thomas wants you to meet all three of them."

"No! No! Are you serious? I'm not meeting anyone—"

Elizabeth paused, horrified. "How am I supposed to meet the finalists when their identities are confidential?"

Elizabeth's alarm was tangible, and for once, Marianne didn't know how to proceed.

"Dad did something illegal, after all," she murmured, and Marianne remained quiet, prepared to fulfil Thomas's final wish regardless of his actions.

"But why?" Elizabeth eventually whispered.

"Because we suspect that one of these last three is Darcy Egerton."

"It's absurd, you know. Absurd, illegal, even unprofessional and immoral!" Elizabeth exclaimed, looking at Marianne with concern. "But then again, even if we entertain Dad's folly, we can't be certain Darcy Egerton participated. It's merely a guess."

"As you said, the competition centred on Jane Austen was Thomas's response to Egerton's interview. Surely, he got the message that this year's contest was designed for him, and Thomas says that he accepted the game."

"Please refer to Dad in the past tense. He's dead, Marianne. He won't be coming to the office today. So, Dad believed, in his last moments, that Darcy Egerton was asking, 'Having once dismissed the value of my work, will you repeat the mistake now?'"

"Something along those lines," Marianne concurred. She'd promised Thomas she'd persuade Elizabeth to meet the finalists, believing that Darcy Egerton would reveal himself not accidentally but because he enjoyed the game. With Thomas gone, Elizabeth was the most important person at Collister. Only she could confront Darcy Egerton.

"No, you can't place this burden on me."

"Just meet each of them and try to identify the man who's managed to evade us for nine years."

Marianne grinned, confident in her persuasion.

"And if I agree, how am I supposed to meet three unknown men?" She looked at Marianne and found her answer.

"Ah, yes! *He* knew their identities! And you claimed nothing was unlawful!"

Marianne's expression revealed a mixture of emotions. Her grimace was comical and vexed at the same time, akin to a child concealing her latest misdeed. Yet, this was real, and Elizabeth wasn't angry or frustrated with Marianne or Olivia but with her dead father.

"Marianne, explain!" she pleaded.

"It's not that simple. But yes, we've got some information about the twenty-five finalists."

"Was MI5 involved?"

Marianne smiled weakly without denying it. "Currently, we're focused on just three men."

"Because you're certain Darcy Egerton is male."

"Yes, after nine novels, it's not too difficult to deduce his gender."

"So, in commemorating Jane Austen's legacy, we discriminated against women."

"Yes. The gender outcomes are definite."

"At least you're being honest."

"I'm not hiding anything. The competition might have an astonishing result—persuading Darcy Egerton to write a Jane Austen-related novel and presenting it to Thomas…to Collister," Marianne uttered.

"And thus, our whole celebration has only this one purpose—Darcy Egerton. It's madness, can't you see? To involve Collister for nearly a year, expending all this effort and money, just to locate one man and orchestrate an event grand enough for him to contemplate revealing his identity.

"And what if we identify Darcy Egerton, yet the Collister Commission selects a different winner?" Elizabeth posed the question, not waiting for an answer. "We kill the commission members and have you, Marianne Beaumont, crown Darcy Egerton."

"Please, don't mock me," Marianne implored, her tone so sorrowful that Elizabeth ceased.

And they lapsed into silence. The meeting concluded, and Marianne sighed in relief as Elizabeth hadn't outright rejected meeting the three men…and she'd refrained from enquiring further about how they'd obtained the details about the contestants.

Chapter 3

"If he wasn't already dead, I'd have killed him this morning," Elizabeth told Arthur Johnson, Collister's financial manager and her maternal uncle, who had hurried to meet her, not only due to her request but also some other urgent matters. They had one golden rule at Collister—to never let their family relationships show at work. But today was an exception. Elizabeth fell into her uncle's arms and wept. It was unexpected—if she ever shed tears for her father, it was never in front of her family or at the office. His wife probably knew more, but he wouldn't be able to extract a single word from her—Elizabeth was Olivia's child, even more so than Cybil's.

"Come, princess," he said with much tenderness. "Come, don't cry."

"I'm crying for him, but I'm also furious."

Arthur laughed, as it perfectly mirrored his sentiments for his late brother-in-law and boss.

"I understand. I feel the same. Especially today."

Elizabeth wiped her tears. "Let's go outside, walk, eat, or perhaps get a bit tipsy. I can't stay here any longer!" she exclaimed, gesturing around her father's office.

They ambled for a long time in a nearby park, then entered a small restaurant by the Thames. It was a sunny autumn day, so beautifully London-like.

"Can you believe we used to splash about in the Thames as children?" Arthur said. "No one cared for us like they care for their kids now."

"Even Mama?"

"Of course. Cybil was a rather mischievous young girl, always the first to run off and play or swim."

Elizabeth could scarcely imagine her mother—perpetually dressed in Hermès—frolicking in the Thames.

"Now, my dear, I'm sorry, but we need to discuss an issue."

"Are we facing bankruptcy?" she asked, her anger and sorrow still palpable.

"No, good heavens, no. We're in better shape than ever. Last year was the best in a hundred and fifty years."

"A hundred and forty-nine! Then, what's happened? Why is it so urgent?"

She observed her uncle sighing deeply, and her mind raced, fearing that either he or Olivia were unwell.

"Tell me you're not ill or considering leaving Collister!"

"Ill? No! Leave? Absolutely not. I love what I do, and you need me until we find someone trustworthy enough to take on the role…in a few years."

Elizabeth nodded. That was all she needed to hear. Her father's death had thrust her into a sea of uncertainty and fear she'd never encountered before. Arthur was the anchor she needed to rebuild her confidence for the days ahead.

"We need to discuss the property Thomas rented to use as Pemberley during next year's festivities."

"I don't know much about it," she admitted.

"Of course you don't. Just like the rest of the Jane Austen plan, he did exactly as he pleased. It was all shrouded in secrecy. He gave Fabien the rental contract to review a day prior to signing, and I only saw it afterwards."

She couldn't fathom how this was possible. Her father had always respected and upheld the longstanding rules at

Collister. The financial manager was the god, while the Collisters were only kings or queens. And Fabien Griffiths, the legal officer, was always present to oversee and approve contracts.

"How?" she queried again, unsettled by tales of a father she barely recognised.

"He insisted that the funds for that property, the entire sum, came from his personal account."

"As a loan to the company?"

"No, he donated the money. It's not to be reimbursed by Collister."

"That's highly unconventional. Why would he do that?"

"Because this way, he didn't need to involve Fabien or me in the negotiations. He wanted that property, even if it's in a state of utter disrepair."

Elizabeth reclined in her chair and shut her eyes. First, she had to engage with those three writers and track down Darcy Egerton—an undertaking burdened with immense pressure. How could her father ask her to shoulder such a responsibility? And now this—to add to her worries!

In brief, she recounted the conversation with Marianne to her uncle.

"Imagine," she sighed, appearing tired and apprehensive, "Dad and his acolytes pursued this man for nearly nine years. I even suspect Dad occasionally employed his connections at Scotland Yard or MI5. Undoubtedly, the finest private investigators in the UK. He had an army of followers dissecting every word the poor man ever wrote. Then, all of a sudden, Dad vanishes into thin air, leaving me to unravel this enigma in just three meetings. It's unjust. It's absurd. What if I make the wrong choice and pick another author?"

"Enough, my dear. Firstly, these absurdities Thomas left behind aren't your burden to bear. If he wanted you to meet these individuals, then do so, but you're not obliged to pick a winner."

She looked at him gratefully. Arthur was brilliant and possessed a quality that few did—offering solutions to the most complex issues in an instant. He was right; she would meet them, but she wouldn't be the one giving Marianne an answer.

"You're right, my goodness, you're absolutely right. I'll meet them and then leave for Patagonia or Tasmania for an entire week. No internet, no phones, and if possible, with one of the contenders." She finally chuckled. She gestured to the waiter and requested champagne.

"And what can we do about that cursed Pemberley contract?"

"You'll need to take a look for yourself. You've got a meeting tomorrow at twelve with the earl. It's been on your schedule for a month."

"Earl?" she asked.

"Yes." Arthur looked at the papers he'd brought with him. "Rowan Stafford, the 15th Earl of Warminster, the owner of Thomas's new Pemberley," he stated, handing her the folder. "Here's the contract. It's all we've got since Thomas never shared the preliminary conversation or anything else."

"Very well. But why's it so urgent to meet the earl on my very first day at the office?"

"Because your father intended to invest a minimum of fifteen million pounds."

And Elizabeth choked; the waiter rushed over with a bottle of water and stood nearby to ensure she was alright. Likely, he was trained in the Heimlich manoeuvre.

"It can't be true," she eventually managed.

"It is!"

"But how did you allow it?" she asked, devoid of reproach.

"I told you—I saw the contract the day after it was signed. His money didn't require my signature."

"And when did this happen?"

"In March. The earl came to Collister, and they signed it in Fabien's presence. Thomas told the earl some tale about Austen's sister supposedly being invited to the estate in 1819. That story is your father's sole reason for choosing that house." He handed her a document to look at.

Elizabeth read the half-page about Cassandra Austen's hypothetical visit to Wiltshire, where the estate was located. It wasn't implausible, considering Southampton—where Cassandra lived—wasn't too far from the southern part of Wiltshire. Nevertheless, there were no documents, merely a mention in a letter of a visit to a nearby mansion.

"Most likely, Dad concocted the story."

"Yes, that's what Fabien said. The landlord didn't appear to be familiar with the tale, nor did he seem willing to acknowledge it as part of his family's heritage."

"Naturally, he wasn't interested in Jane Austen and was eager to sign a contract that would transform his ruin into a grand estate. So, what exactly do you expect me to do?"

"Read the contract. Thomas also secured significant funding from the Department for Culture, Media, and Sport. Once restored, it can receive state protection and even be listed as a scheduled monument. Thomas believed that after our celebration, it would become a site of pilgrimage for Austen's fans—the new Pemberley."

"Pemberley was in Derbyshire—"

"Who cares? This is closer to London, and it could attract a substantial number of visitors. Your father even envisioned a Jane Austen festival every summer. In any case, he estimated that he would recoup his investment in—"

"A hundred years?"

"Yes, something like that."

"And what am I supposed to do?" she asked again.

"The construction began in April. Your task is to convince the earl that while we're compelled to spend this exorbitant amount, it'll be under our conditions. Going forward, we'll hire teams and oversee the work. I'll meticulously track every penny—past, present, or future."

"Of course, Uncle, I'm now in charge." Elizabeth smiled, feeling a twinge of sympathy for that old earl who thought he was embarking on a splendid venture, only to have to contend with Arthur. Arthur was ruthless, and she couldn't recall any instance in history when someone had managed to secure a single extra penny beyond the budget.

"But what has happened in the months since Dad died?"

"Much work has already been carried out. First, significant upgrades to the sewage system and the electrics, and currently, repairs to the roof in preparation for winter."

"These funds didn't come through dad's will."

"No, they were deposited in May, and all the necessary formalities were completed then. To receive funding from the Department for Culture, Media and Sport, a dedicated foundation was required for the project—"

"The New Pemberley!" she exclaimed. "I'm the president after Dad's death. I've seen the documents."

Arthur merely nodded. He wasn't pleased that Elizabeth was largely uninformed about her father's recent activities, but it had been Thomas's decision. They'd clashed over the matter, but his health had already deteriorated so severely that it felt cruel to argue or oppose him. Ultimately, it was his final wish.

"I would have preferred more time to discuss this with Fabian," Elizabeth murmured.

"I understand, but trust me, there's nothing you can do. There's no way to challenge the contract. Your father took precautions to prevent any interference." Arthur paused, and Elizabeth saw the grief in his eyes.

Arthur and her father had been inseparable for the last thirty years. They'd fished, played golf, engaged in constant competition, and argued fiercely about Collister's financial affairs. Yet, at the end of the day, they were like brothers. "This is his final wish. He wanted this blasted mansion in

Warminster to be his Pemberley, and we're going to make it happen. We'll be exceedingly cautious with our investments, but we'll stick to his approach."

They sat in silence for a long time, weighed down by their grief and memories of the extraordinary yet peculiar man Thomas had been.

"He could have lived for many more years," Elizabeth remarked. "Naturally, we'll honour all his requests. But I'm not certain how we can turn his sole, all-consuming dream—Darcy Egerton—into a reality. I doubt he's one of the three authors, regardless of Dad's hopes."

"Don't be so certain. The last time I spoke to him, he said that he'd found Darcy Egerton."

"He was already on morphine," Elizabeth said.

"No, I believe Darcy Egerton could be among the men he wants you to meet."

Chapter 4

Elizabeth reclined on her aunt's sofa, finally feeling the depth of her exhaustion. The weeks following her father's death had been an unending nightmare. She had been forced to take charge as Collister's manager, despite her every fibre urging her to grieve in the comfort of her armchair at home. In a peculiar way, she'd been luckier than her sister and mother. She was obliged to be at the office, working tirelessly for fourteen hours each day. The transition wasn't too arduous, considering she'd been overseeing Collister's affairs since her father first fell ill the previous year.

Nonetheless, a significant shift occurred after his passing. While he was alive, she'd followed his leadership, ideas, and decisions. Every step was taken with his guidance and consultation, and when they disagreed, his presence had assuaged her uncertainties.

She had envisioned steering Collister in a different direction, independent of her father's influence. But, confronting this new reality, she grasped the difficulty and peril of her new role. The responsibility for numerous individuals rested on her shoulders, and her choices could either uphold Collister's standing or plunge it into unfathomable depths. She was utterly alone.

"One thing is evident," Elizabeth remarked, breaking the silence, "I should have commemorated Collister's hundred and fifty years differently. Not that I dislike Jane Austen, but the concept originated in Dad's fixation on Darcy Egerton."

"You might not be entirely right," Olivia interjected from the other end of the sofa.

"How can you say that?" Her aunt's house was the only place in London where Elizabeth allowed herself to succumb to her grief. In Olivia's embrace, she had shed countless tears over the course of many days and nights. She affectionately referred to her aunt as 'Mrs Gardiner', reminiscent of Elizabeth Bennet's aunt in Pride and Prejudice—the only Jane Austen novel she'd honestly liked.

Olivia, an Emeritus Fellow at Oxford's Somerville College, was rumoured to be a strong contender for the principal position. A specialist in twentieth-century literature, her course on female authors titled 'From Aphra Behn to Virginia Woolf', drew participants from around the globe. It was a dynamic and diverse course that presented women not as passive victims of history but as resilient and effective crusaders for rights, emancipation, and active political engagement. Jane Austen occupied a key place. Located in the middle of the period, she was considered a tipping point that changed English literature and heralded the first women's rights movement—the Somerville suffragettes.

"Thomas may have been obsessed, I grant you that, but using Jane Austen is brilliant. I've deliberated extensively with him and Marianne, and this convergence of celebrations is to Collister's advantage. In 2017, it wouldn't make sense to commemorate one hundred and fifty years of a publishing house without using Jane Austen."

"Nevertheless, it's rooted in his obsession."

"Yes, but for once, that fixation aligns perfectly with Collister's needs."

"So you're suggesting that we would have done this even without Darcy Egerton?"

Olivia smiled knowingly. "Perhaps not to this extent, but yes. It's far too compelling an opportunity to pass up. If you recall, your publishing house and others released affordable editions of her novels for train passengers in the late 19th century."

"I thought that was a legend."

"No, it's a fact. We studied it—perhaps the first significant impact of the industrial revolution on culture. Making those novels accessible to everyone at an affordable price. We analysed Collister's sales, and data from other publishers who embraced the popular format, geared towards 'train reading', as it was termed."

Elizabeth nodded absentmindedly, her thoughts returning to the daunting task her father had left her to fulfil.

"I suppose you know that Dad asked me to meet three of the finalists…before the winner's announced."

Olivia paused briefly before responding. "Yes."

"And you agreed? I thought you were on my side."

"I'm always on your side, Elizabeth. You are like my own child."

Elizabeth was astonished. It was a direct statement, something her aunt had never said before.

"You and Kath are like our own children, but I strongly disapprove of Kath's recent behaviour. Being late this morning was such an immature move. She's thirty. It's time she grew up. I talked to her, but she questioned my right to get involved in your lives to that extent."

"I think she's struggling to cope with Dad's death," Elizabeth said.

"Yes, I understand that, and I've followed my instincts, which told me to concentrate on you. And God knows, you need all the support you can get these days."

"Then, my dear aunt, fill me in on everything you know

about those candidates for the role of Darcy Egerton. I'm sure you didn't undertake this *essential* endeavour without thorough research and consideration."

"I'm happy that your father's sarcasm isn't lost," Olivia jested. "Yes, you're right. I've often been your father's consultant in the past. He never doubted my professional skills and integrity, and he preferred those who challenged him. I understand how *fixated* he was on Darcy Egerton. Still, the latest findings on that man are quite remarkable.

"Darcy Egerton has such diversity in his writing. Different styles, genres, and periods. This diversity has provided us with an excellent framework to work with. I'm certain that Darcy Egerton is a man, beyond any doubt. Then there are the other findings, which I also think are accurate. He's around forty and has a background in IT. He attended a humanities-oriented college. He definitely writes regularly for a magazine, although not as a staff writer—"

"You've drawn many conclusions. Are you confident they're accurate?"

"Profiling isn't an exact science, but it offers remarkable insights. It's an overview of an individual. There might be some variations, but they don't change the overall picture significantly. And then the most interesting part—your father was convinced that Darcy managed his own marketing and promotional campaigns, and that he'd found out that after nine years that his readers had grown tired of the secrecy and demanded something fresh. Your father was certain the man would reveal himself next year with his 2017 novel."

"I agree it's plausible. But to assume that he'd choose our publishing house to release a novel, and that novel would happen to be the one we've been longing for about Jane Austen…honestly, I find that hard to believe."

"Well, the expert, a genuine profiler who collaborates with Scotland Yard, indicated that Egerton's looking for an event, a major literary event, to mark his unveiling."

"And Dad orchestrated this plan to fit the importance of the event."

"Yes, he wanted something grand enough for Darcy Egerton."

"But he didn't need to win a literary competition for that. He could've just come forward, and Collister would have rolled out a red carpet for him."

"Yes, but they—Thomas and Egerton—wanted to play a game! And they did play it, even if we haven't seen all the episodes."

"So you're convinced he knew about Dad's obsession with him?"

"Your father's investigations were so intricate and thorough that a person like Darcy Egerton would have stumbled upon traces of Thomas's pursuit."

"A person like him?"

"Well-informed and undoubtedly amused by the attention he garnered in cultural circles. He was well aware of the efforts to locate him. And then there was that interview—he practically acknowledged Thomas as his competitor in this intricate game."

"I see," said Elizabeth, then suddenly came to a decision. "I won't meet those men under the assumption that Dad probably set it up—like some sort of date for me to find this Darcy Egerton and end up marrying him by the end of the story."

Olivia grinned. At one of their recent meetings, Thomas had discussed exactly that, but in more discreet terms.

"I hope not!" she answered brusquely, not wanting to continue the conversation, but Elizabeth spoke further.

"Dad knew I read a lot, but I'm not an expert on Jane Austen or Darcy Egerton. He wanted me to meet these men, hoping Darcy Egerton would want to get to know me better."

"I don't think he truly intended that. He mainly wanted your opinion because you're a good manager, not a literary expert. He wanted an outsider in our field to evaluate the candidates. But it's your call. You won't be cursed if you don't fulfil his final request." Olivia chuckled, concluding the conversation on an optimistic and light-hearted note. "Do what you want, Lizzy. I'm sure, for your father, it was enough to know that his company was in capable hands."

∞∞∞

"Did she agree to meet the Darcy Egertons?" Arthur asked his wife later that evening.

"Not exactly. I won't allow her to take on any further burdens besides Collister. However, she does need to meet some decent men eventually."

"Are you certain they're decent? This Darcy Egerton doesn't strike me as nice—he seems more like a fanatic."

"They're not serial killers if that's your concern. I don't know what kind of man she's interested in. Over the years, we've hardly seen her with any men. Kath has too many, and Elizabeth works too hard to have time for socialising. She won't find love among her business associates. Meeting those candidates means she'll escape her office…at least three times in the coming months."

Yet, Arthur wasn't pleased with the idea. "But you agree that using Elizabeth as bait to attract the Darcys is absurd? The entire search was and still is ridiculous. The way he planned this venture, then the investigations, some of which were…questionable. Does she know everything?"

"No! Absolutely not. She would never have agreed if she'd known how he found the finalists."

"This is the last game, Olivia! We'll continue because Thomas wanted it, but only until next summer. Then, hopefully, we can put this Darcy Egerton nonsense behind us. Tomorrow, Elizabeth is visiting the earl and his estate."

"The new Pemberley." Olivia grinned.

"Whatever! I'm just curious—although it doesn't matter anymore—how Thomas settled on that ruin."

"He didn't tell you?"

"I asked him once, and he put on that annoyingly superior expression while going on about cultural and literary criteria."

Olivia laughed heartily. It was true—Thomas could be that way. Nonetheless, they all forgave him because he was amusing, generous, and an exceptional leader and manager.

"They placed an advertisement that Collister was searching for a candidate for Pemberley. They got about fifty responses back, with all sorts of mansions and castles, and Thomas chose that house near Warminster in Wiltshire," Olivia said, and Arthur looked at her, shocked.

"Isn't it odd that I wasn't aware, and you know more than me?" Arthur queried.

"No, there's no way you could possibly know everything that happens at Collister. Only the folks from Collister Press who put out the ad and a few of us from his working group knew. But we didn't have anything to do with his choice. He told us nothing until he settled on Warminster."

"I'm sorry, but he was completely obsessed with that man," Arthur said, peering into his glass, still filled with anger and sadness. He longed to have Thomas in the room, engaging in an all-night argument with him.

"Yes, but Thomas was clever and innovative, not delusional. He had a strategy to track down this writer—"

"For all those years?"

"Alright! He had many approaches and changed tack when he didn't get a result."

Olivia spoke about him so enthusiastically that her husband set down his glass and gazed at her for quite a while. "Like many women, you were probably in love with him too."

Olivia laughed and moved closer to him on the sofa. Her husband's words held a touch of jesting, but she suspected he was finally voicing one of the fears he'd never showed when Thomas was alive.

"Actually, no," she replied from within his embrace. "I admired him a lot, but I'm far too self-centred myself to fall for a self-centred man."

Her husband smiled, strangely relieved. It was the best reason; Olivia needed a man like him who adored her and allowed her to win all their arguments.

"Do you regret not having children?"

"No, I have the girls. Unfortunately, Kath has been incredibly disappointing lately. She is spoiled, and her privileged upbringing shows in all her decisions."

"Yes, she was late to the meeting because she only arrived from New York at nine this morning."

"Still not a good reason to be late for such an important event."

Chapter 5

"Good morning, Clarice." Elizabeth greeted her chief assistant, who had just entered the room.

"Would you like me to go to Warminster with you?" Clarice asked.

Elizabeth hesitated. She valued having Clarice with her in meetings. Efficient and with excellent attention to detail, Clarice noted every minutia and served as an invaluable witness to discussions. However, it was a Friday morning, and Elizabeth wanted to think of the forthcoming meeting as more of a mini holiday. There were no negotiations or preparations involved, just a trip to Wiltshire. A meeting with the architect was scheduled for Monday, and some teams were set to arrive the following week. Yet, she wished to see the location beforehand, not through photos but by visiting the house and its grounds. In truth, she craved a day alone in that unfamiliar territory that oddly connected her to her father.

Clarice appeared concerned as she squinted at her tablet. "There might be an issue. You're supposed to take the M3 and A303, but there's been a massive accident due to fog, and the M3 will be closed for at least two hours. You won't make it on time. Shall I call and reschedule the meeting?"

Clarice was Elizabeth's personal assistant because she

knew her better than anyone else. A mere glance at her boss conveyed that Elizabeth wasn't pleased about being late or postponing the meeting, and a solution had to be found.

Clarice tinkered with her tablet briefly before saying, "The helicopter will be ready for you in half an hour."

And so, her impromptu getaway began.

She didn't mind meeting the earl; on the contrary, she felt curious as to why her father had chosen that property out of fifty potential options.

She enjoyed flying and had even obtained a light aircraft licence five years ago. Unfortunately, time constraints prevented her from continuing it further. However, the view as a passenger was far more delightful than paying strict attention to controls. The pilot, Nolan Lloyd, an Iraq war veteran, was the only pilot her father trusted. She rarely used the helicopter, given that she hardly ever left London.

"Have you flown my father to Warminster before?"

"Yes, Miss Collister, a couple of times. We've even got a suitable landing spot. There's a platform where Mr Collister intended to build a stage."

The pilot wasn't chatty, and Elizabeth relished the lack of pressure to converse, as well as the clear sky, the landscape below, and her thoughts. Her life was undoubtedly about to change, not necessarily for the better. Amidst her regular work, she now bore the enormous responsibility of preparing a flawless celebration to elevate their name and reputation. Her existence revolved around Collister.

While she had a group of friends, they had all coupled up recently. The last outing with them had been more vexing than enjoyable, dominated by discussions about marriage and property prices. Soon, children would come into the picture, making her prefer solitude over spending time with them. They were kind and tried to introduce a single friend each time, which was even worse than being alone at their table.

At one point, the pilot pointed out the accident. It was a gruesome scene involving at least twenty cars, numerous ambulances, and fire engines.

"It'll be another hour at least before the traffic starts moving again. I don't know how long it'll take for your driver to get through. Shall I wait for you?"

Without hesitation, she replied, "No, thank you."

She yearned for freedom, unburdened by the thought of someone waiting on her. She could call her driver and wait for him as long as necessary. The estate was hers for at least five years.

Suddenly, the house materialised, almost magically, and from the sky, it appeared charming. However, during the helicopter's circuit around the property, she observed that the roof had collapsed in two places, and a team was working to restore it.

"It's not in the best condition," Nolan remarked.

"Yes, a lot of work to be done, and only ten months until July."

"Mr Collister was quite enthusiastic. He was convinced you'd manage to have it ready for the event."

Her father's enthusiasm for difficult causes was characteristic, and it seemed Nolan had been a trustworthy confidant. Undoubtedly, there was an old story between her father and Nolan, given his role in assisting veterans from various wars.

But as they landed, she forgot everything, engulfed in the beauty of the day and the decrepit romanticism of the estate.

Chapter 6

A s she strolled along the path to the main entrance, she observed the place with a curious sensation of gliding from her hectic real life into a glorious past. Unfortunately, the former grandeur and elegance had faded away, leaving a facade with crumbling plaster on the upper levels and decrepit marble steps. She spotted a man approaching the house across the vast lawn in front. Drenched from head to toe, mud even splattered in his hair, he appeared disgusted with his soiled hands.

Uncertain of how to proceed, Elizabeth contemplated running up the steps and pretending not to have noticed him. Yet, their eyes met, making that plan impossible. She ultimately offered a smile and said, "Good morning, I'm in search of Lord Warminster." The man didn't smile back, but she was accustomed to morose men she frequently encountered in business meetings. Nonetheless, the man advancing towards her seemed not gloomy but angry.

"I believe you're looking for me," he responded after a brief pause. Unexpectedly, he then smiled, significantly changing his demeanour.

"Do you not know for certain?" she enquired as they entered a spacious hall where a man and a woman hurriedly arrived, only to halt and gaze at them with curiosity.

"Do something, Soames," he said to the man.

"I apologise, sir," the man replied, and Elizabeth assumed 'Soames' was the butler.

"Mrs Evans, please show Miss Collister to the living room while I have a wash. And kindly assure her that I am indeed the Earl of Warminster."

The woman nodded amiably. She exuded warmth and friendliness as she regarded Elizabeth. "I'm sorry, Miss Collister, for the reception. It appears Mr Stafford had an accident. There's been a lot of work going on lately."

Mr Stafford? Elizabeth mused with a hint of amusement. *Not his lordship or Lord Warminster!*

But then, as Mrs Evans opened the door, all her previous thoughts, curiosities, and concerns evaporated. The scene inside mesmerised her. They had not entered a contemporary living room but rather a spacious, if not colossal, parlour that had remained unchanged for at least a century and a half. It bore characteristics of the Georgian or Victorian era—she couldn't quite discern which, but it was clearly from a distant past. Not pristine but unchanged, with many pieces of furniture in disrepair, stained, or worn, mirroring the general state of the house. She gazed in dismay at the decaying chairs and threadbare carpets, the wall coverings stained and peeling. Elizabeth was surprised to see that the room was not unoccupied. Several people sat around the room engaged in various activities. Had it not been for their clothing, she might have believed herself transported into a Jane Austen novel.

Mrs Evans introduced her, and Elizabeth caught fragments of responses amid the murmurs, with the only distinct phrase being, "Join us for whist?"

Politely declining the peculiar invitation, Elizabeth was immediately ignored by everyone.

Two women chatted, while a man engrossed in his book barely glanced up. It was surreal, implausible, yet undeniably real.

Yes, shouted her mind, *if Dad was invited here, he would have instantly believed he was at Pemberley in 1812.* A dilapidated Pemberley, centuries old, yet a place Thomas could imagine restored to its former glory.

Why did you leave me? she scolded her father. *I need you here, so we can laugh and jest about this scene you surely relished.*

Tears welled in her eyes as she made her way to the tall French doors. She hesitated to step out onto the terrace, which had obviously once overlooked a splendid garden—the doors appeared too fragile to be opened. The room was chilly, and everyone was huddled near the fireplace, where a fire burned, although it was insufficient for the huge space. Surprisingly, the room was clean and well-maintained, albeit old and worn.

The windows gleamed, and Elizabeth surmised that Mrs Evans was responsible for maintaining the space, at least to the best of her ability. Still ignored by the others, she returned to the hall. Doors flanked each side, and she tried the one opposite. It was locked, so she pushed another one, revealing an almost empty room—only a modern, large sofa and a television. Unlike the parlour, the exquisite old parquet flooring was immaculate. She approached the bare windows, wrapping her coat tightly around her shivering form. She sat on the sofa, using the cushions for warmth.

Elizabeth only realised she had fallen asleep when a voice called her name, pulling her into that liminal space between dreams and reality. She finally opened her eyes to find the earl smiling at her. He was dressed in clean clothes, with no sign of mud in his hair, extending his hand to help her up.

"I apologise," he said, his smile unwavering. "I assumed you'd stay by the fire in the other room."

"I fell asleep despite the cold," she admitted, looking at him, not at all embarrassed by the situation.

In the hallway, he opened the closed door she had previously tried. Once again, she found herself in a different time and space. It was a beautifully preserved library, warm and inviting. He settled her near the fire, making sure she was warm with a blanket over her knees.

"Mrs Evans will bring hot chocolate and biscuits. Continue to rest," he said in a tone meant to sound jesting, yet it sounded strangely tender.

"Don't tempt me," Elizabeth replied, glancing around the room. This place surely must have been what her father believed to be Pemberley, the location he sought for his plans.

"I'm sorry for your loss. Mr Collister was a rare gentleman," he said.

"Thank you!" She wanted to add that he was also quite reckless with his money, but she kept silent.

They sipped the excellent hot chocolate in silence for a while. Then, he spoke, looking at her intently. "Would you like to discuss the contract?"

Seeing her confusion, he continued, "When I saw you arriving in the helicopter, I thought you were here to renegotiate the terms." His voice dripped with sarcasm, prompting her to respond in kind. "Apologies if my arrival in the helicopter disturbed your game of whist!"

He maintained his smile as he replied, making Elizabeth wish she could wipe that haughty expression from his face. "Well, Miss Collister, when I found you on the lawn, I was actually opening the main gate for your car…but you arrived by helicopter."

This is Darcy, the genuine one from Jane Austen's book, not poor Darcy Egerton whom Dad has been futilely searching for in recent years, she mused. And the arrogant aristocrat was preferable to all her father's Darcys.

But in this modern tale, she owned Pemberley without having to marry him. And, despite his attitude, she would be the mistress in this house for at least a few years.

"Did you forget about the sprinkler during the turmoil caused by the card game?" she asked. She could discern his thoughts from his expression—the London lady arriving in her helicopter with her Christian Louboutin boots. He probably wasn't familiar with Christian Louboutin, she speculated.

But then, observing him as he added wood to the fire, she realised he likely knew about her favourite shoemaker. His jumper and trousers weren't from just any shop. His shoes reminded her of her father's, which she'd enjoyed helping him select on Savile Row. This man's shoes came from a similar place. What did that signify? She wasn't entirely sure. He had the means to maintain the library in excellent condition and had bespoke shoes, yet he hesitated to carry out crucial repairs on the house, which was teetering on the brink of collapse. And then, there were all those people in the living room she had glimpsed only moments ago—so odd that she pondered whether they were real or if she had dreamt them during her brief nap.

"Are you hungry?" he suddenly asked, changing the subject.

"Yes, actually, I am quite hungry."

"Would you like to have lunch with me?"

"What about your guests?" She gestured across the hall, where the strange gathering likely still lingered.

"Them? We have our meals separately."

She detected annoyance in his voice, not the sarcasm he had directed at her, but something deeper and more bitter.

"Mrs Evans will serve lunch here, in the library."

"Isn't that a form of desecration?"

"Desecration?" He chuckled. "Coming from the Collister heiress who's accustomed to revering books. No, it's just a room, and I can assure you, there aren't many places in this house where we can dine properly. Here, it's warm, and we can address all our issues."

"Issues? Do we have issues?"

"Don't we?" Fitzwilliam Darcy re-entered the conversation, gazing at her while standing before her. "The team I hired to locate and replace the water pipes did an 'excellent' job, managing to puncture one right in the middle of the lawn. You saw the result yourself."

"Please, have a seat," she suggested. "Your restlessness is making me dizzy."

She was sincere, and despite knowing each other for less than an hour, she spoke to him like a friend. He finally took a seat in a large leather armchair opposite her.

"You asked if I came to renegotiate the contract. No, this project is my father's last wish, and even though I may disagree, I'll honour his request."

"You don't agree, then?"

"Would you?" She gestured around, encompassing everything she had observed—the sagging roof, the waterlogged lawn, and the living room that seemed to have endured at least two centuries of heavy use.

"You're right. I was surprised by your father's choice, but I'm not complaining."

Of course not, she thought. *Who would turn down such an incredible offer?*

"Our only condition is that we supervise the renovations from this point onwards," she stated with a hint of concern that he might object. Initially, she had suspected him of intending to pad out the final bill, but his expression dispelled her uncharitable assumptions.

Leaning back in his chair, he rolled his eyes. "Thank goodness! I didn't want to do this. Your father insisted I assemble the teams and supervise the work, but you've just given me excellent news."

"So, we've resolved this matter?"

"Yes, absolutely. Feel free to add any clauses you want to the contract in that regard."

"I think it's unnecessary. A gentleman's agreement between us will suffice."

Once again, Fitzwilliam Darcy from Jane Austen's Pemberley emerged. Setting aside all their troubles and the purpose of her visit, he looked at her and remarked, "It's rather difficult for me to have a *gentleman's* agreement with you." His eyes were dark and had a daring glint in them, making her feel simultaneously hot and cold—a sensation she hadn't experienced in quite some time. She wanted to recall Elizabeth Bennet's words about Darcy but couldn't. Her mind was blank before his eyes, the colour of which she struggled to discern.

As with any situation involving a man, she felt out of place and as awkward as her teenage self. Elizabeth Collister hadn't truly evolved beyond those days. Occupied with her work, she lacked the time for idle romantic games and had forgotten what the subtle cues between a man and a woman looked like. She wanted to project the image of a confident young woman, but in reality, she was more akin to a nervous teenager. She breathed deeply as he continued to look at her, and the silence felt eternal, but he was in no hurry. And surprisingly, she didn't feel flustered, as she was sure he *imagined* her as a confident woman. Being the head of Collister enveloped her in an assurance she didn't have in reality. However, she could rely on it.

It's like I'm playing a role, she thought. *A confident woman of the world*.

"Sorry," he eventually said, interpreting her silence differently.

"What for?" she asked, surprise evident in her voice.

"Because…well, because I was flirting with you."

"Were you?"

"Yes, I suppose I was!"

And finally, they both laughed.

He might be referred to as Mr Stafford by his housekeeper, but he was Lord Warminster in every aspect of his being, body, and soul.

Every Elizabeth has the right to choose her Darcy, she said to her father, as she was sure his presence was hovering around them somehow, perhaps irritated that she had already chosen a Darcy before encountering his genuine contenders. *I no longer care about your Egertons, Dad. I'm thoroughly enjoying this Darcy.*

"I'll need to call someone to pick me up from here," she said, hoping he might offer to drive her back to London.

"I'll take you to London." His response echoed her thoughts, and an odd excitement overcame her, though she was too close to the fireplace to identify its exact source.

She hesitated, and once again, he misread her hesitation. "I assure you, my car can manage the journey."

"Well, that's reassuring," she answered in that tone that conveyed they were playing a game that only they knew the rules to.

They shared a strange moment. Only an hour had passed since they'd met, yet their rapport seemed far older and more profound. She'd anticipated a struggle, intending to assert her uncle's decision. While, certainly, he had awaited her arrival, determined to oppose the new head of Collister. And both had been…'disappointed'. Neither had foreseen they would connect to such an extent. *You're here for work, Elizabeth Collister*, she chastised herself, yet she found herself relishing everything that was happening. The silence was so profound that she stood and scanned the bookshelves. "May I?" she asked.

"Yes, please, it's a genuine library," he responded, his tone devoid of any sarcasm or jest.

"Have we settled on the work to be done?" she asked, browsing the bookshelves. "I was thinking about the roof. We should finish it before winter."

He nodded, but she detected a reluctance, as if he wished to avoid discussing the matter further.

"It's your decision, but yes, logically, the roof should be a priority. I do have one request, which I discussed with your father, and he agreed to. You'll find it in the estimate. We need to protect the library shelves with glass. If this place is turned into a luxurious Austenesque resort, we need to safeguard the books. I've ordered the glass, and they've already come to take measurements."

Elizabeth nodded. She had indeed noticed the great expense, but given the context, it made sense. They needed to preserve the room and its books, while the mahogany wood needed good quality glass to complement it.

"Yes, certainly, the roof and the books!" she affirmed.

They reached an agreement. She attempted to retrieve a book from a higher shelf, and Rowan stood to hand it to her. The encounter was fleeting, yet that brief closeness stirred her, and she nearly dropped the book, which he swiftly rescued from her.

"It's *Elizabeth's Diary*,[3]" she murmured, trying to focus on the book, with his presence still lingering nearby.

"Yes, my great-grandmother received an autographed copy." Opening the book, she recognised the Duchess of Lancashire's exquisite calligraphy.

"I must admit, my introduction to Jane Austen came not through reading her but via *Elizabeth's Diary*. Have you…?" he enquired.

"Yes, of course. It's an essential part of our literature, and you may be right—after reading this book, I too approached Austen's works with greater attention."

And Dad expects me to find a man who can write a modern reply to this incomparable work, she pondered. A sudden urge to confide in him surged. But she decided against disclosing that she was meant to meet three men and evaluate their Darcy-like qualities.

"So, you're saying you've read Jane Austen?" she queried, book in hand.

"Yes, I have," he responded, though his answer was lost as his butler and Mrs Evans entered with lunch. Evidently, he dined here often, as they efficiently arranged a cosy table with candles and a bowl of roses. The butler poured a little wine into his lordship's glass, awaiting his judgment. He gave a slight grimace. "Is this the one we bought in Saint-

Laurent?"

"Yes, sir."

"Is it any good?" he asked, and Elizabeth observed a similar grimace on the butler's countenance. "Bring us another wine, please, Soames."

"Is it for—?" the butler gestured towards the living room.

"Absolutely," the earl confirmed, and they exchanged smiles, a light-hearted jest rather than any malicious intent.

"May I taste it?" she asked. "I'm simply curious to see what you don't like," she explained, addressing their surprised expressions.

The butler poured the wine, a smile playing on his lips that she couldn't quite decipher. It was far from impertinence—a butler of his calibre would never be impolite to his master's guests. His smile held a deeper sentiment Elizabeth could easily discern—he liked her and was pleased to comply with her gentle request, perhaps sympathetic to his solitary master, whom he regarded, for sure, in a paternal manner.

She sampled the wine, finding it agreeable. "It's quite good!" she remarked.

"Exactly. Now wait for the other one." They had fresh glasses, and the butler filled hers. "Wow!" she exclaimed.

"Yes." The earl smiled. "That's the distinction—between good and wow."

"I'm not an expert," she declared with candour.

"How come? Your father was a connoisseur. I had the privilege of spending a few afternoons with him, sampling some of my wines. Of course, my cellar is nowhere near as extensive as his."

"Yes, I suppose he had some real gems. My sister and I used to sneak bottles of wine, but only from one section of the cellar. There were some that were off-limits…I wonder what'll happen to them now."

Unexpectedly, he touched her hand to ease her apparent

pain. For the first time, their gazes locked, leaving them both breathless and suddenly bashful. They sipped their wine silently, yet she felt compelled to speak—an overwhelming urge to tell him more, everything, about her.

"We replaced the bottles with a small sticker with our name and a cheeky emoji. Once, my father told Kath that if she ever took one of *the special* bottles, she should leave her credit card instead of the sticker."

He laughed, and they both felt relieved.

"We weren't prepared for guests, madam," the housekeeper apologised as if the meal might fall short of her standards.

"Come now, Mrs Evans. I know that's not true. Our cook is always ready for guests and often complains that we don't entertain enough."

The lunch was extraordinary—a Niçoise salad Elizabeth devoured hungrily; tasty lamb chops accompanied by the most delicious mashed potatoes she'd ever tasted. When the butler appeared with another dish from the hall, laughter and voices wafted in.

She turned her head, her curiosity piqued by the noise. The library was magnificent, but recalling the Austen gathering reminded her of the strange situation they were experiencing.

"Are they guests?" she asked, her curiosity no longer hidden. Then, realising she might be prying, she added, "Sorry, it's none of my business." Nonetheless, he dismissed her apology with a gracious gesture.

"No, I understand your curiosity. It's indeed quite peculiar. They're my mother's relatives. My father never liked them and limited their visits to a few days a year. But when my father fell ill, my mother took her revenge and invited them to stay here. It's been more than a decade now. My father passed away, and they still reside at Warminster most of the time."

"Is your mother here?" she asked, no longer attempting

to conceal her interest.

"No," he replied. "The irony of the situation is that she couldn't stand her own relatives and now lives in London. She visits perhaps once a month or even less. They're on her side. A brother and sister, along with their adult children—fortunately, only some of them—and their partners. Some are absent on weekdays and only come for weekends."

"Are they paying for—?" She cut herself off, realising she was indeed prying. But he waved away her intrusion as he answered, a hint of exasperation in his tone. "No, of course not. At least I imposed separate kitchens. My staff handle the cleaning. My sole contribution—after my mother left, this place started resembling a pigsty. I tried to evict them, but they returned with my mother."

"But why—"

"Why didn't I employ other means to get rid of them?"

She nodded like a curious child.

"It's hard to explain. They aren't people—they're like a plague." She gazed at him as he spoke, forgetting her meal. He seemed both mad and sad at the same time. "Initially, my mother lived here for the first couple of years or so. That's when they settled in. After her departure, I took some measures—closed off the library and my apartment and isolated the west wing from them. It's strange, isn't it?"

She didn't respond, but she smiled.

"What's really weird is that I don't feel the strangeness of the situation anymore. It's become an accepted status quo for me. Only my logic tells me I should get rid of them. I know the significant amount your father committed to restoring the house, and as you saw, it desperately needs renovation. Yet, one of the reasons I agreed was the possibility of stipulating in the contract that only I would be allowed to stay here during the work while you rent it."

He was sincere; she could tell.

"So, I'll be the villainous tenant who disrupts their

lives?"

"Yes, precisely," he replied, and they both laughed again, feeling entirely at ease.

"But it seemed they didn't recognise who I was. They invited me to join them, then ignored me. All of them!"

"As I explained, they aren't individuals but a collective organism. It's an instinctual response to a potential threat— they saw you but dismissed your presence, hoping the danger would vanish."

"When I entered that room, it felt like a time machine transporting me into Mrs Bennet's parlour."

"Well, Mrs Bennet's parlour wasn't this spacious, but yes, the ambience and decor resemble it. It's what your father intended, restoring the place to its former beauty. After all, it was meant to be Pemberley."

Soon, dessert arrived. A glass bowl contained eggnog topped with delicate white clouds. Once again, she exclaimed, "Wow!" like a child, and Mrs Evans beamed with delight.

"It's a Romanian recipe called 'bird's milk'. Our cook whipped white egg foam onto the eggnog to create these clouds."

The taste was so delightful that she momentarily forgot about him, relishing the dessert.

She was living out the fantasy of many girls—dining with a handsome gentleman surrounded by candles and a crackling fireplace. She had experienced such a setting a few times before, but never with the right man, watching her from the other side of the table with what seemed like genuine interest. He wanted to be there with her. No rush, no outside world, just the warmth of the fire and them. And the delectable meal. The cheese that concluded the simple, yet delicious meal came from France, not the nearby supermarket.

It's working, she thought. *I can play the role of a confident woman in front of this arrogant aristocrat. With the 'Collister director' label stamped on my forehead, people—not just him—won't perceive my shyness.*

"I'd give anything to know what you're thinking," he remarked.

A swarm of butterflies seemed to flutter in her chest and heart, a sensation close to pain. As soon as it passed, she yearned for more—more of everything, especially him. She felt wonderfully exhausted, not accustomed to indulging so much during lunch or letting her self-control relax, and she gazed at him as though he were a man she'd known for a long time.

"You're looking at me as if I'm the managing director of Collister—"

He attempted to interject, but she didn't let him speak. "Please, let me finish." She saw him ease back into his chair, taking a sip of wine; they were now onto the second bottle, and his sharp eyes encouraged her to continue.

"That's how people perceive me—the Collister heiress, now the boss. The image is already established: a proud and privileged young woman who has everything in life."

"And?" he asked, smiling. "Aren't you all those things?"

"I am. I'm also over thirty and have never really dated. Somewhere along the way, I lost the ability to flirt. I can't tell when or if a man's interested in me—"

"I wouldn't say that," he responded, but his voice was a quiet murmur, difficult to catch. She understood his words more with her heart than her ears. She felt he liked her, probably never imagining that the woman he'd initially disliked as she descended from the helicopter could be the same person now eating with visible enjoyment and sharing these vulnerable confessions. She trusted him.

"It's not that I don't attract men. It's more about how I feel inside—I can't tell when a man's interested or flirting with me. Lost in my busy life, I've forgotten the rules of the game."

Silently, he approached her and helped her stand, the

sequence of events unfolding in slow motion, like a dream. He gave her the space and time to step back or stop what he was about to do. But she didn't move. Her inner self merged with his in an explosive collision as she found herself in his arms. Then, his lips pressed against hers, and she clung to him, overwhelmed by the intensity of the feeling.

It's probably the wine, she thought before the reality around her faded. They kissed like two desperate beings. As if this were the final kiss in the universe. Their mouths opened with hunger and complete acceptance of the other's intrusion. Eventually, he trailed kisses along her neck and ear, eliciting such delightful sounds that he held her even closer, making her seem utterly lost in him. "Do you remember the game now?" he asked, aiming for a touch of jest but only sounding hoarse with excitement.

He gazed at her, yet their bodies remained close.

Her eyelashes strived to hide her excitement, and she replied, "To some extent. Please show me more!"

He took her hand and almost pulled her along with him. She knew what awaited her from the first step, but it was what she wanted.

"Please don't slam me against the wall like in American films," she teased, causing him to pause again, enveloping her in his arms. However, his hand sought her breast this time, and she nearly melted in his embrace. "I've got a king-size bed. Is that acceptable, Miss Bennet?"

She didn't answer as he pushed some of the shelves away, opening a door to a well-lit wooden staircase that ascended to the next floor. *Still Pemberley*, she thought briefly, looking around the room, but then she forgot everything again as her eyes fell on his bed. It was indeed the first time this had happened to her. From acquaintance to bed in no more than three hours, but it was the breathtaking adventure she had always fantasised about.

She'd taken off her boots at some point, and he lifted

her onto his bed like a precious burden, and there they kissed again. But this time, his hand wandered over her body, under the blouse he unbuttoned, and then he discovered her secret place under the soft fabric of her skirt. She cried out and trembled, and she made him take her into his arms only to feel him ready to love her.

"We will see later about the prelude," he said while he undressed. Under his eager eyes, Elizabeth showed the same haste as she undressed, watching him put on a condom, and all she could think of was having him inside her, or she would die waiting. He entered her in one fluid movement. "My goodness, you are ready for me!"

"Yes," she whispered as he conquered her, relishing the incredible sensation. It lasted a second or an hour. Neither of them could tell as, at the same time, their orgasms overcame them, making them both cry out in wonder.

"Good or wow?" he asked, looking at her after a long while.

"Wow!" she said, stroking his face.

"You're still wearing your bra. I need to see your breasts," he whispered in her ear.

"Well? Are you shy? Undress me!" She laughed.

"I confess my biggest failure in life is women's bras. I have fought a continuous battle with those tiny—"

He was suddenly silent in front of her naked body.

"You are perfect," he said, slowly caressing her bosom.

"Maybe a little fat," she said, touching her belly.

"Women are so foolish. They don't understand what a man wants. Do you think I enjoy a bag of bones?" he asked, caressing her belly and legs, his fingers skimming over her sensitive parts and driving her close to another orgasm.

"This is what I like," he whispered, his hand on her belly.

"Says the man with zero fat on him."

"Would you like me to be fatter?"

"No."

"Then we're both happy. The inconvenience of

condoms is that I need to leave you and wash while you wait for me here, unwashed."

"Pervert!" she said, looking at his naked body. "Do you have a proper bathroom, or is it the Austen type?"

He turned to her and said before disappearing, "Exasperating woman!"

He found her under the duvet, nearly asleep, and he gently took her into his arms.

"Elizabeth," he said.

"Darcy," was her answer, making him pull back a little so he could see her face.

"Darcy?" he asked, surprised.

"Yes. Haven't you read *Pride and Prejudice*?"

"I know who Darcy is."

"Then you understand that it's only natural that I call you that. Me—Elizabeth, you—Darcy, it—Pemberley."

It only took a look for his passion to reignite; he yearned to know her body. It was impossible to restrain his eagerness while she, like a marvellous instrument, let him play his tune to blissfulness.

"In this Regency bed with you, I completely agree with my father's plans for next summer. Hooray for Jane Austen!" she exclaimed and chuckled. "I'll write a fitting speech."

"About what?"

"About what I appreciate the most in my new role as a woman two centuries after Jane Austen."

He still wanted her, but he also liked Elizabeth talking. It was as gratifying as lovemaking.

"And? What do you value the most among all the things women have achieved or gained?"

She didn't hesitate. "This!" And she indicated their naked bodies beneath the covers. "At last, we're equal in love. I've made love to you as you have to me. I don't need to conceal anything. Lovemaking doesn't disgrace me. I could have a child without marriage, and everyone would admire my bravery. I can sleep with anyone, just like any man, with no worries, remorse, or fear.

"Elizabeth Austen, a hundred years after her great-grandaunt's death, made love to Darcy Lancashire, and she had to marry him[4]. Even if she had other immediate plans for her life."

"So you think sleeping around is the most significant freedom women have gained."

"Yes, because it's something for us, unrelated to politics like voting, or to the family like working eight hours for pay. It's about pure pleasure and freedom. The freedom to love, to decide what you want to do with your body without interference from the state, men, church, or society."

"You might be onto something. It's a compelling speech," he remarked. "Stay!"

She wanted to stay, yet she remained silent while observing him. And then he embraced her, whispering, "Stay, please stay." Making her tremble, as again she felt him ready to love her and her body answering that incredible call.

"I need clothes," she whispered.

"You don't. I have a kimono for you. It's all you need."

She laughed, tempted. It was the perfect sequel to the novel she was living, yet she hesitated, inclined to leave. *It's too perfect to be true.* A vile thought clouded her mind, but it lasted just a second, and a wave of fury overwhelmed her. *I'm always running from my happiness. Who cares what'll happen on Monday?*

"Yes, I'll stay. But I need my clothes." He got up stark naked with no hesitation. Her longest relationship had ended some time ago after three years. She didn't remember Robert getting up naked from bed. He always had boxers on, but the earl was happy with his *whole* body and didn't seem to have any complexes when he wasn't aroused. He brought her a sumptuous silk kimono, inviting her to get out of bed in his arms to help her dress.

"No," she said, admiring the black kimono with cherry blossoms. "I'm dirty."

"Shush, your body's covered in love's juices, and you call it dirt?"

He enveloped her in the fresh silk and showed her to the bathroom.

It was as exquisite as the rest of his apartment—a perfect combination of old and new. She had been wrong initially; it wasn't a replica of a Regency apartment but old, reinterpreted in a modern vision. That room, and most likely the whole apartment, was a masterpiece by a designer who plainly understood what was required.

She closed her eyes in the large black marble bath, waiting for him. She was sure he would come. "I have some orders to give," he said, "while you make your calls."

He didn't wait for her to say yes to his invitation. *Damn aristocrat*, she thought, *he is so sure of everything.*

But she liked his attitude, and *that* was no longer a secret.

With its soaked park and fallen roof, that ruin of a mansion could be restored to look like his apartment—2017 Regency. She accepted the costs were fair and, for once, agreed with her father. Mostly because Rowan Stafford, the Earl of Warminster, had slept with her.

"Did you ask for clothes?" he said while undressing and approaching her in the bath. She smiled, as it perfectly fitted two people.

"Yes, the road is open again and my housekeeper has sent the driver with my luggage."

"Which road?"

"There was an accident on the M3."

She couldn't see his expression from her position in his arms, but he was surprised. "It was an accident!" he murmured.

"Yes, a bad one, lots of cars involved."

"That's why you came by helicopter."

"Of course, desperate to be on time for my meeting with

Lord Warminster, who was waiting for me in the middle of his soaked lawn with his trousers covered in mud."

He laughed heartily. It was the first time in her life she'd shared a bath with a man. One moment she was in his arms, but then, helped by the water, she escaped and floated above him, resting on his chest. They gazed at each other for a long moment and tried to kiss, which proved to be deliciously complicated.

"*You* are Elizabeth Bennet after all!" she said, and as he didn't understand, she continued. "This is *Pride and Prejudice*—the 2016 version. I'm Darcy, rich and prejudiced, you're Elizabeth Bennet, proud with a mansion in ruins and a crazy family, coming to meet me with your petticoat soaked from your stroll through the fields."

He laughed again and kissed her because, by now, they knew how to do it, surrounded by water.

"You did read Pride and Prejudice," she said.

"Of course I did. I've read all her books. It was the least I could do to know what your father's project was all about, and besides, he almost imposed it on me as a condition."

Elizabeth wanted to tell him that the celebration was not about Jane Austen but her father's obsession. Yet she forgot her thoughts as his hand searched again for her secret place and once again set it on fire.

"I want to make love to you," he murmured as he helped her out, drying her with a huge towel, but it was more a caress than anything else.

"Stop. Let that place stay wet," she whispered, amused by his drying efforts that had turned into foreplay.

"I know other methods to moisten it…" he said, and she felt him plunging into her with such power that she cried out in pain, but then everything turned to elation.

∞∞∞

"I'm famished," she finally said. He helped her dress in the beautiful kimono, showing her to the dining room where the table was set.

"My staff leave at six. I usually eat leftovers for dinner."

"Great, I want to taste the lamb again," she said, licking her lips in an erotic manner.

"Madam, I forbid you to have an orgasm away from me!" he said, smiling at her hunger. He poured the wine, and she rolled her eyes again.

"Does your lordship, undress himself at bedtime then?" she asked while she mixed the meat with the cheese.

"Not tonight, I hope!" he replied.

"So you would like me to undress you?"

He looked at her, incapable of eating. "Yes, absolutely."

"What's the wife of an earl called?" she asked suddenly, and he smiled as he grasped her words.

"A countess. Why do you ask? Planning to marry me?"

She paused, her fork in the air, and gazed at him. The light was on, allowing him to see her blushes, though she appeared surprised rather than embarrassed.

"Perhaps," she replied in the same manner.

"Well, Miss Collister, I'm probably not your best option." As she continued to look at him, he carried on. "You're on the list of the most sought-after single women in the kingdom, even in the Commonwealth."

"I am?" she enquired, genuinely surprised.

"Of course you are. Don't you read glossy magazines?"

"No, but it's surprising that you do."

"I don't, at least not usually. But I wanted to gather some information about you before you arrived."

"And the chauvinistic lord searched for me in glossy magazines rather than on LinkedIn."

"Yes, what better way to uncover the flaws of a wealthy girl?"

"And?"

"And I came across a lot about your sister and even your

mother—"

"But not me."

"Yes, that was quite disappointing. No scandals, no outrageous behaviour. A proper and well-behaved princess."

Elizabeth brushed off his words with a gesture he was already familiar with. "You're well-informed while I…"

"You?"

"I didn't find much about you, but obviously, the Earl of Warminster isn't a poor man."

It was a statement not a question, as she gestured to their opulent surroundings.

"No," he agreed.

Elizabeth laughed at his obvious hesitation.

"I'm not asking you to show me your bank statement."

"You're right, but I remember how honest you were…I want to be the same. Let's say that it's Rowan Stafford who possesses the wealth, not the Earl of Warminster."

"Is there a distinction?"

"Yes. Forty years ago, when my father became the 14th Earl of Warminster, he inherited a decent estate and a substantial amount of money. Ten years ago, I inherited a ruin."

"And money?"

"Perhaps enough to maintain the house for a few years. Well, my mother took a larger share, but it's incomparable to the wealth my father inherited. Everything you see around us was achieved with the money I earned. Rowan Stafford doesn't intend to invest more in this property. It's my home, but it's not meant to eat up all my earnings."

"And what's Rowan Stafford up to?" she asked.

She had a vague idea, as his company name was also in the contract—a small business of no more than twenty people specialising in cybersecurity.

"I'm sure you're familiar with my company."

"Yes, I saw it in the contract and googled you, but it's

quite mysterious, nearly impossible to grasp what you do. Your company uses some rather unconventional marketing."

"I agree, but in our industry, we're well recognised. Cybersecurity is so critical that no one in any sector can thrive without us."

"And precisely what do you do?" she asked, surprised that discussing such matters felt natural, even though they'd just made love. Their connection had grown deep enough for them to become acquainted beyond the bedroom.

"We protect computers, servers, mobile devices, electronic systems, networks, data—essentially anything digital—from malicious attacks. And now, we've expanded into safeguarding important applications and even video games."

"Fascinating," she remarked.

"We serve major players, on the Korean digital market."

"Perhaps we could go into more details—"

"Sorry to interrupt you, but it's a firm 'no'. We're collaborating on the Jane Austen project, and now we have a personal undertaking..." He grinned at her.

"And you're not keen on mixing—"

"Exactly. I think it's wise to maintain a boundary. Your father hinted he was prepared to introduce us to your IT department, but I declined."

"You're right. Let's restore Pemberley to its former splendour, and then we'll take it from there."

Chapter 7

They slept until Soames rapped on the door with her luggage received from London.

"He won't come in. He'll leave it in the other room."

And they didn't move, enjoying the darkness, wrapped in each other's arms, talking when they were too tired to make love.

"I haven't felt this peace in a long time," he said. "Remarkably profound, unlike any other experience."

"How's that? An earl like you must have had plenty of relationships."

"That's the problem. I didn't want relationships. Never did. I preferred escorts to relationships."

"Prostitutes? No!" she exclaimed, shocked, which made him chuckle.

"The innocent princess is taken aback. Don't think I pick up someone from the street. A weekend with a high-class hooker, including a supper or the theatre."

She couldn't say a word, and he laughed before her obvious shock; many questions were visible on her face—he could see them in the starlight that invaded the room.

"Yes, most of them do it to fund their education or start a business. Once their goal's achieved, they move on."

She still seemed unsure, looking up at him from his

chest, her head resting on her palm. She wanted more explanations, and he continued revealing things he had never shared with anyone before, all within twelve hours of their first meeting.

"Attraction is risky. It's like a lamp that illuminates your life and then switches off, leaving you with an unpleasant situation to deal with. I've been attracted a few times, but it never lasted. I had to end it the next day or month. I'm not overly sensitive, but I prefer that the lady agrees to break up or at least not hate me."

"Interesting! But has attraction never lasted for you?"

"No," he calmly replied to her defiant question. "Has an attraction ever lasted for you?"

She wanted to challenge his outlook on life, to destroy his philosophy which she found self-centred, cynical, and macho. However, as she rested her head on the pillow, distancing herself from him, she begrudgingly admitted his solution might be better than her cycle of failed relationships that often ended in bitterness and intense resentment. That had occurred at least three times in her past.

"I'm right." He smiled, observing her in turn, propping himself up on his elbow, close to her. "I can tell from your expression that you remember some painful break-ups."

"Yes, I do. But that doesn't mean you're right."

"I'm not trying to impose my views. It works for me."

Yet a slight distance appeared between them, which hadn't been there in the previous hours.

"I've lost you," he murmured. "I could make love to you, but I prefer to win you over through different means. Come on, let's get dressed. I want to show you something."

He admired her as she emerged from the bathroom, loving her new look—jeans, a jumper, black trainers, and her lovely black hair pulled into a ponytail, giving her a schoolgirl charm. He pulled her into his arms, and they kissed—their second standing kiss in between so many changes that had occurred in their lives.

His hand slipped under her jumper. "No bra, you little pervert!" he whispered in her ear.

She giggled and slipped away from his embrace. "He calls me a 'pervert' when I'm just trying to make things easier for the clumsy lord!"

He caught her again, and they kissed, their resolve nearly faltering as they considered returning to the bedroom.

"You're the pervert. After ten hours, we just got out of bed, and you're ready to return. Come on, show me what you promised."

She tried to open the door and then turned back to him. "How do we escape from your luxurious prison?"

As he approached, the door swung open. "The master's presence opens all doors," he joked, though there was some truth to his words.

"How?" she enquired.

"How does the door open? With my phone, my left eye, or my palm," he revealed.

He led her to the park facing the library and bedroom windows, leaving her wondering what he could show her at this late hour. Despite the cold, they relished the gentle breeze as they strolled.

It was not wholly dark. She could see the garden and the trees in the distance, and when he eventually stopped and pointed upwards, she understood why. Millions of stars shone as she had rarely seen in England. She sighed at the breathtaking sight, and he wrapped his arms around her from behind, allowing her to fully appreciate the sky. They took their time, the spectacle too magnificent to interrupt with kisses or caresses.

"Maybe it is Pemberley, after all. This could be what Elizabeth and Darcy saw two centuries ago—this starry sky we've lost in our cities and busy lives."

"Elizabeth and Darcy aren't real. They existed only in Jane's imagination."

"Then it's what Jane Austen saw before she died, throughout her life."

"Rarely. England's always been known for its clouds—"

"You really know how to crush a girl's dreams."

"You're right. Ultimately, we share this sky with them. Even your father's tale about Jane Austen's sister coming here might hold some truth on a night like this."

"Yes, imagine that Cassandra stood here one night and beheld this sky. How old's the house?"

He paused for a moment. "It was originally a medieval castle, but around 1750, one of my ancestors transformed it into what it is today. There have been two other significant renovations, but the main structure dates back to the mid-18th century."

"Remarkable!" she murmured, clearly impressed.

"Yes, being near you, I almost feel the same way. I've considered selling it a few times and ending everything."

"But you didn't."

"No, there was a moment when I was on the verge of selling it, but it didn't feel right."

"Then you let it fall into disrepair."

"If it weren't for your father, I might have explored ways to restore it. I'd made plans and enquiries, and then your father arrived. I toyed with the idea of turning it into a museum or a hotel. It's too much for a family nowadays."

"So Dad was here?" she said, turning in his embrace to face him.

"Yes, several times. He placed an advert in a magazine, and I responded. Then I received a call from his assistant, and he came. I don't quite understand why, but it felt like Pemberley from the moment he stepped inside. He told me then that he wanted to organise a grand event here for the two-hundred-year anniversary of Jane Austen's death."

To catch Darcy Egerton, she thought.

Whenever she discovered something new about her father's actions during his search for that man, she worried that he might not be entirely sane. She was ultimately relieved he kept some secrets, but she wondered if she would ever escape the maze, he had built to lead her to Darcy Egerton.

"What's wrong, honey?" Rowan asked with incredible tenderness. Never had she been addressed that way, that beautiful word and his voice that made her feel he liked her. She tried to push her worries aside and smile at the earl who dazzled her with his presence.

"It's so beautiful," she whispered, determined not to let thoughts of her father's obsession taint their relationship. "Dad crosses my mind every now and then, and it's hard to imagine never seeing him again."

It wasn't a lie but only half the truth. Nonetheless, she needed to rescue that place from her father's obsession.

"I understand. He spoke about you, quite a lot, and I could see how deeply he loved you. I admit I was a bit envious of the bond you shared. I never had anything similar with either of my parents. I'm glad your father chose Warminster."

"Yes, I can picture Elizabeth and Darcy living here happily ever after."

"Though, it's curious that you decided to combine your anniversary with this two-hundred-year commemoration. I got the sense that Collister was committed to 21st-century progress."

"Yes, but progress thrived in writers like Jane Austen. She was among the first ten authors we published. Our wealth and literary reputation are built on a simple idea my ancestor, Louis Collister, had. He understood the era and the signs of progress, addressing the need for affordable books for everyone."

"The train readers!" he interjected.

"Yes. The Duchess of Lancashire was one of the pioneers in discussing how industrialisation had cultural consequences—people moving around the country more often, suddenly needing something to do while travelling. The cheap books earned us a fortune, but it wasn't just about money. Those writers and their stories contributed to an unprecedented cultural revolution."

"We find ourselves in somewhat similar circumstances," he mused as they strolled through the park.

I'm in love, and I think he feels the same way, she thought, captivated by his words, reassured by his arms around her, as proof of his sentiments.

"We put in so much effort in the past to convince various professional groups that the digital revolution had begun, and computers are essential in their work, but we hardly saw any results...until smartphones came along. Until Steve Jobs, really. He sneakily introduced computer usage by making everyone need a smartphone—much like the train books."

"True, I hadn't thought of it quite that way," she admitted.

"Your publishing venture is also moving to digital, not just through e-books, but also by inventing new ways of creating and experiencing art," he said. He looked at her and smiled. "I've never met a woman I wanted to love and someone who listened to my words with such genuine interest. Making love used to be a way to relieve stress, a physiological necessity, but now it's a dependency. I crave more and continuously. Come, I need to make love to you!" he declared, making her ache to feel him deep within her— an overpowering and uncontrollable need.

∞∞∞

They made love again and fell asleep, utterly exhausted, unable to even bid each other good night, only to wake up and be together again.

"You're going to exhaust me!" he exclaimed in the

morning. "Keep your distance from me. Wear something thick. I get aroused just from seeing you, despite my fatigue."

"Are you complaining?" she wanted to know.

"I am not! Yet I wonder if you haven't turned my life upside down…forever…"

He didn't say anything else, but she understood as if she could read his mind.

"The earl's wondering if he would ever be able to have a casual fling in his bed, *engaging* in lovemaking exactly twice a night, fulfilling a basic physiological need."

He looked at her, almost scared.

"Perhaps," he said hesitantly.

"Well, your lordship, be reassured! I'm as scared as you are."

She couldn't sit comfortably on the chair, but she grinned, recalling the cause of her discomfort.

"This happens, madam, when you don't hold back your desires and let lust control your life."

"I can't believe you're proud of your accomplishment," she remarked, looking at his cheerful face as he observed her attempt to sit.

"I am. After all, I'm as primitive as any man in the world!"

They fell silent as Soames entered.

"Well?" Rowan asked impatiently.

"It's done, sir! They've left."

She saw a sense of relief on his face that she couldn't comprehend.

"What's going on?" she asked curiously, though still hesitant about getting involved in matters that weren't hers.

"It's not a secret." He smiled. "I wanted to show you the house, but with that crowd around, it was impossible. Soames did the impossible. He managed to get them out." He let out a deep breath. "It's the first time in years they're not around on a Saturday morning. And it wasn't as difficult as I thought."

They ate in silence, yet he couldn't contain his eagerness. "Please, come. I have to show you the miracle!"

Chapter 8

Far from intending to hide any secrets from her, he appeared enthusiastic about being together in the unexpected situation.

They paused in the hallway and looked around. Besides the birds chirping in the 'parlour', an unusual quietness pervaded the space.

"Mrs Evans has finally opened the windows," he whispered, and the room looked different. Inside, it felt cold, but the air was fresh. Upon entering, they found three young women cleaning the place. They cheerfully greeted them, a stark contrast to the gloomy atmosphere that the strange gathering had imprinted on the room when they were present.

"Good morning, ladies," he greeted them. They continued working, stealing quick glances in their direction, obviously curious about her.

"Miss Collister is the new mistress of Warminster," he announced. It felt as though the earl wasn't merely introducing the tenant, but rather Fitzwilliam Darcy was presenting his wife to the staff at Pemberley. She tried to snap out of her daydream. Everything regarding Jane Austen was still connected to her father's obsession. And she loathed to indulge in such thoughts.

"But *they* will eventually return," she murmured.

"To get their things. And by then, this room and many others will be locked."

He surveyed the room and then tested some tiles around the fireplace, which easily came loose.

"It's in ruins!" he muttered, and she could sense his regret. "I hope it's not too late."

The library door stood wide open, an unusual sight even for her.

"I need to breathe, and the house needs the same," he explained as they ascended the stairs.

"I have a feeling that *you* were the prisoner. They had free rein over the entire house, while you were confined in your gilded cage," she remarked, instantly regretting her words.

However, he simply shook his head. "No, wait and see. It's far stranger than you can imagine."

He guided her to the first-floor landing, where only the wing to the left was accessible, while the wing to the right and access to the second floor were blocked by grilles.

"This was the most I could do to limit their access only to the living and dining areas on the ground floor and their bedrooms."

"But why? Why?" she enquired as he opened the grilles.

"I couldn't get rid of them. Dozens of times I kicked them out, and they returned with my mother within a week or a month."

Suddenly, the lady residing in London was no longer just his mother; she seemed like a sorceress determined to annoy her only son in every conceivable way.

"It's insane! How could she do this?" she muttered, again feeling bad for her words. After all, that lady was his mother.

"Yes, without any doubt. She is afflicted by some kind of ailment, wanting to keep me under her control— indirectly, though, through this insane scenario. I suspect she wanted me to leave and let this place become her family's residence…or some similar plan."

"And I thought my family was crazy!" she exclaimed.

"No, Miss Bennet, your family is just odd, while mine is eerie, like something out of a horror film."

He took her hand and led her into the wing to the right, leaving the doors and grilles behind them wide open.

"Today, I'll remove the grilles. They've left for good this time."

"And if they refuse to accept it and come back?" she asked, concerned for the Collisters' plans but deeply entangled in the chaos caused by his strange family.

"They will leave, rest assured," he declared. "I spent a long time in London before the grilles and doors were installed. As you can see, they were confined to their part of the house—" He paused and drew her into his arms. "Do you see how I speak? Their part, my part! My God, they drove me crazy!"

But with her in his arms, he forgot about the house. They kissed, remembering the night and their lovemaking. It was splendid to escape reality again into their world of passion. They ran, and he opened a door at the far end of the hall into a lovely bedroom, not refurbished but kept in an acceptable state and clearly looked after daily. The door closed behind them, and he took her into his arms, heading to the bed.

It was what she had wanted all along. That crazy house made her yearn for passionate love, and his hands on her body drove her to orgasm even before he took her.

"You are nuts, Miss Collister, to come before I have taken you!" he murmured while they looked at the ceiling, tired out by their incredible encounter that had made their energies explode in one single expression of bliss.

"Your hands, sir, have this effect. Your hands caressing my skin."

"Oh, and what about that certain significant part of me

that comes into you? Does that have any role in your satisfaction, madam?"

"Whenever you take me, I die!"

That was too much of a confession; all he could do was make her die while his hands revived her.

∞∞∞

"This room looks quite nice, and so does the bathroom," she remarked much later, just before continuing their journey down the hallway.

"I did some work, but nothing essential. Some apartments don't have bathrooms, which is the most pressing issue."

"How many rooms are there?"

"About one hundred and thirty, but only a hundred will be renovated; the rest will be turned into bathrooms or dressing rooms."

"Some of them have lovely furniture."

"Yes," he replied, admiring the Collister lady who already seemed to be the mistress of the place. "The cabinetmakers will arrive next week, and we've found a nearby factory that will produce similar pieces in the Regency style."

"It's not as much of a disaster as I thought," she said, trying to come to terms with her father's substantial investment in the property.

"You're trying to defend your father." He chuckled, reading her thoughts.

"Yes, but I must admit that the earl's prowess in the bedroom has had a significant impact on my current state of mind."

"You're quite the libertine, Miss Collister! It seems you like me."

I more than like you, she thought, a feeling escaping her

heart and stirring up her emotions. And they had known each other for only a day.

His phone had been unusually quiet. He had turned it off, yet at one point, as they walked up to the top floor, he showed her the caller ID, which read 'Countess'.

"They've already told my mother about me. I should take the call." As she moved to step away, he gently grasped her hand to make her stay.

"Yes, Mother! You're right. I asked them to leave as the tenant from Collister came to see the place."

He waited silently for her to respond, and then his tone turned unexpectedly sharp, like a razor blade. "I told them to leave a month ago. Their belongings will be gone by Monday, or I will toss them outside the gates. Mother, this circus has gone on long enough. They're moving out for good. You can have them at your London house."

As he turned back to Elizabeth, his anger had subsided. On the contrary, he seemed jovial.

"I planned to do this as soon as your assistant confirmed the meeting, but I hesitated to do it on Friday when your arrival was scheduled. I didn't know how they'd react, and I didn't intend to frighten you. As you saw, Lady Catherine[5] called within an hour."

"Lady Catherine," she repeated and burst into laughter, infecting him with her mirth. "We're in the middle of *Pride and Prejudice*. You asked why we still celebrate Jane Austen after two hundred years. This is why—what the duchess said a hundred years ago still holds true. Our feelings and lives haven't changed much. We might travel to the moon and carry pocket-sized computers, but we still have drawing rooms where fathers, mothers, daughters, and Lady Catherines play out their peculiar old stories."

"Yes and no. I agree that many things remain unchanged—but look at you! You're a successful manager of a significant business—"

"True, but then Dad decided to restore Pemberley to its

former Regency beauty, while I was dishonoured in the bedroom by the master of the house. Same old story, as I told you."

"In our times, nobody cares that you slept with the earl."

"You're mistaken! Maybe my reputation won't suffer in a Regency sense. Still, we could end up on every glossy magazine cover, and for once, my privacy will be blown to bits. So you see, not much has changed, and in the end, Dad was right. We ought to adore the old lady and declare her a national treasure."

He gazed at her intently. They stood at the top of the house on a spacious terrace, surrounded by a stone balustrade with views for miles.

"I'm in a dangerous situation," he confessed as she admired the view. "I'm tempted to confess my feelings beyond the bedroom and the evident passion you've ignited in me."

"Is that so terrible?" she asked, aiming for sarcasm but radiating excitement and curiosity about his confession.

"Yes. In bed, passion can cloud one's judgment and lead to impulsive words, but here, with all my mental faculties intact, I can't help but tell you how deeply fond I am of you."

He glanced at his watch. "After just a day! And look at you blushing, Miss Bennet."

"I'm simply excited, Mr Darcy, but our roles are reversed from today onwards. I believe I will propose to you, but I must admit that I have reservations about your family," she quipped and laughed.

"Then tradition dictates that I mustn't accept your proposal and should instead be cross with you. Nonetheless, I'll hold off a bit before uttering that categorical no," he said as he caressed her.

"Is it too chilly here to make love?" he enquired, not waiting for a response before pressing her against a wall. "Just like in American films," he whispered in her ear.

"I can't believe you have a whole pack of condoms in your pocket," she exclaimed, and gasped as he removed her trousers and knickers.

"You've led me to prepare for unexpected situations, madam."

Chapter 9

Olivia gave Elizabeth an enigmatic glance, or at least that's how it appeared to her. In reality, her aunt was simply happy. Elizabeth had finally let her guard down, and her expression reflected the events that had transpired. At seven o'clock on Monday morning, she looked radiant. Exhausted but radiant. Olivia had sent down luggage for two days—the only person in the world her niece could ask such a favour from, but that also meant Elizabeth owed her the whole story. Elizabeth glanced around, searching for her uncle.

"He's having breakfast in town," Olivia explained without further detail.

"At seven o'clock?"

She suspected that Olivia had persuaded her husband to leave the house at an ungodly hour to give her a chance to talk to Elizabeth alone. But the news was so significant that no sacrifice seemed too great. Elizabeth sat at the kitchen table and ate like Olivia had never seen her eat at that hour before.

"Tell me, dear! Don't keep me in suspense!"

"It was magical! Something I never thought could happen to me!"

Olivia remained silent, captivated by the transformation

that had occurred. She thought her niece was a wonderful woman, but that was one woman's perspective, not a man's. Her experience had taught her that men looked for something different, a certain sparkle that some women possessed, and others didn't.

"An implicit invitation to be bedded. Something related to hormones, in fact," she had once said to her husband, who had agreed with a hearty laugh.

But that morning, the hormones or that special spark radiated from Elizabeth. Finally, her little girl had become a whole woman.

"I've always felt there must be a man for you beyond the Kenneths and Martins you've dated."

"What was wrong with Kenneth or Martin?" Elizabeth enquired, though she already knew the answer.

"You needed a man to undress you the first time you met and love you to complete oblivion."

Her aunt had hit the mark, causing Elizabeth to blush slightly as she recalled the earl and how they'd undressed, eager to make love less than three hours after their first meeting.

Elizabeth recounted everything to Olivia, and even in the retelling, she felt a surge of excitement and happiness.

"I'm in love," she whispered, and her aunt hesitated briefly amidst her joy. Eventually, she decided that falling in love and feeling alive was what Elizabeth needed, regardless of what the future held.

"And he?"

"He told me he liked me!"

Olivia nodded, satisfied. She already had a 'profile' of the Earl of Warminster. For two whole days, they had googled and discreetly asked questions about him, mainly Marianne, who seemed to have a gift for investigation.

He studied at Cambridge, Corpus Christi College. He graduated in linguistics, a prestigious department with only a few graduates each year. He wasn't part of the jet-set crowd, was the owner of a small but well-established company, and had no scandals attached to his name. He seemed almost too good to be true. But he was precisely what Elizabeth needed.

"Alright, one more question," Olivia interjected. "Why did he accept money from Thomas to renovate his family estate? Is he…struggling financially?"

Elizabeth laughed.

"What? Struggling financially? Are you turning into Mrs Bennet now? I thought you were my aunt Gardiner," Elizabeth exclaimed playfully, but her joy remained undiminished. "Remember that conversation between Dad and Arthur about a Patek Philippe not too long ago? The earl had one, a simple gold one. It might be the one Dad wanted. You can tell a gentleman—"

"—by his watch and shoes," Olivia finished, completing Thomas's favourite saying.

"He's not after my money, that's for sure." For the first time in her life, a man was crazy about her body and how she made love.

"I'm the same person I was three days ago. I can't quite grasp what he saw that others missed for so long."

"It's called love, attraction—no one really knows. It's a heavenly mix of hormones."

"He drove me home late last night but left me on my doorstep. I appreciate that he let me rest since I was exhausted. Starting today, I need to function at my best. I'm not sure how to manage all this. Balancing my first days as Collister's big boss with having a man in my life feels overwhelming."

"You'll manage. Love is a wellspring of energy, you'll see."

Both women startled as Elizabeth's phone rang as if awakened from a dream. Elizabeth's face flushed, then turned pale as she spoke with a light on her face that brought tears of happiness to Olivia's eyes. "It's him, and it's only seven-thirty."

"Yes," she responded, her voice unrecognisably deep with excitement and anticipation.

"Good morning, honey," he greeted her. It was their first call, and she didn't recognise his voice on the phone.

"Good morning to you too." She wanted to add *my love*, but Olivia's presence restrained her.

"How did you sleep?" he asked, and she was nearly lost for words, so entranced was she by his voice.

"Like a baby. I'm at my aunt's," she added to explain why she couldn't be more intimate.

"Ah, then please don't mention Lady Catherine to Mrs Gardiner. I want her to like my family and me."

And they both chuckled at Olivia, who had transformed into Mrs Gardiner for the occasion.

"I'm on my way to Warminster for a ten o'clock meeting with architects and your colleagues, but I'd like to invite you to dinner tonight."

"To Warminster?" she asked, a bit worried since she didn't expect her first day at the office to end before dinner.

"No, I know you're busy. In London. Is eight, OK?"

"Yes," she agreed, and he hung up, leaving her slightly disappointed not to hear more words of love.

"Why did you laugh?" Olivia asked, but then she regretted it. She didn't want to delve too deeply into Elizabeth's personal life. Her role was winding down in one way or another. Since Elizabeth had been a teenager, she'd listened to her niece's confessions of love, from her first hesitant kiss with Martin at fifteen to this day of profound happiness and fulfilment.

"Because he asked me not to tell Mrs Gardiner about Lady Catherine." She chuckled.

"Oh, is there a Lady Catherine to oppose you?"

"In the modern version, Lady Catherine is his mother, and he's worried my family won't approve of her."

Elizabeth kissed her aunt and dashed to the car, as her

driver had arrived to take her to the office. She was elated for the twenty-minute journey, a chance to relive the road from Warminster to London they had taken the previous evening.

She relished every page of *Elizabeth's Diary*. Elizabeth Austen's journey to becoming the Duchess of Lancashire remained one of the most cherished love stories, inspiring generations of girls to dream. Elizabeth Collister loved every word of that book, but the part that resonated most deeply was the lovers' car rides. In that confined space, the future duchess tasted her first thrills of love. Later, the car became the setting for an exhilarating prelude to her first experience of lovemaking.

Elizabeth had begun her sex life at nineteen with an Oxford friend. After that, she'd had several other relationships, some short, some longer. But at the beginning of each affair, she'd waited impatiently to get into her lover's car, dreaming of his hand on her leg or those restrained gestures filled with the urge and passion a car inflicted on the lovers. And she'd shivered in anticipation before climbing into the earl's car to be taken to London.

Olivia had told her once that a car was a man's second penis. She'd grinned at the earl's silver Aston Martin. It was indeed like his penis—exquisite, sensitive, and fast.

"His lordship has James Bond's car," she said with loving sarcasm.

"Yes, because it belonged to my grandfather, whom I deeply loved."

His answer made her smirk, as her grandfather had owned the same car—that was now Kath's, as she always got what she wanted. No matter how many cars she could have, she had wanted the one Elizabeth had driven at eighteen.

She intended to tell him about Kath and their Aston Martin, but when he started the car, the magic just happened. His hand on her leg made her come close to orgasm, a dream coming true. The duchess had been right—there were few better places to experience passion than in a small car.

They stopped twice and kissed, while the air between them vibrated with lust every time they touched.

"I adore your car," she whispered, with the duchess and her duke in mind.

Rowan laughed with that guttural sound that she'd come to recognise when he was excited and said, "A man's car is his—"

"Stop!" she cried, "I'm a romantic girl with romantic dreams!"

"Of course you are, honey!" he said. "And I'm a vicious aristocrat who wants crazy things from you."

"You're right," she said, looking at him intently.

"Of course I am, you perverted rich girl who knows I want to love you," he murmured.

"Yes, perhaps I am perverted…I adore your dick. It's just like this car!"

∞∞∞

"Miss Collister, we arrived five minutes ago." Her father's driver roused her from her reverie. He was the one who had brought her home from the hospital when she was born, and her choice to retain him as her driver had filled him with joy.

"Thanks, Albert," she replied, swiftly heading to her office. She lacked the luxury of daydreaming but hoped for a nice cup of coffee before the chaos of Monday commenced.

"A leader always arrives first in the morning," her father had emphasised, and he was indeed correct. Occasionally, that hour of serenity was her sole opportunity to contemplate and plan the day.

Chapter 10

Elizabeth sat at her desk feeling quite uncertain as she thought about her first day at Collister. Indeed, it felt like her very first day.

It didn't matter that she had been her father's right-hand man for the past few years or that she had practically run the company on her own during the previous year. The only thing that mattered was her father's perpetual absence and her new overwhelming role as the boss. She was alone, just like her father and grandfather had been at some point, and she wondered why she'd never asked either of them how they'd felt on their first day.

She phoned her uncle. He'd come to the office immediately after his wife had thrown him out that morning.

"Good morning, Elizabeth," he greeted her, and they both remained silent for a moment.

"Would you join me in the Grand Hall?" she requested without further explanation, confident that her uncle understood the difficulty of that first morning.

A glass atrium on the second floor connected the old part of Collister's headquarters to the new part. Her ancestors had been successful publishers and shrewd real estate investors. When the company had begun to expand almost twenty-five years ago, they'd built a modern building adjacent to the old one on land that had been theirs for over a century. Yet the 150-year history of Collister was encapsulated in the Grand Hall, adorned with portraits of all her ancestors who had guided the company since 1867.

Her uncle kissed her hand and smiled. Dressed elegantly and holding a bouquet of hibiscus, he had anticipated her call.

"Welcome, Elizabeth Collister," he proclaimed, presenting her with the flowers that unofficially represented Collister's coat of arms.

"Elizabeth Collister, in the 149 years of Collister's history, twice Collister ladies have managed the business while their husbands were at war."

And he pointed to the pictures of Amelia Collister, who had managed the company between 1916 and 1918, and Louisa Collister, who'd assumed that difficult task from 1942 to 1944.

"However, dear niece, you are the first lady Collister *to inherit* the company and be the boss in your own right. Isn't it a perfect way to celebrate 200 years of Jane Austen?"

"Please don't be angry with him," he added, his voice wavering as he gestured towards the portrait of Thomas Collister on the wall.

"I'm not, Uncle. Who could be angry with him?"

They sat at the table, but Elizabeth occupied her father's chair this time.

"Back to business," she said. "The earl has agreed to entrust us with the reconstruction. You can hire the project supervisor."

"I already have, my dear. He's got a meeting in Warminster at 10 o'clock," Arthur replied before departing, casting one last glance at his beautiful niece. He felt happiness and sorrow at the same time, yet he was confident that she was the best choice Thomas had made. Thomas had only hesitated because he loved her and knew that such a responsibility could jeopardise her personal life.

"Women are not like us," he'd told Arthur more than once. *"She might want to have children and be a mother, which is a vastly different role from being a father."* Nevertheless, they'd accepted that Elizabeth was strong enough to balance family and Collister.

She gazed at her ancestors for a while, familiar with each of them by name. When she reached her father's portrait, she whispered, "You've placed an enormous burden on my shoulders, Dad."

Yet, that ancient room and her ancestors made the magic, and suddenly, she felt better, while her fears and hesitations all transformed into excitement about the future.

∞∞∞

"Could you please call Marianne?" Elizabeth asked Clarice as she crossed the hall.

And Marianne arrived only a few moments later, as if she had waited for the call.

Elizabeth was sure her aunt had involved Marianne in searching for Rowan's profile, and indeed, her friend seemed to have grasped the entire story with just a few hints.

"We'll have lunch together tomorrow," Elizabeth promised.

"That means you're occupied tonight," Marianne replied, a smile playing on her lips, as they often went to dinner when work kept Elizabeth busy.

Elizabeth simply nodded.

"That's great news for you!" Marianne exclaimed, and that was the end of it. When Elizabeth spoke again, she fully embraced her role as the boss.

"I've considered the competition. Marianne, I won't be

meeting the Darcys—"

Marianne wasn't prone to over reactions; when deeply irritated or concerned, she typically maintained a blank expression, precisely what she exhibited now. "But you agreed," she stated, still unsure whether Elizabeth's decision was final.

"I said I'd think about it. I don't know what choice I'd have made under different circumstances, but that's no longer relevant. This is my decision now. I can't meet man after man and pretend to be interested enough to get them to reveal their secrets."

"Elizabeth, we never asked you to do anything like that. Just to have a business meeting with each of them."

"I won't do it! I have even less time now, and I intend to dedicate every spare minute of it to my personal life."

"We could ask Anna to go."

"Anna? The project manager we hired, who was so nervous she wanted to run away after our first meeting?"

"She's got a degree in communications."

"She might, but we need someone who understands—really understands—the scenario. This is a difficult task. Someone who sees the authors as a peculiar group of even more peculiar individuals. Someone who knows about Dad's obsession… She can negotiate contracts but not extract secrets deeper than the Vatican archives from three egotistic people. When's the first meeting scheduled?"

"It's in less than two months, during the Jane Austen event in Oxford—"

"No, please, spare me the details."

"We're in a bind here. It's urgent. No! Actually, it's a desperate situation."

"I understand, and I'll find a solution, I promise. Just give me a few days."

Elizabeth was taken aback by how distressed Marianne was about her refusal. Since learning the whole story, Elizabeth regarded it as one of her father's whims she had never taken seriously. When it came to Darcy Egerton, Thomas Collister had been nothing more than a boy. However, it seemed much more significant to Marianne. Elizabeth's decision was an unexpected blow to the flawless plan she had intended to carry out in Thomas's memory.

Her father's little scheme hadn't panned out, but he could never have foreseen that she'd find her own Darcy.

∞∞∞

"What shall I do about Anna?" Elizabeth asked Clarice as they awaited the arrival of the new project manager.

"I like her," Clarice responded. "I told her it was an informal meeting, but she just couldn't grasp the concept." They shared a smile, recalling the gathering in the Grand Hall.

"I'll leave you two alone," Clarice said as soon as Anna arrived, appearing more at ease this time.

Elizabeth gestured for her to sit in one of the armchairs away from her desk.

"Anna," she began without preamble, "Collister is built on the publishing house, and everything we've been doing in this modern world is influenced by the books we create. We live in the digital age, and we embrace progress, but at our core, we're publishers. It's crucial to immerse yourself in this atmosphere and mindset.

"Forget what you know about project management or communication that you learned at university or applied in other companies. Engage with the people here, learn about their projects, and read Jane Austen. A lot. Even at the office. This Austen project is unlike any other, even for us. Firstly, because my father didn't have the time to fully communicate all his ideas and plans. But also, a cultural project like this can't be meticulously planned from start to finish—it evolves and develops as it's implemented. It's like a living structure that shapes its own path and objectives. You heard my father assigning tasks to each department. We've now got distinct plans that you need to meld into a coherent, astonishing structure that will captivate everyone. Can you handle that?"

Elizabeth appreciated that Anna didn't reply immediately; her uncertainty was evident when she finally did. "I admit, I was scared at the initial meeting. I want to be honest with you. I don't know if I'm up to the task. I can't say for sure if I can do it right now. I know time's short, so please give me a few days to talk to everyone."

"And you'll come back with a decision?"

"Yes."

Suddenly, Elizabeth found herself liking Anna; her honesty was endearing. She'd even feel a pang of disappointment if the young woman decided to leave. As Anna stood up, Elizabeth spoke warmly, "Stay, and you'll experience a unique mix of enjoyment and frustration. There's no better place for you to get training that'll serve you well in any future job!"

Chapter 11

At eight o'clock, his car was parked outside the office. She'd finished her work around seven and then had a restless hour that felt unusually long, almost like a week. He'd occupied her thoughts throughout the day, regardless of her tasks, conversations, or contemplations. His presence didn't bother her until the last hour, when it turned into torment.

"I waited for an hour in the park," he told her once she was in his car, and she chuckled.

"I thought eight o'clock would never come, wandering around my office! Why didn't you call?"

"Because I know how irritating it is to pressure someone busy with work. Why didn't you call if you finished earlier?"

Explaining was hard. There were specific rules a woman followed if she wanted a relationship. He didn't want to distract her from her work, while she followed the holy precepts about dating.

"What nonsense," he retorted when she explained.

It sounds like nonsense only when the man has feelings for you, she wanted to convey, but she remained silent. After a day without him or his calls, she fell back into the typical behaviour that young women usually followed.

"So, which restaurant are we heading to?" she asked,

changing the topic.

"Restaurant?" he queried, looking at her. They were at a traffic light, making eye contact for the first time. "Are you serious? I haven't seen you all day and night, and you're thinking of putting a table between us? We're going to my place."

"We could've gone to my place."

"Do you have Soames and a cook there?"

"No," she admitted with a smile.

"Then hush and put aside your emancipation for the night."

"Yes, your lordship," she said while his hand on her leg made her close her eyes and forget everything else; then, he kissed her at the next traffic light.

"I hope you don't live in Wembley," she commented.

"No." And within another five minutes, they were on a quiet street in Belgravia that seemed to belong to another era.

"Regency?" she enquired.

"Almost. Perhaps a few years before."

As soon as he closed the door behind them, they kissed. She glanced around quickly, noting a distinct décor, very different from Warminster—exquisite minimalism. However, her view was obstructed as she was enveloped in his arms.

"I hope you've got a proper bed," she whispered.

"Good Lord, Elizabeth," he murmured close to her ear, making her tremble. "Have a little faith in me."

When they finally lay down, the Japanese bed had a perfect mattress where they made long and tender love, different from the storm they had experienced only two days ago.

He already knew her body, but that night it was like he discovered it again, lingering on each spot until she cried out, incapable of waiting longer for him to invade her.

"I've never met a woman more obsessed with beds," he

finally said with her in his arms, still caressing her body as he talked, making her wonder how it could be better each time he took her and where those feelings had been hidden all those years.

"Yes. Your houses each seem to be from an entirely different era and place. And the beds were no good in the Regency, nor are they in Japan."

"What? In the Regency they had impressive four-poster beds with enormous mattresses."

"Wrong! They mostly had iron-sprung mattresses filled with wool that hurt your body in every possible way. While in Japan…it's the opposite—a thin layer of rigid material. Or perhaps a Japanese man prefers his woman directly on the hard floor to toughen her character."

"An interesting idea!" he said. "Not to harden your character—that's already strong enough—but so I can love you anywhere in my houses. And I'll make a note not to forget the living room futon. I need a plan and a schedule."

"I need food," she said, pointing to the kimonos hanging on the back of the door. "I haven't eaten all day."

"I wonder why," he teased, guiding her to the bathroom.

"Your bathroom's designed for two," she remarked.

"Are you already jealous?" he joked.

As she didn't say a word, he faced her and planted a gentle kiss on the tip of her nose. "Is it because a certain someone made a lasting impression on you?"

"Perhaps," she replied as they dressed. "Are we going to dine like this?"

"You want to have dinner naked?"

"No, you fool. I'm naked under the kimono…and Soames is around."

"Soames isn't here."

"So, you lied and enticed this innocent girl into your debauched earl's apartment?"

"The enticing part is true, but Soames was here to set the table."

Indeed, on the glass table near the terrace door, there were metal bowls warmed by small blue flames to keep the meal hot.

"Ah, it's good to be a countess," she quipped, inspecting each dish under his amused gaze.

"Do you plan to propose to me?" he asked playfully as they sat down to eat.

"Maybe," she said while she served them in haste, her hunger evident.

"Then, madam, I want a watch—"

"What watch?" she asked, already eating. "You already have quite a spectacular Patek."

"How many pairs of shoes do you have?"

"I'm not sure."

"It's the same with my watches."

"Yes, but a pair of my shoes costs around £1000, while your watches…"

"I understand, but you're a wealthy heiress, and when you propose, you need to do so in accordance with your status."

"My 'status' on the London Stock Exchange, I presume."

"Exactly!"

"Well, Lord Warminster, if my feelings progress to a proposal, I'll keep that wish in mind. But what kind of watch do you want?" she enquired.

"A certain Vacheron Constantin…"

"Do I have to sell the plane to afford your watch?"

"Not quite," he reassured her. "But what would *you* want?"

"If you were to propose?" she asked hesitantly, recognising that discussing marriage on the second date was a departure from the norm.

"Yes," he affirmed, and she felt he was also approaching the subject cautiously.

"I'd like a ring like Lady Diana's—the one with a

sapphire and diamonds but with a red diamond and platinum."

"I appreciate that you won't make me negotiate with Prince William for his mother's ring. You're a reasonable woman."

They continued their meal in silence, mainly because she was concentrating on eating while he observed her, captivated by her speed and efficiency.

"What happens in novels when the main characters declare their love and get married?" she wondered aloud, which seemed to unsettle him even more than before. He gazed at her with a troubled expression, a departure from the passionate look she'd grown accustomed to. His green eyes were anxious, and she worried she'd crossed the line by bringing up the topic of marriage. She resolved to avoid the subject, even if he were to broach it later on.

Then he smiled, and the cloud of doubt dissipated as he responded, "Honey, everything changes when love is revealed and accepted. Films conclude with that famous final kiss, while novels tend to end just before the marriage or within ten minutes of it. Novels about marriages usually delve into their failures rather than glorifying their happiness."

"It's odd how happiness often seems dull in literature," she remarked.

"You might have a point there. Consider Jane Austen's *Pride and Prejudice*—Darcy proposes, and the last few chapters consist of just over fifteen hundred words."

"How do you know such details?" she asked, surprised. "You said that my father made you read Jane Austen."

Her words prompted Rowan to let out a deep laugh, making her inner body stir in expectation.

"Yes, he did. He shared much of what I know about her. He discussed Jane Austen's character, life, and habits in a way that resembled the methods profilers use for serial killers."

Elizabeth held her breath, sensing his response to her reaction. She couldn't determine whether her father had told him about his obsession and relentless pursuit of that accursed Darcy Egerton, which had cast a shadow over countless moments of her life.

"I'm sorry," he said. "It's still difficult for you to talk about...your father."

She exhaled, relieved that he'd chosen a simple explanation and hoping he remained unaware of the truth. It was easier for her to be seen as someone struggling with her father's memory rather than his fixations.

"I hear his name countless times at work, but he's the late director there. Here—"

"He's your father."

"An obsessed father who sought to invade writers' privacy, dreams, and lives. I found that method horrifying."

"Delving too deeply into someone's private life can be unsettling. However, analysing their writing style can be quite interesting. I recall a fascinating discussion about Jane's influence on the women's liberation movement."

He observed her to gauge her reaction, but she continued eating, indicating her eagerness to hear him discuss Jane Austen. She'd chosen to believe that Darcy Egerton would never be a topic between them, hoping that her father's profiling was limited to Jane Austen.

"Any insights Dad had about Jane Austen could be interesting for me. Maybe he told you more than he revealed to us. I need a fresh perspective on Jane Austen for this challenging 2017 event, which will focus entirely on her."

"He had some interesting perspectives on her life and work. Having two daughters made him feel a kinship with Mr Bennet, the father of five daughters."

Elizabeth nodded, having always seen her father in that light. "Yes, Dad often said that Jane didn't advocate for a specific cause in the modern sense—"

"And she portrayed a woman who wanted more than being a simple housekeeper or mother…and just like that, the modern lady was born without much fuss," he mused. They both laughed, recalling her father's flamboyant words.

"I remember some rather long conversations with my aunt and Marianne about women's education and marriage."

"Can you imagine that your father had every quote related to these topics?" he asked.

Elizabeth hid her eyes, not allowing him to detect her frustration. She was well aware how her father amassed those quotes, and a plethora of others related to Jane Austen and Darcy Egerton's works. He employed a legion of Oxford and Cambridge PhDs to assist him.

"I'm naked," she finally said, looking at him. "Under this kimono, I'm not wearing anything—"

"You started this conversation, honey. And to tell you the truth, I'm fascinated by the idea of eating this dessert off your belly while talking about Jane Austen."

She dipped her finger into the chocolate soufflé and held it out for him to lick.

His eyes met hers, he grasped her hand, and before licking, he whispered, "Don't stop talking. I find myself strangely aroused by your voice and words."

"While my father spoke to Olivia, I was sometimes bored, but with you, every subject becomes fascinating…even exciting." She smiled, deciding to cast aside the old rules.

"Because you want to make love to me."

"Probably. Or I know that at the end of each of those boring discussions, I'll receive a prize for my patience." She laughed. He moved towards her to taste the last bit of chocolate soufflé on her lips. His roving hands searched her body under the kimono. Then he loved her on the futon while the lights dimmed and music began, with apparently no intervention on his part.

"Everything is prepared for the master's amorous games."

"Be silent, woman, and move. I want to feel your stir in my body."

∞∞∞

"We can't do this every evening," she said, a mixture of happiness and concern apparent in her tone, as sleep was crucial for her to function during the day.

"Of course not. We'll figure it out later—"

"How life will continue after the kiss concludes the novel."

"Well, that's a matter for profound reflection. So, I'll take you home this evening."

"To contemplate," she quipped.

"To sleep, honey."

While it was tough to leave his embrace, she appreciated his assistance in dressing and leaving the apartment she adored, much like everything associated with him.

"We can't spend every night like this," she said again just before they reached her apartment.

"That's true. We'll find a solution," he responded, "but tonight, you need your sleep."

Yet she couldn't help but murmur, "We could never simply sleep together."

"It would take a concerted effort," he agreed, "but we'll figure something out in the end. Maybe ski suits…"

Chapter 12

Anna was ready to give her final answer much sooner than Elizabeth had anticipated, which could only mean one thing.

"I didn't need much time to decide that I wanted to take on this project," she said, her eyes already sparkling with excitement.

"I gather you no longer find us weird." Elizabeth smiled, gesturing for her to take a seat in the meeting room. She knew well the feeling at the start of a new project.

"Let's just say I regard Jane Austen at Collister as a challenging project from all angles."

"That implies you still consider us eccentric, but in a positive way that could lead to professional excitement," Roger Chapman from Collister Advertising chimed in as he joined them, taking a seat at the meeting table.

"You knew I'd accept," Anna said to Elizabeth.

"Of course I did. Somerville ladies don't back down from a challenge."

"Quite the opposite, they initiate challenges," Roger added.

Anna smiled, feeling so different from the first meeting. She was still dressed in a businesslike manner, but instead of a formal suit, she was wearing loose trousers and a stylish green blouse.

"I've put together a concise presentation with my ideas, or rather, my idea," she announced as she connected her laptop to the projector. "I've met with each department, and the discussions were quite satisfying."

Elizabeth already had reports on her desk from her colleagues about those meetings. She'd asked each of them if they thought Anna would stay, and they'd all answered in the affirmative. Anna posed exciting and relevant questions, making the conversations meaningful and enjoyable.

"We needed an external perspective to assess our efforts and bring something new," Roger remarked while observing the young woman engrossed in her laptop.

"Absolutely," Elizabeth agreed. "This project is, after all, my father's brainchild, but unfortunately, his health deteriorated long before he could formulate a plan for the grand finale."

"I understand that. Every department has its own project, but it's essential to interconnect them, to have a unified Collister project."

There was a brief pause following her initial words, and she didn't try to conceal it.

"We're here to find a solution, Anna," Roger encouraged her. During their first meeting, he appreciated how the discussions had evolved into lively debates about the project and his department's strategy.

"There's no need to sugarcoat things." Elizabeth smiled.

"Nor to make it seem like everything is perfectly settled," Roger added.

Anna hesitated before speaking. In other workplaces, a specific filter often existed through which issues reached the upper management's ears. Not falsehoods but a kind of embellishment. Yet at Collister, the former boss was deceased, and Anna sensed that the new leader, Elizabeth Collister, was different from the other managers she'd known.

"I've learned that each department has an ambitious project. They're impressive in scale—" she paused, glancing at Elizabeth, who appeared highly interested.

"Comprehensive works—literature, film, even music—alongside Pemberley and a grand Austenesque celebration to cap off the festivities. All designed to showcase Collister's breadth."

"I sense a 'but' coming," Elizabeth quipped.

"Yes. I'm genuinely impressed by the work that Collister has undertaken over the past hundred and fifty years, while this project demonstrates that Jane Austen remains one of the world's most widely read authors—these are the two dimensions of the project."

A pyramid labelled Collister appeared on the projector screen. Scattered within were books, film stills, posters—various manifestations of how Jane Austen's literary legacy persisted in modern society. Bees buzzed in the Collister pyramid, each item illuminated. Eventually, the pyramid shone, although the light was relatively modest. The things rearranged themselves into a hive structure, forming a honeycomb filled with books.

"But?" Roger grinned in response to such a visual concept.

They all gazed at the screen with interest; Anna's presentation was vivid.

"While the analogy of bees and honey is remarkable, honey is still just for breakfast. The Collister content is valuable and engaging, and the pyramid is impressive as a whole. Yet it falls short of being astonishing, incredible, mind-blowing, extraordinary—pick any of these words that the Collister project is not. To truly amaze with this pyramid, we need—"

Each item on the screen gained a new glow, and a magnificent firework display erupted from the top in vibrant butterflies.

We need fireworks. It was written in capital letters on the screen, conveying a sense of urgency in the digital world, much like shouting.

"We need fireworks to illuminate with their explosive power all the work that has ever been done at Collister. We need an extraordinary conclusion to a hundred and fifty years of outstanding work and to put into perspective everything that will be achieved in the coming months…and those fireworks we do not have…yet," Anna said.

"Unfortunately, we're aware of this," Roger concurred. "Without the fireworks, we'll have nothing more than attractive displays."

Elizabeth took a deep breath to steady herself—a ritual she performed every time discussions centred on her father's project and Jane Austen. Since the project's inception, she'd known one undeniable fact—the project was interesting, colossal in scale, but it lacked the unexpected, those fireworks Anna had talked about so rightly. She feared that her father had pinned everything on Darcy Egerton and his tenth book being published by Collister. For Thomas Collister, the ultimate fireworks— the grand finale that Anna had referred to—depended on Darcy Egerton. Yet, ten months before the celebration, they remained clueless about his identity or intentions for that year.

Elizabeth had urged Marianne to disclose the truth to Anna. Nonetheless, it was difficult to admit that Thomas Collister had an obsession that might spell disaster for his company.

"No use in hiding it," she eventually said, her resolve to reveal her concerns firm. "I asked Marianne to share everything about Darcy Egerton and…my father's fixation."

Anna simply nodded. That revelation solidified her trust in the people she'd encountered, recognising that they wanted her to become part of their team.

"Yes, she did."

"Unfortunately, for all of us, the fireworks my father imagined were centred around Darcy Egerton and his tenth book being published by Collister."

A tense silence hung in the air. Roger had thoughts he wanted to voice but hesitated. Thomas Collister was dead, and harsh words could be perceived as disrespectful and ultimately fruitless. Nonetheless, a simmering frustration resided within him. In some way or another, they all shared the sentiment—Thomas Collister's cherished project was hurtling towards disaster, as he had staked everything on an improbable event.

"Marianne probably informed you about our finalists for the Collister Fiction Prize," Elizabeth said.

"Did Mr Collister ever entertain the possibility that Darcy Egerton might be among the competitors?" Anna asked candidly, observing their sombre expressions. Even though not a word had been uttered, Anna had sensed the deep crisis gripping the project during those three days of discussions. In a way, her choice to stay was predicated on that issue. Finding *fireworks* for the Collister project posed an immense challenge.

"Do you believe that's possible?" Elizabeth enquired, knowing that neither Anna nor Roger had the complete truth, and the extent of her father's endeavours to locate Egerton should remain a secret for eternity.

"No, absolutely not!" Anna replied with conviction. "I genuinely believe that Darcy Egerton would never participate in a contest. He's an unequivocal star, globally renowned. He's got no need to win a prize, not even one from Collister."

Elizabeth nodded. From an external perspective, Anna's assessment held true. However, Marianne was correct that Darcy Egerton had played games involving her father.

"At this point, the best strategy is to assume that we won't have Darcy Egerton in June and engage in brainstorming sessions to find an alternative."

Both Elizabeth and Roger concurred.

"I've discovered that we have potential fireworks, albeit spread out from December to June, in the conferences and events we're organising. The Oxford conference will be remarkable, a completely unexpected point of view on Jane Austen's work, as will be the 'train' conference and the one on marriages from Gretna Green. Roger's developing vibrant promotional campaigns for the Austen Game slated for release in April and for the Austen Encyclopaedia. The events are noteworthy, and the promotions are captivating. However, they're not unique and merely set the stage for the grand finale."

"I'm so angry with Dad," Elizabeth whispered, evoking sympathy from them for her, both as a person and as the head of Collister. "So frustrated. For everything, particularly for leaving us in this situation. He crafted a labyrinth, and increasingly, I'm convinced it has no way out."

"No!" Roger declared firmly. "You're grieving his loss, we all are, but here we are, some of the finest minds in our respective fields. We'll find a solution, or several. And fortunately, we have Anna with her fresh perspective on our work and her background in cultural projects."

"The first item on my agenda is now a trip to Warminster," Anna proposed. "I believe that seeing the place might spark some ideas. In the coming weeks, I suggest spending a full day in Wiltshire with the team. Have our brainstorming session there, at Pemberley."

It was an excellent suggestion, yet Elizabeth found herself curiously hesitant. For the first time, she looked at Anna as a woman. She seemed younger than her actual age and possessed a vivacity that added to her allure. They'd all misjudged her during that initial meeting, but she'd swiftly revealed her true nature and substantial potential.

Am I jealous? Elizabeth thought while sipping her coffee, alone, waiting for her next meeting. Most certainly, she was. But then she remembered the earl and their first week together. They had met three nights out of four, always at his apartment, still unsure of finding another solution for them.

"What will happen after they bang and marry?" She asked the same question she'd asked some nights ago—the one that remained unanswered.

"Sleeping together then getting married is the right order in our time, Miss Bennet!"

Elizabeth shrugged as she needed an answer, and he seemed unwilling to provide it.

"They live their life," he finally said.

"Boring!"

"Life is mostly boring, honey!"

They were still in bed, and it was so good to be in one another's arms that they couldn't even be bothered to get up and eat.

"You stayed in London for me, and I feel guilty," she said.

"Why? I've always lived in London half the time, before you. I can work in both places equally. But you have to be here. It's only normal to do what's best for you."

"Thank you," she whispered, while he smiled in the darkness. "You're such a polite girl. That's what people think about you."

"And?" she wanted to know.

"And I hope I'm the only one who knows that savage woman who devours me in bed."

"Is that what I'm doing?" she asked, incredulous and happy.

"Yes, absolutely!" he said. "It's so strange that instead of being satisfied each time we make love, I want more even before it's over. Stop...I didn't mean right now!"

But it was too late to stop.

Chapter 13

Late on Friday evening, as they approached Warminster Park, they saw the main gates wide open, ready to welcome them.

"Please, stop," she said, impressed by the house's grandeur. With all the lights on, the view was spectacular. "Oh my goodness!" she exclaimed. "It's incredible. What a mistake to have come by helicopter at noon and seen the roof first. It's magnificent," she whispered to herself, and Rowan nodded, gently touching her neck. The damaged steps and fallen plaster on the facade were nowhere to be seen; the house appeared elegant and majestic under the lights.

"However, something still seems odd. These imposing gates belong in a high wall…which is missing."

"Most of it collapsed many years ago."

"Will we restore it?"

"No, the costs would be astronomical, but the Department for Culture will place markers every five yards to mark the property's boundary."

"We should hold our celebration at night," she suggested, looking up at the house. He chuckled and opened the car door for her. "Even during the daytime, everything will look splendid."

She still had reservations, but some of her worries faded as they entered the hall. The doors to his library were open, but it was the parlour that caught her attention. She could hardly believe how much the room had changed. She struggled to remember the shabby interior and its contents. The beautifully restored parquet floor looked fit for a grand ballroom; from the ceiling, sparkling chandeliers hung, their hundreds of tiny bulbs lighting up the room.

"How?" she asked, almost in disbelief.

"They were waiting for approval to begin, and I insisted on refurbishing the parquet, the walls, and the lights in this room. The furniture workshop took all the pieces to decide what to repair and what to replace, and they'll recreate any missing items."

To Rowan's surprise, her reaction was to cry rather than smile. Seeing her eyes glisten with tears was so unusual that he pulled her into his arms. "What's wrong, honey? Don't you like it?" Instead of answering, she burst into sobs, and he held her even closer.

"Dad," she managed to say between sobs. "He wasn't foolish."

"No, honey, he was a visionary, a man who knew what he wanted and how to inspire his team to achieve it. Come on, let's sit in the library."

Dinner was ready, but he settled on the sofa by the fire, holding her in his arms.

"Lately, I've been feeling that I almost despise him for burdening us with a fantasy, even ruining our chance to do something significant for Collister and Jane Austen."

"He knew what he was doing, I believe. Despite my limited knowledge of him, he seemed confident in his plans for Jane Austen…and his Pemberley."

"I resented him for thrusting this project onto me," she murmured.

"No, you didn't. You were concerned, and that's natural. It's a massive responsibility. It seemed almost impossible to complete without him. But he believed in you…and I do too."

"I lack confidence in myself," she admitted as he wiped away her tears.

"That's not true! You're Jane Austen's heir—even if not by blood, it's a spiritual filiation that's even more significant. When people see you, there's no need to explain Jane's legacy. You're her legacy and the duchess's—every woman who fought battles, big or small, contributed to making you, Elizabeth Collister—who you are today."

"You speak so well for an IT geek. I'll put you down to give the final speech in July."

She gazed up at him from his arms, and for the first time in months—perhaps since learning her father was going to die—she felt a sense of peace about the present and the future.

"Let's eat and—"

"—go to bed?" she interjected.

"You're obsessed, my dear. I didn't intend to take you to bed but to show you how the place looks now with us as the only residents."

"Goodness, you're right! How did you manage with your relatives?"

"It was simple. On Monday morning, they came back thinking that it would work like in the past, but the site manager arrived, and we gave them a day to get out before lorries came to take away the furniture."

"And they just left?"

"There were many calls from my mother. I had to explain to her that Warminster was no longer ours for at least five years. She even tried to ask me to keep some of their belongings here, but the answer was again no. As long as Collister's the tenant, they can't live here or leave any traces behind."

"And they just left?" she asked again.

"My phone had sixty-two missed calls…from them.

Almost everyone tried five times to reach me. Their presence has been obsessive, and I'm sure they had many requests, only to ensure their return."

"That'll never happen."

"Absolutely not. Regardless of Warminster's status five years from now, they won't be returning. You've brought healing not just to me but to the house as well. I was under siege for all those years, trapped in an unbelievable situation. I even considered seeing a therapist to figure out what was happening to me."

Elizabeth laughed. "I know a therapist nearby. Just take her to bed, and you'll find your cure."

"The therapist's office is between your legs!"

"Goodness, you're getting quite cheeky!" she exclaimed, though her happiness was evident.

"No, you misunderstood. I wasn't referring to *that* area. It was a metaphor. But my overly obsessed woman seems to interpret everything as a sexual innuendo."

In the still of the night, they made long, passionate love. No longer strangers but lovers in search of life after *the novel's end*.

∞ ∞ ∞

Yet again, she held back from sharing the entire story the following day. Olivia encouraged her to discuss it with her, believing she might have ideas about the fireworks, which were referred to as the plan to crown their celebration.

"I don't want to exclude Darcy Egerton, but it's rational to have alternatives. A solid backup," she said—a sentiment Elizabeth shared. Olivia didn't work at Collister, but she'd been their literary advisor for the past three decades, as Thomas had complete trust in her.

However, Elizabeth chose not to heed her aunt's advice this time. Her reasoning was simple: she wanted to keep her love life separate from her work for as long as possible. She enjoyed discussing Jane Austen with him, but that was a different domain. She maintained a distinction between their love and her professional commitments.

"What do you enjoy doing in the winter?" he asked during breakfast.

She grinned.

"Why the smile? Is that all the answer I'll get?"

"I'm smiling because this is what people do in relationships—they get to know each other."

"Yes, but there's no strict plan to follow, at least not consciously. It's about how we feel about continuing to be together. I want to know everything about you beyond your Louboutin shoes."

"My Louboutin shoes have a special place on Elizabeth's comprehensive map of the future."

"Agreed! I already know what Santa will be bringing you for Christmas."

She looked at him curiously. Until now, their relationship had mostly revolved around their passion. Suddenly, they were talking about a future together.

"I enjoy the sun and sea. I'm not particularly fond of mountains. But I have a feeling you might be into skiing."

"That's true, but I won't force that on you. However, there's a track in Finland, about ten miles long, with a twenty-degree slope."

"That sounds intriguing. Dad used to take us to Italy or Switzerland every year, and I despised almost every moment spent on those cold, frozen slopes."

"And your mother? You rarely mention her."

It was true. They had a distant relationship. In a family dominated by Thomas, there was little room for a close mother-daughter bond.

"My mother lived for my father and her so-called 'cultural circle'."

"'So-called'?" he laughed, a glint in his eyes that she

hadn't seen before. She appreciated how their passion transformed into everyday life when they were out of bed. She was his love and sex partner, but they also enjoyed talking, which was rather rare. For the first time in her life, she felt no need to censor herself. Apart from her father's obsession, there was nothing else she needed to hide from him.

"Yes, 'so-called'. She'd bring struggling artists to her gatherings as if they were exhibits in a zoo. It's not about discussing art—it's more about satisfying a sense of snobbery, where the wealthy support artists as long as they play their part at social events."

"You might be too harsh. Being seen at Mrs Collister's parties can be a springboard for young artists to achieve greater recognition."

"True, it's possible. But for a long time, I had to endure dinners and cocktails. More than once, I had to rescue some poor soul from the clutches of women circling my mother."

"Well, clearly, neither of us has the best relationship with our mothers."

"It's not that I dislike her. We just don't have that mother-daughter bond. I suppose she fears me now because she'll have to approach me for more money."

"Ouch," he said playfully. "Are you being hard on your mother?"

"I won't take revenge for all those wasted dinners—if that's what you're insinuating. Dad left her half his personal fortune. She gets dividends from the company and a monthly allowance. We're not talking about clothes, shoes, or holidays, but mostly money she donates to frivolous causes. Dad mostly helped veterans, and we sponsor scholarships every year at major universities worldwide."

"So, my darling, sun and sea for our holiday?"

She nodded, momentarily distracted, as she didn't feel their conversation had concluded.

"Can I ask a question about you now?" she asked.

He looked surprised but playfully mocked her serious expression when he replied, "Is that how it works? One answer in exchange for another? Are we still playing by those old-fashioned rules that a lady must follow?"

"Perhaps! It's hard to break free from the old ways that dominated my life."

"In that case, yes, it's only fair to answer a question. Then it'll be my turn again," he continued in a playful tone. "Carry on!"

"Have you ever been in a serious relationship?"

She didn't meet his eyes as she asked, so she didn't expect his laughter.

"Is it Mrs Bennet or Mrs Gardiner enquiring about your Darcy?"

Elizabeth closed her eyes briefly. He already knew that little expression on her face. She was slightly abashed as he had guessed right—Olivia had pressed her to ask him.

"What kind of man has frequented prostitutes for years?" Olivia hadn't elaborated more, but the question had lingered in Elizabeth's mind, as she wanted her lover to be flawless.

"Yes, you can reassure Mrs Gardiner that I've had more than one relationship and that I'm quite sure about my sexual preferences. I was in a seven-year relationship with a woman called Laura. I won't reveal her full name. You'll have to take my word for it."

"Rowan!" she cried with reproach.

"Oh my! Is this the tone I'll get if I forget our anniversary?"

She looked up from her plate to find his teasing gaze, full of love and amusement at the same time. She wanted to ask, *"Are we really speaking about one of our anniversaries?"* But she held back. It felt too soon to talk about such things. There were still restraints and even superstitions she harboured about a seemingly perfect relationship developing too rapidly.

"We were the same age, and at 29, Laura proposed to

me, and for a while, I thought I was prepared. However, in the end, I wasn't. Or more precisely, I wasn't convinced I could spend my entire life with her. I enjoyed her company but couldn't envision a future with her in ten or twenty years."

Elizabeth wanted to enquire whether he could picture himself with her in ten years, but they'd only had a few days together, not years. And then, she suspected that due to their intense passion, it wasn't the ideal moment to make long-term decisions. She aimed to prolong the passion, and for once, she set aside all other uncertainties and questions.

"She's now married and has got three children."

"Do you regret it?"

"Regret her or just regret not being married at forty?"

"Both."

"Well, just like in Jane Austen's world, marriage is one thing and love is another. They often don't align."

"Even in our times?" she enquired.

"Yes, even in our times. Do you think all marriages today are based on love?"

He continued, as she didn't respond, "I suppose you have a queue of bachelors, eager to marry you. And not just bachelors. Many men would leave their wives for your wealth."

"You're being cynical."

"I'm simply a realist aware of the world around him, even if I spend most of my time in virtual reality. If I've preferred the company of escorts in recent years, it was for that reason as well. Maybe I'm not as wealthy as you are, but my title's attractive to some women.

"And no, I do not regret Laura or not getting married. What Jane Austen observed two centuries ago still holds true today. Many people enter into marriage for reasons beyond love, and that kind of marriage, without deep feelings on both sides, didn't appeal to me."

"Not much has changed," she said. "And, like in

Regency times, the opposite is also true. Not all women are gold diggers. There are still Elizabeths and Janes who value love.

"But then we haven't found solutions to all the old problems. While we have a lot more rights now, and divorce is legally simple, many abused women can't divorce due to financial constraints. They struggle to make ends meet, and escaping an abusive relationship through divorce is out of the question."

"You're speaking as if only women face such situations. Men have similar problems too. But feminists tend to highlight the persecution of women then and now."

"What do you mean?"

"Jane Austen, my darling! Some men marry for financial security—like Colonel Fitzwilliam in *Pride and Prejudice* or John Willoughby in *Sense and Sensibility*."

"Wow, you're well-versed in the details. Did Dad quiz you?" she asked with a mischievous smile that he loved because it showed she could tease him despite their deepening love.

"Madam, I have a photographic memory. Unfortunately, I also remember a lot of rubbish. But it has advantages—I've got pictures in my mind of every place *on* and *in* your body. I just close my eyes and touch you—"

"Oi! We're eating!"

"And? Don't I have the right to make love to you during dinner, breakfast, or after, as I've certainly done so before. I'm sure that Elizabeth and Darcy screwed before the wedding."

"What?"

"Yes, I picture Elizabeth like a daring young lady who relished not following the rules of that crazy society they lived in. While Darcy was a grown man, not a youngster to be satisfied by a mere kiss. I'm sure he took her on the sofa in the Netherfield library before they married, and she enjoyed it."

"Stop, you obsessed and vulgar person!" Elizabeth laughed. "You should write variations of *Pride and Prejudice*."

"Are they also hot?" he asked.

"There are about seventy variations published on Amazon every month, and I'm sure that Elizabeth and Darcy screw in some of them. Porno Jane Austen Fun Fiction for the Earl of Warminster."

"Yes, I would definitely enjoy writing a detailed narrative about everything that happens in our bed!"

And before she could answer, he grabbed her out of her chair and loved her on the sofa, eager to hear her moans and cries.

"So, darling, do you want to come to the sea and make love to me deep in the water?" he asked.

Chapter 14

"He wants to take me to Morocco next weekend," Elizabeth told Olivia.

"And I order you to take at least two days off after the weekend," Olivia said.

"I'm not sure…" Elizabeth hesitated, mindful of the pending work waiting for her.

"You haven't had a single day off this year, and how many weekends have you spent working?"

"Before Rowan?"

"You've only known Rowan for a few weeks."

"Yes, but my life feels divided into 'before' and 'after' the Earl of Warminster."

That was a strong affirmation, and Olivia looked at Elizabeth with concern. She didn't want to dampen her happiness, but Elizabeth's eagerness to love and be loved made her see Rowan as the only man in the world.

"You are afraid I will…suffer. You think I'm overly confident," Elizabeth murmured, looking at her; she knew her aunt well enough to read the concern on her face despite her efforts to look indifferent.

"Who isn't at your age?" her aunt answered enigmatically.

"We've decided to get our medical tests done—"

"What?" Olivia exclaimed, revealing her concern this time.

"We're not getting married," Elizabeth laughed at her aunt's expression. "But we're now in an exclusive relationship."

"The polite way of saying you want to stop using condoms."

"Yes, it's only natural, as we're already thinking about a future. Why don't you trust him?" Elizabeth's voice held a hint of exasperation.

"It's not about him—it's about you."

"Don't you trust me?"

Olivia sighed and smiled. "I just want to see you happy. Enjoy the intensity of the moment yet give your relationship a little time to clarify. Let it become *forever* on its own terms. Don't rush, please."

"You're not consistent. You say *live intensely* yet *be cautious*—those are conflicting statements."

"I know, but I mean—experience the passion fully while being cautious about what you want next. Smaller steps…perhaps."

"Right now, I want him to marry me."

"That's the haste I'm concerned about."

"I'm in love."

"You are *in passion*. You've only had friendships with some physical involvement before, and now this man's opened up a new world for you. Passion's what we all desire, but few truly find it. It's wonderful yet perilous."

"People do think of marriage when they fall in love. Darcy proposed to Elizabeth, and they married quickly. They didn't wait a year."

"Yes, because in 1800, they couldn't live their passion like you can now. You're free to indulge in passion without obligations. Adjust to one other, understand each other deeply, and let your relationship evolve."

"You're sounding like my mother now."

"You've told your mother about all this?" Olivia asked, surprised.

"No! But I would have expected her to say these things, not you."

"I'm just a concerned mother figure."

And that, Elizabeth knew, was true.

"Now, tell me about Morocco."

Morocco had slipped their minds amidst their intense conversation.

"I will, but please let me know if you've found anything concerning about…Rowan."

"No." Olivia said sincerely. "Absolutely not! I would never hide anything from you."

"I know you did your research."

"Yes, I did. But people who know him have only good things to say. My concern was him being a forty-year-old with no stable relationship—"

"Luckily. Otherwise, I'd have taken him from any woman on the planet."

"You're quite fond of him!"

"Yes, and I'm going to Morocco with him. Speaking of which, do you think I can use the company plane?"

"Are you serious?" Olivia asked, studying her.

"Why? Is it possible or not?"

"My dear, you're the big boss at Collister. You've got unlimited power within the company, just like your father, grandfather, and all your ancestors have had for the past hundred and fifty years. Why even ask?"

"Kath's made a reservation for the same day."

"Then open the app and make your own reservation. You can override any booking if you need the plane. Get on the app," Olivia instructed in her authoritative tone.

Elizabeth complied and opened her phone, though an uncertain smile lingered on her face.

"Yes, it's possible. I've cancelled her reservation, and now it's mine," Elizabeth reported, surprised. "How did you know?"

"Because we had a conference in New York a few years ago, and Thomas found out that Kath had booked the plane on the same day, for the third time that month. He was angry—I could tell. He had a serious conversation with her. He forbade her from using the plane for holidays and her crazy parties in New York or Dubai."

"She's already used the plane fifteen times this year," Elizabeth read from the app. "I can't believe it. And the year isn't even over."

"I know. Arthur planned to tell you to rein in her expenses."

"He never said a word."

"He had other issues to address first. While Kath took advantage of your father's illness."

Elizabeth's phone rang as they spoke, and she glanced at Olivia. "It's her. She probably got a notification about the change."

Despite the awkward conversation ahead, Elizabeth's voice remained composed and pleasant.

"Yes, Kath," she answered, putting the call on speakerphone.

Kath sounded clearly annoyed.

"I think one of your idiot assistants booked the plane on the day I want it."

Elizabeth's benevolent expression vanished, and she breathed deeply to calm herself.

"My assistants are all nice and intelligent people, and I won't tolerate you speaking that way about any of our employees. I booked the plane."

"Even if I need it and made the reservation two days ago?"

"Yes."

"That's outrageous! I'll talk to—"

A heavy silence fell between them. She wanted to say 'Dad', but the painful reality struck her. The two sisters hadn't been getting on lately, but they shared the immense regret of losing their father.

"I understand," Kath said. "You're taking advantage of the fact that Dad isn't here to defend me."

"Defend you?" Elizabeth responded in a sarcastic tone. "It's me who needs the protection—and the company. You've used the plane fifteen times this year when Dad clearly stated you were only entitled to five. His rules stand."

"The rules that work for you. Others will be changed."

"You can claim for tickets on a normal flight."

"I don't need plane tickets. I need the plane. I've got friends coming with me."

"Well, they can buy their own tickets for once. You won't have any more access to the plane this year."

The blow was so strong that Kath ended the call without a word.

"You've angered the beast," Olivia remarked, surprising Elizabeth. Her aunt had always been impartial between the girls, loving them equally. Lately, though, Olivia had shown resentment towards Kath more than once.

"She's not on the right path. I love her like I love you, but I'm seriously worried about her association with those frivolous people who are always partying. You need to intervene before it's too late. I've seen her in glossy magazines, and I asked Emily Robertson about your agreement with them."

Emily Robertson was the head of Collister Magazines. Years ago, influential magazine owners had agreed not to publish information about their family.

"And?" Elizabeth enquired.

"She told me that they discussed the issue. But they feature Kath on their pages when she's with those constantly followed by the paparazzi. They don't print individual pictures of her, but it's hard to keep her out of a photo when she's with Paris Hilton or others from the jet-set."

The phone rang again. Elizabeth answered, showing the phone to Olivia. She whispered, "Rescuing the baby seal from the villainous shark."

She put the phone on speaker again. "Hi, Mum."

But her mother was far from being in a benevolent mood.

"You made Kath cry. I don't know what's going on between you two. You need to let her go wherever she wants and end this feud."

"Are you serious, Mother?" Elizabeth retorted, her voice as sharp as a razor blade. "Kath's used the plane fifteen times this year, and I haven't used it even once."

"Just this one time, dear."

"This time, I'm going on a short holiday—the first in a year. Kath can have plane tickets if she still wants to go."

"You're so selfish!" her mother exclaimed, causing Olivia to turn red. Afraid that Olivia might intervene, Elizabeth silently urged her not to say anything.

"This conversation is over. Have a good evening, Mum."

"I can't believe it!" Olivia shouted. "I feel like the whole world is upside down. You accused of being selfish, while that little rascal only thinks about herself, indifferent to everyone else around her."

"Dad left a letter about Kath. He regrets that he couldn't change her ways to something more normal or at least eccentric but not the kind of wastefulness that involves travelling from Paris to Milan to New York and back."

"Where's that letter?"

Elizabeth emailed Olivia the letter, and she began speaking as she read. "He's asking you to do what they couldn't do in thirty years. Look here—*five trips each year*. I told you he knew about the plane issue. Ha! *Pay her for her projects according to their performance indicators at Collister, with no extra money except her dividends.* Interesting. Has your mother seen this?"

"No, I wanted to let her cope with Dad's death first, but I was wrong. I'll give her a copy first thing in the morning, as Dad's written words can be considered an amendment to his will."

"Definitely."

Olivia turned off her tablet and remained silent while looking at her niece. Although Kath and Elizabeth weren't her blood relatives, she cared for no other people in the world more than Thomas's daughters. It was impossible not to like Kath and be concerned about her. While Elizabeth had proved to be the person that Collister needed. Confirming all their expectations, Kath was in free fall.

"Regardless of what I've said…sometimes I'm a little too forceful when it comes to your problems…and burdens. Don't get into a feud with your sister—or your mother. It's not what Thomas would have wanted. You used to be such a loving family."

"I don't want to fight with them, but we were never truly happy as a family. We appeared content because we always avoided topics that could cause conflict. We were experts at putting on smiles and being polite despite our inner feelings. But that mostly applied to Dad and me. I think Mum and Kath enjoyed it."

"Because your lives revolved around them."

"Yes, probably. Olivia…"

"Yes, dear?"

"Thank you. I'm so grateful that you're a part of my life."

Chapter 15

"Where do you make love in here?" Rowan asked with that passionate gaze that showed he wanted her. They were sitting face to face, a table between them, yet Elizabeth already knew his eagerness well.

"Lord Warminster, you will not ruin my reputation in the company plane."

"Come on, managing director, don't be so stiff. Just let me know where you've done it with other men."

"Rowan, you've never asked me anything like that before!" she said, midway between surprise and comic fury.

However, Rowan was not easily dissuaded. "I have this sad epiphany that my woman isn't accustomed to the most important rule of flying."

And as she didn't say a word, he continued, "Come on, Elizabeth, don't tell me you've never done it in a plane, this one or another."

"No! I haven't," she said, but she wondered how it had never happened to her, what sort of men she had dated. But then, it was not their fault but hers.

"OK, Miss Purity! I admit that in the past, you didn't know the rules stating that at least once in a lifetime, everyone has to have sex in a plane, it's called joining the mile high club, and *it* doesn't count if the plane's on the tarmac—it's just an experience in the skies. But now that you know it's compulsory…where's the bedroom?" he asked and began searching around.

"Ta-da!" he sang as he opened the door. "This is the bedroom."

"No, it's the resting room," Elizabeth protested. Though she remembered her father and mother going there 'to rest' while she and her sister slept on the reclining chairs in the main cabin. And she slightly blushed.

"What is it, Miss Bennet? Why did you blush? I've never seen you so red. Did you remember a shameful episode?" He was joking as he leant over her and tried to undo her seatbelt.

"Stop," she said. "I'm not going to have sex with you on the plane."

But then he kissed her, undid her seatbelt, and gently dragged her into the other room while his eager hands caressed her in indecent ways so familiar to her earl.

"There isn't a proper bed," she murmured, but his hands greatly corrupted her will.

"We don't need a bed, honey. Not on a plane."

And he loved her on the sofa, murmuring, "My little woman doesn't know that this sofa is a king-size bed, but who cares?"

He loved her half-dressed, in haste, but it didn't matter, as he liked to love her in all circumstances and ways. She wanted to undress, but he stopped her, laughing. "Don't spoil the game, Miss Bennet. Most people attempt this in the plane toilet and don't have room to undress!"

"You know far too much about sex for my taste," she said.

"And you object because…you don't want to experience more of my knowledge—"

"No, it's because I'm inexperienced, while you seem to be an expert in the matter."

"I prefer it this way, my lady."

"I'm sure you do, Mr Darcy, with your arrogance and impertinence. You prefer the lady to be nearly a virgin, while your own experience is as vast as an ocean."

"A sea!" he replied, touching her gently.

"A sea? Not an ocean?"

"Yes, technically, I've had many experiences, but with you, they're something else. I've dived into the depths because of you. And since we haven't got any barriers between us, the emotions are explosive. I can't help but want to be with you. I can't think of anything but to get inside you."

"Oh," she said, and he couldn't tell whether she was scolding or encouraging him to continue.

"Do you think of anything else apart from…that?"

"Rarely," he admitted. "Like most men, I suppose."

She looked at him with the gaze he had playfully dubbed 'Jane Austen's face', imagining how a 19th-century virgin might react to a naked and aroused gentleman.

"I find it hard to believe that all men only think about sex."

"It's not a secret, but women choose not to acknowledge it."

"Tell me, where are we headed?" she asked, pulling him back to the present moment and momentarily diverting the conversation from their sensual musings.

"To Tangiers. We're going to Ibn Battuta Airport, where a car's waiting to take us to my family."

He had once despised intrusions into his privacy, but he was now willing to open all doors for her, even the most secret ones. She was curious, and he didn't intend to hide anything from her.

"Are you an Arab then, my lord?" she asked, attempting a joke.

"Yes, because of my milk and my upbringing—and my own choice. My nanny was from Tangiers. She gave birth on the same day as my mother, but unfortunately, there were complications, and she lost her baby. You can imagine that the countess didn't breastfeed me. It was incredible that she even had a child. I was lucky to have Yadira. She breastfed me on my first day, and later my parents convinced her and her husband to come to Warminster. They stayed there for nearly thirty years, but we always went to Morocco for holidays. When I first visited Tangiers, it felt like coming home. My father always said it was due to Yadira's milk. They never had another child, and they worked for us until eleven years ago when they decided to return to Africa. They now live in a beautiful house on the hill, and from my bedroom window, I can see both the Atlantic Ocean and the Mediterranean Sea."

"And will you invite me to your bedroom, or shall I have my own?"

"Good question," he replied, looking at her. "Perhaps it would be more exciting for me to come at night and whisk you away or passionately seduce you…"

"Are you sure you're my earl from Warminster and not his vile twin?"

"Yes, his vile twin, how splendid!" he exclaimed. That evening, as they descended towards Ibn Battuta Airport, she found herself wondering once again how little she truly knew him.

"Ibn Battuta is a mall in Dubai," she remarked, and he chuckled. "Me, Tangiers, you, Dubai, long live Ibn Battuta," he said, his tone not sarcastic but genuinely joyful.

"Just breathe," he told her as they stood on the steps of the plane, and the humid African air enveloped them, carrying scents she had never experienced before. "It's a mix of floral fragrances, spices, sea, and the Sahara wind," he explained as he held her in his arms as if they were newlyweds. "Welcome to Africa, my love!"

It felt like a dream, like reality had momentarily slipped away, leaving her in a magical realm of new sights, colours, and scents. She had been to Africa before with her parents, who were avid travellers. However, this time was different, as if she were entering another dimension.

Damn you, earl, she thought playfully, *you're much more than I thought.* But then again, he was hers, and every gesture of his was for her. He presented the city to her with the pride of ownership, and finally, she understood that Tangiers was where he had found his happiness.

"I've been coming here since I was a child. My parents never took me on holiday with them, which turned out to be a blessing because I spent every summer and most of the winters here with Yadira's family. But thirty years ago, my father bought a house, and to my everlasting gratitude, he put it in Yadira's name. My mother wanted it after my father died, but it had been Yadira's from the start. When they permanently moved here, we transformed that place into a—"

"Into a what?" she asked, intrigued by the story and the winding streets they traversed, after getting out of the car at the foot of the hill.

"You'll see," he said, leading her onwards. "We're here," he finally announced.

"Is this it?" she questioned, eyeing the house before her.

"No, my dear, we must go up the hill."

Hand in hand, they explored the labyrinth of alleys with charming houses. Some appeared to be fortresses with small windows, while others were painted in striking hues—terracotta red, blue, or vibrant yellow—though white was the prevailing colour in the neighbourhood.

"I've been here before," she suddenly realised, surprised that she hadn't remembered the sense of enchantment Tangiers provoked in her. Then it dawned on her that she was experiencing the town through his love. Clearly, he was in love with Tangiers…and with her.

She found charm in every corner, even in the worn streets. It was astonishing how grand houses with intricately designed wrought-iron window grilles coexisted with more modest dwellings. The old and the new, poverty and prosperity, merged harmoniously, forming the city's enchanting tapestry.

"I like what the men wear here," she whispered.

"No need to whisper, my dear. Here, people speak Arabic and French. English is uncommon."

"Do you speak French?"

"Of course I do. I also speak Arabic. They were my first languages, from Yadira and Driss, her husband. My parents were uninterested in me." He waved away memories of his birth parents, focusing on the city that had brought him happiness.

"The men wear djellabas." He pointed out an elderly man ahead of them.

"I love the colours and the hood."

"The loose-fitting hood is called a qob."

"Qob," she repeated, fascinated by his enthusiasm for sharing his knowledge of the place with her.

"The hood isn't just decorative—it shields the wearer from the sun, and in the past, it protected against sand carried by strong desert winds. In the Moroccan mountains, it serves as a winter hat, guarding the face from snow and rain. The roomy hood can even function as a pocket, holding loaves of bread or bags of shopping."

"I'd like to have one," she said.

"You'll have your djellaba, my love," he assured her, planting a kiss on her temple as they paused in front of a white house, similar to several others they'd passed. "We've arrived."

"It looks like a fortress," she commented, a touch of disappointment in her voice. She'd hoped for a sea view, something the high walls seemed unlikely to offer.

"It's paradise, my dear," he said, detecting her scepticism.

"Welcome to Tangiers," he continued as the door was swung open by a young boy of perhaps ten years old.

"You didn't ring," she whispered.

"They were watching for our arrival," he explained.

As he ushered her inside, she momentarily forgot about the outside world. The presence of Rowan even seemed to fade, and she felt as if she was stepping into a fairy tale.

"It's a riad!" she murmured to herself, awestruck by the trees and flowers surrounding them and the walls adorned with windows that opened onto the courtyard.

When she next looked at Rowan, he'd embraced an older woman who was elegantly dressed and beaming at both of them.

"Allow me to introduce you to Yadira, Elizabeth," he said.

That was all it took for Elizabeth to feel she was becoming part of the family. She and Yadira exchanged the customary French kisses. Amid the enchantment of the surroundings, it felt fitting.

"Go on, go on," Yadira encouraged, gesturing towards the house. "Show Elizabeth her room, freshen up, and then come to dinner."

Hand in hand, they ascended the stairs to the top floor. Rowan opened the door for her. "Your room, Miss Bennet."

She found herself in what could have been Shahryar's bedroom—the very place where Scheherazade wove her tales to evade death.

"Will you spare me after this night?" she teased. Rowan let out a guttural laugh that told her he was ready to love her. He showed her the canopy bed in carved wood, and she reached out to touch the diaphanous white curtains swaying gently.

"Yadira is expecting us for dinner," she whispered.

"Shush, my love. We're free to do whatever we want here."

They took a shower together in the marble bathroom with its huge bath, and then, hardly dried, he led her to the bed.

"Scheherazade told stories." She tried to stop him.

"That's fake news. Do you really believe the king merely listened? Let me show you the true story of each night."

And so, in the opulent surroundings that had witnessed centuries of luxury and leisure, he loved her. They danced to the rhythms of the ornate decor, their bodies entwined in a passionate embrace.

"Feeling you is the most overwhelming experience I've ever known," he confessed.

"Overwhelming? Not delightful or exquisite?"

"No, no," he protested, gazing at her intently. "It's like a hurricane's force."

"And the pleasure, Darcy? Where does the pleasure come in?"

"It's difficult to explain. Pleasure resides within the pain."

"You're quite complicated for my taste. I prefer simplicity."

"I know, but you'll get used to me, I hope, Miss Bennet!" He laughed, urging her to join him at the window.

"I promised you the ocean and the sea. They're right before you," he said, opening the window to reveal a panoramic view. She hadn't imagined the seemingly austere house could offer such breathtaking scenery. The entire bay spread out before them, illuminated by countless twinkling lights. Only then did she realise how high up they were on the hill. She shivered with excitement and awe, unable to tear her gaze away from the mesmerising view.

"Come, my love, let's go down for dinner," he suggested. "We'll return later, and you can spend the entire night admiring the bay."

Two robes awaited them on hooks, though hers was remarkably splendid. Still, she seemed somewhat disappointed. "Mine doesn't have a hood."

"No, because yours is a kaftan. It's a robe for

celebrations, fit for a desert princess."

And indeed, she appeared regal, as if preparing to address her subjects, her hair up in a bun and her body enveloped in the green kaftan adorned with intricate embroidery and crafted from exquisite fabric.

"Does Yadira live alone in this house?" she enquired as they descended for dinner.

"No, her sister's family lives in one of the buildings, though they rarely appear when I'm here unless I invite them for dinner. They're discreet, respectable people. Tonight, it will just be us, Yadira, and her husband, Driss."

The table was set outside, beneath the trees, with a simplicity that contrasted sharply with elaborate English dinners. Each place consisted of a cobalt blue plate adorned with white geometric patterns, and a glass.

"It's so refined," she remarked.

"Yes, it's Fassi pottery, well known in Morocco."

She instinctively spoke French as she heard them talking.

"You speak excellent French," Yadira said while serving her a copious portion of couscous.

"We spent many holidays in France. I really don't know how or when I learned."

"Rowan told me about your father. I'm sorry for your loss."

"Thank you. And thank you for the kaftan."

"Oh no, that's from Rowan. He had it tailored in Marrakech."

"She was disappointed," Rowan explained, "because she wanted a djellaba, as she liked the hood."

"We'll go tomorrow and buy you a djellaba. You know, the djellaba was originally a man's garment," Driss chimed in. Though he rarely spoke, his presence was palpable, his calm smile in perfect harmony with the surroundings.

As they dined, it was as if they were in one of Scheherazade's stories, and the nearby marble basin whispered its secrets, lending an air of freshness and mystery.

"It's a tale fit for Jane Austen's legacy," Rowan commented, observing how Elizabeth savoured each bite—the best way to honour Yadira and her house.

"How so? Is there a connection between Austen and Morocco?"

"Not directly, but the changes in our world, in Europe, gradually permeated across from Gibraltar. A few decades ago, it was socially unacceptable for women to wear djellabas outside their homes. Then, wearing the djellaba outside became a symbol of independence, signifying a woman's desire to work and engage with the world alongside men. Now, wearing a djellaba is utterly commonplace, you'll see."

"Another reason to get me one. I don't need anything fancy, just a simple one like the old man I saw on the street."

"That one was made of wool."

"Doesn't matter. I'll wear it on cold winter nights with the hood up."

Chapter 16

They spent four wonderful days immersed in a culture Elizabeth believed she knew from her travels. Still, she realised she had only experienced the tourist's perspective. She came to understand how shallowly one perceives a country or its people while staying at a fancy hotel and driving an air-conditioned car.

Their Moroccan journey concluded in Olivia's kitchen, just like every joyful experience in Elizabeth's life. They parted ways at the airport; Rowan had to return to Warminster that evening. Though the real reason was different: they each needed a moment alone to comprehend the significance of what they had lived. Those four days in Tangiers had brought them closer to a relationship they couldn't yet put a name to.

"Besides the earl, what did you enjoy most?" her aunt asked.

"It's difficult to say. There were amazing places like the Hercules Cave near Tangiers, at Cape Spartel, right at the entrance to the Strait of Gibraltar—a remarkable experience, a guided journey to the underworld—

"But I'd already been to that place with Dad. It's for tourists. I absolutely loved an early morning at the market with Yadira. That was stunning—the fruits and vegetables had different colours and textures. The tomatoes and even the salad looked enticing on the stalls. Yadira told me they were local vegetables that grew in the local peasants' gardens, and they're rarely sprayed with pesticides. As a result, they can't be exported due to their perishable nature. Like all beauty."

Olivia was eager to know everything, captivated by Elizabeth's visible happiness. She was gifted a luxurious kaftan and spent a while admiring its elegance as she listened to stories about Tangiers and the places they'd visited.

"We spent a day at sea. He's got a small yacht—nothing overly elegant. I think Yadira's relatives use it for fishing."

"And you had couscous."

"Yes, for lunch and dinner—I shocked everyone with how much I ate. It was enchanting. Every moment was delightful and unique, and the earl…well, he was perfect. But the journey back—"

"Goodness, what happened?" Olivia exclaimed. Drawn into Elizabeth's elation, she finally accepted that the man was right for her niece.

"You won't believe who spoiled our trip."

"Oh, I hate bad news, especially now when you're so happy."

"Kath sought revenge for not getting her toy."

Olivia observed the anger on Elizabeth's face—a stark contrast to the happiness she had exuded since her return.

"What did she do?"

"Two evenings before we left, we ate at Alain Ducasse at The Dorchester. I'd made a reservation six weeks in advance, for a meeting. My meeting was cancelled, so Rowan and I decided to go together. While we were eating, my sister turned up with one of her friends, and I invited them to join us. I thought it was a coincidence…poor naive me. I introduce them—a big mistake."

"She made a scene?"

"No, I wish she had. She was with Valery Wilson, the singer."

"Oh," Olivia said, anticipating the worst. She vaguely remembered that girl; she had some notoriety, as her name was all over the place.

"As we left the restaurant, the four of us together, a group of paparazzi appeared, seemingly waiting for Valery. My fault! I should have seen through her trick and her inability to forgive. Remember when she wanted to annoy Dad and did the same—a photo with a rock star in a glossy magazine?"

Olivia nodded, relieved that it wasn't so catastrophic. A photo in a glossy magazine occasionally happened to all the Collisters, even to Thomas.

"On the plane ride back, Rowan saw the pictures. His name, my name, and Kath and Valery—the jolly group leaving Alain Ducasse."

"But how did she find out where you were?"

"Kath was searching for me that afternoon, and one of the assistants told her where I was. It took her just ten minutes to plan the ambush."

"And? It's not a disaster—his reputation is intact," Olivia attempted to joke, trying to bring back the light-heartedness to the kitchen.

"No, but it seems Rowan resembles Dad in more than a few ways. He was furious, and he tried not to show it, but I'm starting to know him. After the wonderful times we'd had, it was shocking to see him agitated. I was upset too, but I wasn't about to let it ruin my best holiday, whereas he—he was really bothered. I couldn't do anything to fix the situation. I just apologised to him and kept silent, but rest assured, I'll arrange a meeting to redefine our agreement about my picture in magazines."

"Yes, do that. But why was he so angry?" Olivia wanted to know, but then she served her niece dinner and decided to steer the conversation onto other topics. Tangiers had to remain the idyllic journey she had heard so much about.

∞∞∞

"I think Kath's crossing the boundary between callousness and irresponsibility," Olivia told her husband that evening. "And I don't know how to prevent her from hurting Elizabeth."

Her husband nodded, concerned. "She's got involved with a group of useless wealthy people and has lost all sense of decency. Sooner or later, she'll cause irreversible damage, and it won't just be Elizabeth who suffers, but Collister in general."

"Your sister isn't any help in this. I talked to her yesterday, and she just thinks Kath's enjoying her life."

"But why was the earl so angry?" Arthur asked the same question that had been troubling his wife. "It wasn't such a terrible situation, leaving a restaurant in the company of three lovely ladies."

"Perhaps his work in cybersecurity enforces certain rules."

"Yes, that must be it."

"Remember how furious Thomas was when it happened to him? It was as if he'd been physically attacked."

That was true. It was the only time they'd seen Thomas yell at Kath, blaming her for the indiscretion.

"I hope Elizabeth and Rowan will discuss it. I have a feeling she was really worried about his reaction. I know that Elizabeth's finally ready to confront Kath, but I can't see anything positive arising from that conversation. It might be better for you to impose some limitations on the money."

Arthur nodded; he felt the same way. He didn't like the idea, but he was, after all, in charge of the Collister finances—both private and for the company.

"Kath can certainly hurt Elizabeth, but I won't worry too much about Collister, no matter what Kath does. The other day, someone told me that there's no bad or good publicity...everything that promotes the company is good."

Olivia looked at him and smiled. "Perhaps we're getting a bit outdated, my dear!"

Chapter 17

Elizabeth pushed open her office door, a mix of intense emotions swirling in her soul—nervous about discovering potential disasters that might have unfolded during her absence and burdened by a sense of guilt for leaving her responsibilities behind just a few weeks after assuming the role of the boss.

"Nothing happened," Clarice responded to her worried face even before she could utter a word. "You haven't received a single phone call in that time, have you?"

That was true, and Elizabeth was grateful for Clarice's efficiency in acting as a barrier between her and the rest of the company. "Marianne will be here in five minutes. It's your first meeting of the day and the only one."

"Alright, and please ask Emily to join us in half an hour."

Emily was the manager of Collister Magazines, and they needed to address the paparazzi situation definitively. Elizabeth needed to resolve the issue promptly if this was as crucial to Rowan as it seemed. She decided to postpone a confrontation with Kath, even though it was inevitable. She needed time to prepare a strategy. Their father had left guidelines, knowing how complicated it would be to manage Kath in his absence. And first of all, Elizabeth was keen on not appearing angry, not wanting to provide Kath with ammunition for future conflicts.

Marianne entered the room with a cheerful smile. She was genuinely happy for Elizabeth, having already heard about the Moroccan story the previous night. But that morning, it was all about work.

"We need to set a date for the celebration," Marianne stated. "July the eighteenth falls on a Tuesday. Is a midweek day suitable for such an event? There'll be overnight guests and the ball as well."

"Yes, we can discuss the details with Roger and Andrew, but not today."

"Roger's anxious to get the date finalised."

"I know, and he's right. However, I'm more concerned about not having the bloody fireworks. Let's decide to brainstorm in Warminster next weekend."

"Can we stay there?"

"No, but Anna will arrange a hotel nearby for Friday night, and we'll come back on Saturday. She's already drafted the invitations. Throughout the year, each department will have an all-staff meeting. We don't know who might have a brilliant idea, and we've discussed offering a £10,000 prize for the winning idea."

"That's quite something!"

"Courtesy of Dad's funds." Elizabeth chuckled. "Also, I spoke to Olivia about bringing in the 'secret group' that's been searching for Darcy all these years—profilers, professors, police—"

"Police?" Marianne asked cautiously.

"Yes, police, MI5 agents, anyone who contributed to Dad's crazy plans." Elizabeth laughed once more, in high spirits. "Unfortunately, the obsessed one is dead."

"Yes, unfortunately. It would have been much simpler to let Thomas handle everything and not burden ourselves."

"Without Darcy Egerton, even Dad would have struggled to organise a spectacular celebration."

Nonetheless, Marianne was less daunted by the prospect

of a celebration without Darcy Egerton. "I disagree. I think there are other fireworks we could arrange to add consistency and grandeur to July 2017."

"I hope you're right. We were blinded by Dad's fixation that Darcy was the only answer to a magnificent two-hundred-year Austen commemoration."

"We've become fixated on this idea, but our younger colleagues might come up with some fantastic fireworks."

Elizabeth nodded, hoping for an alternative finale to Darcy Egerton for their celebration. "We could have a magically lit lawn with torches instead of fireworks, each of our achievements lit well enough to contribute to the general sense of splendour."

"Or Thomas was correct, and Darcy Egerton is among the finalists," Marianne suggested, but Elizabeth didn't fall into her trap, as they had other problems to discuss.

∞∞∞

"Come in, Emily," Elizabeth welcomed, preparing to tackle an issue she disliked.

"I know why I'm here." Emily smiled. "And I completely understand." Her husband was the youngest member of parliament and faced similar problems. "But there's little to be done as long as they hide behind the fact that you happened to be in a photo meant to feature a rock star. You weren't targeted, as we agreed a while ago. They didn't break the understanding. Moreover, it was based on a 'request' for the paparazzi to be there."

"A request?"

"Yes, it's the polite term when a celebrity announces where they can be found, seeking free publicity. That's what Valery did."

Of course she did. It probably cost Kath a Vuitton bag or three pairs of Blahnik shoes, Elizabeth thought. However, she refrained from saying it aloud. Despite their differences, Kath bore their family name.

"The only thing you can do is to avoid being near any of those 'requests'," Emily advised.

"Almost impossible unless I want to stay at home forever."

The conclusion was both disheartening and concerning. This wasn't just a random picture taken by a lucky paparazzo; it was a scheme devised by Kath. The divide between them was widening, as her sister was no longer concerned about *their* shared interests, whether pertaining to the company or the family.

∞∞∞

"What should I do, Arthur?" Elizabeth questioned her uncle as they ate sandwiches for lunch.

Arthur appeared visibly concerned, not concealing his state of mind.

"If Thomas couldn't rein her in, and your mother supports her, I'm not sure what we can do."

"That sounds rather desperate," Elizabeth remarked, attempting not to absorb her uncle's deep apprehension.

"It seems to me that she's out of her senses. She's been unleashed. Nothing happened that night because it wasn't a compromising situation for you or Collister—it was just dinner. Still, I detest her plan, seeking revenge on you for stopping her from having fun with her loser friends. It's utterly terrifying."

"I agree, but if she doesn't grasp the dangers of such situations, talking to her won't help. It'll only make her more entrenched, leading to an open conflict," Elizabeth said.

"We need to talk to Olivia, and I'll speak to my sister, though I don't have much hope from that front. But I must tell you everything…" Arthur hesitated, and Elizabeth looked at him, slightly anxious. Her uncle wasn't one to hesitate—he was usually quite direct.

"Oh dear, what is it?" she enquired.

"It's not as dire as all that." He smiled weakly. "But this issue is troubling me. I don't understand your relationship with your mother."

Elizabeth breathed a sigh of relief. She didn't understand their relationship either, but it didn't worry her so much.

"I see her at least once a week."

"I know, but you don't share things like you do with Olivia."

"Really?" Elizabeth looked surprised. "We never did."

"But I remember those cheerful dinners where you used to talk and laugh."

"Arthur, I told her about Rowan—that I was in love and happy. She practically cut my revelation and asked me to bring him to her Wednesday dinner."

Arthur stood still, not saying anything.

"Sorry, what you remember was us, united by Dad. He was the one who brought the family together, who made us laugh and enjoy each other's company."

"No, you can't say that."

"I'm sorry, but that's the truth. Perhaps in the future, once her pain subsides, she might change. But for now, I don't intend to bring Rowan to her Wednesday events. I'll continue to visit and dine with her but refrain from discussing my own personal matters. The latest Hermès bag is a suitable topic for us."

Chapter 18

Eager to discuss the paparazzi issue with Rowan, Elizabeth was also curious to grasp the reason behind his intense anger. Perhaps it had been a fleeting bout of frustration, and his mood had improved since Wednesday. They hardly spoke on Thursday. Both swamped with work, they disliked communicating through texts or phone calls. Their relationship was too intense for that; they preferred not to have any technology between them and had planned to meet on Friday night at her flat. She was pleased to order food and play the host in her apartment that she cherished and felt matched her personality.

Clarice, who knew everything worth eating or seeing in London, helped her.

She arrived home just minutes before he did, barely having time for a quick shower. Still wrapped in a towelling robe, she hoped he wouldn't rush her to get dressed. Instead, he poured himself a whisky, an unspoken signal for her to change. She wasn't overly concerned; they had their repertoire of games, and infusing their lovemaking with everyday gestures was one of the most gratifying aspects of their fledgling relationship.

While she dressed in her bedroom, she anticipated him

watching her from a distance, as he often did. But he didn't appear.

He's still angry, she thought, wondering why he was mad at her. She'd called Clarice from the aeroplane as soon as she'd seen the picture in the magazine. Clarice quickly confirmed that one of her assistants had leaked the information to Kath. She recounted the incident to Rowan with honesty, and he seemed to understand and accept what she said. Back then, on the plane, she'd imagined it had been a mere indiscretion that Kath had taken advantage of, not a calculated plan to irritate her. Nevertheless, it was an annoyance, not a catastrophe.

She was ready to listen, find a solution, and rekindle their happiness if he was still furious.

However, the man she encountered in the living room was a mere shadow of her lover. He stared out of the window with his glass in his hand, leading her to question whether he had come with a chauffeur or in a taxi, as he never drank when he was driving.

Determined to let him speak, she suppressed her urge to rush to him, even though she yearned for his embrace after nearly two days of separation.

"Please, Elizabeth, have a seat," he said, and her name sounded cold in his mouth.

"I was preparing dinner."

"I won't be staying for dinner," he replied oddly, in an even stranger tone. And all she could think of was what to do with all the food Clarice had ordered. Yet, this was a diversion from understanding with her mind what her heart already felt. She wished to cry even before he spoke, but she remained silent, hoping it was merely a mood or the start of their first argument.

She settled into an armchair, far away from him again, hoping he'd protest and urge her to come closer.

But he didn't.

"What's happening, Rowan?" she asked at last, fear

coursing through her body like venom, creeping from her feet to her brain in an agonising surge.

"Elizabeth, I loathe myself for this, but I came to tell you we can't continue our relationship."

She looked at him, seeming not to understand. His words refused to arrive in her mind. Then, her beautiful face froze in shock, revealing her agony and immense suffering.

"No!" she said in a steady voice. "No, what are you saying? We can work through any problem we might have."

"We can't. I'm sorry, but we can't," he whispered. His voice struck her like thunder, cleaving her soul in two. She physically felt like she was bleeding from the wound.

"No, I won't accept this."

"Please, I'll go now. There's nothing else to say. It's over, Elizabeth." But he didn't move to leave. Despite all the evidence, she still hoped that she could dissuade him or at least prompt him to tell her more.

"Why? Just tell me why."

"We come from different worlds. I'm not prepared to live in your world."

She laughed, finding his excuse absurd. "Different worlds? What nonsense is this? If that's your excuse, it's feeble. You're a wealthy earl, and I'm a wealthy heiress—what 'different worlds'?"

"It's about our lifestyles. While you thrive in the spotlight, I'm a private, secluded man."

"No! I don't. Remember, you said you never found me in glossy magazines. It was an isolated incident that won't happen again."

He seemed to ignore or reject her words.

"I'm sorry."

"You're breaking up with me?" she asked, still in disbelief.

"Yes," he said, meeting her gaze as if he expected her to gasp at his decision. Her agony was so palpable that he seemed on the verge of taking her into his arms to console her.

"But why didn't you do this last week before Tangiers? You introduced me to your family there," she pleaded.

"It was a mistake—"

"No, it was wonderful. How can you call it a mistake?"

She followed him with her eyes as he rose, like an old man preparing to depart.

"No, you can't leave it like this. I need an explanation."

"There's nothing more to say, Elizabeth. I despise myself for causing you pain."

"Yes, you should," she agreed. "I love you in a way no other woman ever could."

"I know," she thought she heard, but uncertainty lingered. She buried her face in her hands, unwilling to witness his departure.

He didn't play around with such sentiments, yet he had toyed with her heart and life. The pain was so atrocious that she remained immobile for a long time, frozen in despair. The shock was so intense that it felt as if her body would cease to function without his love.

No explanation, she repeated obsessively. *What he told me isn't an explanation.*

She struggled to recall whether he'd left looking pained or relieved, but her anguish clouded her perception.

Ten times she contemplated going to his home or even Warminster, yet each time she retreated to the armchair she now loathed. He wasn't pretending; that was the only certainty of that night.

And then, when she finally stood up, she called a taxi to Olivia's country house outside London—the only place in the world where she could seek refuge that night.

Chapter 19

Elizabeth hesitated outside Olivia's house. Glancing around, she had the feeling that his car was parked in the distance, but she compelled herself to ring the doorbell. It was merely her heart playing tricks, refusing to accept reality.

"He left me," she said, falling into her uncle's arms. It didn't matter anymore that he was also present. When Olivia asked him to leave and give them some privacy, Elizabeth mumbled, "Let him stay." She needed both of them to restore her world, even if it seemed like an impossible thing.

They were having dinner, and the aroma of food made her sick. She rushed to the bathroom to vomit, with Olivia following her quickly to help and comfort her until she could return to the living room, where Arthur was waiting, seething with anger. He paced the room with a glass of whisky in hand. Through her exhausted eyes, she saw Rowan instead of her uncle, and tears welled up once again.

She wept until there were no more sobs and tears left. When Arthur stood up to refill their glasses and declared, "I'll grab my rifle and go and kill him!" she managed a pale smile. This was the reason she'd turned to them.

"Please, sit down," she whispered. "You can take care of

that later."

"The scoundrel!" her aunt exclaimed, tears in her eyes. She'd shared in Elizabeth's joy, and she could feel the loss in her heart. "I lived with that fear until you left for Tangiers. But that holiday helped dispel all my worries. He seemed ready to commit to a serious relationship. But he couldn't."

Elizabeth stood to face them, finding her aunt and uncle just as tormented as she was. For a brief moment, the pain eased, seeing how deeply they understood her anguish. She was grateful to have them now that her father was gone. She'd never felt close to her mother, and Kath likely hated her. Olivia and Arthur were her family—a safe haven where she felt shielded. They wouldn't allow her pain to consume her life entirely and plunge her into utter despair.

"Why?" Arthur enquired.

"I don't know. I'd say the incident with the photo was the cause—"

"No, that was the trigger," Olivia hesitated before revealing more, but ultimately, Elizabeth had to confront the truth. "It merely showed him that he had to end the relationship—"

"You swore you didn't know anything about him!" Elizabeth cried with a hint of reproach, sensing her aunt knew more than she'd disclosed.

"And I didn't lie. We gathered all the information we could find on him. He only told you the truth—he led a reclusive life and owned a cybersecurity company. He's financially well off and hasn't been in any known relationships for years, definitely not in high society."

"He didn't lie!"

"No, but I found it hard to fully trust him. He seemed too perfect. He painted the ideal love story for you. Perfect love doesn't exist. People disagree and quarrel, even in the early days of a relationship. He left you, I hate him, but against all the odds, I'm certain his feelings were genuine."

"We even discussed marriage. I didn't sense any hesitation or rejection, and it wasn't me who initiated that conversation."

Observing Elizabeth closely, Olivia struggled to manage her own pain. It was terribly unjust for her niece to have to endure such trauma. Elizabeth was honest and loyal, and Olivia had hoped the earl was the right man for her. No man had ever succeeded in making her happy before; the earl was the only exception, yet also a source of anxiety. From the beginning, that man had made her content and anxious at the same time. He had given Elizabeth the love she deserved, yet from her accounts, Olivia could detect an odd restraint that seemed to hang over their relationship.

"Please, Olivia, please tell me everything you know."

"She doesn't have any concrete or rational details. You know how your aunt is. She's guided by feelings, and her instincts have never steered her wrong."

"You didn't approve of Rowan," Elizabeth said, her resentment towards her aunt for not approving of the love of her life briefly overshadowing the pain of their breakup.

"I did like him, quite a lot, actually, but—I'm not sure how to explain it—I couldn't entirely trust him. Not in the same way I didn't trust that Steven you dated some time ago. With Steven, I had clear reasons for my distrust. He was overly eager to win favour with us, your family. On the other hand, Rowan was the opposite—he didn't want to know us."

"We were just beginning the relationship, yearning to be alone," Elizabeth tried to defend him again, no matter what.

"Perhaps you're right, I don't know. That story about his family living in Warminster seemed incredibly odd, almost like a collective delusion. Don't expect a logical explanation."

The brief moment of tranquillity dissolved as Elizabeth's tears resurged. "No man can love me," she sobbed.

"Don't speak nonsense," Arthur intervened. "Even

Olivia found someone."

Despite her tears, Elizabeth managed a smile—a mixture of despair and a strong desire to move forwards, leaving the earl behind.

"Bastard! Why say that?" Olivia addressed her husband, aiming to shift the conversation.

Surprisingly, Elizabeth also wanted to know, seeking any insight that might help her comprehend what had transpired and why she'd been abandoned in the midst of happiness.

"Olivia was impossible. I met her when she was writing her first PhD, and she had only two short breaks during the day to socialise. Not an hour, but two half-hours separated by eight hours. She expected everything to fit into those breaks—friendship, romance, strolls in the park, even—"

"Enough, old man, you've made your point!" Olivia interjected with affection. Elizabeth observed them. It was the kind of relationship she yearned for, distinct from her parents' marriage. However, now she had nothing, and no man would ever measure up to the earl.

"How will I live without him? We were only together for a few weeks, yet my entire life had already rearranged itself around our love. I hadn't considered marriage until then, but I was daydreaming about it. Imagining what it would be like. Not just our marriage but living together. I hoped we would be living together very soon."

"I'll kill him," Arthur repeated.

"Unfortunately, my dear, duelling is no longer an option," Olivia responded, and curiously, those sorts of conversations were soothing. They were striving to pull her out of the shadow of despair that descended every time she thought of the earl. Unfortunately, he seemed to loom over them that night like a dark, sinister figure.

"I don't know how I'll go on without him," she murmured.

"It'll take a while to forget him. But the good thing is

that you won't run into him unless you want to. You don't inhabit the same worlds."

Elizabeth looked at Olivia, shocked by her words. *You don't inhabit the same worlds.*

"What is it, dear?" Olivia asked, concerned by her peculiar expression.

"He said the same thing—we don't inhabit the same worlds. But how's that possible?"

"Perhaps that's the explanation, and you don't need to search for another. You're the big boss of a major company now, and your life will revolve around that role. The woman, the wife, even the mother, will need to adjust to your position at Collister."

"I never thought about that. Dad managed it so effortlessly. At least, I didn't feel like he was trying hard to balance being a boss and a father."

"Yes, because all of you were content living around Collister. With her never-ending cultural and charity events, even your mother contributed to his role. Maybe the earl didn't want to be known as the husband of Elizabeth Collister, the managing director of Collister Publishing."

Elizabeth stood motionless, struck by that excruciatingly painful revelation which finally made some sense.

"But if that's the real reason, why didn't he tell me?"

"Perhaps because he isn't as aware of it as I've explained. Different worlds—likely that's the core of it. Your mother embraced your father's mission, while a man might not be so eager to be simply a consort."

"My God," Arthur murmured, "Olivia, you're truly wise. Look at me—I'm a consort!"

"Be quiet, Arthur," Olivia chided, and their complicity was evident once more. How did her uncle manage his relationship with a brilliant woman, a globally recognised expert in English literature? That was a secret the earl didn't want to unearth, a life he didn't wish to embrace with her.

But at least that thought was a starting point for her

healing. She longed for Rowan, yet she understood he wasn't a man to become a consort as, for sure, her life would impose such a role in the future. No matter how they lived at home, he would have to agree to accompany her in society and help her in her career.

Yet, despite the solace, her pain surged back like a hurricane. Even though her mind comprehended and respected the explanation, her heart yearned for him, and her body felt the pain of the loss of his caresses and lovemaking.

"I'll never make love again," she whispered to her aunt as they finally found themselves alone in the living room.

"For a time. But the earl opened the door to a place you didn't know existed. Passion is like a drug. You'll crave that feeling and search for it, even without him."

"I doubt it. How can I fill this emptiness within me?"

"Work, work, work—at first. Eventually, you'll look around for a new man."

∞∞∞

They discovered Elizabeth in the kitchen the following day, making breakfast with their housekeeper. She'd been crying and had likely confided in Rosa about what had happened, as the normally cheerful woman also appeared teary-eyed. Elizabeth and Rosa had a longstanding relationship. Rosa often looked after the two sisters when their mother was feeling overwhelmed by the 'responsibilities' she didn't particularly enjoy. Their nannies had willingly let Rosa take the lead during their stays at the Johnsons' country mansion or London house, which had been frequent during their early years.

"Good morning. Why are you up so early?" Olivia asked. She enjoyed sleeping in during the morning and wasn't the most pleasant person until she'd had her first cup of coffee.

"I'm going to work," Elizabeth replied, placing a cup before her aunt.

"It's Saturday, dear." Olivia sighed. "I'm going fishing with Arthur."

"No," Arthur objected as he entered. "*We* are all going fishing."

And that was settled. Even Rosa, who worked until noon on Saturdays, nodded in agreement. She couldn't let Olivia cook for her Lizzy, as she still affectionately referred to Elizabeth.

The fishing excursion had become a ritual that Elizabeth didn't quite understand. However, that morning, she had a clue for the first time in her life. Her uncle was evidently the consort in their outside relationship, while Olivia had established domestic rules that made *her his* consort. It was an equilibrium that a couple needed for their relationship to function.

The Johnsons' mansion was fifty miles from their London house, situated by a river where Arthur liked to fish. He waded into the river in tall rubber boots while Olivia followed in a boat, paddling, or she waited for him in a gazebo where she read. Occasionally, they had friends who joined them for fishing weekends. However, Arthur was well known in their social circle for his biannual fishing parties around the world—an event Olivia didn't participate in. That was considered men's business.

In one way or another, they made their marriage work. Seeing them together was heartwarming, as their love for each other remained strong.

Not long ago, Olivia had admitted to Elizabeth that her husband wasn't her first love. They were attending a conference in Oxford organised by Collister.

"Reginald Morrison," she pointed out, indicating an older man seated at a distance. "He was the man I was passionately in love with when I was twenty-five. He showed great promise as a poet and left me because he wanted to pursue a destiny that didn't involve being a husband or father."

"And?" Elizabeth asked.

"Have you heard of him?"

"No," Elizabeth replied hesitantly, glancing at the man. "But I'm not well-versed in poetry."

"Well, I am, and I can tell you he's a mediocre poet who gave up on his *destiny* about fifteen years ago. Since then, he's been teaching at a school near London. It's the first time I've seen him in years."

"Did you suffer?" Elizabeth asked, curious but secure, as she believed the earl to be the love of her life.

"Yes, but not for so long as you imagine."

Yet remembering their conversation a day after her break up, she wondered whether she would have the same strength as Olivia to forget.

∞∞∞

They hadn't expected any memories about the earl to come out in that rural landscape away from London. But they were mistaken. She still wore the jeans she'd been wearing on the fateful evening when their love was certain. She wept because of the jeans and because of a car parked in front of their house that resembled his. She cried when Rosa informed them that they'd run out of *honey*, and then she cried for no reason, simply because the pain in her chest was unbearable.

"Imagine having to communicate with the earl because of our work in Warminster," Arthur said as Elizabeth hurried to the river after breakfast.

"Ask someone else to handle it. You can simply oversee them," Olivia suggested.

"Perhaps. Otherwise, I might forget my manners and punch him."

Olivia sensed that was a genuine possibility, as she might have done the same.

"Why take her to Tangiers?" she asked for the umpteenth time. "He wasn't convinced about their relationship from the start."

"How can you say that? You haven't met the man."

"It's a feeling I had, considering his lifestyle. A geek, living and working alone in a house divided in two by a wall he had built. He didn't seem like the kind to compromise or get frustrated, yet he couldn't resolve his family's problems for so long. Then, suddenly, it was sorted out within a few days once he decided to address it. No, he needed those people in his house for some unknown purpose I can't fathom."

"Stop, Olivia, just stop. I've always said you should write mystery novels. You find strange connections in the most innocent situations. People are like that—they get accustomed to living in unconventional circumstances without realising their lives might seem weird to outsiders. Do you think our family is normal? Elizabeth runs to you when she's happy or sad, hardly talks to her mother, and look at Kath—travelling the world with a group of idiots. After all, she's the trigger for this situation. I still believe the earl decided to leave after seeing his picture in that blasted magazine."

"Maybe that hastened the decision, but it wasn't the cause. No, the earl struggled with his desire to have a relationship with Elizabeth, but his way of life prevailed."

Arthur regarded his wife with intensity. "Don't tell me you've profiled the earl."

As Olivia remained silent, he got up, almost furious. "You've gone as crazy as Thomas!" Yet, he sat down again and asked, "So, what was the result?"

"67% likelihood that he wouldn't commit to a lasting relationship." She heard her husband sigh, frustrated with her, the profiles, and the earl.

"Come on," Elizabeth called from a distance, "let's go fishing."

∞∞∞

The silence and the water cast their spell. Elizabeth could finally sit at the dinner table and eat toast with butter and eggs after over 24 hours of fasting.

"I can't eat anything else," she said, recalling that the earl liked her belly.

After a whole day without him, she managed not to cry in the presence of her uncle and aunt when a memory assaulted her. But suddenly, his eyes or his touch on her belly brought tears, making the pain impossible to bear. She was sure he loved her, but his feelings weren't as profound or intense as hers. She'd given herself entirely to him, body and soul, with astonishing trust, while he had always ensured there was a way out of their relationship.

"There's a saying that it's better to experience passion and suffer than to live without knowing it exists."

Olivia remained silent, waiting for her to continue.

"But today, I wish I hadn't experienced it. I wish I could let him go without this feeling of being torn in two, with a part of me forever his. If I'd known his doubts, I wouldn't have placed him in that consort role."

"Yes, I believe you're wise enough to handle it, but he felt like you inhabited different worlds. He couldn't find a way to be with you and accept he had to think first of your job and mission in life."

"Isn't it strange? Two hundred years ago, every woman was a consort. Like you said, that was the norm in Jane Austen's time. A woman married and became the shadow of her husband. For thousands of years, in fact. Even though society has made progress in terms of liberty and rights, the mentality hasn't changed much. Men are still the providers, and women are still expected to be mothers and housekeepers."

"No, you're wrong, the changes are evident," Arthur interjected. "For me, and many others, it wasn't a shock to accept that I had an exceptional wife and to adjust to her needs."

"No, I don't think it's the same. You weren't a consort from the beginning. Olivia was finishing her studies. She had enormous potential but hadn't fully realised it yet," Elizabeth suddenly said.

"Yes, my dear, Elizabeth's right. Back then, you were working at Collister, and you were a rich man—"

"Did you marry me for those reasons?" Arthur grinned. He was glad to see Elizabeth engaged in their conversation. He and Olivia had enjoyed over thirty years of marriage, and the reasons for them marrying hardly mattered as long as they found happiness together.

"Definitely for Collister. Having Thomas as a brother-in-law was a big incentive," Olivia joked.

They smiled with great fondness, remembering Thomas, whose presence cast a certain calm over their table.

"Queen Elizabeth the First didn't dare take on a consort in the 16th century. Any man married to her back then would have compromised her independence. But our queen had a formidable consort who paved the way for this 'consort-hood' of men."

"And what about Queen Victoria's Albert?"

"You're right. Though he was more active and less satisfied with the consort role. But Prince Philip is different—he clearly supports the queen in her mission. I admire him for how he's managed this role in a society still dominated by men."

"What are you saying, Olivia?" her husband asked, intrigued. "You have the same rights as we do. We attend the same schools and apply for the same jobs."

Olivia shook her head. "Have you ever seen the board

of trustees at a bank? It's all men. Women are left to fetch the coffee. While we certainly have more rights than before, even in 1900, there's still much to change for genuine gender equality to exist globally."

"Uh-oh, the Oxford feminist is attacking the poor fisherman."

"No, we're not feminists," Elizabeth said. "But if he left me because I'm the boss at Collister and he couldn't be my partner…I might just consider becoming a feminist and fighting for a shift in mindset."

Chapter 20

On Monday, at eight o'clock, Olivia and Marianne joined Elizabeth in her office. Despite Olivia's wish for her to stay, she had gone home to sleep. In his subtle way, Arthur had convinced his wife to let Elizabeth go home and face her pain alone.

While Olivia hardly slept all night and she appeared more worn out by morning than her niece, Elizabeth's makeup did a remarkable job. She looked, as usual, maybe a bit slimmer since she hadn't eaten much for three days, no matter what they tried to give her.

Thanks to Olivia, who briefly gave her the news, Marianne already knew what had happened. Aside from Clarice, who managed her schedule and understood on her own what was happening with the Earl of Warminster, only Marianne knew about her relationship.

"Please, don't open the discussion if she doesn't. It's best not to dwell on it," Olivia had advised the night before during her conversation with Marianne.

∞∞∞

"I'm so sorry," Marianne murmured, uncertain what to say or do. Elizabeth nodded and invited them to sit. From her composed demeanour, it seemed she had decided not to discuss herself, at least not in the office.

"I've asked both of you to be here to let you know that I've decided to meet the *contenders* for Darcy Egerton's title," she said calmly, but a hint of sarcasm was evident.

"No, absolutely not!" Olivia exclaimed while Marianne nodded in agreement.

"No? You were the ones who suggested it to me."

"We were just following Thomas's plan. But since you chose not to meet them, we agreed to wait for the Collister committee to decide the winner and just hoped it would be Darcy Egerton."

Elizabeth waited for more, but neither of them spoke. Through the wide windows, she observed how the beautiful morning had transformed the usually grey London into a fairy-tale place. *So inappropriate with my pain,* Elizabeth thought, considering pulling the blinds down. However, she felt such a glorious day deserved celebration, even if it reminded her of the magnificent Tangiers, shining like a precious gem under the African sun. *I hate you, and I love you at the same time,* she mused, continuing to live in a world where she could still converse with him and scold him for leaving her. Both women watched her, sensing that she was thinking about him and unsure how to proceed with the difficult conversation.

Marianne gestured to Olivia, tacitly saying they should let Elizabeth do whatever would help her and alleviate her pain.

"You said that you wouldn't be able to gather crucial details about the writer in a casual conversation with the man," Marianne said.

"Yes, but that was in the past. Now, I plan to study the profile you've created, and with those details in mind, I'll likely find some clues."

Still concerned, Olivia eventually nodded, though it was not an entirely enthusiastic acceptance.

"Olivia, I need to do something—"

"You have your work, and you have us when you want to talk…"

"I need something more. Anyway, my mind's made up. Please give me the details."

As neither of the two ladies spoke, Elizabeth turned to Marianne, who seemed more convinced and said, "Let's pick up the discussion from where we left off. Marianne…"

"We have three potential candidates," Marianne sputtered, secretly pleased that Elizabeth was continuing with Thomas's plan.

"Yes, candidates for the real-life role of Darcy Egerton," Elizabeth quipped lightly, showing more interest. This newfound attitude marked a considerable improvement from the despair that had consumed her until then.

"Three men, all around forty years of age, producing excellent literature," Marianne continued, more at ease.

"Producing excellent literature! That I understand. The question is, how do you know other details about anonymous competitors?"

Suddenly, the two women she considered the most honest in the world seemed flustered.

"Goodness gracious, Dad involved both of you in his dirty business." She gave a weak smile, feeling better, her pain not diminished but manageable. Olivia had been right—work was her salvation.

She intended to arrive home so exhausted that she would fall asleep instantly, lacking the energy to dwell on her lost love. Although any mention of him was still painful. Even during peaceful moments, memories of him cut deep into her body and soul. Returning to everyday life after thinking about him was a struggle. Fortunately, Olivia and Marianne were ready to move at her pace.

"And not to mention that you're willing to manipulate the outcome of a literary competition that has been Collister's pride for over a century. Something Hugh

Collister refused to do a hundred years ago."

In 1915, when it began, the competition proceeded like all others. They selected the winner from novels published the previous year. Whether it was by Virginia Woolf, James Joyce, or an obscure newcomer, all had equal chances. But in 1917, there was immense pressure to choose a winner—specifically, a lady, the wife of a prominent figure. Hugh Collister was at the forefront while his wife, Amelia, served as interim director. She wrote to him, and his solution was to not award the prize that year. Upon returning from the war the following year, he established a new rule that remained unchanged for a century—they demanded unpublished texts or texts published that year. In light of the celebration, they added a requirement for 2017—the book had to be inspired by Jane Austen's life, work, or legacy.

"No," Marianne objected. "No, the committee will decide the winner, regardless of whether he's Darcy or not. The Collister Commission will reach an unbiased verdict…while we could have a different winner if we're sure he's Darcy Egerton. That's why we need you. Only the head of Collister could approach Darcy Egerton and offer him an alternative arrangement, independent of the competition."

Elizabeth let her head drop onto the back of the armchair. "It's a nightmare—multiple commissions, multiple winners…so you are suggesting there's a chance the esteemed Collister Commission might fail, and someone other than Darcy Egerton could win?"

"That wouldn't be a failure. Literature's subjective, not a science. Perhaps he hasn't created such a masterpiece this time, and someone else might outshine Darcy Egerton."

"You're driving me crazy!" Elizabeth exclaimed, but she turned to Olivia for more details.

"Professor Markson and his research group worked independently, using their methodology. Marianne, your father, and I picked our finalists. Then we compared them with the Collister Commission's finalists. The commission selected the best five purely based on literary merit, while we…we knew Darcy was a man—"

"So, you excluded the women," Elizabeth stated.

Olivia nodded. "And that man had to meet certain criteria, including age. There was a woman and an older man among Collister's top five. He was around fifty."

Elizabeth sighed, but this time, it was due to the peculiar situation, not the earl.

"Only one woman out of the five?" she eventually enquired.

"Yes, we were quite surprised because we initially thought that Jane Austen's works would mostly resonate with women…but that wasn't the case."

"And what's next for Collister?"

"We'll select and announce the winner as usual. We'll sign the publishing contract with the winner by the end of February. However, the launch date will depend on our overall celebration plan."

"So, we've got until the end of February to figure out if Collister's winner is Darcy Egerton and whether we'll have the fireworks at Pemberley—"

"But if he's not Collister's winner…" Olivia continued hesitantly.

"I understand," Elizabeth replied. "Then he might be one of the three men I should have met by then. But how did *you* choose…your finalists?"

"If Darcy sent in a manuscript, he must be among the finalists. His talent is undeniable, and any judging panel in the world would recognise it. We have no doubt about that, and he should be among the ones we've chosen."

Elizabeth nodded, finding it logical. "The three."

"Yes, but I agree that the commission could choose one of the remining two…they are all five so good!" Olivia said.

"But with all the tools you've developed over the years,

how is it possible not to identify his writing style?"

"Because as a writer, Darcy Egerton is a 'transformer'. That's how I've described him in this modern context. He constantly changes his style and literary genre. We admire and appreciate this aspect of his writing. Undoubtedly, it's the foundation of his success. However, it's problematic for our purposes since we couldn't create a consistent profile of his work to use in the competition. For instance, he writes from different perspectives and in the past, present, and even future."

"And what role do you want me to play?" Elizabeth asked.

"If—aided by you—we find concrete evidence that one of the three is Darcy, you'll approach him again and propose an alternative arrangement...different from winning the Collister Fiction Prize 2017."

"As you said, because there's still a chance he might not win," Elizabeth said, finding the situation somewhat amusing this time, unlike Olivia or Marianne.

"Anything's possible when it comes to judging literature," Marianne grudgingly agreed.

"Goodness gracious, ladies, what a maze. We're in quite the predicament regardless of the circumstances."

"That's why we need you. If Darcy Egerton is among the three, we must identify him before the official results are out."

"Or we'll face another disaster."

"Yes, imagine if he's one of the contenders but doesn't win. What happened nine years ago would seem like child's play compared to the ridicule we'd endure. People would once again mock stupid old Collister who couldn't recognise the talent that had conquered the world...and that would be for the second time."

"But there could be other talented winners," Elizabeth suggested.

"Of course, but who would care?" Marianne responded,

her concern evident.

"Dad's struck again. He's left us with a problem that could ruin our company and completely tarnish our 150th-anniversary celebration. He was mad. His crazy games could lead to disaster. How could he jeopardise the company and all of us like this?"

"Now, my dear," Olivia interjected into their conversation. "Thomas loved Collister too much to lead us into disaster. I'm certain that if we follow his plan, we'll find Darcy Egerton. When I last saw him, he took my hand and said, 'Don't worry, Olivia, everything will be fine.' He knew what he was talking about."

"Let's hope so," Elizabeth said. Her father had almost said the exact same words to her, and he'd remained lucid until his final moments. "Can I sleep with one of them if I'm interested?"

Both women rolled their eyes and exclaimed, "No!"

"No? Then why do you think I'm going out with them?"

"You're not going on a date," Olivia corrected. "You're embarking on a mission."

"Alright, not a date, but I need more details about them. First, how did you even learn their names?"

Once again, silence settled in the room.

"So, ladies, there were twenty-five people in the final phase. How did you manage to find out who they were?" Elizabeth enquired, sensing their hesitation.

"We don't know their real names—they used pen names. However, we have photos," Marianne finally confessed.

And that answer made Elizabeth jump from her seat. "What? Do you realise that what Dad did is illegal?"

In the silence that followed, they all pondered deeply.

Dad would have been an ideal sect leader, as he could manipulate even the most intelligent people in the world, Elizabeth thought, looking at her aunt and her friend while the ladies, for the first time, froze in fear.

"Obtaining photos of strangers like *he did* can only be done by breaking the law—hacking to be more precise," Elizabeth continued, amused by their expressions of considerable worry.

"The manuscripts were sent by registered post, and in every Post Office there are…security cameras. It's a matter of matching the registered letter to the security camera's registration—" Marianne murmured.

"No, no, no!" Elizabeth cried, shocked.

Suddenly, everything Thomas had done appeared illegal and perilous. What if it placed Elizabeth in a dangerous situation?

"I assume there's a risk of ending up in jail," Elizabeth joked, while the two women no longer cared about Thomas's scheme, worried about the potential danger they had entangled Elizabeth in.

One thing was clear—until that moment, neither of them had truly contemplated Thomas's words or actions. While he was alive, it was his plan. Afterwards, they'd simply accepted it without giving it much thought, assuming they had time to discuss it with Elizabeth. And when Elizabeth had refused to meet the contenders, they'd buried the matter and put their trust in the competition, hoping that if Darcy was among the finalists, his talent would secure his victory. Otherwise, they would face a catastrophe.

The earl, once again, had disrupted their plans. They silently agreed that if Elizabeth still wished to meet the men, they'd provide her with all their information and let her decide afterwards.

"If I decide to go, I need the whole story. I need to know what I should conceal from Scotland Yard when they arrest me," Elizabeth quipped.

Marianne nodded; she knew details that Olivia didn't, as, in the end, her responsibility was only the literary value of the texts.

"He"—and it was clear Marianne referred to Thomas—"used the usual private investigators, so there's no danger from that angle. As we told you, from all the candidates, the committee selected twenty-five."

"The best entries," Elizabeth noted.

"Yes, naturally. If Darcy Egerton participated in the competition—as your father led us to believe—he must have been one of the best. The finalists were then asked to submit additional chapters. Thomas only mentioned that he had the photos…" Marianne spoke with apparent difficulty, glancing between Olivia and Elizabeth as if realising the illegal nature of their actions.

"He hacked the Post Offices' recordings," Elizabeth mused, amused again, causing Marianne to pale. "I might end up in jail."

"Then perhaps you shouldn't go. We're not accountable for what Thomas did, but if you decide to go on, you will be using stolen data."

Both Olivia and Marianne appeared fearful. They'd never attempted to understand how Thomas had obtained the images of the finalists. Surprisingly, Elizabeth found the entire situation rather entertaining.

"I've made up my mind to go. Tell me more. After all, we've got the finest lawyer in the UK. Go on."

"We've got their photos taken by the security cameras, and I suppose Thomas's private investigators did the rest." Marianne attempted to sound composed, but as Elizabeth buried her face in her hands, Marianne's composure crumbled in the face of her friend's evident amusement. They loathed seeing her distressed, yet her mirth was also scary.

"It's Monday morning, and I—the managing director of Collister—am discussing a crime with the manager of the *Books* department, Marianne Beaumont, and Emeritus Professor Olivia Johnson from Oxford. Well done, Dad!"

"Enough," Olivia interjected. "Let's approach this

problem calmly. I agree it's peculiar—"

"Insanity, Olivia. It's madness and risky, really. Perhaps Dad was on morphine in his final days, without us knowing."

"No, he wasn't. He took some sedatives, but he wasn't delirious or drugged."

"Then how could he believe that a man who'd eluded all searches would participate in his literary contest, among a thousand contenders, and personally post his manuscript at the Post Office right next to his home? We're talking about someone so secretive that he evaded all attempts to uncover his identity for eight long years."

"I told you—it was a game between them," Marianne declared firmly.

"Between Darcy Egerton and Thomas Collister—his most obsessed pursuer? If it was a game between them, Egerton wouldn't risk appearing at a post office, assuming that Dad would have discovered a way to discover his identity. If he hid his chapters among the thousands of texts, someone else likely posted them."

"We reached the same conclusion. It's rather naive to think the real Darcy Egerton is among the three men we chose…"

"Ah," Elizabeth interjected again, amused. "And yet, you were urging me to meet them."

"Yes, because we sensed that Thomas knew who he was. When he asked you to meet those three, he probably suspected that you'd somehow end up with the real Darcy."

"How? He left no other clues." Elizabeth exhaled sharply. "So, the detectives somehow obtained—God only knows how—photos of the twenty-five individuals of varying ages, colours, and genders who submitted the second part."

"Yes, among the twenty-five were men, women, young, old—nearly all categories," Olivia confirmed.

Marianne nodded and continued, "We read all the texts,

yet our finalists were exclusively male."

"The competition committee announced two weeks ago that they'd selected the finalists," Elizabeth recalled.

"Yes, they determined the five finalists who would proceed to the final evaluation. Five external editors will be involved," Marianne said, sounding more confident as she delved into her expertise.

"And among their five, three are our picks!" Olivia exclaimed with apparent enthusiasm.

The three women fell silent at the same time. They felt as exhausted as if they had scaled a mountain. The entire situation was dangerous and deeply obscure, yet it was crucial for Collister. Thomas had laid a heavy burden upon them.

"Thomas wasn't a fool, nor was he under the influence of morphine or painkillers. We both had the feeling that he knew who Darcy Egerton was. Even if he didn't reveal the man's identity, he left a trail to find him when he arranged for you to meet them."

"Another part of his game," Elizabeth said with reproach.

"It was his final wish, and he knew that if we had Darcy Egerton, our celebration would be an unprecedented triumph."

"We now have three photos." Elizabeth took charge in her resolute and organised manner.

"Yes, and we know where each of their manuscripts was posted—London, Swindon, and Carlisle—"

"Carlisle in Cumbria?" Elizabeth queried, irritated.

"Yes, but there's something extraordinary about that place. Carlisle's only ten miles from Gretna Green," Olivia explained, and Marianne nodded.

"And? Do you expect me to elope with the man on the spot?"

"Not exactly, but Gretna Green holds significance in Jane Austen's works. By Jane Austen's time, elopements to

Scotland, particularly to Gretna Green, were so common that they're mentioned in several of her novels."

"Wow!" Elizabeth exclaimed. "And you think Darcy Egerton went to Carlisle to play games with Dad?"

"It's an intriguing coincidence. Since Pemberley's a fictional location in Pride and Prejudice, perhaps he chose a real place that held significance in Jane Austen's work. If you go there, you might find a clue."

"Or perhaps it's just a coincidence."

But Olivia shook her head. "I'm entering the realm of unfounded speculation now. However, if you meet these men, even if none of them is Darcy, one of them will lead you to him."

"Dad set in motion an extensive operation. You now have twenty-five photos," Elizabeth pondered.

"If he's not among those three, we'll still have the other twenty-two."

"Yet, I can't believe that Darcy Egerton wouldn't have made the top five if he did participate," Elizabeth stated. Her rational mind urged her to stay out of the game. However, her father hadn't been foolish or reckless, and he wouldn't have endangered his family or the company.

"But even now, Dad's plan's unclear to me. We've got five Collister finalists, and among them, three correspond to the profile. One of them might be Darcy, and he may or may not win the prize."

"Yes," Marianne agreed.

"So, by February, I must confirm for certain if Darcy Egerton is among those three, or we're in deep trouble. Suppose I meet them and no information about him emerges. In that case, I might shut down Collister and flee to a country without a UK extradition treaty."

"We must trust Thomas's plan and stick to it, even if the current situation's bewildering," Olivia urged, and Marianne nodded.

"Perhaps, but regardless of how Dad's spy scenario plays

out, we still need a Plan B if we don't find Darcy Egerton. That's why we'll brainstorm next week—"

She stopped midway through her sentence, overcome by pain.

"What's wrong, dear?" Olivia enquired with concern.

"We planned the brainstorming session in Warminster," she murmured. "In Dad's Pemberley."

The meeting had concluded, and so had her respite from suffering. She could hardly fathom that love could hurt so intensely, like a physical wound oozing from every part of her being.

"I've got another meeting soon. Please leave me alone now," she requested, and Olivia followed Marianne, stealing one last glance at Elizabeth.

"We didn't tell her how she'd meet the men," Marianne whispered.

"We will. Perhaps at lunch tomorrow."

Chapter 21

A few days ago, in Tangiers, she'd thought about marriage. Now, all that remained was a void in her heart and a constant ache that radiated from head to toe. The most effective remedy was work, and she immersed herself in her daily tasks until she felt ready to face Clarice and then Anna and settle the problem of the earl.

"Please inform Lord Warminster that we require him to move out. I plan to use the house for our brainstorming sessions. He can lock up his apartment, but we need access to the rest of the house, including the library."

Clarice wrote notes on her tablet as she usually did. Nothing in her demeanour betrayed any inkling of knowledge or suspicion. Yet she was an extremely intelligent lady. And Elizabeth knew her assistant assumed there was trouble in paradise, as the familiar spots where her boss could usually be found were missing from her schedule for the week.

Then Anna entered. Work served as a refuge for Miss Collister in many ways—she was the managing director at Collister, unlike Elizabeth, the unfortunate lady left behind by the Earl of Warminster.

"Anna, I'd like you to take charge of Pemberley." They shared a smile, both amused by those words.

"I hope you won't push me into marrying the owner." Even though the conversation maintained a light and jesting tone, Elizabeth's heart turned a perilous somersault. She had to admit that jealousy enveloped her, whether directed at Clarice or Anna. They could still see him, while she pondered whether he could be attracted to either of them. Anna was good-looking, but she projected a somewhat overly corporate demeanour.

However, in the earl's presence, women seemed to shed their inhibitions and transformed into ladies who sought admiration or affection. And, if Anna didn't genuinely alarm her, Clarice was a different matter. With her substantial clothing budget, she always appeared impeccable. Whether radiant or refined, she knew how to converse and behave flawlessly at work and elsewhere. An interesting man occasionally awaited her in a luxurious car, but that didn't soothe Elizabeth's unease. In the earl's proximity, any woman might lose her head…just as Elizabeth had done not so long ago.

She wondered again whether the adage about it being better to regret a love than to live a life devoid of such emotion was true. But the agony was excruciating—a sensation she could have done without and not regretted.

∞∞∞

"He's like a drug," she confided to Olivia during lunch the following day. "I can't put it any other way. Remember how Roberta felt after she got out of rehab?"

"Yes, she mentioned constantly having physical pain," Olivia recalled, thinking of her niece who had struggled with a cocaine addiction.

"Love is a self-inflicted drug."

"It fades over time."

"How can you be so sure?" Elizabeth questioned, toying

with her food, much like she had as a child.

For a moment, Olivia was tempted to say, "don't play with your food," but Elizabeth was thirty-two years old, suffering from the pangs of love.

"I just know. Do you think you're the only one who's gone through this?"

"That man we met in Oxford?" Elizabeth said.

"Yes, I felt like I'd die when he left me, but the pain gradually subsided. I'm not sure how or when, but one morning I woke up and he wasn't on my mind anymore. When I went to work, I didn't ache for him. Love is like a drug, but your body also knows how to neutralise its effects over time."

"Good to know," Elizabeth replied, though scepticism lingered. "Have you ever regretted him?"

Olivia laughed. "Let's just say my situation is different. Would I have preferred a life of constant turmoil with a poet who had lost his talent? No, absolutely not. But at the time, I felt differently. I saw a gifted man driven by his brilliance in bed and in poetry. He shone brightly among us, and I had the privilege of being his partner for a time. When I last saw him, I felt compassion, appalled that I could have stayed with him. Leaving was the best thing he did for me. Then your uncle came along, made me laugh, and offered me this leisurely life that's essential for a scholar. When we were engaged, and I had a conference in Princeton, his secretary handled the arrangements. It was my first experience flying first class and staying in a top hotel, and to be honest, I came home and married him. I enjoyed the luxury of first class and a man who would give me the moon if I asked, even after thirty years of marriage. He's affectionate, humorous, and supportive of my career. I'm fortunate."

"I fly first class," Elizabeth said, her words tinged with regret.

"I know." They shared a sad smile.

"You'll find something else when you're ready to move on to another man. Ultimately, even when you have a man, you still need the reality of everyday life, not an illusory continuous state of bliss."

"The earl helped me discover the meaning of lust, desire, and passion."

"It's a valuable gift. Make use of it and be thankful to him for it."

"At the moment, all I feel is pain and regret. How should I approach the Darcy Egertons?" She evidently sought to shift the conversation and return to work matters.

Olivia didn't respond immediately, and Elizabeth felt like they had entered a crime zone.

"Dad made all of us offenders. In the end, this is like a scenario from one of Jane Austen's novels."

"Why do you say that?" Olivia asked, intrigued yet wary that, like all other discussions, this one would return to the earl.

"We've got all the characters—aristocrats, commoners, Darcys, Elizabeths—"

"An heiress," Olivia added, lightening the mood.

"Yes, like Emma."

"No, you're quite far from being Emma."

"Then who am I?"

"You're definitely Elizabeth Bennet, but also Elinor, who has to care for her mother and sisters when Mr Dashwood dies—"

"Yes, you might be right. But I lack Elizabeth's courage, even though I share her name. But the earl is undoubtedly Darcy. What if he left me because of his family?"

Then she smiled; she knew that was absurd. She hadn't met his mother, but that woman likely had little concern about him marrying a commoner. If anything, the Collister fortune and influence might be appealing to her.

"I never met his mother. Odd, given that we spent most of our time in London, and I'm fairly certain she lives nearby. Nonetheless, he avoided introducing us."

"Did you introduce your mother…or me?"

"No, you're right. It was too early. We were revelling in being just the two of us. Why are we discussing the earl?"

"You're right! Let's talk about Thomas."

"Yes, Mr Bennet, the criminal version." Elizabeth smiled, and the conversation took a safer turn. "Do you see how I suffer? I am, after all, Jane Bennet. Jane Austen's novels are replete with suffering, all of which still exists in our world…just like her characters."

"I agree that Austen was brilliant at depicting human emotions and how we experience them. She provided an exceptional and timeless portrayal of human nature. And you're right, not much has changed. However, we aren't the same characters. You possess some of Elizabeth Bennet's qualities, you may suffer like Jane Bennet, but you are Elizabeth Collister—a Somerville College graduate, the managing director of Collister, and the tenant of Pemberley. Two centuries after her time, the *backdrop* of our lives has considerably changed."

"But inevitably, we are Jane Austen's Elizabeths or Emmas."

Olivia wasn't as concerned about the coherence of their discussion as she typically would be. For once, she simply wanted Elizabeth to find a way to alleviate her suffering. If they had to use Jane Austen, so be it.

"I don't quite grasp your point, Elizabeth," she said, attempting to steer the conversation onto lighter topics, wishing for her niece to view the earl as an Austenesque character rather than the real man who had hurt her.

"My point? When the duchess wrote her diary at the beginning of the 20th century, things weren't vastly different from a century prior. I'm referring to the situation of women. There was a modest thawing that primarily benefited women of the upper classes or artistic circles. Life remained unchanged for the rest, even if they could travel by train from Oxford to London."

"Mostly unchanged," Olivia corrected her in the manner she would correct a student. "You can't equate a housekeeper from 1922 to one from 1813 when *Pride and Prejudice* was published. By 1920, women already enjoyed certain freedoms. Their lives had evolved. They could attend school, as education had become more common over the last century. There were women's colleges at Oxford and Cambridge, some ladies had the right to vote, and others drove cars. They could apply for a divorce, own property and money. But you're right—the change wasn't universal. It didn't touch the lives of ordinary working-class women significantly."

"But Austen's characters aren't working class. In her books, they all had handsome properties and comfortable lives. That was the society she portrayed, and the duchess also referred to it a hundred years later."

"I must disagree," Olivia interjected. Elizabeth seemed to have momentarily forgotten her pain for the first time that day. "This is a common misconception when interpreting Austen—the idea that she depicted a specific social group or class—and this is where your argument falters."

"And didn't she?"

"Her novels revolved around the same type of people—those of middle-class society who admired the aristocracy and sought to imitate them. But take any character or situation and transpose it to any social stratum, from the working classes to the royal family. You'll encounter the same events, the same emotions—hatred, love, envy, gluttony—along with a great deal of gossip, suffering, and joy in remarkably similar circumstances. They marry, have children, are afflicted by similar tragedies and elated by the same happy events. That's what the duchess saw a century after Austen, and it's what I too perceive today—two centuries after her passing. You can shift the social setting or the century, yet human nature, feelings, and actions remain largely unchanged when confronted with the same experiences. However, it would be erroneous to assume that we're still her characters."

Elizabeth didn't catch the final words, already consumed by her anguish.

"He isn't Darcy. He's Bingley, and he's leaving Netherfield."

"Perhaps not for the same reasons, but in a similar manner—ending a relationship that wasn't fulfilling enough. Yet, you can't strip your character of electricity, running water, your bank account, and your managerial position. You are Elizabeth Collister, and even though you may suffer like Jane, two centuries of progress have shaped your *reactions*."

"I don't believe so," Elizabeth disagreed.

"So, are you suggesting that nothing's truly changed?" Olivia queried.

"Yes, I'm the same old Jane weeping over her Bingley."

"Not really. More like Elizabeth pining for Darcy."

"That's not true. I think Jane Austen might scold you. Elizabeth Bennet *rejected* him."

"And do you think that's any easier? Or that she suffered less when she realised her mistake? I think Elizabeth's suffering runs deeper than Jane's tears, precisely because she turned him away just as she finally understood that she loved him."

"Perhaps. Though she didn't grapple with this awful feeling of helplessness."

"Helplessness? How so?"

"Because I've always been accustomed to controlling my own life, even from a young age."

"You often said 'no' when it came to love—but out of fear, not control. Besides, all your experiences are important. The earl gave you confidence—"

"And I promptly lost it."

"No, absolutely not. That's how you perceive it now, less than a week since…"

"Since he abandoned me," Elizabeth declared, anger in her tone.

"Yes, since he abandoned you—because he's a fool," her affectionate aunt affirmed, bringing a faint smile to Elizabeth's lips. At least one other person in the world loathed the earl as much as she did. Perhaps two, if you counted her uncle. "But this anger and frustration will eventually subside, and you'll realise that this experience has brought something positive into your life."

As always, Olivia was correct. Unlike anything before, her extraordinary experiences in the bedroom with the earl had allowed her to embrace love and sex without constraints or reservations.

"He liberated me," she murmured.

"Yes, and that's evident now. Even to someone like me, a woman. For a man, it's as if those words are written across your forehead."

"Dirty words?"

Olivia erupted into heartfelt laughter, and she affectionately stroked her niece's hand. "Words that show you are an uninhibited woman, exuding pheromones. And, my dear, in the 21st century, those words are a badge of honour if you're seeking change!"

"Interesting. I want to include something I once told him in my final speech about Jane Austen. About where we now stand, two centuries after Jane Austen witnessed the rise of the uninhibited and liberated woman. Not in terms of civil or social rights, but in fully embracing life, with physical love now morally acceptable, justified, and even celebrated. And that, indeed, is a triumph!"

When she momentarily forgot about the earl, Elizabeth radiated vibrant energy, causing Olivia to hate and appreciate the earl at the same time. He had wounded Elizabeth like no one else ever had. Yet undeniably, he had permanently changed her, giving her what she had long lacked—her self-assured womanhood.

"We tend to romanticise the Regency era, envisioning their leisurely lives. But that's false. Even the very wealthy endured horrible conditions compared to ours. And that marks another significant change."

"So, we've changed," Elizabeth said, as she wanted her aunt to continue speaking, even about Jane Austen.

"Some social rules have changed, mentalities, social interactions, yet Jane Austen's portrayal of human nature captured its core behaviours in the basic situations of everyday life. In this aspect, she was accurate, and we're almost unchanged. That's why we continue to read her novels without finding them outdated—fundamentally, we still experience love and hatred, betrayal and folly, in much the same way. We're burdened by the same age-old sins. Her art encapsulates the basic characteristics of humanity. Every era and even every group of people has contributed to confirming Jane's narrative, resulting in a comprehensive and timeless image.

"But each era also brought changes…to everything. And for those changes regarding a woman's place in society, we must also thank her."

"She was a fighter!"

"No, absolutely not. In her time, a woman's situation was terrible compared to a man's. Yet Jane Austen only provided hints and allusions rather than a resolute or confrontational stance. She painted the colours on a canvas without going deeper than an image. Still, for the women of the future, her work became a mirror reflecting their predicament. No education, no civil, financial, or social rights. You find everything in her novels. She's a keen observer and has mastered the written word impeccably, yet she's not a crusader. She digs deep, instigates a fight."

"She digs deep?" Elizabeth asked, surprised, suddenly more interested than she had ever been in one of Olivia's speeches.

"In the 120,000 words of *Pride and Prejudice*, she uses the word 'smile' as a verb or noun sixty-nine times and 'laugh' forty-four times. In a contemporary novel of the same genre, 'smile' and 'laugh' appear twice, maybe three times. Our tendency now is to focus on action. Instead of explicitly stating 'she smiled', Austen allowed us to discern her amusement or joy over two pages, relying on context to convey the smiles or laughter. Her immense talent was to insinuate ideas into her reader's conscience. And this is why we consider her a forerunner to the fight of women for their rights."

Elizabeth followed Olivia's speech, resting her head on her palm, her lunch forgotten. Olivia was a persuasive speaker. Elizabeth had even heard whispers that crucial political speeches from recent years had been penned by her. Olivia knew how to captivate her audience, whether at lunch or in a packed auditorium.

But Jane Austen was not such a safe subject as Olivia imagined.

"He was the only man in the world who made love to me and then engaged in discussions about any topic under the sun a mere five minutes later. Even your Jane Austen seemed interesting when I was with him. I'll never find anyone like him."

"He's not unique."

"No, but he was the one who loved me."

Olivia thought his love might not have been strong enough, but she refrained from voicing this, as it would have only fuelled the fire. He needed to remain an enigma.

He was a Soviet spy, married, someone who preferred men, or terminally ill. Elizabeth had thought of everything. Still, it was impossible to determine which, if any, was genuine, and in the end, it hardly mattered.

"What did you say to your mother?"

Thomas's passing hadn't brought Elizabeth and Cybil

closer as Olivia had hoped. Instead, it had created a wider chasm between them.

"Just that we split up. She wasn't really interested and remarked that this wasn't an ideal time for me to be in a relationship."

"What?" Olivia exclaimed, visibly distressed.

"Yes, it appears I'm now expected to dedicate my entire life to Collister and ensure its prosperity with remarkable dividends at the end of the year."

"You both hold such strong prejudices against each another."

"When a mother openly favours one child over another, such animosity is only natural."

"She once confided in me that she felt you judged her for not having a job."

"I don't," Elizabeth responded with an unexpected smile. This was a fresh perspective on her lukewarm relationship with her mother. During the last month of her father's life, she'd lived in her old room in their house. Eventually, she'd sensed that her mother wanted to be alone. The following months had only deepened their estrangement.

"I struggle to communicate with her. While Dad was alive, I thought we had a decent relationship. His presence, humour, and constant conversation bridged the gap between us. He loved us all with equal intensity, continually nurturing our family. Without him…"

Elizabeth fell silent, overwhelmed by the grief her father's absence had left.

"I feel so guilty now. I forgot about him during the time with…Rowan. I no longer suffered, and I didn't yearn for Dad."

"Don't talk nonsense. What guilt? You were happy, just as Thomas wished. Speaking of Thomas, it's time to plan how you're going to meet the Egertons. Time's running short. Let's go back to your office. Marianne's waiting for us."

"I finally enjoy hearing you speaking about Jane Austen," Elizabeth said.

"Finally?" Olivia asked, somewhat surprised.

"Yes, when Dad was alive, it was only a prologue to talking about Darcy Egerton. Now the old lady can have a life of her own, free from Egerton's tyranny."

Olivia didn't answer; she was not so sure.

Chapter 22

But as they entered Elizabeth's office, Clarice announced that Kath wished to speak to her.

"So, she's at work!" Elizabeth said, attempting to conceal her frustration.

"Yes, and she asked me to let her know when you got back," Clarice responded.

Elizabeth turned to Olivia, her aunt's concern evident, ready to shield Elizabeth from any potential danger or individual, even Kath.

"Let's postpone the meeting with Marianne until tomorrow," Elizabeth suggested. "Don't worry, I'm fine. I promise I'm fine," she added quickly, though her aunt was unconvinced.

"Are you sure you don't want me to wait?" Olivia asked.

"No." Elizabeth's firm tone only heightened Olivia's concern. She feared the worst, while she hoped that Elizabeth wouldn't lose the battle with her sister for once. The situation was far from the unity they had hoped for after Thomas's passing. They'd wished for the three women to find solace together and uphold the family bond Thomas had built. Yet, Thomas's death seemed to have increasingly driven a wedge between them rather than fostering understanding or cohesion.

Elizabeth waited for Kath at her desk, half facing the stunning view from her windows.

"London's so beautiful!" Kath exclaimed as she came in. She was dressed casually in jeans and a white shirt, her makeup almost subtle.

Sitting down in front of Elizabeth, Kath's sadness was palpable, and she didn't make any effort to hide it.

"I'm sorry for what happened at the restaurant," Kath said unexpectedly. It was unprecedented; Kath never apologised. However, it seemed she had actually recognised the consequences of her actions.

"If you're referring to my breakup, there's no need to apologise. It likely only sped up the inevitable."

"You seemed happy together," Kath remarked wistfully, while Elizabeth struggled to maintain her composure.

"Kath, there's an unspoken rule about not discussing our private lives at Collister."

"Oh, don't be so uptight, Lizzy," she retorted, using Elizabeth's childhood nickname. Still, Elizabeth wasn't in the mood for nostalgia and affection.

"What do you really want, Kath?" she asked, instantly regretting her harsh tone. Yet, it had become instinctive when conversing with her sister recently.

"Nothing. I want nothing, Elizabeth. I just came to tell you I'm sorry for any role I may have played in your breakup. But it seems you're not willing to accept my apologies."

"I've told you there's nothing to be sorry for. It wasn't your fault."

"I'm in love, and I want to get married," Kath suddenly said, and Elizabeth was lost for words. "Finally, I've got your attention," she continued, rising from her seat. "But talking about such personal matters in *your* office isn't appropriate apparently."

And just like that, she was gone, leaving Elizabeth feeling deeply distressed.

Elizabeth didn't wait for Clarice to tell Arthur about her arrival. She barged into his office, hoping to find him there.

"What's happened?" Arthur exclaimed. "I will kill him!" he continued, but Elizabeth shook her head.

"It's Kath. She just told me that she's planning to get married." And she slumped into the chair across from her uncle. "Dad used to say that misery never came alone—it brought its companions."

"Your father was wise and too willing to give advice without being asked. Tell me more," Arthur replied, concerned despite his attempts to appear composed. "Let's not panic. Marriage isn't such a catastrophe."

"It is when we're talking about Kath, just a month after she received her inheritance."

That was true. Probate had concluded on Thomas's estate recently, and the bequests had been distributed. It was no coincidence that love had emerged at this time; besides, they were unaware of any man in Kath's life.

"You should talk to her," Arthur suggested.

"Unfortunately, I'm not the right person. She came to me to make some sort of confession, and I wasn't patient enough to listen. Lately, her mere presence irritates me."

"I don't like that, and you know it's not OK."

"I'm only human, and right now, I can't do any better."

"I know, I know. Forget about Kath, and I'll handle her. Now, go. And be good!" he said, as he often had when she was a child. Elizabeth left his office, leaving Kath's issues behind.

She regretted not being closer to her sister and missed the times when they'd been on good terms, but they'd never truly been friends. She remembered Olivia talking to her own sister, their closeness evident. In that light, her relationship with Kath seemed unusually distant. However, they hadn't attached much significance to it while their father was alive.

Unfortunately, Kath was a troublemaker; their lawyers had been forced to resolve difficult matters where she was concerned multiple times.

I don't need her to complicate my already intricate life, Elizabeth thought, yet Kath was someone who considered only herself.

∞∞∞∞

"Do we have a real problem with Kath?" Olivia enquired of her husband that evening. He'd told her earlier about the potential marriage, and she'd gone out to buy a collection of magazines to see if there was any public gossip, but none mentioned Kath with a partner, or a wedding.

"Her personal money is at risk. Otherwise, she can't do much. She can't sell her shares or bequeath them to her husband in the event of her death. The company's safe legally. Yet 2017 isn't the best time for her reckless actions. In fact, it's the worst, considering Collister needs to shine this year."

"Maybe it's her way of grieving, but I'm afraid she might do something irreparable."

"Did you find anything in those magazines?" Arthur asked.

"No, nothing. But we need to check tomorrow's papers. However, I did find this." She handed Arthur a magazine containing the photograph of Elizabeth, the earl, and the two young women.

"It's not the end of the world," Arthur said. "It can't be the real reason."

"No, it's just a single photo in a second-rate magazine. However, it represents the life Elizabeth appears to have—under the spotlight."

"But we know that's not true. A simple search through the papers from the last year would reveal the same. She's a hardworking woman, not part of the jet-set that fascinates Kath. Let's hope Kath isn't entirely reckless and chooses a respectable man."

But doubt clouded her husband's eyes. Over the years, few of Kath's ventures had been respectable. Only Thomas's immense reputation had shielded them from more significant turmoil.

"Did you consult the lawyers?"

"Yes, although I was already familiar with the legal situation. The only issue is her personal accounts. Thomas insisted on giving them full control. Kath and Cybil can manage their money, but I have to approve any expenditures exceeding £50,000. It's a way to oversee significant transfers to third parties."

"Did she inherit a substantial sum?"

"Yes. However, it won't last if she buys planes, luxury yachts, or palaces in Dubai and throws parties for all her friends."

Chapter 23

The next day, Elizabeth met Olivia in Marianne's office. She hadn't slept well, but at least there were no happy dreams or terrible nightmares to remember.

"I can't shake off this constant feeling that I'm living in *Pride and Prejudice*," she said.

They waited to see what she meant, as it was hard to gauge from her calm face that morning.

"The earl left me at the end of November, the same time Bingley left Jane Bennet. It's all so proud and prejudiced, isn't it? And Kath's practically Lydia Bennet!"

Olivia shook her head, already in a better mood. "No, we decided you're not Jane."

"But I'm definitely not Elizabeth—"

"Why not? It's a common theory that Mr Darcy advised Bingley to leave Netherfield because he already had strong feelings for Elizabeth," Olivia explained.

"A theory, not an Austen fact," Elizabeth countered.

"Jane Austen leaves room for interpretation. The novel's mostly written from Elizabeth's perspective. And even if we often get insights about other characters' thoughts, Darcy remains an enigma, leaving readers to imagine his actions and feelings until he proposes at Rosings."

"This is a scholarly debate," Elizabeth added with a

smile.

"But I agree that Kath's dangerously close to becoming Lydia—" Olivia said.

"Enough about her. I'm meeting Mum this afternoon. So, ladies, let's lighten up my day with our twenty-first-century adventure novel."

As Marianne began speaking, she handed them a schedule. "We've planned an event every two weeks from December the sixteenth, Jane's birthday, to the end of June. The first one's in Oxford, organised by Olivia, which we announced a while back. It's quite fitting for our goals—"

"Criminal goals," Elizabeth chimed in, already intrigued by the plan. For Marianne, though, it was a serious matter.

"It's possible that one of…*them* might attend the Oxford event," Marianne said in a conspiratorial tone.

"So, my dear comrades, you're suggesting that at least the London-based Egerton will be in Oxford. But why? It's merely a guess," Elizabeth said.

"Of course it's a guess. But think about it—if you were shortlisted for the Collister Prize, and the publishing house organised a symposium where you could meet people, even those on the panel, incognito…"

"But they can't reveal they're Writer X and ask for opinions on their writing."

"No, of course not, but you can gauge their reactions, even ask some subtle questions."

"Alright, let's say you're right, and curiosity drives a writer to that event, and we have a rather blurry photo of him…"

"All participants have to register with a name."

"Why?"

"Because we'll give away a pack of books to everyone who's registered."

"Oh God! Such a setup!" Elizabeth laughed and then she said, "Fine, we'll have a name and a photo. Possibly not their real name—"

"My God, Elizabeth, this is an event in Oxford, not a rave!" Olivia said.

"Anyway, ladies, I was wrong. This isn't *Pride and Prejudice*. It's more like an Agatha Christie novel. The *Three Little Darcy Egertons*. But I need to forget about the earl and Kath. At this point, any means are justified, even some covert actions during my aunt's speech about Jane Austen's era and work."

"Remember, there's a press conference in Oxford."

"Yes, I've seen the schedule. Roger asked me to prep some answers for likely questions."

"Then, on December the thirtieth, we've got an event in Swindon—"

"That's in Wiltshire!" Elizabeth exclaimed. "I hope the earl won't turn up." Despite her words and her expression suggesting otherwise, she secretly wanted him there—it would be a sign he was still interested in her.

Marianne, however, didn't seem to hear her as she continued, "Yes, in Swindon, at STEAM, the Museum of the Great Western Railway. We've got a colloquium organised by one of Olivia's PhD candidates, focusing on the industrial revolution—"

"*Sir Isaac Newton's Science in Service of Culture and Empire,*" Olivia interjected with a professorial air.

"Sir Isaac Newton's admired by Oxford alumni?" Elizabeth asked.

"We've moved beyond past animosity. Sir Issac Newton, the Lucasian Professor at Cambridge, is a national treasure now. But this is a good idea, this eternal competition between Oxford and Cambridge that undoubtedly contributed to the excellence of both of us! I like the idea!"

"We've lost her," Marianne joked.

"You see, my dear," Olivia finally said, addressing Marianne as if Elizabeth wasn't present, "that's why she'll be a great leader and an astute manager. Her world isn't confined to objects—it's a web of relationships. She grasps the connections and the bigger picture."

"Really? No need to flatter me," Elizabeth responded with a smile. "I've already signed up for your criminal activities." She aimed for nonchalance but craved Olivia's words, not for praise, but to redefine herself amidst the impossible task of managing Collister alone. "Do you think then that I'm up to this Herculean task?"

"Yes," Olivia affirmed, as someone who wouldn't deceive her. "I do. You're still so young. That was my only concern, because you haven't had enough time to live fully. Although being young isn't just about lacking experience, it's also about forging new paths that aren't dictated by past experiences."

"I could make mistakes on this new journey."

"True, there's a risk, but progress often emerges from the bold souls who carve their own paths. And I'm so happy that you unfolded your wings in your private life—"

"And then lost them."

"No, not at all. Sexual energy is far too underrated. You lost a man, not your capacity to love."

"We're delving into personal territory at Collister HQ," Elizabeth teased.

"No," Marianne interjected, "we're discussing Collister's leader, the woman named Elizabeth Collister."

"At long last, after 150 years, a boss who's a woman," Olivia quipped.

"An unhappy woman," Elizabeth muttered.

"For a while. The pain will subside."

"So, circling back to our problems, one way or another, our first presumptive Egerton will search me out in Oxford."

"Or we'll help him find you, depending on the circumstances. You'll tweak a few words. The sessions will be recorded…" Marianne hesitated.

"Oh my!" Elizabeth exclaimed.

"But not by you."

"I thought you would make me wear a wire like in those crime programmes."

"No, the whole conference is recorded. However, the profiler must assess his reactions to specific questions."

"Ah, because I've got some questions for him."

"Yes," Olivia confirmed, convinced that Elizabeth wasn't only amused by her assignment but genuinely intrigued by the authors she'd meet.

But Elizabeth shook her head. "I'm still convinced none of them is Darcy Egerton. It'd be too simple, and there was never a simple game between Dad and Darcy Egerton."

She tried thinking like her father for the first time since it all began. The ladies were right. Thomas Collister's fixation on Egerton went beyond Collister's fame or wealth. It was a personal quest; Darcy Egerton was Thomas's Holy Grail.

"Poor Dad. He died without knowing that man's identity."

"Don't be so certain," Marianne countered, and Olivia nodded.

"Then why didn't he tell us? Why this elaborate charade? What if we can't find him, and we face failure in July?"

"There won't be any failure," Marianne stated firmly. "We've planned the next six months as a continuous celebration centred around Jane Austen. No dull or recycled events. Take Oxford, for instance. Next week, Olivia has orchestrated something truly exceptional. It might start as an education-focused event on Austen's era but explode into something quite different."

"Seems rather mundane for a kick-off," Elizabeth commented, and Olivia laughed.

"Wait and see!"

Elizabeth's inquisitive look prompted her aunt to continue.

"My lovely female students, dressed as Jane Austen characters, will share where they 'studied'."

"Studied? Elizabeth Bennet never went to school."

"No, but Georgiana Darcy did. They even arranged for her education in London, including that infamous Mrs Younge—"

"Infamous?" Elizabeth grinned. "Seriously? Who is she?"

"She's the one who convinced Georgiana that Wickham loved her."

"Education and elopement," Elizabeth grinned again, enjoying their exchange.

"Caroline Bingley and Louisa Hurst, who hailed from a socially rising family, were sent to 'one of the first private seminaries in town' to build connections while honing proper etiquette. Harriet Smith from Emma is an illegitimate child, taken care of by her father from afar. He sent her to school, albeit without acknowledging her as his daughter. Anne Elliot from Persuasion went to boarding school after her mother's death. And just when boredom sets in, a flurry of excitement awaits. We suddenly change tack as this conference takes a surprising twist. The Oxford event is in fact about…gentlemen."

"My God, where was I during all this planning?" Elizabeth asked, feeling more at ease. "And the train conference? I read about each event, but only a brief summary."

"On December the thirtieth, we're taking an 1867 train from Paddington to Swindon—a journey of 70 miles in four hours. Part of the conference will happen on the train. We had to add extra carriages to accommodate everyone who's confirmed they're coming."

"Robert's doing a fantastic job."

"Yes, everyone's doing their best. You said we needed excitement. Every time Jane Austen's name is mentioned in a symposium, seminar, conference, or casual meeting, it'll trigger fireworks."

"And at Gretna Green?"

"We've got four seven-minute sketches with significant actors from London. Notable ones, I promise.

"The first's from *Love and Friendship*, a youthful Jane Austen tale—Laura and Sophia convince young Janetta, who's set to marry a man her father chose, that she's in love with Captain M'Kenzie. They also manage to convince Janetta's suitor, leading them to elope to Gretna Green."

Elizabeth smiled, imagining the sketch. "Then?" she asked, caught up in Marianne's effervescent mood.

"From *Mansfield Park*, Julia Bertram and Mr Yates elope to Gretna Green to marry. Of course, we can't forget *Pride and Prejudice*, where Lydia and Wickham are rumoured to be heading to Scotland. Lydia confirms Gretna Green as their destination in the letter she leaves for her friend Mrs Forster.

"Lastly, the tragic love story between young Colonel Brandon and Eliza Williams, his father's ward, from *Sense and Sensibility*. Before Eliza's compelled to marry Brandon's brother, the ill-fated couple plan to elope to Gretna Green. Unfortunately, they're betrayed by Eliza's maid."

Elizabeth smiled, swept up in the excitement. "And then I'll marry Darcy Egerton, secretly at Gretna Green, thereby preventing him from accusing me during my trial that I stole his photo from the Post Office. It'll be the perfect conclusion to the story and the celebration."

Elizabeth didn't feel haunted by the earl's lingering presence for the first time in days.

"There's no risk of such an ending," Marianne jested. "We're confident that, one way or another, we'll decipher your father's intentions. And these three events are our strategies to find the Darcys. But the series will continue with captivating, unexpected gatherings and conferences. We're revealing an unfamiliar Jane Austen—unknown works, fresh perspectives on well-known events, like marriage. March will be dedicated entirely to love and marriage. Was Jane Austen in love with Thomas Langlois

Lefroy? We'll answer that with a resounding yes."

"Who's Thomas Langlois Lefroy?" Elizabeth asked.

"Her only known…or supposed love," Olivia explained. "When she was twenty, a neighbour called Tom Lefroy visited Steventon from December 1795 to January 1796."

"I like that. Maybe that young gentleman served as the male prototype in her novels. Why didn't they marry?"

"They were both poor, and his family had other plans for him."

"Poor Jane!" Elizabeth sympathised, identifying her own heartache in every unhappy tale. "What will happen after March?"

"We're presenting 'The Game' in May, followed by the 'Digital Encyclopaedia' in June."

"I'm trying to see the positive side of our efforts and not obsess over Darcy Egerton's absence," Elizabeth finally conceded. "Alright, let's do this!"

Chapter 24

Elizabeth hesitated to get out of her car outside her parents' house. It was always hard to face her mother and her apparent inclination to defend Kath under any circumstances, yet taking into account recent events in her life, it had become pure torture.

She'd worked for long hours during the last few days and had slept poorly, while the earl still consumed her mind almost every second. Instead of finding a peaceful atmosphere in her parents' house, she anticipated the worst—a confrontation that had been lingering in the air since that incident with the plane. Perhaps it would have been more honest to recognise that they didn't share the same perspectives and find a way to be close without being intimate. However, given everything happening in her life, Elizabeth had hoped for more sympathy from her mother.

If not for Kath's announcement, Elizabeth would have postponed her visit for a later time, but Arthur had asked her to investigate the situation. His own attempt had yielded no results; his sister's animosity had made him realise that his involvement was an unwanted intrusion into her life.

Fortunately, Elizabeth found her mother preparing to leave for one of her events. With only half an hour to spare, she invited Elizabeth into her bedroom while continuing her preparations.

"If it wasn't for Kath's impending marriage, you wouldn't have come," she stated without any preamble.

For once, Elizabeth chose to forgo niceties or diplomacy. "Most likely," she replied, sitting on the end of the bed.

Cybil Collister paused her perusal of dresses and turned towards her daughter.

"What's troubling you, Elizabeth?"

"Troubling me, Mum? Alright, I'll tell you what's troubling me. At thirty-two, I'm the CEO of a two-billion-pound company that I have to manage on my own. The man I loved just broke up with me because he caught a glimpse of the life he'd have with me—paparazzi ambushing us on quiet evenings or me working twelve-hour days."

"It's no one's fault, Elizabeth. You knew it wouldn't be easy when you took over your father's position."

Elizabeth made a concerted effort to avoid exploding. She finally understood that they didn't share the same reality, and arguing about their differing viewpoints was futile.

"Yes, I knew—"

"You accepted it for yourself, not for me or Kath."

"I accepted it, Mother, because I'm a Collister. Dad's been preparing me for Collister my entire life, ever since I was a little girl. At ten, I was at the Frankfurt Book Fair while other little girls were still playing with dolls."

"Are you complaining?" her mother asked so aggressively that Elizabeth stood up and faced her. "Yes, I am, and no I'm not, all at once. My life was mapped out from the moment I was born—"

"You're mistaken. Your father waited for Kath to be born, hoping for a boy. Only after seeing we had another daughter did he prepare you, as you put it."

Elizabeth let out a forceful sigh. She couldn't believe her

mother was intentionally trying to wound her, but she was. All because that spoiled girl wanted a plane and a marriage, and her father wasn't around to fulfil her wishes.

"You're fond of the money, Elizabeth."

"I'm fond of the money?" she retorted, moving swiftly to the dressing room, which was nearly as large as the bedroom. "My dressing room is the size of a wardrobe, but how would you know that when the only time you visited me and I wanted to show you my new home, you were in a hurry to get to one of your events?"

"I can't say I was warmly welcomed into your…home."

"And what did you expect when you breezed in, eyes on the clock, calculating exactly how many minutes the visit would take? Anyway, I accepted this exceptional mission Dad entrusted me with, and I'll strive to make *him* proud. But your other daughter needs to understand that we both have responsibilities. So, dearest mother, here's the letter in which Dad instructs me to manage Kath."

Cybil didn't even glance at the letter Elizabeth placed on her dressing table.

"And to sum things up from 2017, Kath can use the plane for five return flights, she won't have a blank check for her expenses, she'll settle her debts with her own money…or yours—"

"You can't do that—"

"Yes, I can. I've already adjusted her budget, and I expect her to discuss her marriage plans with me. Our lawyers will determine the financial terms of her marriage once I know everything about the man. During the challenging months ahead, I'll do my utmost to maintain Collister's standing where Dad left it. Still, it'll be an uphill battle if you and Kath don't help me. If she continues to behave—"

"How?" her mother exclaimed, growing exasperated. "How is she behaving?"

"Three years ago in March, she wasn't on a month-long

business trip to the Middle East as Dad led you to believe. She was in jail for 27 days in Dubai because they found a bong in her luggage at the border."

"No!" Cybil cried out again.

"Yes. Dad spent four hundred thousand pounds on lawyers to rescue her. She's banned from entering the Emirates for five years. In May of this year, Dad paid a fortune to Hotel Danieli in Venice, where your beloved daughter and her group of misfits vandalised a historic apartment. Want more examples? The recklessness stops now. I'm not afraid of negative publicity. In fact, Rogers told me that any publicity is good publicity. Next time, she'll settle her own debts or end up in jail. Her fortune won't last more than two years at this rate."

"You've ruined my day," her mother whimpered, slumping down onto the bed, tears streaming down her face.

"I've ruined your day?"

"When Thomas was alive, we were at peace, a happy family—"

"Only because Dad bought his peace of mind from both of you with vast sums of money."

"Me? What do you have against me?"

"Dad compiled a list of charities you can represent on Collister's behalf. That's when you use Collister's money. Your personal finances are your own business. I'm waiting for Kath to work with me, to help me with Collister. She's incredibly talented in her field. But rather than leading a respectable life, she's endangering her future. And Mum, you've ruined my day too."

∞∞∞

The burst of courage and adrenaline faded as Elizabeth left the house. In half an hour, she was sobbing in her aunt's embrace after crying all the way there. She didn't know why she was suffering—for her father, her earl, or simply because enforcing rules that Thomas Collister had evaded his whole life for a tranquil existence was proving tough. She comprehended her father's leniency but disagreed with it.

"His inability to say no is why Kath's the way she is. He never had the strength to refuse, and now it might be too late."

"Yes, perhaps it is too late, but she displayed such audacity as long as her father's wealth backed up her actions. She'll either self-destruct or find her way out of this chaos she's created."

"She might drag us into her self-destructive lifestyle."

"No, she can't. We're not in Jane Austen's era or in 1900. Her actions will only harm her."

"I don't like playing the bad guy," Elizabeth admitted, feeling the weight.

"I understand, and I'm so proud of you," Arthur reassured her. "I'll start enforcing the new rules from now on. I just needed you to communicate with your mother."

"Wait, I haven't spoken to Kath yet."

"Alright, once you talk to her, forget everything. I still have authority over their finances, as specified in Thomas's will."

"I'm apprehensive about Kath."

Olivia simply sighed sorrowfully. She disliked seeing Elizabeth burdened with further responsibility when she had to bear Collister's weight alone.

"Do you remember what Mr Bennet told Elizabeth about Lydia going to a town full of officers alone?"

Elizabeth didn't respond; she was too drained to interrupt her aunt.

"This is just a continuation of our conversation about what's changed in the modern world compared to 1800."

"I read *Pride and Prejudice* what feels like a century ago,"

Arthur chimed in. "Have mercy on us, Professor Johnson!"

They all smiled, and Olivia continued thanking Jane Austen, who could bring some peace among them.

"Elizabeth reproached him for allowing Lydia to go to Brighton, and he said, 'Lydia will never be easy until she's exposed herself in some public place or other.'"

"Goodness!" Arthur exclaimed, concerned.

"So we let Kath destroy herself. The scenario's already written," Elizabeth murmured.

"Unfortunately, we don't have any power, and it seems Jane Austen warned us," Olivia said, leading her towards the car.

"In one way or another, this period will make you so strong that nothing will ever break you in the future," Arthur said to Elizabeth as she left them.

∞∞∞

On her way home, Elizabeth imagined herself in bed with a sandwich and a cheesy film, but the dream soon died. Sandwich in hand, she opened the door to Kath. She anticipated her sister to be furious and for a huge row to erupt, but her first words were, "I didn't come here to argue."

Elizabeth remained silent. They settled onto the large sofa. "I love your home," Kath remarked, glancing around the elegant penthouse with terraces on four sides.

"I also own the apartment below, but I haven't done anything with it. The last two years have been hell."

"Yes, but any hell with Dad's better than a beautiful world without him."

Elizabeth was grateful to still have their father's presence. They both loved him deeply, and his absence was a tragedy they shared.

"Each of us mourns in her own way," Kath

acknowledged.

"I know."

"I'm not thrilled you told Mum about Dubai or Danieli."

"Dad was an exceptional man and a remarkable manager, but he was soft when it came to his family. He believed that problems would vanish if he ignored them long enough."

"A rather cynical perspective," Kath commented, yet she wasn't angry—she was almost smiling.

"I can't be like Dad. Or at least not for a few years."

"What will you do when you have my fiancé's name? MI5, Scotland Yard?"

"Most likely." Elizabeth finally smiled, relieved that the evening wasn't turning into a disaster.

"I've sent you an email telling you everything about him. I don't want you to dislike him like you dislike me."

"Jesus, Katherine, I don't dislike you. I love you. I'd be happy to work with you and have you by my side managing Collister. But you need to make a decision. I can enforce certain rules, but they relate to finances or material assets. What you want to do with your life is your choice."

"I'm in love, and Adam wants a normal life for us— home, jobs. He's not part of the jet-set."

"I'm starting to like him," Elizabeth admitted.

"I'm sure you will. And Elizabeth…I'd like to work with you."

"Then come on, there's so much to do this year."

"I will, but it's difficult when I'm met with caution."

"I'm sorry, Kath, but that's all I can offer at the moment. I won't shower you with kind words like Mum and Dad did. If you want to work with me, I'm more than willing. But you hold a position at Collister that can't remain vacant indefinitely because you're not yet ready for the real world."

"I am ready."

"Alright then. I'll see you in the morning."

Elizabeth sat on the sofa long after Kath's departure.

Ultimately, the day hadn't ended on such a sour note. She had to admit that her mother hadn't been one of her favourite people lately, but Kath had every chance of becoming one.

Chapter 25

At six o'clock on the morning of the Oxford event, Clarice arrived at Elizabeth's door with a large team, ready to prepare her for her debut as the managing director of Collister.

"My goodness, Clarice, I thought *you* would help me," Elizabeth said, still sleepy.

"Hush, boss, I'm here to make you look flawless today, and I can't do that on my own." And she introduced the people accompanying her.

They'd bought a navy-blue trouser suit a few days before that Elizabeth would never have dared to wear. Nevertheless, Clarice was resolute, and eventually, she entrusted herself to her hands.

And, after only half an hour, the result exceeded Elizabeth's expectations.

"Is this really me?" she asked, somewhat tentatively, making Clarice's team smile. They appreciated her unpretentious demeanour and lack of arrogance.

"Yes, madam, it is indeed you."

Her hair was elegantly curled on her shoulders, and her makeup made her look almost rested, despite not sleeping much the previous night.

Whilst preparing, she couldn't shake off the feeling that

participating in that game, which was ultimately illegal, was a mistake. She imagined being arrested during the event, whether in Somerville's main hall or the Sheldonian Theatre.

Thankfully, Clarice and her team made her feel better.

When she learned the event would be streamed online, she grinned, hoping the earl would see it and regret her. *Don't be foolish, Elizabeth Collister. He broke up with you and has got no reason to regret anything about you.* Yet, despite that nagging voice insisting he didn't love her, a part of her still clung to the hope that there was another motive behind the breakup.

Elizabeth arrived fifteen minutes before ten o'clock, welcomed by the principal of Somerville College and Olivia at the Sheldonian Theatre. She'd accompanied her father to numerous significant events, but she'd never felt as nervous or excited as she did now. Since she hadn't accepted any invitations during her father's illness, this was her first solo experience, at the centre of attention and curiosity. They all wanted to catch a glimpse of the new head of Collister, even though she'd been by her father's side in his final years.

"Goodness," Olivia murmured, "you look absolutely stunning! Kath's here by the way. How did you do it?"

Indeed, Kath appeared, with Roger from Advertising, evidently overseeing the preparations. She was dressed impeccably, a sight Elizabeth hadn't witnessed in a while, wearing black trousers and a green shirt that matched her heels. As she approached Elizabeth, they exchanged a kiss. However, this wasn't just for show; Kath genuinely seemed ready to support her sister.

"Thank you," Elizabeth whispered, but Kath had already moved on.

Escorted by the Somerville principal, Elizabeth entered the auditorium. To her surprise, a hushed silence enveloped the room as everyone turned to catch a glimpse of her.

Clarice and Olivia followed behind.

"I'm slightly concerned about the earl…" Olivia confessed, unable to hide her worry. She had noticed Rowan's name on the guest list the day before, likely added before their breakup, and feared his presence might unsettle Elizabeth.

In the seven years since Clarice had been Elizabeth's assistant, she had never initiated or participated in a conversation about her boss's personal life. Nevertheless, she looked at Olivia and saw the concern etched on her face.

"He's not coming. I received a thank-you note from him yesterday, politely declining," she said, and Olivia visibly relaxed.

"But—" Clarice hesitated.

"Both of us only want what's best for her, Clarice," Olivia said, inviting her to speak.

"I met him three days ago in Warminster, and he seemed as troubled as she is. What's really going on?"

Olivia turned to Clarice, the same anxiety evident in their eyes. Her question seemed like a plea for Olivia to intervene somehow. Regrettably, there was little that could be done. They joined the others in the auditorium, illuminated by lights with its windows cast in shadows.

"I want you by my side when I speak," Elizabeth told Kath. They positioned themselves on either side of the screen beneath the organ. As they looked around, they marvelled at the sight of the venerable hall, now filled to capacity.

Elizabeth took hold of the microphone at precisely ten o'clock, and the lights dimmed.

"Ladies and gentlemen," she began, "my sister, Katherine Collister, and I welcome you with a mixture of joy and sorrow. 'Jane Austen—Two Hundred Years Later' was my father's most cherished project. Sadly, Thomas Collister isn't here to celebrate with us."

On the screen behind her, Thomas Collister was shown

navigating through the shelves of books in his office before reaching his desk. The sight of the wall behind it—bearing Jane Austen's portrait, notes, and a picture of the Warminster house—embodied the 'organised' chaos that defined his approach to projects. He then turned towards the camera, and the image froze.

"Let us take a moment of silence in Thomas Collister's memory," Elizabeth requested.

Kath's cheeks glistened with tears, yet Elizabeth remained composed, though Olivia sensed the inner turmoil she must be suppressing.

"I hope my father's watching from wherever he is," Elizabeth continued once the audience had settled.

Suddenly, something unexpected followed. Kath gestured briefly to Elizabeth, silently asking for the microphone. The event had been meticulously planned for a month, with many people at Collister working to ensure its perfection, and Kath wasn't among the scheduled speakers.

Nonetheless, Elizabeth knew Kath's chance to return to Collister and a normal life would be forever lost if she didn't grant her that moment. As much as she cherished Collister, her love for Kath outweighed everything else. So, she handed over the microphone, causing Olivia and the rest of the team to freeze in surprise and fear.

Kath wiped away her tears with a visible motion before speaking. "Two centuries ago, Jane Austen was compelled to publish her first novel under a pseudonym she didn't select—A Lady. This was not merely a pen name but an emblem of the anonymity and indifference that was shown to women's destinies in her era. In 1917, in this auditorium, Nevin Darcy Lancashire, the future Duke of Lancashire, presented *Austen Integral*, commemorating one hundred years since her passing. While signing the introductory study alone, he acknowledged that nearly every word had been inspired by his wife, Elizabeth Austen.

"Yet, Elizabeth Austen's name still remained absent from the Integral. The future duchess was an expert in the works of her great-great-aunt. She studied at Somerville College, where suffragettes were already championing their right to vote. In 1917, women's circumstances had evolved somewhat, but there was still a long road ahead. Ladies and gentlemen, two hundred years after Jane Austen, one hundred years after Elizabeth Austen, and for the first time in Collister's 150-year history, the company has been inherited and is managed by a woman—Elizabeth Collister. Mission accomplished, Ms Austen!"

To Olivia's astonishment, the audience erupted in applause, clearly moved by Kath's words.

Obviously touched, Elizabeth reclaimed the microphone. "Thank you, Kath!" she said, then shifted her attention to the audience, savouring the impact of her sister's words. They all looked at her eagerly, wishing to hear her speak. She began abruptly, when Jane Austen's portrait appeared on the screen behind her, overlaid with images of Elizabeth Bennet as portrayed in various adaptations of Pride and Prejudice.

"Jane Austen was not an outspoken champion of women's rights, but her cutting wit, realistic portrayals, sarcasm, social commentary, and incisive critique of manners laid the groundwork on which generations of women constructed their struggle for social, civil, and personal rights.

"I can confidently assert that in 1813, when Pride and Prejudice was published, Jane Austen gave birth to the modern woman. Since then, Elizabeth Bennet has served as a model for every girl and woman who refused to accept the roles imposed on them in a male-dominated world. Intelligent, educated, proud, and audacious, Elizabeth Bennet demonstrated the significance of education to the women of the 1800s. She taught them to decline undesirable proposals. Furthermore, she illustrated that a

Regency-era wife need not confine herself to household matters. She could be her husband's partner. Elizabeth Bennet lives on in every suffragette and every woman who has dreamt of or fought for a different life over the past two centuries. Ladies, Elizabeth Bennet taught us how to seek our own Darcy, and she proved that we are free to love and express that love. From 1813 onwards, every enlightened woman has aspired to be Elizabeth Bennet, and I hope our daughters will carry on this tradition."

She paused, and the screen behind her turned black.

"However, today isn't about us, Jane Austen's women. On your seats, you'll find a pair of 3D glasses. When the lights go down, please put them on. Now, I invite Emeritus Fellow Olivia Johnson of Somerville College to take the floor," she announced as Olivia stepped forwards. Elizabeth extended her arms to embrace Kath, and the sisters shared a warm hug.

"Ladies and gentlemen," Olivia began as Elizabeth and Kath exited the stage, "after two centuries of struggle, we have earned the right to revel in discussing...Jane Austen's gentlemen."

And the screen was filled with gentlemen from another era—Darcy and Wickham, Colonel Brandon and John Willoughby, George Knightley, Edmund Bertram—every male character from her novels was there, drawn from all the TV and film adaptations ever made based on Jane Austen's work. Then, it was the ladies' turn to appear. The couples curtsied and bowed, danced and walked, and finally kissed. The entire scene lasted five minutes, but the sketches were so vivid that the guests were reluctant to remove their glasses when it ended. Then, as the lights came on, real characters emerged from all directions, exquisitely dressed in Regency attire.

"Let's be honest," Olivia remarked, "we all want to marry a Darcy or a Colonel Brandon, but who among us hasn't dreamt of eloping with a Wickham or John

Willoughby?"

"Elizabeth Collister spoke about the modern woman who appeared for the first time in Jane Austen's novels. However, we must be truthful to the end. Jane Austen also created the modern man. From the moment Mr Darcy or Mr Bingley, Colonel Brandon, George Knightley, and Edmund Bertram were conceived, they were entrusted with the noble mission of crafting new and improved destinies for their ladies."

∞∞∞

Marianne wouldn't let Elizabeth sit down. She practically pulled her into the hall.

"He's here," Marianne whispered, her excitement palpable. "Sorry, I'm being a bit crazy. Congratulations on your speech…and Kath's."

"Who's here?" Elizabeth enquired, blushing at the thought that Marianne might be referring to the earl. However, she soon realised Marianne was talking about the first candidate for Darcy Egerton.

"You won't believe it, but the Londoner is actually a journalist from The Sunday Times, Lucas Jackson, and he's covering our event."

"I need to sit down," Elizabeth admitted, feeling pressure for the first time that morning. "Has everything been going well until now?" she asked.

"Yes, everything's been perfect. And Kath was so inspired. But can you focus on what's happening from now on? You have a press conference in an hour, then you and the heads of each department have individual interviews of no more than ten minutes."

Elizabeth burst into laughter. "You're unstoppable, Marianne!"

"You'll be meeting three people—"

"Randomly chosen," Elizabeth added, still laughing.

"Almost," Marianne admitted.

"Lucas Jackson is his actual name. How did you wrangle it, so he ended up with me to interview?"

"It wasn't very hard. He was among the first to arrive and the second to choose you for an interview. You've got his photo on your tablet."

"Is this really happening?" Elizabeth asked, looking at the man who could be Darcy Egerton, yet neither her heart nor her mind told her anything.

"Do you think it's him?" she murmured, not waiting for an answer. Laughter echoed from the auditorium. Olivia knew how to blend just the right amount of humour into her academic presentations and then make everybody feel nostalgic or happy, just the way she planned.

"I'm heading back now," Elizabeth declared. She entered the auditorium as Warminster Mansion appeared on the screen. Her heart ached, but she smiled at a young woman, who invited her to sit beside her while Andrew Miller presented Pemberley. Fortunately, the depiction on the screen didn't resemble the house she remembered; it was how Pemberley would look after the work was complete. The house, the way she had seen it two months ago, was old and ramshackle, yet it was her Pemberley, as in that house lived her Darcy. Regardless of what Olivia and others might say, she knew she could never love another man as deeply as she loved the earl. Even if he no longer loved her, he would forever be the love of her life.

∞∞∞

"Are you ready for the press conference?" Clarice asked, scrutinising her with a worried eye, but her boss looked serene when they entered the press room.

"Ladies and gentlemen," Elizabeth commenced her

succinct presentation before the press. "I am delighted to be here in Oxford to launch our project. From now until July 2017, we will celebrate Jane Austen's enduring presence over 150 years of Collister. We intend to use her invaluable work as a backdrop to commemorate the 200-year journey that has carried us, both women and men, from the industrial revolution to the digital era. Now, I can take your questions."

"Marilyn Thompson, The Sun. Miss Collister, what are your immediate plans for your company?"

Elizabeth glanced at her tablet, which transcribed spoken words into text.

"Ms Thompson, our upcoming months will be focused on the project we have launched today. As you witnessed, we intend to take a more unconventional approach."

"Did your father approve of this approach?"

"This was my father's final project, which he regarded as the most significant in his life. *He* opted for an informal and engaging perspective on Jane Austen's life and work and…" Elizabeth hesitated, and a hush fell over the room as all eyes fixed on her.

"And his last words for family and collaborators were about this project."

The questions continued, while she looked for Lucas Jackson and saw him in the third row. He was writing and occasionally glancing at her, although his interest didn't seem as keen as Olivia had anticipated.

Then, a question quickened her heartbeat. She recognised the name of the glossy magazine where her photo with the earl had appeared a month ago. She hated that man from the start as if he were responsible for *that* image. His question about her personal life was sly and insinuating, similar to the comment about that seemingly harmless photo that had probably hastened their separation.

"Mr Milton," Elizabeth responded, her tone steady

despite her racing heart. "Over the past five years, I accompanied my father to numerous events, including press conferences. I can assure you that he was never questioned about his private life, unlike what you are subjecting me to." She hid her satisfaction in front of Mr Milton's rather annoyed face. "I will only *declare* in front of you that I have no private life until the 20th of July 2017. I work fourteen-hour days, then prepare for the next day."

"Yet we've seen you in some glamorous company recently."

Elizabeth smiled, which surprised the audience. "Mr Milton, you didn't *see* us—you ambushed my party as we left a business dinner. If you'd done your research, you'd know that we were in the company of the owner of Warminster Mansion, our Pemberley, which we rented a few months ago. Warminster Mansion requires extensive restoration, unlike the image you saw at the end of our presentation. I am ready to answer any question about *Collister's* plans for the next year as soon as you understand that I am the new managing director and my mission is to present my company, not my private life."

It was perhaps harsh, but her answer was totally in her father's manner, and for the first time, she felt that her father lived within her, and that his legacy was way beyond a company or a name.

Then she heard *Lucas Jackson, The Sunday Times*. But by then, she was composed and calm; nothing could be worse than a memory involving the earl.

"Miss Collister, you mentioned that each lady seeks her own Darcy. Is Collister Publishing House also in search of a particular Darcy?" Lucas Jackson asked.

Elizabeth gazed at him intently, prompting Clarice to gently touch her hand under the table.

"An intriguing question, Mr Jackson," she responded, maintaining her intense gaze. Could it be that she had found the man her father had sought for almost nine years? She couldn't glean much about him; he was standing, yet details were hard to discern. Suddenly, she wished for everything to be over with so she could be in a private interview with that man.

"It's no secret that nine years ago, Collister Publishing lost a Darcy...as you aptly put it. My father lived every editor's nightmare—letting a hugely talented artist slip away. He never blamed the editor or the head of the publishing department. He considered it a consequence of the outdated management Collister practiced back then in the Books Department. Since that time, everything in our Books Department has changed. Under the management of Mrs Marianne Beaumont, we have published every talented writer who has submitted their work to us."

"Miss Collister, rumours suggest Darcy Egerton might be ready to forgive Collister."

Again, Elizabeth locked eyes with the man, attempting to unravel the mystery.

"Mr Jackson, there are countless rumours concerning Darcy Egerton that we could spend the whole afternoon discussing. It's one of Darcy Egerton's tactics. But if he's willing to offer us his novel, my sister and I are prepared to forgive him for disrupting nine years' worth of dinners, breakfasts, and even Christmases."

Laughter and applause filled the room.

"It's a triumph," Clarice remarked, her pride evident as if she were Elizabeth's mother.

"A triumph," Marianne echoed, leading Elizabeth away from the crowd to meet Olivia.

∞∞∞

"No," Elizabeth interjected when they could finally discuss matters further. "It's too simple. This isn't a game of cat and mouse worthy of my father. Darcy Egerton wouldn't simply turn up like that after nine years. This is like a game of hide-and-seek that Dad would never have initiated."

"Wait until you read about him," Marianne replied, observing their surroundings as people prepared to head to lunch.

"My God, you're a true conspirator," Elizabeth teased.

Marianne sent her a short biography of Lucas Jackson. He was a journalist, but no novel had ever been published under his name.

"He sent us a polished novel. It's hard to believe it's his first," Marianne commented. "I've reread all three novels, and I clearly remember his. Outstanding. And he comes from money. His salary as a journalist isn't his only income."

"And?"

"And that's it," Olivia chimed in. "Elizabeth needs half an hour of quiet. We're heading to my office for a sandwich. Where's Kath?"

As they walked towards Somerville, Elizabeth took her aunt's arm. "Could you have ever imagined how remarkable Kath was?"

"I could, and I do. That's why I was so frustrated with her. She was squandering her talents and potential. I was in shock when you handed her the microphone."

"I know, but it was a risk I had to take."

"We need to decide something. I talked about this with Marianne too. About the Darcys…"

"This story remains between the three of us," Elizabeth assured her, and they continued their stroll in silence.

Chapter 26

"Miss Collister, I'm not sure how to bow," Lucas Jackson said, and she instantly liked him. They looked at each other with unhidden interest.

"It can't be that hard. You saw Colin Firth in Pride and Prejudice."

"I think Colin Firth did us men a huge disservice by setting the bar so high as Darcy."

Feeling suddenly at ease, she found herself enjoying meeting this man. He obviously believed he had the upper hand, hiding from her the fact that he was a Collister Prize finalist. But in that room, the only significant secret was whether he was Darcy Egerton.

"I understand, Mr Jackson, that you have an interest in various manifestations of Darcy."

"Not exactly. Like everyone else, I'm a bit bored of the mystery."

"Do you know anything about Darcy Egerton?" she enquired, studying him for his reaction.

"Same as everyone else. Rumours are circulating in every editorial office and around town. You must have your fair share as well.

"Now, Miss Collister, among all the projects you're planning for the coming months, which do you consider the most important?"

"I hesitate to single out one as the *most* important," she responded, inwardly amused as he attempted to lead her towards discussing the publishing contest.

"Then perhaps the one closest to your father's heart?"

The ladies had been correct. He was eager to know more about the contest. During the press conference, the questions about the Collister Prize had been few.

Elizabeth smiled, feeling good. "My father and all our ancestors always favoured the publishing house above all the other arms of the business. It's where we started, after all. He had a passion for publishing books and never believed we had enough. Take the Collister Fiction Prize, for instance. After announcing the winner each year, we also publish some of the finalists. My father wanted to publish many more of them, but Marianne Beaumont always objected. She argued that even five were quite a lot for a single year, considering it's a challenge to find five excellent books besides the winner's."

"But this year, you haven't revealed the number you'll publish."

"No, but we can't discuss the contest in detail. Not that I'm privy to much. The publishing house operates like an independent 'state' within our company. They have their own rules."

"So, you plan to culminate your celebrations with the announcement of the winner?"

Elizabeth was still uncertain about what to think. He was curious, doing everything he could to extract more information from her. However, she couldn't determine whether he was merely a competitor in their literary contest. He was into money; that much was all she knew. His family owned one of the oldest haulage companies in the UK. That's what she recalled from the bio she'd received from Marianne.

"Indeed, that prize is crucial to Collister. But, as I

mentioned, each department has its own projects, and I can't say I favour one over the others."

"Could you give me some examples?"

Elizabeth nodded, almost disappointed that they were moving away from the Darcy subject.

"You can find more details in the press documents we released. We have our *Austen Integral 2017*, matching the one from 1917, but this time it's complete. Every word written by Jane Austen is included. Then we have the *Austen Digital Encyclopaedia*, a modern concept that compiles all forms of art related to Jane Austen into a private repository. Every reader can organise their encyclopaedia based on their favourite books, films, and artwork related to Jane Austen. Naturally, we'll also present our own version."

"Very intriguing and innovative."

"Thank you. You can link a book to paintings or music or watch a film adaptation while reading the novel."

"I'm eager to see it. Have you got a preview?"

"No, we'll be testing it with a group from Oxford in April and plan to release the final version in June. And then there's *Austen Educational*, which is transforming the encyclopaedia into a comprehensive application for educational use. Simultaneously, Collister Digital is working on a game called *Austen Games*."

"I'm impressed," he said, and his admiration was unmistakable. "Do you have more surprises planned?"

"We certainly do. In July, Pemberley will be ready for our final event, the Regency ball. One last question, Mr Jackson," Elizabeth said as their time was coming to an end.

"Do you like Darcy Egerton?" he asked, and at first, she looked disconcerted but then amused, failing to give an immediate response.

"You don't seem to like him." Lucas Jackson grinned at her hesitation.

"No, you're mistaken. I enjoy the writer's work—his novels, I mean. My hesitation was only because my father deplored his loss so profoundly that he developed almost an obsession with finding him. At times, it felt like he was toying with all of us, and I didn't appreciate that."

"Do you believe he won?" he asked.

"No, personally, I consider that losing him made Collister stronger."

∞∞∞

"I think he flinched once or twice," Elizabeth recounted to Olivia and Marianne. They were at Olivia's house, waiting for Kath, and they spoke quickly, knowing they'd have to stop once she arrived.

"We'll only have the profiler's results after meeting all three of them," Marianne explained.

"Results? You speak as if someone can definitively confirm his identity. The profiler will likely make an educated guess, much like we're doing now," Elizabeth said.

"And what's your guess?" Olivia asked.

"I don't think he's the one. He checks most of the profiler's criteria, but it's too simple to be him and find him in this…way. That's my impression."

"We still have two more to meet," Marianne said hopefully.

"This man won't give us what we want that easily. That's my gut feeling."

"Perhaps that's exactly what he wants—simplicity, given our expectations of a complicated move," Marianne suggested.

Elizabeth felt relief as she heard Kath arrive. Arthur opened the door, and they all embraced as she joined them.

"It seems you still love me," she told Olivia, who hugged her without needing to say a word.

"You were exquisite, eloquent, and inspired this morning," Marianne said.

"While all of you were worried." Kath laughed. She'd had time before speaking to study a few faces. "I don't know why you thought I'd ruin the event. I mean…I understand why, but it surprised me that you judged me based on my past mistakes. I love all of you, and Collister's also my livelihood," she joked. "But even if I was crazy or mad at you all, how could you think I'd sabotage Dad's project?" Her tone suddenly turned serious and sad. "Losing Dad was devastating, then I found myself alone, or at least only with Mum, who mourned in her own way."

"I also mourned in my own way," Elizabeth said, almost as if apologising.

"I don't blame you. I tend to cry often, and you couldn't spend all your time crying. I understand. But this world feels so empty without him," she whispered, and Olivia enveloped her in a hug. Kath was finally sweet and easy-going, much like the girl they remembered before she entered the world of the jet-set.

"I want to get married," she announced during dinner, and they let her speak this time.

"And not to Scott," Olivia added. Scott had been her long-term boyfriend, but their relationship had drifted as she'd mingled with the jet-set crowd. Scott was a lawyer, and while he hadn't proposed, they all suspected marriage was on the horizon.

"No, Scott and I are still good friends…but Adam's different. Adam's American—from Seattle."

Indeed, that's all they knew about him. His father had passed away a long time ago; he lived with his mother, and they had a comfortable income from his father's investments.

"I know Arthur made enquiries about him—"

"How can you be sure?" Arthur asked, finally amused.

"Because that's your style. Dad would have done the same. But you won't find much about him except that he's an ordinary man, not like the ones you don't like."

"So, he's not part of your jet-set circle?" Arthur asked again, and it was evident Kath wasn't thrilled with the questions.

"Do I need to call my lawyer?" she joked, trying to ease the suddenly tense atmosphere.

Olivia laughed and patted her hand. "No, of course not. Arthur used to be just your uncle, but Thomas made him swear that he would take on the role of surrogate father."

"I could have told you everything you wanted to know," Kath said rather sadly. Surprisingly, she then refrained from uttering another word—a stark contrast to the past when she always had the final say and was not always pleasant. Even Elizabeth was surprised by this change. She didn't have much time to ponder what had happened; she accepted Kath's newfound attitude as a gift.

"Your marriage…it's quite unexpected, you have to admit, Kath," Olivia remarked.

"Yes, but Dad told us countless times about how he met Mum, and within a month, they were together."

Arthur, for once, remained silent, as the situation had actually been very different. Cybil and he hailed from a wealthy and well-known London family. When she'd met her future in-laws, she'd epitomised the lady the Collisters desired for their only son. In contrast, Adam was just a name, a city, and a mother.

"We'd like to meet him," Elizabeth said, then enquired with genuine curiosity, "How did you meet?"

Perhaps Kath hadn't anticipated such a simple question, as she responded without much thought, "In Monte Carlo."

And that was a blunder. She'd prepared a different story about another town, but Elizabeth's query had caught her off guard.

"Monte Carlo?" Olivia asked in a light tone, attempting to steer the conversation in a more pleasant direction. "At a casino?" she added playfully. However, Kath was again unprepared, and her expression betrayed that her aunt's remark, made in jest, had been accurate.

Arthur sighed, Elizabeth hid her face behind her coffee cup, and silence settled in the room.

Kath rose abruptly and tossed her napkin onto the table. "It's impossible to talk to you. I will marry with or without your approval, though I don't intend to be resentful," she stated, fixing her gaze on Elizabeth. "I want to work at Collister, and I accept all of Dad's terms. If you fail to see the change, then I'm sorry for you."

And with that, she left. Elizabeth silently gestured that she'd go after her, and Olivia encouraged her to do so.

$$\infty\infty\infty$$

"Another unsuccessful dinner," Arthur commented.

"Yes, but at least we dined with both of them, which hasn't happened in months. You don't trust her."

"No, I don't believe in such sudden and significant transformations. Just a month ago, she was willing to hijack a plane, and now she's a docile girl fully embracing the family spirit."

"You can't say that. Maybe love has changed her."

"Love with a man she met at a roulette table in Monte Carlo? It's such a cliché to pursue a wealthy heiress in Monaco. It surprises me that an intelligent girl like her can fail to grasp such a simple truth. We're in for a challenging time. She doesn't understand the conditions imposed upon her upon marriage. She thinks ten per cent of Collister is hers or her husband's, and she can sell it or do whatever she pleases with it."

"And it's not like that?"

"No, Mr Bennet's entail is nothing compared to the complexities of Thomas Collister's will. Perhaps I should tell that to her future husband before they marry."

"No, we shouldn't interfere. It would be pointless. Many

generations of parents can attest to that. Any advice would be twisted to serve a different purpose. Her lawyers will inform her as soon as she officially announces her engagement."

"Yes, her future husband will likely have to sign quite a comprehensive prenuptial agreement."

∞∞∞

Reluctantly, Kath eventually agreed to accompany Elizabeth to her apartment. She trailed her sister's car and sat in an armchair, keeping her distance.

"I don't know what to say or do," Elizabeth initiated the conversation. "I sense that we're in different spaces."

"I'm not claiming that my behaviour was acceptable. However, I also can't accept that I'm a wicked person—"

"No one sees you that way."

"Don't lie, Elizabeth. No one can compete with your perfection," Kath retorted bitingly.

And suddenly, that was too much for Elizabeth. "Perfection? How dare you judge me in such a condescending tone. I've been working since I was twenty. I haven't taken a proper holiday in the past five years, just stolen moments with my phone in my pocket. And this past year…do you know what it's like to wipe away your tears and walk into a five-hour meeting, all while knowing that Dad could pass away during that time? If Collister succeeds and you receive your dividends at the end of the year, it's because of me—working while you and your friends destroyed Danieli. By the way…why were we the only ones who had to pay?"

"Everything's about money with you. That's all that matters."

"And not with you? Fine. We can donate your shares, you can travel economy class and stay at budget hotels.

Collister means working for me, Katherine, not luxury plane trips to Monte Carlo. I've been to a casino once with Dad and a client."

"I don't want to argue," Kath finally whispered.

"Nor do I. But it's difficult when we see life so differently."

"We don't. I want to marry, to put an end to this wild phase of my life. Adam thinks we should settle down somewhere and build a life. I love him because he helped me see my previous life's true colours, and he understood that I needed to change…something you and the family can't comprehend."

"We're trying…I will try. I promise to see your changes, but I'm not prepared to like Adam just yet…because I've lost faith in men lately."

"I understand."

They sat in silence for what seemed a long time before Kath spoke, obviously wanting to change the subject to something they both agreed on.

"That train event was my idea."

"I know. You're impossible yet talented, coming up with remarkable plans."

"I'll step in during the train journey while you stay in London and…I don't know, go to a spa or go shopping."

Elizabeth grinned. "That event isn't the only thing Collister has going on that day. Every day's filled with tens of issues to address or discuss. Plus, my presence has been announced. I have to be there on that bloody train. But I'm glad to be working closely with you."

∞∞∞

"Was she sincere?" Olivia asked that night on the phone.

"Yes, she genuinely seemed eager to work and contribute to our projects."

"My dear, I hope with all my heart that she's on the brink of changing her life."

"Me too. After my talk with Mum, I feared she'd become even more rebellious…but you've seen her.

"I'm utterly exhausted, Olivia. Just worn out by everything. I yearn to just go to work, then come home without thinking about the earl, the Darcy Egertons, or Kath. I'd like to go out for a relaxing dinner with a friend, but I haven't got any friends. I phoned Lydia Barrister yesterday, but she just talked about her baby. She didn't have any other interests."

"I'm sorry, truly sorry. Forget the Egertons and embrace the idea that Kath wants to change for the better and work alongside you."

"Yes, and then next month, we'll have to pay for a jumbo jet she and her gang trash—"

"No, let's give her a chance. It's the first time she's expressed a desire for a different life. Perhaps it's genuine. Why not accept that Thomas's death had this impact on her?"

"Maybe. I can give her credit in our personal life, but I can't trust her at work. I can't be certain that in a month or three, she won't revert."

"Let's take small steps with her. Let her coordinate the train event while you handle the press at the museum, and until then, keep an eye on her…discreetly."

"Like she's ten years old."

"Yes. Elizabeth, she's not your responsibility. In our era, her actions no longer deeply affect the company's reputation. Every family has its black sheep, but that's no longer a stain on the family name."

"I hope so. Lydia never regretted what she did."

"Lydia Barrister?" Olivia queried.

"No, Lydia Bennet."

"Lydia Bennet? Well, at least not by the end of the novel." Olivia attempted to change the subject, and this time, Elizabeth managed to feel a little better.

"In the end, dear professor, I'm right, not you. We're essentially the same people Jane Austen depicted in her novels. Our manners and lifestyles may have evolved, but our core characteristics haven't changed. Is that not true for Lydia? Did she change?"

"No. She remained 'untamed, unabashed, wild, noisy, and fearless'," Olivia responded.

"You know Pride and Prejudice inside out."

"Pretty much like the conductor of a symphony."

"Ha, but Jane and Elizabeth no longer cared because they were already married. And the novel ended…which is not how it is in our case."

Chapter 27

"Do you want to go to…Pemberley together?" Kath asked Elizabeth on the morning of their brainstorming session.

Since waking up, Elizabeth had been trying to find a reason to stay in London. Still, eventually, she accepted her sister's invitation. She had to face his house once and for all. It was impossible to avoid the place, as Pemberley would be central to their plans until July.

Lately, she had successfully avoided thoughts of him for longer periods. The memories of him invading her mind were less painful. But Warminster was where it all began— her love and his. She questioned many things, but not his feelings in those initial days and nights.

"Yes, thank you," she said. "But we need to take Albert with us."

"We won't be able to talk," Kath protested.

"We can talk about whatever we want in Albert's presence. He's taken me to Warminster several times, and he's seen me sad more than once. He knows about everything that's happened."

"Will you be alright?" Kath asked hesitantly.

"I'll try," Elizabeth replied, still uncertain about her emotions.

∞ ∞ ∞

They picked up Kath from outside her apartment. For the first time in their adult lives, it was Kath who was concerned about her older sister. She smiled when they greeted each other with a kiss.

"I really don't know how to cope with this situation. I'm sorry you're suffering, but I do find some satisfaction in being able to help you…"

"Making this trip is difficult. I feel torn…yet happy that you're with me," Elizabeth responded.

She remembered how eager she'd been the last time Albert had taken her there. As soon as the car stopped, she'd run into the arms of Rowan, who had been waiting for her in front of the house.

"I understand. I'm sorry for my stupid behaviour. I didn't mean to hurt you."

"It's not your fault. Or maybe it is, but only to a certain extent. It was the photo that made him run away, but it was just the trigger, as Olivia said, not the deep reason. I think he was scared. He lives a solitary life, whereas mine seemed unbearably crowded."

"It's crazy. You live a solitary life in your own way," Kath remarked. "At least compared to mine."

"He didn't understand that, or maybe there's another reason. He didn't love me enough."

Kath remained silent, realising how painful the subject was. But that evening at the restaurant, she had seen the love in his eyes and his gestures. That man was in love with her sister, and his behaviour was even more puzzling.

"Warminster is still in a state of disrepair. It needs a lot of work."

But, when they stood in front of the house where she had once been happy, Elizabeth's heart skipped a beat in awe. The front steps were now made of elegant grey marble, the windows were all intact, and an impressive chandelier illuminated the great hall. Then she looked towards the door of the library, where she used to spend time with him. It stood open, but she hesitated to go inside.

Instead, she entered the parlour, which had been transformed into a meeting space with a large oval table in the centre with computers and a screen on the wall. It was hard to believe that this room had been the setting of a Jane Austen novel not too long ago.

"It's magnificent!" exclaimed Emily Robertson, welcoming them. "They told me how shabby it was, and now look at this splendour."

"Finally, Dad made the right decision," Kath chimed in, trying to shield Elizabeth from the barrage of questions and exclamations that filled the room.

"And the library…" Andrew added.

"Stunning, isn't it?" Kath spoke for Elizabeth as she smiled and hugged Olivia before sitting beside her.

"There's still a lot of work to be done, but it's going to look fantastic. It's Pemberley!" someone exclaimed, and they all settled in to watch Roger Chapman's presentation on the Oxford event.

"The conference was a success. I must thank Anna, who didn't sleep for two nights, but it was worth it. Kath's presence was a real bonus, and our new manager received such high praise that I swear I didn't pay for any favourable reviews. In the end, all the departments did an outstanding job. Congratulations, ladies and gentlemen!"

Applause and smiles filled the room, and Elizabeth began to relax and feel more at ease. She was here for work, and she needed to regain her composure.

"But the real star was Professor Johnson. Her presentation was fantastic, unexpected, flamboyant, and I'm not saying that just because Arthur's here."

Laughter followed as Roger displayed some images. "Later, we'll have the full conference available for viewing."

From the screen, Olivia asked, *"Do we still have the Regency man among us?"* And Roger paused the video.

"Thanks to Professor Johnson, we've just discovered our project's concept, motif, or recurring theme—*Jane Austen's Gents*. Professor Johnson has joined us, ready to present her brilliant idea. If 1917 was about the ladies, in 2017, we'll focus on the gentlemen. Our upcoming events will, in one way or another, revolve around this theme."

Images illustrating the idea appeared on the screen.

"We've got the logo. We're starting with *Jane Austen's Gents*, which will become 'Austen's Gents' in April once our project gains more recognition. We're still working on the logo, but Professor Johnson likes the idea of Jane Austen's portrait with the silhouette of a Regency gentleman. Please, Professor Johnson, share more about gentlemen and Jane Austen."

"First of all, please call me Olivia," she said. "I'm thrilled to collaborate with all of you. But I have a confession to make. It wasn't my idea. Before he died, Thomas made me read the final paragraphs of *Elizabeth's Diary*. The book was still a project when the duke asked her whether her diary would be dedicated to Jane Austen and she answered, I quote:

'Yes, for so many reasons. Yet truthfully, it is for you and every other Darcy in this world, as without you, all our wishes would have remained nothing but a dream.'"

"Remarkable!" someone said.

"Yes, indeed! Focusing on the gentlemen in Jane Austen's novels might seem unconventional or even shocking. While it worked well for a conference, we must be careful not to sideline the women. After all, Jane Austen is largely considered a women's author, a precursor to the romance genre."

"Did men read her novels during her time?" Andrew enquired.

"Yes, certainly. Mainly because, in households like Jane

Austen's, books were read by all members. There were limited new releases. I can confidently say that many Regency gentlemen, including Jane Austen's father, read her works along with those of other female writers."

"Excellent!" Andrew exclaimed. "We can highlight this during the train event next week."

"Everything's already set up," Anna responded. She wasn't keen on altering an already-agreed concept.

"I'm sure it is, but I think we can add a little touch without altering the core message," Olivia reassured her. "Vinod Laghari, my PhD student, has done a marvellous job for the train event. He's extensively researched the demand for affordable, unbound books for train travellers during the industrial revolution, a period largely dominated by men. For a significant part of the 19th century, it was mainly men who travelled by train—"

"What's the title of his dissertation?" Kath interjected.

"*Sir Isaac Newton's Science in the Service of Culture and Empire*. But don't be put off—it's not boring. It's not his doctoral dissertation but a lively exploration of how advancements in science impacted cultural spheres. He'll have a five-minute dialogue with Stephen Hawking, who held the Lucasian Professor of Mathematics position from 1979 to 2009, a role Newton held nearly three centuries ago."

Olivia glanced around the table and grinned, as everybody was taking notes. "No need to worry. There won't be an exam at the end of the meeting."

Only Elizabeth laughed. "It's the 'Olivia Effect'. Everyone loves her talks but dreads the test at the end of the lecture," she remarked. "Nonetheless, this concept about Regency gentlemen needs further discussion. It's intriguing and unexpected. However, we must handle it with care. I suggest we listen to Olivia as she is *live at Pemberley*. You can always review the recorded conference later if necessary. Olivia—"

Olivia's callings were teaching, debating, and speaking,

and her physical presence was an asset. Her charisma had the power to hold any audience captive for hours with her words.

"The Regency Gentleman," she announced, pausing to gauge her audience's attention. "The Regency gentleman was not drastically different from his predecessors in terms of ambitions, perceptions, or worldview. The innovation in Jane Austen's work stems from the women, who were quite distinct from their mothers and grandmothers. Elizabeth Bennet's perspective on life underwent a transformation. Educated and valuing her education, she considered love a prerequisite for marriage, rather than the choice of marriage partner being solely a decision made by a woman's parents. While education is crucial, a question arises—*Why is love so significant?*"

Olivia smiled at her audience. "Throughout human history, love in marriage hasn't been a given. For figures like Henry VIII, love or desire was such a driving force that it altered the course of history. Unfortunately, for women across eras, marrying for love was often nothing more than a dream. Jane Austen was among the first writers to bring love to the altar. It's a 'feminine' action for personal freedom."

"Feminist," someone interjected.

"Not feminist, but 'feminine'—with the necessary air quotes. Jane Austen wasn't a crusader. Her ideas are subtly persuasive—implied. She's the master of subtext, which laid the groundwork for women's awakening. It took nearly a century for these 'feminine' actions to evolve into the suffragette movement—a journey from dream to struggle." Olivia paused again. "Education and love were the pillars that facilitated this transformation. In her time, around 1800, Jane Austen *informed us* about her heroines' education, while she *included* love and marriage constantly in her characters' preoccupations. Any conclusion we draw is largely our own."

"Did Jane Austen go to school?" Kath enquired.

Olivia nodded, casting a fond glance at her niece. "Not in the way we understand school today. Jane Austen's appreciation for education and the importance of a strong foundation comes from her father, who was an educator as well as being a clergyman.

"The Reverend Austen, akin to Mr Pratt in 'Sense and Sensibility', took in pupils, who lived with the Austen family while receiving instruction from him. Regarding education options for girls in Georgian England, it's a mix of very little and quite a lot. Public schools didn't exist, and attendance of any form of education wasn't compulsory. As a result, a child's education reflected family attitudes, financial means, and the family's general aspirations for the child's future. Austen's heroines hailed from relatively well-off families, where they received some form of education, whether at home, in private schools or academies, or a combination of these.

"Homeschooling was popular among Austen's contemporaries. It could be supervised or performed by the parents themselves, as seen with the Morlands in *Northanger Abbey* and the Bennets in *Pride and Prejudice,* or by a governess, like Miss Lee in *Mansfield Park* or Miss Taylor in *Emma*. In some cases, a 'master' might be hired to impart specific skills like music or drawing to the daughters.

"And this is where we arrive at a significant conclusion—every change in women's lives during that era, and even up to the late 20th century, needed the support and approval of men. Within this framework, the 'Regency Men'—Mr Austen, Mr Bennet, or Mr Pratt—already represent a form of progress by considering women's education as important. They distinguish themselves from their predecessors in actively contributing to women's education."

"Interesting," Kath mused. "You're suggesting a mirror that reflects the men who facilitated change rather than focusing solely on women's incipient struggle for rights. Consequently, this mirror showcases the evolution of gentlemen."

"Exactly, Katherine!" Olivia exclaimed with enthusiasm. "That's precisely what we're aiming for. In Jane Austen's works, the ladies had already progressive ideas, but to turn ideas into a new reality, they needed progressive men."

"We can do that," Anna agreed. "It's a change in perspective."

Everyone at the table began jotting down notes as Olivia and Elizabeth exchanged a knowing look. The enthusiasm for the work was a legacy from Thomas, who had always preached, "Love your job or change it."

"And love?" Henry questioned, looking at Kath. Elizabeth wondered whether the geek was in love with her sister.

"Love is essential." Olivia chuckled. "Whether young or old, the heroines in Jane Austen's novels share a profound interest in love as a premise of marriage. Until their generation, marriage had been a transaction orchestrated by parents, driven by different motives but mainly ensuring the daughters' well-being in a society where women lacked civil and financial rights. However, when Elizabeth, Jane, Emma, Elinor, or Marianne discuss love, it is not only a matter of the heart but also a step towards personal freedom. When Mr Darcy proposes to Elizabeth Bennet at Hunsford, he embodies the arrogance and indifference that was characteristic of the time towards women's feelings. He's confident of her acceptance. Elizabeth's response is such a shock that it's akin to an earthquake shattering his deeply ingrained certainties. Mr Darcy appeared changed after the Kent proposal, which marks the emergence of a new gentleman who observes and cares for a lady's emotions. Mr Darcy wasn't that way until he fell in love with Elizabeth. His most admirable quality is his ability to see Elizabeth as an evolved woman and decide that he loves her and wants to marry her—on her terms. It's not easy, but the transformation occurs seamlessly, and they eventually marry.

"The new women in Jane Austen's world prompted the need for a new gentleman who wouldn't view his wife solely as a homemaker or child-bearer but as an equal partner.

"To sum it up, the archaic female model persists in Austen's novels. Charlotte Lucas is the prime example—she marries the insufferable Mr Collins at her father's behest. Louisa Hurst, Mr Bingley's sister, weds placid Mr Hurst as per her parents' choice. But Elizabeth marries Darcy, and we can imagine them continuing to share a dynamic relationship at Pemberley. The same applies to Emma, who marries Mr Knightley, the owner of the region's largest estate, yet he's the one who moves to live at her residence despite his wealth and status as a landowner.

"These events might not appear remarkable in our modern context, but during the Regency period, some of Jane Austen's gentlemen defied convention with their progressive attitudes towards women."

Elizabeth sipped her coffee and quietly slipped out of the room. Her heart raced wildly as she stepped into the library and settled onto the sofa where she'd once found happiness in Rowan's arms. She didn't want to cry; she closed her eyes instead and imagined his embrace. A sharp pain engulfed her, but she stood up, surveying the surroundings. The shelves were now adorned with glass for protection. The decor had changed, and the room felt cold. Everything reminded her of the earl, but ultimately, that frigid room was no longer her haven.

Chapter 28

The Swindon writer had very few characteristics matching the profiler's description. He had registered under the name Arnold Black and provided no additional information.

"No, he isn't Darcy Egerton," Elizabeth confidently said to Olivia and Marianne on their way back from Swindon.

"How can you be so certain?" Olivia enquired.

The only way to meet him in person had been to select him for a cocktail event with Elizabeth and Marianne, among the twenty winners of a deluxe edition of Austen's six novels published in her lifetime.

"I suspect that Black isn't his real name. I addressed him as Mr Black, and he seemed hesitant to respond," Marianne mentioned.

"Compared to Lucas Jackson, he's simply a timid man who writes secretly," Elizabeth continued.

"But his writing's good," Olivia protested more for the sake of argument.

"You say that this coy writer produces good literature but consider the profile. Darcy Egerton isn't timid. Moreover, he's quite wealthy. Dad and Arthur estimated his earnings. At the very least, he's likely made around thirty million from nine novels over nine years. That's the most conservative estimate. Mr Black isn't a man of significant means."

"Maybe it was an act. He bought his clothes from a supermarket before he arrived."

"No, he was dressed well and seemed comfortable in his clothes. He hasn't earned millions in recent years."

"We've discussed the possibility that Darcy might have sent someone else in his place. You're not convinced—"

"Let's end this conversation," Elizabeth interjected with determination. "I'm confident that the real Darcy isn't among the three finalists. This man has managed to conceal himself flawlessly for years. Even if he agreed to play Dad's game, Darcy Egerton wouldn't easily reveal his secret like this. Unfortunately, we've overlooked something. I don't know what it is, but I'm now sure that Darcy Egerton would never choose this approach. It's too simple for a man who's built such a complex barrier around himself. If Dad knew his identity, he must have left us some indications or clues that we haven't found yet. We need to carefully consider his final words and actions. I intend to go to his office and examine every scrap of paper he left behind. I've told Sonia not to move any papers from his desk."

"How is Sonia?" Olivia enquired. Sonia had been her father's assistant from his first day at Collister until his last.

"She's doing well. She went on that world tour with her husband, a gift from Dad, but retirement doesn't suit her."

"Speak to her. Thomas had immense trust in her. I'm sure she's aware of what her boss did relate to Darcy."

"I will. But first, we need to visit Dad's office and review everything. And there's something I haven't done in a while that I plan to do. Read Darcy Egerton's novels. Perhaps his books contain some clues."

∞∞∞

The following day, Elizabeth met Sonia Roosevelt, an elegant lady who had added a touch of class to Thomas's office—a style emulated by every assistant at Collister since. They met in one of her father's preferred restaurants, and Sonia received a regal welcome.

"It's been difficult. It might have been easier if I'd retired and left Thomas in his office. But his death marked the end of my career in a way I hadn't anticipated."

"You were never pressured to retire," Elizabeth reassured her.

"Of course not, but I was *his* assistant. There's no other position at Collister that I would have enjoyed. Working with him was occasionally difficult, but it was also gratifying. He knew how to motivate people to achieve extraordinary results. I'm sorry, my dear. I understand talking about him can be tough."

"It's still painful, yet at the same time, I feel like I didn't know enough about him."

"I understand that feeling. I lost my father at the same age, and I've spent my life wondering what it would have been like to have him when I was forty, fifty, and now."

They spoke a lot about Thomas, but eventually, Elizabeth enquired, "What do you know about Dad's search for Darcy Egerton?"

Sonia didn't hesitate. "I advised him countless times to abandon that pursuit, so in the last two or three years, he didn't confide much in me. He only shared information when he needed me to do something he couldn't."

Elizabeth sighed, and Sonia regarded her with affection and a touch of pity. She'd watched Elizabeth mature into the remarkable woman she was, yet she knew Elizabeth's life would be very complicated if she agreed to be the head of Collister. "At times, I hoped he'd discover an alternative solution to you taking over from him. But…"

"Dad's death eliminated any other immediate solution. I'm the only one who can ensure a seamless transition."

"I know. I'm also aware of how much your father respected and appreciated you."

"Sonia, during his final days, did he give you the impression that he'd found Darcy Egerton? You knew him better than anyone else."

"I don't think he could've kept such news hidden from me. However, he was absolutely delighted to have found his 'Pemberley'. He was like a child. I visited the place once and couldn't bring myself to tell him it was a dilapidated old wreck that would devour a substantial amount of money. He was already unwell, and I simply wanted to see him smile. I assured him that the property would eventually look incredible."

"Do you know how or why he chose that particular place?"

"The 'how' isn't entirely clear. There were adverts in the newspapers, but he also had a list of stately homes in the southwest. However, I think he was captivated by the owner, an earl. He convinced that gentleman to transform his home into a Pemberley."

Elizabeth averted her gaze. Each time someone spoke highly of the earl, her heart ached. She wanted to despise him and imagine him as a scoundrel who seduced and abandoned women. But that was impossible to believe. The earl was a respectable man with an enigmatic life. She couldn't accept that he'd participated in any scheme, as he had nothing to gain from loving and leaving her.

Yet, he had a reason for leaving her, and her lack of understanding intensified her suffering. She was often tempted to seek him out and demand an explanation, but she lacked the courage. She was gradually healing and encountering him would only reopen her wounds.

∞∞∞

Alone in her office, she read the list of the final five Collister Prize contestants, then called Marianne and Olivia to join her.

"I spoke to Sonia. She doesn't know much about Dad's movements regarding Darcy Egerton in the last year, but I'm convinced we've overlooked something, and it has to be right in front of us. Otherwise, Dad would have told one of us. I agree that he wouldn't endanger Collister due to his obsession.

"I've had an epiphany…there's a flaw in your reasoning. If Darcy Egerton submitted his work, he must be among the finalists who don't fit the profile—like that lady, the elderly gentleman, or anyone else from the top twenty-five list."

Olivia and Marianne exchanged a silent glance.

"She might be onto something," Marianne admitted. "But that opens up countless other possibilities. It's driving me mad."

"What possibilities?" Olivia questioned.

"He could be any man or woman—"

"No, stop. All three panels unanimously selected the same finalists. It's not coincidental. The decision is based on the contestants' merit."

"But *we* specifically selected the men in their forties from the twenty-five and overlooked the others," Olivia pointed out, her concern growing as she spoke.

"Yes, but the Collister Commission evaluated all the contestants, and I've got complete faith in their judgment. The top five are their genuine choices."

"And if he's not among the top five?"

"Then he's either a subpar writer, or he's played a cruel prank on us, submitting a miserable text merely to mock us. Either way, we'll be ready to fight this time," Marianne said, obviously angered by such possibilities.

"I don't think he played any tricks, or that he'd submit a poor text. I see him as someone who respects his writing.

Even if he played Dad's game, it's a respectful confrontation between gentlemen," Elizabeth asserted.

"Why do you say that?" Marianne queried, her turmoil still evident.

"Because he's a talented writer. Submitting a weak piece would tarnish his reputation. I won't hesitate to publish his work if he chooses that path to undermine Collister. No, you should read the remaining submissions and see if you can find any high-quality pieces not penned by forty-year-olds."

"Fine," Olivia conceded. "I personally think it's a waste of time, but Elizabeth's right. We can't discount any possibilities."

Chapter 29

If Christmas had been difficult without their father, Elizabeth expected New Year's Eve to be a disaster. Only two months ago, she had dared to imagine a New Year spent with Rowan, wrapped in his arms at that moment when she was typically alone, gazing out of a window to mask her solitude while everyone around exchanged kisses.

A few days before the end of the year, Clarice arrived with an envelope in her hand, appearing excited.

"Mr Kaiden Cole is honoured to invite you to his New Year's Eve concert. I know many ladies in this town who would do anything for this invitation."

Kaiden Cole performed in Soho, an acoustic concert with only a few musicians, already a New Year's Eve tradition, with tickets sold years in advance.

"You know I get an invitation every year. You can go if you want," Elizabeth said dismissively.

"Thank you, it's tempting, but I want a little sunshine for the end of the year. We're heading to the Maldives."

"Well then, find someone else at Collister to give them to."

But for once, Clarice broke their tacit agreement and said something akin to what Olivia would say. "I think you should go to the concert. I'm sure Kaiden Cole would be impressed to see you. Or, at the very least, don't give away the tickets…yet."

Elizabeth decided not to go but heeded Clarice's advice and kept the tickets on her desk. Her invitation was for four people, so she could bring guests.

∞∞∞

"Go," Olivia urged. "Ask Kath. Perhaps you'll have the chance to meet Adam and learn a bit more about him."

She hadn't given the concert much thought, but her loneliness became unbearable as New Year's Eve drew nearer. She despised that night, spending it alone almost every year. Even when she'd been seeing someone, something would come up, and she'd find herself alone while her friends were all in stable relationships or marriages. With the earl being such a significant part of her life, it seemed like she might finally have that New Year's kiss for the first time. She'd made plans for just the two of them, even considering skiing if he enjoyed it.

And suddenly, the idea of being utterly alone in her apartment or even with her old friends felt dreadful. So, she asked Kath if she would come, with Adam, to the concert.

"I'm on my own, and I don't have any plans. Adam's spending time with his mother. I think he wants to bring her to London for—"

"Goodness, Kath, you're really planning to get married."

"Yes, when Adam gets back, you can meet him and help us choose a wedding date."

"And so you'll be alone on the 31st?"

"Yes, why does that surprise you?"

"Because you've always had numerous plans and friends around you."

Kath didn't respond. They were alone in the little kitchen off Elizabeth's office, eating sandwiches, sharing a calm moment that had become increasingly common between them. Kath sighed as she picked the pickles out of the sandwich, a habit she'd had all her life. "Why not order a sandwich without pickles?" Elizabeth asked.

"Because," Kath answered, "I like the taste but not the texture." She took a large bite and chewed thoughtfully for a while, looking at Elizabeth.

"You still doubt that I want to change," she continued eventually, and it was Elizabeth's turn not to respond.

"I *have* changed, Elizabeth. You don't need years to change. I don't believe in those anti-smoking patches. You just decide one day to stop smoking. I wasn't so entrenched in that lifestyle that I couldn't change."

"I know. I'm trying to accept it. But less than two months ago, you tried to get revenge on me for not letting you use the plane."

"I was furious. I'd planned a romantic getaway with Adam and—"

"I had the same intentions with…"

And she recalled Morocco as if the earl were still a part of her life. "He took me to meet his friends in Tangiers. I thought we were in it for the long haul. Those people were more than friends—he considered them family and introduced me to them."

Her voice quivered, but she didn't shed a tear.

"I'm so sorry. I keep apologising because you seemed so happy together."

"Please come with me to see Kaiden Cole."

"If you promise to knock him out with a karate kick," Kath said and laughed. "Yes, I will. Perhaps you could also invite some of your annoying friends," she continued, smiling, while Elizabeth playfully tossed a pickle from her plate in her direction.

"Or you could invite those guys who caused trouble at Danieli's."

"We didn't cause trouble at Danieli's. There was some

damage to an apartment. It wasn't even mine."

"Then why did you pay?"

"Because I made the reservation. I don't know why. Venice was the last time I saw them."

"Who?" Elizabeth enquired.

"Those friends."

"But what about when you were late for Dad's commemoration?"

"I was only with Adam. It was foggy, so we had to land in Paris and drive from there."

"When you've got an important meeting—" Elizabeth began, her words tinged with nostalgia as she remembered their father's repeated advice.

"—you arrive a day early," Kath finished and laughed. "We couldn't come earlier. I was so happy with Adam then."

And Elizabeth saw in her sister's expression that she was in love and wanted to change for that man.

"I'm genuinely happy for you."

"And I'm furious with the earl for making you unhappy. You'll forget about him. There's no way you'll cross paths. As he said, you live in different worlds."

Chapter 30

Kath was right. Meeting someone by chance in a city like London was nearly impossible. Yet, against the odds, it happened.

Elizabeth and Kath entered the club along with their childhood friend Henry Marshall. Kath, being the first to step inside, froze in anguish as the first person she saw was the earl. She stepped in front to create a barrier between his table and her sister, but Elizabeth also caught sight of him. She didn't utter a word, almost pretending he wasn't real. But she took a seat at the table with her back turned to his, signalling that she had indeed noticed him.

The turmoil within her soul was hard to decipher. After the initial sharp pain, an odd calmness washed over her. He was there, fulfilling her secret desire that she had held onto during weeks of suffering—to see him again.

Is he really here? Elizabeth wanted to ask Kath to ground herself in reality, but she refrained, feeling his gaze on her neck.

Then, by chance, their table became the centre of attention as Kaiden Cole materialised next to them. And after kissing her hand and meeting the others, he invited Elizabeth backstage.

Elizabeth followed him without hesitation, again

ignoring the earl's presence. Surprisingly, the pain had faded, replaced by Kaiden Cole's evident delight at having her at his concert—a sentiment witnessed by everyone present. Elizabeth couldn't help but think that, finally, there would be some juicy photos of her.

"Jesus, Elizabeth, it took you quite a while to forgive me!" Kaiden exclaimed, looking at her with admiration. "You look stunning! I was such a fool to lose you!"

"Enough, Archer," Elizabeth replied, feeling better under his warm smile.

"Only you and Mum call me Archer."

"When we first met, you were still Archer. How did you know I was here?" she asked, looking around his dressing room, covered for that night in posters from his past concerts.

"My assistant was in the hall, keeping an eye out for you."

"For me? Why?" Elizabeth enquired, her gaze meeting his in the mirror surrounded by lights.

He turned to her, and she remembered the man she'd loved most before the earl. "Because, Elizabeth Collister, I owe you a lot. When we met, I was Archer, as you said. The violence was just part of life where I came from. You transformed me into Kaiden Cole."

"Well, Archer Kaiden Cole, you've repaid me tonight."

"How so?"

Elizabeth caught a glimpse of herself in the mirror on the wall. She hadn't really looked at herself lately, considering the mirror just a tool for checking her clothes.

"You look stunning." Kaiden confirmed what she was seeing. Her green dress was exquisite in its simplicity, complemented perfectly by the ruby necklace, her father's last gift, while the Louboutin pumps matched the red hue of the gems. She was slimmer than she'd been two months ago when the earl had admired her belly.

"Your necklace is stunning as well. I suppose you've got

a bodyguard with you?"

Elizabeth touched the stones with a pang. To her, that necklace held the memory of her father's farewell. He didn't want to have his family near him when he died, and he let them go in his own way.

"It was Dad's last gift. He had a penchant for precious stones and was quite knowledgeable about them. You should see my sister's necklace with Padparadscha sapphires."

"Is she wearing that tonight too? Elizabeth, I might need to ask for a police escort," he joked while applying makeup. "You said you'd forgiven me, and I've returned the favour for the gift you gave me that night I ended up in hospital." He smiled, stealing glances at her.

Archer, or Kaiden, was a friend from when she was just a girl like many others, so she spoke without restraint. "At one of the tables out there is the man who broke up with me two months ago."

"And you still love—"

"Yes," she whispered, the ache and yearning returning.

"Well, Lady Elizabeth, if he's still in the club, he'll regret it."

∞∞∞

Once she returned, she didn't dare look at the earl's table. But Kath's worried expression and constant glances in that direction told Elizabeth he was still there. They couldn't talk because of Henry, yet, for once, the silence was perfect.

"You, crazy lady," Henry joked. "Half the UK's population wishes they were in your shoes tonight. Did you do anything your mother would disapprove of?"

Elizabeth laughed. Archer hadn't made any advances during the evening, but that was her secret. Perhaps the onlookers imagined a passionate encounter between them, which also brought a little comfort to her heart. If the earl still held any feelings for her, he must have felt uncomfortable seeing her with another man.

"He's just a friend. Now I regret sharing that old story with you," Elizabeth said in a nearly normal tone, matching her appearance.

"It's not much of a secret. He once told that story in an interview, like it was an essential lesson in life. Of course, he didn't reveal the lady was you," Henry said.

"I had no idea," Elizabeth replied, and for the first time, she glanced at the earl. Fortunately, he wasn't looking her way. The dim lights made it difficult to see him properly, and soon Kaiden's band appeared on stage, and the concert began.

For a while, Elizabeth forgot about the earl's presence, listening to the man all the ladies adored, who'd just told her with genuine admiration that she was stunning. It was how she felt. And Olivia's words came to mind—Rowan had unleashed her womanhood.

"I'm going to sleep with Archer," Elizabeth whispered to Kath. While it might not be true, or she might not be ready for sex again quite yet, she felt good just thinking it was possible to be with another man. And Archer was the only man she could picture.

"I think you should wait another month before you sleep with someone else," Kath replied, strangely sounding like Olivia.

"Is that the protocol for ladies who've been dumped? Wait three months before—"

"Something along those lines."

Elizabeth regarded Kath with curiosity. Her usually unconventional sister had spent a quiet evening elegantly dressed, offering maternal advice.

"Ladies and gentlemen, this is a special night for me," Kaiden Cole suddenly declared. Elizabeth blushed slightly, suspecting what was coming next. "I'm delighted to perform a song I penned long ago for a lady who holds a special place in my heart."

He didn't say more, but many eyes turned towards their table, having witnessed Elizabeth leaving with Kaiden not long ago.

The song spoke of friendship but was perceived as much more by the audience, and as she listened, she forgot about the earl. And when it concluded, she silently thanked Archer for repaying his debt to her in such an unexpected manner. That night, she didn't appear sad or despondent, alone or grieving the man who'd abandoned her and who, she hoped, had been watching her throughout the concert.

Then the earl was gone. Elizabeth failed to notice when he left. Despite the unease his presence had caused her, she felt a twinge of regret at his departure.

Their night continued until dawn, the first time in years that Elizabeth had enjoy midnight, when she and Kath shared friendly kisses with Henry, revelling in the moment.

"It's a sign that 2017 will be alright for me…for us," Elizabeth whispered to her sister.

"Yes, I almost forgot what it's like to start January sober." Kath chuckled as they retired to their parents' house together.

∞∞∞

They came down for breakfast at nine, a ritual in the Collister household, to find their mother already seated. She looked surprised, even though she'd known they'd slept at home, as the table, laid by the housekeeper, showed she had guests. Faithful to tradition, they were still wearing their pyjamas but had put on the jewellery gifted to them by Thomas.

"Please sit, I'm famished," Cybil spoke—the words

typically uttered by her husband. "Olivia and Arthur are on their way. They'll be here in ten minutes."

She spoke casually, yet Elizabeth could sense her mother's happiness at her brother and sister-in-law's impending arrival. It was the first time since their father's passing that Elizabeth truly empathised with her mother, imagining the solitude that followed years spent with her partner. Her grief was different from theirs. Submerged in her sorrow and problems, she failed to see her mother in the proper light.

Still enjoying their breakfast, they listened to the Vienna New Year's Concert, which Thomas adored doing every year, surrounded by family and often also by friends.

"We're not going to cry. Dad wouldn't have wanted that," Kath declared with energy. "Last night, we won the Thirty Years' War, the Wars of the Roses, Star Wars—pick any war, and we triumphed."

In her characteristic playful manner, she recounted Elizabeth's victory.

"I almost felt sorry for the poor man," Kath remarked, laughing, recalling his expression when Elizabeth had disappeared into Kaiden's dressing room. "This outrageous little lady, whom you all see as perfect, vanished for fifteen minutes with the lead singer. And there were no paparazzi around!"

"But what was the earl doing there?" Olivia asked, more intrigued by the earl than by Kaiden.

"An incredible coincidence. Or God's work," Kath mused, but Elizabeth was no longer in that merry mood.

Seeing him had been a true test of her self-control. She was better not only because of Archer's help but also because she didn't hate him anymore for leaving her. Yet once her resentment had gone, all that remained in her heart was love. She saw only his shadow, but that was enough to make her regret him even more. The earl had been accompanied by an older couple; it could mean he hadn't found a new woman to take her place yet. Elizabeth speculated that he might still have feelings for her...in his own way.

"When will we meet Adam?" Cybil asked, and a radiant smile appeared on Kath's face, suggesting that the meeting would happen soon.

Chapter 31

Unfortunately, Kath's radiant smile didn't last. On January the fifth, Kath rushed into Elizabeth's office wearing a tragic expression never before seen on her face. With a single leap, Elizabeth enveloped her in her arms. Kath wasn't crying, but she seemed deeply shocked. Clarice arrived shortly after, silently asking Elizabeth what should be done.

There was little to do but wait for her to talk. Her profound distress didn't relate to their family, as Elizabeth would have already known.

"Speak, little sister," she said with unbridled concern.

"It's Adam," Kath murmured, then fell back into a sort of numbness.

"What happened? Did he have an accident?"

Kath simply shook her head, and suddenly, Elizabeth suspected the truth. "He broke up with you!" she exclaimed, angrily adding, "What's wrong with these men?"

But once again, Kath shook her head. "He emptied my account and disappeared."

"What?" Elizabeth cried, relieved for a brief moment before succumbing to anger and concern. It was about money, but that could also be perilous.

"Which account? Kath, which account?"

"My inheritance."

Elizabeth let her slump onto the sofa cushions. This was no trifling sum.

"But how? Arthur has to authorise any transfer above a certain amount."

Kath shrugged and buried her face in a cushion, as she used to do when she was just a toddler. Yet, it wasn't a time for giving comfort. Elizabeth rose and opened the door to the outer office. "Clarice, please get Arthur and Fabien here now, along with our lawyers—all of them."

Arthur was the first to arrive and headed directly for Kath, finding her still with her face buried in the cushions.

"What on earth happened?" he asked, alarmed.

"Adam took her money!" Elizabeth exclaimed as Fabien joined them.

Kath protested weakly, still hoping with all her heart that it was something else, though her rational mind knew the truth. The bank confirmed that the transfers were made by her using her own credentials.

"But how? Any large transfer needed my approval," Arthur muttered hurriedly, opening his laptop only to discover he had no message from the bank authorising the transfer.

"The scoundrel hacked my computer," he murmured, distressed.

He immediately called the bank, which confirmed that the transfer had taken place at nine after he signed his OK.

A deep silence engulfed the room, as they had no words to talk about such a predicament.

"Let's compose ourselves and find out what happened," Arthur said, but the girls hardly recognised his voice.

"Did you make any transfers or payments that required Arthur's approval when he was nearby?" Fabien asked as Arthur showed him the transactions.

They saw Kath almost faint. She was so pale that Elizabeth became concerned and made her drink water.

"We're all here, Kath. We'll figure this out."

"How? He's a swindler, and everything we lived was a lie."

"Kath," Fabien spoke sternly, "I empathise with you, but please tell us what happened."

"She did a transfer," Arthur replied in her stead, his voice cracking. "At the end of December, she made a purchase from Cartier for £54,000. Any transfer over £50,000 requires my authorisation."

"Good heavens! What did you buy?"

"A ring, my engagement ring," Kath answered, revealing the beautiful blue solitaire.

"You bought your own engagement ring?" Arthur queried, stunned and angry.

"Yes, he claimed his funds were frozen until the end of the year and promised he'd return the money. How could I have suspected, especially when he bought the ring for me?"

"Is it authentic?" Fabien asked.

It was indeed genuine; Kath had received it in a Cartier box, accompanied by a bouquet of red roses that still adorned her room.

"Did you choose the ring?" Elizabeth asked.

Kath hesitated, tormented by her own mistakes. "Not entirely. He liked this one very much and convinced me it suited me." She removed the ring from her finger and cast it onto the floor. "It's a fake. He switched it when he left on the twenty-ninth. I took it off when I showered."

Elizabeth summoned Clarice and handed her the ring. They had a jewellery specialist in the magazine department. Meanwhile, Donald Palmer, the family lawyer, arrived with two assistants. Fabien briefed them on the situation, and they began questioning Kath, who, surprisingly, was regaining her composure as she recounted the events, willingly answering every question.

"Miss Collister, did you ever provide your account

credentials to that individual?"

Strangely calm, Kath responded, "Yes."

Elizabeth couldn't believe her ears. She remembered the numerous times their father and Arthur had cautioned them against using their personal accounts for any transaction. She couldn't fathom why Kath would willingly giving out account details.

"Never use your personal accounts," Thomas had advised them since they had their first account. "Always use your credit cards." This was exactly what Elizabeth did, even for substantial sums.

"You need to tell us exactly how this happened. Every detail is crucial," the lawyer urged in a concerned tone. There was no room for feigning confidence in an easy solution.

Kath remained silent for a moment, appearing more composed, although Elizabeth sensed her inner turmoil. So much had gone horribly awry—not only the massive sums of money lost but to be deceived in such a despicable manner was terrible. Finally, Kath spoke, her voice and demeanour slightly recomposed. It was such a horrible occurrence. Elizabeth still held affection and respect for the earl, while Kath already loathed the man who'd deceived her.

"I was conned," she admitted. "Yes, I was conned.

"On the evening we bought the ring, we spent over an hour looking, and eventually, we settled on one. I didn't have the funds on my credit card, and we were in a hurry, so I used one of my personal accounts. But not for a moment did he tell me what to do. Every decision was mine," she recounted, her voice trailing off as she slowly pieced together what had occurred.

"Of course, he planned every step, giving you the impression that he didn't intervene. He wasn't in a hurry."

"After the transaction, the online banking app stayed open on the tablet."

They made love, elated to have bought the engagement ring that signified their commitment. Yet, Kath now dismissed that memory with frustration and continued her story.

"I was getting dressed, and I needed to make a deposit for—"

"My God! You asked him to do the transfer," Elizabeth murmured.

"Yes."

"And he asked for the login details," Arthur concluded. "Good Lord, you never use those accounts for everyday transactions. You have your cards."

"I know. I've never done it before," she choked out, overwhelmed by desolation.

"He's a master of deception. It's plausible that he even drugged you," one of the lawyers suggested. "It was a meticulously devised plan. Not a single move seems to have been arbitrary or spontaneous."

Then Clarice returned with the ring. "It's a three-thousand-pound ring, white gold with a semi-precious stone."

"He's good," Fabien commented. "He had a three-thousand-pound ring made to replace one valued at fifty-four thousand. He's not cheap, and he had a solid plan. And he decided to take it all."

"I authorised the ring purchase from home," Arthur admitted, tormented.

"But why did you give your approval?" Elizabeth asked with a hint of reproach.

"Good grief, Elizabeth, you're grown women. My role is to prevent you from making dubious transactions, not to supervise your shopping."

"Sorry," Elizabeth mumbled to her uncle, evidently more shocked than she already had been because of his direct participation.

"That Cartier payment was made solely to hack Mr

Johnson's computer. He was already aware of the sum requiring authorisation," one of the young lawyers explained.

"I usually receive a confirmation when I approve a payment," Arthur stated. However, on that morning, no confirmation message had arrived.

"He executed the transfer early this morning and stopped the message from the bank," Kath whispered.

"We need to officially notify the bank, then the police."

Yet Kath couldn't fully grasp the complete reality. "Perhaps he needed the money and intends to return it. Please, let me wait a day." She gazed at them with pleading eyes, though within that room, all knew the truth.

"Every day is crucial, Kath," Arthur said, addressing her almost as a child because, for once, he felt sorry for her. She'd lost her money and a piece of her heart.

"Please, Kath, urgency is essential. Most likely, he's already in Argentina," Elizabeth said, then abruptly rose. "Excuse me for a moment. I've got an idea. Please wait for me here."

A sudden insight ignited within her mind—an unclear idea—but she didn't hesitate. Maybe Rowan didn't love her anymore, but he would surely help her if he could. And who could be of more help to her than a cyber security specialist?

She didn't call him to announce her arrival, wanting to surprise him and perhaps stir within him even a fraction of the turmoil in her heart as she approached his house. As he opened the door, she sensed his shock that he didn't try to hide. He appeared both content and concerned, yet her own turmoil made it hard to ascertain.

"Elizabeth," he addressed her. "What's wrong?"

Her anxious face conveyed a tale, and she sought his assistance.

"I need you," she murmured. Only once seated in his living room did she manage to breathe again, relieved to be there, even if the circumstances weren't ideal. She yearned to close her eyes and, if only for a brief moment, imagine that she'd dashed from her office purely to see him.

"Would you like coffee, water, or tea?"

"Yes, a glass of water, please." She watched him pour the water, and when he handed her the glass, his aftershave hit her with countless happy memories. Then, he sat a fair distance away in his favoured armchair.

She relayed to him a condensed version of events, observing his growing concern.

"I know why you've come to me, but I'm not a hacker, Elizabeth." His tone was gentle and composed, much like when conversing with her.

She was there on behalf of Kath, but deep down, she simply wanted to be near him, regardless of the reason. Their eyes locked, and she finally responded in a slightly shaky voice. "I understand, Rowan. But your expertise is in that area."

He nodded, a faint smile playing across his lips, and again, Elizabeth found herself uncertain. Did this man still love her, or was she avoiding the truth?

"I do have experience, but I can't use it for any unlawful purposes. My company's integrity is at stake."

Elizabeth sighed and downed the water in one gulp, just to do something that might temper the stirring inside her.

"I need to escape it all," she whispered. "If only for a short while. I wish I could erase this world around me." And she rose to leave, distressed beyond measure.

But he didn't let her go, his gaze fixed on her with intense fervour. She felt he'd almost pulled her into an embrace, though he stopped himself at the last moment. But her mind couldn't be trusted, eager to interpret each gesture as an expression of love.

"Wait for me," he implored. "I want to speak to your lawyers. I can offer some guidance. That I can do. Let me dress. Will you wait, Elizabeth?" His tone harkened back to when they were happy together. He had a unique way of saying her name—a way that no one else could replicate. She nodded, words evading her.

As he vanished into his bedroom, she reclined on the sofa, reminiscent of the day months ago when she'd waited for him in Warminster. Much like then, she closed her eyes, suspended between reality and a dream. His voice roused her, and she opened her eyes, unsure whether she'd heard correctly. Had he called her 'honey', or was it merely wishful thinking?

They didn't speak in the lift, then upon opening the car door for her, the fragrance of his aftershave enveloped her again, transporting her back to those happy times when he'd come from the bathroom to make love to her.

"Did you enjoy the concert?" he suddenly asked, his voice rough, causing her to look at him with curiosity.

"Of course I did," she replied. "Kaiden's an old friend."

And then they lapsed into silence until they reached her office.

Clarice's satisfied smile upon their entry spoke volumes. Her assistant cherished their love story and still clung to hope for them. Rowan returned the smile, and Clarice offered him a drink as if in a play, but it sounded more like a vaudeville than *Romeo and Juliet*.

Once in her office, Elizabeth introduced the earl to her uncle. Overwhelmed by the whirlwind of events, her uncle's anger and apprehension were barely concealed. He held a greater animosity towards Rowan than Elizabeth did.

Seeing Rowan in a professional setting was peculiar. She remembered his body and his love, but now, in her office, she encountered a man she didn't know.

"I specialise in cyber security. I have a small firm, and I believe that's why Elizabeth asked for my help," he stated.

"Yes, indeed, as this is a cyber offence," Fabien confirmed.

"We must be cautious with the distinctions. There are two kinds of events," Rowan explained, and Elizabeth only loved him more for his way of talking and behaving, of saying 'we' when discussing her sister. "If Katherine willingly provided him with the login details, which weren't obtained by force, then he had your consent to manipulate the account."

"Not exactly," the lawyer interjected. "Only a power of attorney would grant him authority for a transfer."

"Legally speaking, yes, but I assure you he'd win in court. He had the login details, and Katherine provided them while in her right mind. On the other hand, hacking Mr Johnson's computer constitutes a criminal offence. Yet, the degree of my involvement depends on the circumstances. I can't touch that computer unless the police request it."

The lawyers nodded. "So, what's your recommendation?"

"You should go to Scotland Yard with Katherine's and Mr Johnson's computers. They've got a division that handles cyber offences."

This time, Kath remained silent. It seemed she finally understood that Adam, her love, was a swindler who'd stolen her money.

"I can assist with Scotland Yard—if they ask me. I've collaborated with them before."

And then they left, leaving Elizabeth with a jumble of conflicting emotions—relieved and devastated all at once.

That bloody earl still cares for me, she thought, allowing her inner voice to say what she hadn't allowed it to before.

∞∞∞

"That crazy lad has feelings for Elizabeth," Arthur told his wife when they met later that evening.

"No way! How can you say that?"

"He looked at her like a love-struck fool, his feelings evident in his eyes. And he rushed to her aid like he was at her beck and call. I had half a mind to push her into his arms."

"Why did he leave her then?"

"Maybe he's impotent."

However, Olivia burst into laughter instead of responding.

"Or perhaps he's a spy. I noticed the way he spoke to those folks at Scotland Yard. They're familiar with him. Perhaps he's on an undercover mission, and—"

"Enough. I married an honest accountant, not a writer of cheap crime novels. It doesn't matter why he left her, nor does it matter if he still loves her. What matters is that Elizabeth is alone and hurting. I hope she doesn't indulge in the same kind of reasoning, worsening her pain."

Chapter 32

Elizabeth used the same logic when she learned from Kath that the earl had spent nearly five hours with them at Scotland Yard, and the agent they encountered knew him quite well.

"The man loves you, but he's got a reason for being unable to continue your relationship."

And what better reason than a secret mission for Scotland Yard or MI5? Elizabeth didn't dare to share her thoughts with Kath, but she felt a glimmer of hope in her heart. Perhaps in the future, once his mission was complete, he'd think again of her and their relationship.

She wanted to know in detail what had happened at Scotland Yard, and strangely, all the action and commotion eased her pain. The man she still loved had agreed to help her and be a part of her life, even if indirectly.

But then Adam was also known at Scotland Yard. They might not have known his true identity, but he was on the list of most-wanted criminals in multiple countries. Kath hardly recognised him in the photos they showed her, so changed was he from one role to the next.

"From one identity to another, he's completely transformed. He's a true chameleon—an impeccable actor. They don't even know how old he is. A year ago, he convincingly played the role of a fifty-year-old man. Can you believe it? And I thought he was thirty. The agent told me they think he's around forty."

Kath spoke rapidly, as if she wanted to expel that man from her heart and mind, finally revealing the enormity of the situation. "I loved him so much, and now all I feel is an overwhelming anger."

"It's better than feeling pain, trust me. Anger compels you to take action, even seek revenge, whereas I just want to—" Elizabeth stopped herself. She wasn't sure of her own desires anymore. In less than a week, she'd met the earl twice. London didn't seem so vast anymore, and they were part of the same world after all.

"We're in different situations," Kath said bravely. "Your earl is a decent man who certainly still loves you, while Adam…he never loved me. He's a criminal. He took my money, and he even planned to steal the ring. Luckily, Arthur's incredibly clever and insisted that I deposit most of my inheritance in my Swiss accounts as soon as I received it. Adam didn't know about that."

She shed tears, then angrily wiped them away. "I'm crying over my money, but I don't feel any pain for that man. I hope they catch him, and I want to testify at his trial. They asked if I would testify against him, and of course, I will. It seems some other women refused to testify against him if he was caught. He's a brilliant manipulator. I'm so ashamed to have been such a fool. The rich, naive girl…such a cliché. But at least I gave the police a good lead. An officer came to my house, and I gave him some of the handbags and shoes I remember wearing when I was with him."

"Do they have fingerprints or DNA?"

"They didn't tell me. But I'll go home and think hard about where else his fingerprints might be." She paused, then continued, "I wanted to buy a house for us…"

"You can still buy a house. You can do anything you

want."

"Yes, I suppose so. They asked so many questions about him, and I realised I knew nothing substantial, just fragments of an untrue story. The apartment where we met in London was rented through a phantom company. It was paid for until the end of February. He said he owned it."

"You didn't take him to your apartment?"

"No, he had a rented Bentley, and we hardly used my car. But at the time, nothing seemed suspicious. It was more in line with his persona—a rich man interested only in me as a woman." Kath laughed bitterly. "And in truth, he was only interested in my money. Can you imagine how easy it is to steal? I always thought my money was secure in the bank."

"It is, as long as you haven't shared your login details with anyone," Elizabeth said.

"Yes, I've learned that now—the hard way!"

"It's a bizarre situation. All the normal and honest people around you were trying to help you live a less tumultuous life. Yet, the only one who succeeded was a crook named Adam."

"You're worried I'll return to my old life," Kath said with a pang of sadness.

"Yes," Elizabeth replied honestly. "I like this version of you—involved in our business and enjoying our time together."

"I've always enjoyed our time together."

Elizabeth remained silent. If Kath continued behaving as she had in the past month, the financial loss wouldn't be so devastating. She'd paid a hefty price for a lesson. Some people pay with their lives or freedoms, Elizabeth thought, recalling the nightmare when Kath was arrested in the Emirates.

"I can't promise anything, at least not right now, but this life isn't so bad. That Adam guy made me want to get married, have my own house, and…I don't know, even work regularly. And now that I'm broke—why are you laughing?" Kath asked, looking at Elizabeth.

"Because you're far from broke…you still have plenty of money."

"Yes, but what Adam took was from the money Dad left me. I'm so ashamed."

"Kath, what Dad left in this world is us—you and me. We're half Dad, and it's up to us to use that legacy for good."

Long after Kath had left, Elizabeth stood by the window, watching her plants swaying in the rain and wind like they were dancing. That day, filled with drama, had disrupted her relative peace again. But truthfully, she'd been feeling melancholic since the concert. All it took was to see him, and her suffering engulfed her soul again. And the visit to his apartment hadn't helped.

On the contrary, being in that place where she'd once been so happy only intensified her longing for him, just like in the beginning. She recalled how he was dressed, his bare feet when he answered the door. The way he gazed at her and helped her to remove her coat. And again and again his aftershave that drove her nearly to orgasm.

He had nicked himself the first time he'd glanced at her while shaving.

"You're not very good at that," she remarked, slightly concerned about the blood.

"I'm not used to having an audience while carrying out this intimate operation. Actually, I can't recall ever having company while shaving."

But he let her tend to the cut and seemed to enjoy her care. Then he lifted her onto the edge of the sink to make love to her. "It's cold," she shivered when her skin touched the marble.

"Good," he responded in that raspy voice he always used when he was making love to her. "I nicked myself because of you."

Tears welled in her eyes, definitively the best way to go on was to avoid him, and that was what she intended to do.

Chapter 33

Gradually, life returned to the familiar routine it had assumed before meeting him. She dedicated long hours each day to work and often returned home late, only to catch up on sleep.

A few days later, shortly after arriving home, the telephone rang on her private line, reserved for close friends and family. She looked at the number flashing on the screen; Sonia, her father's assistant, was on the other end of the line. She hesitated before answering, and it rang off, but eventually, after fetching herself a plate of cheese and crackers and a glass of wine, she returned the call. Sonia had known her father the best. Their relationship had been so close that Sonia had been privy to most of his ideas, worries, and even fears.

"Sorry, Sonia, I'd just stepped into the house when your call came through."

"No, I'm sorry to disturb you in the evening. I did send you an email, but I thought it would be best to discuss this over the phone. About the documents your father left behind. Shortly after he died, I put two envelopes on your desk with a message from Thomas to read both of them."

"Yes."

"You asked me about some papers from the first

envelope, but you didn't mention the second—"

"It was a manuscript. It didn't interest me. I must tell you the truth—I put it back in the envelope when I saw it was a manuscript," Elizabeth said.

"Oh!" Sonia said slightly disappointed. "Your father wanted you to read both, did not tell me the reason. Anyway! It's Darcy Egerton's manuscript that he sent to us. I assume you're more than familiar with the story, but I remembered an aspect you might not know about. This dates back to about seven years before Henry Marshall joined Digital. Since the inception of Collister, we've kept all the manuscripts received from authors, even those we rejected for publication. In 2000, a decision was made to also receive texts in digital format and to digitalise all that we had, and we organised them into yearly folders."

Elizabeth remained silent, her interest piqued. Sonia was known for being efficient, and she never wasted her bosses' time.

"When Henry Marshall arrived, he restructured everything and informed your father of a security breach. The folder containing unpublished works from 2007 had been deleted. And I can remember how shocked your father was."

"2007?" Elizabeth asked, troubled, as that year was well known by everybody at Collister. "The same year Egerton submitted his manuscript?"

"Exactly. Thomas was convinced that Egerton was responsible for deleting the folder."

Elizabeth let out a breath, unsure whether to interrupt Sonia or continue listening.

"I know you loathe the subject much as I do. However, it's such a strange coincidence that only one folder was deleted, and that it was for the year we received Egerton's novel. Thomas was already deeply obsessed with him, and so—"

"He'd already printed the manuscript," Elizabeth

interjected, her interest growing.

"Indeed, the only remaining copy within Collister or any other publishing house was the one he printed."

"How can you be certain?"

"Thomas reached out to other publishers who had rejected Egerton's initial novel, and they reported similar experiences. Two other publishers who held digital copies of the manuscript had suffered the same breach. In one instance, where manuscripts weren't organised by year, the entire folder of rejected works had been wiped."

"Goodness, Darcy Egerton is a digital criminal," Elizabeth commented, both of them sharing a chuckle.

"The manuscript I left on your desk is that very copy. Your father kept it in his safe—that's how significant it was to him. It's signed Colin Barnes—"

"It must be the pseudonym that Darcy Egerton ultimately didn't use."

"Yes. Thomas scoured the country for any real Colin Barneses, hoping Egerton had used his true name, but no luck. Just another pen name."

"And why did Dad want me to have the manuscript?"

"He didn't tell me anything else. He only asked that you should have it, along with the other envelope and his message."

Suddenly, Elizabeth recalled her father's final words—after gifting her the necklace, he had said, "Please read *everything* Sonia gives you."

While the green post-it on the envelopes had said, 'Read ALL, my love!'

"Oh God, he did tell me! He wanted me to everything he left behind."

"And?"

"And I didn't. I didn't do it. But even the title differs from the final one he used for his first novel."

"Elizabeth, just read everything. Your father was scarily lucid in those last days."

"Thank you, Sonia," Elizabeth said, finally convinced her father's words held weight and weren't mere ramblings from his final hours on earth.

That envelope could contain crucial information communicated in her father's enigmatic style, which she often admired when it didn't concern the company's future.

∞∞∞

Hastily, she got dressed and headed to her office. She remembered where she'd put the envelope, but, as usual, it wasn't where she thought it would be.

Anxiety gripped her—Thomas had left that document for her to uncover something crucial about Darcy Egerton. And again, like every time it was about that man, she loathed how her father had decided to act. If he knew Egerton's identity, why not just tell her and put an end to the uncertainty? Yet, that was how he operated in life. And even in death, he was toying with her and Darcy Egerton.

Thankfully, Clarice's impeccable, clear mind came to the rescue. She never lost a piece of paper and knew the whereabouts of every document.

With a sigh of relief, Elizabeth located the envelope. Aside from the manuscript, it contained nothing else—not a single word to show her how important it was. And she was certain that envelope was the answer she had searched for in vain since her father's death.

She sat on the sofa, too impatient to go home, eager to delve into what her father had meant. She had read the novel years ago, but her memory was hazy. On the first page, she remembered Lucas Jackson from the Oxford event but dismissed his image. Deciphering her father's riddles was never straightforward, and Darcy Egerton wasn't the type to casually send in a manuscript for a contest.

With every page turn, she wrestled with despair, wondering how the initial editor at Collister hadn't recognised the brilliance of Egerton's writing. The novel had charm, and its plot unfolded at such a pace that she couldn't fathom any reader setting it aside.

She poured herself a glass of whisky and decided that none of the finalists were Darcy Egerton—that was certain.

Then, a tremendous lightning bolt struck her, causing her to leap from the sofa and pace the room. "You didn't do that, Dad," she whispered to the memory of her father, convinced that if an afterlife existed, he was watching her at that very moment. She resumed reading hurriedly, skipping and revisiting passages. "What were you thinking, Dad?" she cried, waves of emotion overwhelming her.

Her face flushed and then paled as she continued reading, the pages scattering on the sofa. She closed her eyes, attempting to steady herself, before bolting down the corridor, passing the incredulous doorman, and flagging down a taxi waiting outside. She directed it to her aunt's house, oblivious to the late hour. Trembling and shaken, she felt her heart on the verge of explosion, needing someone to confirm the truth or risk losing her sanity.

Her uncle answered the door, and she almost knocked him down in her hurry to find Olivia. Despite his attempts to guide her to the living room, Elizabeth was unstoppable. She burst into her aunt and uncle's bedroom and proclaimed, "It's him!" even before her aunt was fully awake. Collapsing onto the bed, she repeated, "It's him."

Finally awake, Olivia and then Arthur regarded her, awaiting an explanation.

As she didn't speak, Olivia said, "What is it, my dear?"

Only an hour ago, they had discussed how difficult it was to be parents. Since Thomas's death, so much had happened, and it was them who had to take the brunt of parenting his adult daughters.

"Speak, Elizabeth," Arthur said, quite annoyed. "What's

happened this time?"

Elizabeth passed the manuscript to Olivia. "I've found Darcy Egerton," she cried, prompting Olivia to snap fully awake.

"Who is he, my dear? Speak, you're killing me."

"Tell us more, girl. Don't keep us waiting."

"It's him! My earl! Darcy Egerton is my earl," Elizabeth said.

$$\infty\infty\infty$$

They sat in the kitchen around the table, each grappling with their own shock. Olivia was reading the novel, trying hard to understand what these recent events would mean for English literature. It was a historic moment very few would know about in the future, yet she was only the second person to find out who he was. Or the third, as she was sure that Thomas had known. Arthur was already thinking about the benefits to Collister, while Elizabeth was dreaming of his arms around her.

"How did you find out?" Olivia asked, taking a break from reading as she must have clearly missed some crucial context.

"Are you absolutely sure it's him?" Arthur asked cautiously.

"Yes, I'm certain. I failed to listen to Dad's instructions. He asked me to read everything he left behind, but I overlooked the manuscript. I should have read the novel the day I found it on my desk."

"It's his debut novel," Olivia added.

"It's more than that. It's the first version, unedited—the one he submitted to publishers. I think he never planned for this elaborate ten-year spectacle, but repeated rejections led him down this path. In his first draft, he described his estate. All the elements that amazed or shocked me were right there: the drawing room full of his family members, the gate without walls— Whisky!" she exclaimed, and Arthur fetched a bottle and glasses for everyone.

"Oh, my goodness," Olivia cried. "This is how Thomas found him. He wasn't searching for Pemberley—he was looking for Egerton."

"Yes. If I'd read the manuscript as Dad asked, I would've gone to meet the earl, recognised the place, and solved the riddle instantly. All this nonsense with the Darcy Egertons from our contest would have never happened."

"But in the beginning, Thomas agreed to the contest idea."

"Yes. Then, during his interview, Darcy Egerton sent a message to Dad. *Doubting Thomas* was obviously a message for him, and the real game between them began at that moment. Initially, Dad considered the contest, and he formulated the Jane Austen Project specifically for Darcy. He aimed to give a significant opportunity for him to come forwards. I think only then did Dad reread the manuscript and begin suspecting that Darcy Egerton had described his own estate. He started the search for the house resembling the one in his book. The advert in the newspaper described it—the park, how many rooms it must have, and details from his novel. And the conceited aristocrat walked into Dad's trap. He answered the advert. Dad visited a few estates then, but when he arrived at Warminster... The poor earl had given some unmistakable details that Dad didn't miss. And he found him."

"But why did Thomas persist with the riddle involving the three finalists?"

"Because he wanted to ensure that you and Marianne wouldn't suspect anything. Moreover, that absurd quest would never have taken place if I'd simply read the novel. During my initial visit to Warminster, the truth would have been apparent.

"Strangely, I'm unnaturally calm for a future criminal.

I'm only unsure about how to kill him."

Arthur smiled and stroked her hand. "Go on, my dear. You'll fill us in come morning."

"Go where?" Elizabeth questioned, her confusion evident.

"To Darcy Egerton. Make him pay for what he did to you!" Olivia cried.

Within moments, Elizabeth was in her uncle's car. He didn't trust her to be alone, feeling her apparent serenity was just the short period of calm before the tsunami. He drove away only when she'd entered the earl's home.

Then he returned to Olivia, finding her on the verge of an explosion. It was one of the most important events of her life, but it was impossible to predict the future.

"Fireworks or murder?" she mused, gazing at her husband.

He sat next to her, the manuscript scattered on the table, and began making calculations on his computer. "My budget had just exploded," he said smilingly, and then he considered his estimates while Olivia began reading.

Chapter 34

Her uncle had got it right. A flood of emotions overwhelmed her like a giant tide in the lift. She found him in only his pyjama bottoms, as he habitually slept, while wild anger and love surged from her eyes as she yelled, "It's you, you bastard, it's you!"

Still sleepy, he took a moment to comprehend, but then he ushered her inside and attempted to embrace her. However, Elizabeth dashed off, poured herself a whisky, and downed it like water.

"That's my third," she murmured to herself, then she turned to him again and shouted even louder, "You bastard, it's you!"

As he tried to coax her to sit, she evaded him once more upon hearing him say, "Yes, it's me, honey, forgive me!"

"Forgive you? I nearly died when you abandoned me. I suffered like a dog. Forgive you for placing your damned secret over us? Never! You lied to me with every word you uttered."

"No, I loved you, and look at me, I don't eat, I don't sleep, I haven't written since—"

"Since you left me, you bastard!"

"Since I left you. Marry me!" he proposed and disappeared into another room, returning with the ring she had wanted—Lady Di's red diamond ring. However, she struck the box from his hand, and it tumbled to the ground. "I won't marry you, not now, not ever—"

"Do you need the book?" he teased, momentarily diffusing her anger.

"What book?" she asked.

"*Pride and Prejudice*, Miss Bennet. To know exactly how to reject my proposal."

"You—" she cried, suffocated by her rage. "You're ridiculing me, you—Darcy Egerton!"

"Marry me, Elizabeth Collister."

"No!"

"Then live with me, be my mistress, girlfriend, or whatever you prefer."

"No, nothing, ever."

He sat down, but she turned to him again, unrestrained. "Where do you write?" she cried, scanning her surroundings and flinging open all the doors. "Where?"

He rose slowly and indicated the bedroom door.

"No, I won't go into your bedroom," she protested, but her head was spinning and weary. He then took her arm and led her through his bedroom into a room with computers and screens that twinkled in the darkness.

"I slept in that bed—"

"You did more than sleep, honey," he said. He was finally at ease, with no more secrets to hide. He felt as though he had taken a huge step forward.

"Bastard. I can't remember anything I did in here with you. Your lie has erased it all."

"Marry me," he pleaded.

"You've got an obsession."

"Yes, you. I loved you long before getting to know you, as your father was the ultimate manipulator. Please marry me."

"No."

And suddenly, Elizabeth saw clearly, like a mountain

spring. She scrutinised him—he had lost weight, looked worn out, and she remembered her father's guilt in that situation too.

"I want a novel about Jane Austen."

He looked taken aback. Just moments ago, his love was before him, nearly drunk, splendidly furious with him, and now she was someone else, the managing director of Collister Publishing.

He nodded. "Alright, you'll have your novel under my terms."

"What terms?" she asked cautiously, prepared to negotiate.

"I assume your aunt already knows about me—"

"Yes."

"Then only Marianne Beaumont will be informed about me and the novel—"

"Are you trying to deceive me?"

"No, certainly not. Elizabeth, I'm Rowan Stafford."

"I don't trust that bastard who left me."

"Then I'm Darcy Egerton." But she shook her head, unconvinced. "Another bastard who hid for almost ten years. But go on," she said, still glaring at him angrily.

"Marianne or your aunt will edit my book."

"OK."

"Nobody at Collister besides them will know about my book until the day of publication."

"Yes."

"Are we even?"

"No, I need you to come forward on the day of publication," she said, never averting her sharp gaze. She noticed his hesitation. A struggle was playing out within him, clearly visible.

"Alright," he mumbled. "I intended to come forward anyway. Doing it at Warminster is only fair."

"My ring," she said, searching for it on the floor and placing it on her finger.

"Why are you putting on the ring?" he asked, curious.

"Because it's mine."

"But you don't want to marry me."

"No."

"So you have your book, Darcy Egerton revealing his identity when and how you want, and you've taken the ring too. It's too much for mere forgiveness. I was away from you for less than three months. What do I get to be even?"

"Me," she said, and the next moment, he took her into his arms, and like in the American movies, he pushed her back against the wall, with her legs around him. "You're wearing trousers," he whispered in her ear.

"Yes, you idiot. In American films, the girls wear short shirts."

"And no knickers," he said, his eyes boring into hers.

"You can have that in your bedroom."

He carried her in his arms like a precious trophy, and then slowly, no longer in a hurry, undressed her. First, he unbuttoned her shirt, and when he uncovered her breasts, he sighed in relief. She was his again.

"I hesitated ten times a day to call you and tell you the truth."

"Bastard. Idiot!"

"I love you!"

"I hate you…I hate Darcy Egerton, in fact."

"OK, then the Earl of Warminster will love you!"

He slipped off her knickers then stopped in horror. "What did you do, crazy woman? Where's my belly gone?" She wanted to answer angrily again, but he sealed her mouth with their first kiss, and what had happened in the previous months was no longer important. All that mattered was in that bed. He kissed her and turned her to see every inch of her white and maddening skin. He conquered her only when her breathing became heavy with arousal. Then, he lost his mind in the happiness that waited for him inside her. They didn't speak, and it was Elizabeth's turn to caress him and remember how her hands had traced burning paths across his skin.

"You are so skinny now. I don't like you," she said.

"Then give me back my ring," he said and tried to take it by force, only ending up loving her again in the middle of the fight.

"Is it genuine?" she asked, observing him with wary eyes.

"Of course it is, woman."

"How much did it cost?" she asked, still looking at her ring.

"I am not telling you how much I paid for your engagement ring!"

"It's not an engagement ring!" she said.

"Then what is it?"

"You're paying me for having sex with you."

Rowan smiled, exasperated. "In that case, it's a little bit too much just for sex."

"I dreamt of sleeping with your arms around me," she said abruptly, forgetting the ring and everything else besides him.

"That's no longer a dream, honey," he murmured.

"Where's my kimono?" she asked.

"Your kimono?" he asked, surprised.

"Yes, everything here is mine—the kimono, the man in the bed, the ring…" Then she remembered the rest and, smiling, she continued, "The new novel, Darcy Egerton, even Pemberley is mine."

They didn't sleep for a single moment, but they weren't tired; they were eager to caress and kiss and make love and then speak as they had always done as a marvellous way of crowning their passion.

"Dad knew who you were," she said.

"Yes. Now, I'm sure he knew, but he didn't say a word and didn't make a single allusion or joke. From time to time, I had the feeling he knew, but I didn't understand his game anymore."

"Because, after all, it was a game between the two of you?"

"Yes, it was a game. All these years, I followed his desperate attempts to find me. I enjoyed hiding from the world, but that was just a marketing gimmick. Hiding from him—that was a game."

"Like two toddlers playing."

"More like two wolves who weren't enemies yet were engaged in the ancient fight for power in a gentlemanly manner."

"But for so long, you didn't participate in the game. You merely followed my father's obsession with Darcy Egerton."

"Perhaps. But at the end of last year, I decided to give Thomas the 2017 novel, the tenth one. He was the only one who deserved it."

"But not to reveal your identity."

"Perhaps also that."

"But how?"

"I wasn't entirely sure. A press conference maybe. I even considered creating a game, a quest, but that felt a bit excessive. Too grandiose. Ultimately, it would have been a press conference."

"You chose to reveal yourself because you realised the hidden game was losing the interest of your readers?"

"Yes, precisely." He looked puzzled in the dim light around them.

"Don't look so surprised. Dad was just as intelligent as you are."

"I'm sure he was, but how did he know about my decision?"

"He saw that the bets on your last two novels had dropped, and he interpreted it as a signal for you to reveal yourself, especially since it was your tenth book."

"I need a cigar," he said. He rarely smoked and never in bed, but they had no rules that night.

"Thomas was brilliant. He was remarkable. I never imagined he'd followed my actions so closely. And to know about the bets…that's impressive. It means he was almost inside my head."

"You were his obsession."

"I decided to reveal myself and finally give Thomas his answer. Many people had searched for me, but none like him. And in the end, this game represented more than money or fame. Thomas wanted to find me for the sake of the game he'd initiated. I merely participated without playing openly all those years. So, I chose to become an opponent in his game for the first time."

"The interview, *Doubting Thomas*…Dad got your message and interpreted it correctly," Elizabeth stated.

"Yes, his response was the novel contest. In the announcement for the contest, there was a message meant for me."

Now, it was Elizabeth's turn to regard him with profound astonishment. She hadn't realised the extent of their intricate game.

"He mentioned that 2017 marked a *triple* anniversary."

"Oh my God! We only had two. The third was yours."

"Yes."

"But you didn't participate in the contest," Elizabeth said.

For the second time that evening, she assumed the role of Collister manager rather than the woman in love. She stared at him intently, still unsure whether he was one of the participants, and the answer came, as the earl remained oblivious to her tactic.

"No," he responded, "there was no longer a need for more concealment. The first chapters had to be submitted in April, and in the beginning, I wrote something—"

"You wrote?" she enquired.

"Yes, in January, as soon as I saw the announcement. But I would never have submitted the text myself. I was considering prolonging the game somehow when I came across the Pemberley ad. From that point onward, everything became clear. I had the Pemberley Thomas wanted, which was the authentic way for us to play. Just the two of us, not me among hundreds of contenders. By then, my decision was made. The novel was intended for Thomas. I admired Collister and how Thomas had transformed the publishing house by recognising its outdated style. Marianne Beaumont is a genius."

"We'll meet her first thing in the morning," Elizabeth said. Again, she shook herself out of the haze of love to return to the reality where she, Elizabeth Collister, had found Darcy Egerton, the most wanted fish in the editorial ocean.

"We'll meet here," he said.

"Here, as in London, or here as in…?"

"My apartment."

"What are you saying?"

"My darling, the only way you'll achieve enormous success in July is to keep Darcy Egerton a secret. I never intended to leave you—just to be apart for a few months until I determined my course of action. But the book was yours. Without Thomas, the game made no sense. I maintained an impeccable secret, shielded by those scoundrels in Warminster, merely to create a diversion, to have a smokescreen. I made every step according to plan. I've navigated treacherous waters for years and nearly drowned on the shore when I fell in love with you."

"You talk as if I were your adversary. But *you* were my enemy when Dad's fixation disrupted countless meetings, dinners, and Christmases, leading to endless arguments about you."

"So, I'm already a character in your family."

"Darcy Egerton is."

"I'm Darcy Egerton, honey. You'll have to get used to that. Do you enjoy my novels?" he asked as he extinguished his cigar and pulled her into his embrace.

"Yes, last night, as I read the manuscript—"

"What manuscript?" he interrupted, and the room's lights suddenly turned on, his interest shifting from their love story to her story.

"The manuscript of your first novel."

"But—"

"But you deleted the file."

To Elizabeth's surprise, he didn't utter a word, merely gazing at her.

"You won't tell me everything, will you?" she enquired, attempting to leave the bed, but he pulled her back.

"I'm sorry. Thomas was obsessed with me, and I was obsessed with keeping my secret. I once told you that I led an unconventional life. It was all due to the secret. But eventually, living like that became untenable. The past two years have been incredibly difficult. In some tormented way, I waited for Thomas to deliver me from my confinement. I didn't want to have secrets anymore. Just understand that, like Thomas, I've taken actions that aren't quite…ethical."

"Illegal, you mean."

"Illegal," he reluctantly admitted.

"Fine, I can accept not knowing those particulars."

"Thank you," he replied, kissing her gently, his fingers caressing her body as if memorising every contour.

With her head cradled in his hands, he studied her for a long moment, smiling contentedly to have her back in his bed, no secrets dividing them.

"Thomas stored my first novel elsewhere," he said, deeply shocked.

"Yes, he printed it."

He collapsed beside her, seemingly torn between laughter and tears.

"I regret he's not here to share a drink and decide how to publish my novel."

And Elizabeth began to cry. Clutched tightly in his arms, the intensity of the past hours was washed away by her tears for her departed father, who'd planned their meeting, allowing her to get to know Rowan and, finally, Darcy Egerton.

"I'm sorry. I was an idiot for making you suffer. Thomas isn't far away, my love."

"Oh, I hope he can't witness everything, or if he can, he's got the decency to avert his gaze from everything you did to me tonight."

"It's called love and desire and longing. My body ached without you. Tell me about the manuscript."

"I can't talk with your hands on my body," she said, and to her astonishment, he withdrew.

"So, your game with Dad still outweighs our love." Despite this, she no longer cared, laughing at him as she replied, "Dad printed the file long before you deleted it."

"Of course! He printed it as soon as the Darcy Egerton frenzy began."

"Likely. But I'm certain he only understood its value near the end. He connected the original manuscript to the file deletion, but only sometime last year. If that file was erased, it was because it contained information about you."

"The description of Warminster," he remarked, finally completing the puzzle.

"Yes. He compared the published version with his own, and the only missing part was…the description of Warminster. And he placed the advert with…the description of Warminster. Poor you. Thomas Collister finally caught you! I'm so pleased for Dad."

"This is the best story. My writing's rubbish in comparison." Rowan laughed. "He made me. That old rascal made me. He would have discovered me even if I hadn't answered the ad. The book centred around a mansion in southwest England, replete with those confounded details about the gate, the steps, and the people in the living room."

"Yes, I'm sure he would have scoured every mansion in southwest England, but you served yourself up on a platter when you responded."

"All along, I believed I held mastery over the game, but Thomas outsmarted me in the end."

"He finally bested you after years of relentless pursuit. The last time I saw him, he almost ordered me to read everything he left behind. There were two envelopes, one containing some papers and another a manuscript. And I didn't do what he told me. That manuscript was written by Colin Barnes—"

"Colin Barnes. God, I'd forgotten about him. And that initial version was called *The Snake's Bite.*"

"And—my mistake—I didn't read the manuscript. And that's where Dad's plan fell apart. I should've arrived at Warminster prepared, recognising the house from your novel immediately."

"I'm grateful you didn't. I have a feeling that what's happening between us now would have been impossible in that scenario. And I adore this story with you in my life. I chose to come forwards, to give you Egerton and whatever you wished, simply to be able to make love to you. Just as I want now."

"Later, my love. You've pushed this body to its limit, and it hurts, truly hurts."

"I'm entitled to push you. You're mine,"

"Yes, but you've got my body while I'm left with only promises."

"You still doubt me. It's a gentleman's agreement between us." He smiled, recalling their initial meeting. "You planned everything."

"I didn't have a plan. Dad made up this game, and only he understood the rules. Olivia and Marianne kept insisting the answer would come, but I was sceptical. I'd witnessed too many failures in locating you. I had no idea how to find

Darcy Egerton. Strangely, I have a sense that Dad knew Darcy's identity but never exposed your secret—"

"Because he wanted us to meet!" he exclaimed, pulling her into his embrace to love her.

Yet, Elizabeth freed herself, remarking, "It's not over." She noticed his concerned expression. "I want to know more," she added.

"Then ask quickly," he urged. "I want you so much I'm going crazy."

"Later," she said, her voice stern. "When did you buy the ring?"

"Alright, let's wrap this up quickly and resume our lovemaking. I'm starving for you." Rowan sighed and flicked on the light. "I admit, I was rattled by that photo. I hadn't evaded Thomas and the others for nine years only to be discovered by a journalist from a glossy magazine. I needed time to make a plan. Briefly…I continued the novel I'd begun in January and was determined to submit it to Collister sometime in March."

"Without revealing your identity—"

"I hadn't planned that bit out yet. I just wanted you back. I'd have brought you the novel myself in March."

"In March? That implies your love isn't as profound as you believe."

But she suspected how difficult it was for him to reveal his identity and give Darcy Egerton to the world. What had transpired no longer mattered.

"It doesn't matter anymore," she murmured.

"No, all that matters is that you came and saved me, Elizabeth Collister!"

Chapter 35

"Are you with the earl?" Marianne asked over the phone, trying to sound calm when, in truth, she was dancing round the table, prompting her husband and son to burst into laughter.

"Yes, at his apartment," Elizabeth confirmed.

Marianne entered the earl's apartment with evident curiosity, joining them for the meeting. Elizabeth's earlier call had provided no clues about the subject at hand. Nonetheless, it was a business meeting, and Marianne was present as the manager of the publishing house, not as Elizabeth's friend.

The news was wonderful, and a joyous Elizabeth smiled to see her, but despite her efforts, her lingering sadness was noticeable. Finally, the love birds were back together, but the reason for their meeting at the earl's residence remained unclear.

Elizabeth made the introductions, and after a handshake, they took their seats at the table.

"Rowan has a book for publication with Collister," Elizabeth explained, smiling at Marianne's composed expression. Although Marianne displayed no emotions,

Elizabeth knew her aversion to such interventions. Marianne never greenlit a text without the approval of her committee of editors.

An awkward silence hung between them briefly, only to be broken by Elizabeth's laughter. "Let's not keep you in suspense, Marianne. May I introduce you to Darcy Egerton?"

Marianne's heart skipped a beat. She glanced around in surprise, expecting someone else to walk in. But it wasn't a joke, and she struggled to believe that the long-sought-after dream of every editor in England might come true for her, and in such an ordinary manner. Like everyone else, she had fervently wished to know who he was, yet the notion of their meeting had never truly crossed her mind.

And out of nowhere, Elizabeth's voice announced his presence in the earl's apartment on that grey day in London—no fireworks, no thunder and lightning, not even a noisy fanfare.

"Don't look for him to come through the door. He's here. Rowan Stafford is Darcy Egerton."

And that truth seemed scarcely possible in the morning light even to Elizabeth. Wrapped in her happiness at having the man she loved, she'd failed to grasp the magnitude of meeting Darcy Egerton. The author that her father had relentlessly pursued for years was the very man who'd offered her a ring and a proposal. Her gaze sought his. Darcy Egerton remained a stranger, even if her earl smiled at her.

Marianne couldn't move, frozen, afraid to look at him as she wished. Nine years ago, an unknown writer had submitted a novel to six publishers. One after the other, all six had refused his text. Then the seventh had accepted it. His debut novel had been published a year later, exceeding all expectations. Eight books later, he remained a mystery— a dream and secret desire for every editor and publisher. However, Darcy Egerton had only become an obsession for

Thomas, who never gave up the search.

"This can't be real," Marianne whispered. Her silence was awkward as she struggled to find the words to convey her shock and lingering doubts. Her heart ached amidst the turmoil of her mind.

"It is him, Marianne," Elizabeth spoke as if he weren't even in the room.

"Please, believe her," Rowan added, offering a gentle smile in the face of her tremendous shock.

Marianne took a deep breath, striving to comprehend the situation. Could Darcy Egerton be sitting at the head of the table? She studied him, attempting to overlay her idealised image of the writer onto the actual man. She looked around; the room was elegant and refined but still hardly the decor for such a revelation, which would have been better suited to the Hall of Mirrors in Versailles. It was an overwhelming triumph disguised as a simple breakfast meeting.

"Poor Thomas," she finally managed. Elizabeth nodded, moved by Marianne's need to include her friend and boss in this glorious moment of her life. "It should be him sitting here, not me."

"Dad wanted us to find Darcy Egerton and relish the moment as he would have done."

"He knew who you were?" Marianne asked, addressing Rowan directly for the first time.

"Yes, he knew. I'm certain of it," he answered.

"But then, why…?"

"We're not sure why. Elizabeth suspects that her father decided to let her discover Darcy Egerton for herself. A game between father and daughter, in the end."

"Please forgive me," Marianne mumbled, beginning to regain her wits. Suddenly, her mind was consumed by plans, and all of them revolved around Darcy Egerton. "I'm struggling to keep my composure. I'm trying to act normal, but it's impossible. You were my Holy Grail. At one point,

I even doubted your existence. I've always pictured your revelation as an earthquake, never imagining I would be among the first to know."

"I understand," Rowan replied, inviting Marianne to accept the reality with a smile. "But I'm as shocked as you are. For all these years, only a few people knew who I was. It's strange to stand before you as Darcy Egerton. If it weren't for Elizabeth, I doubt I'd have found the courage to stop hiding. Thomas wasn't the only obsessed one in this story. I was also trapped by my decision to stay hidden, which eventually became my only way of life...and my prison."

With each word, they attempted to adjust to the new circumstances. He grappled with the idea of starting a new life, wondering whether Elizabeth understood his turmoil. For now, Elizabeth was consumed by her own fears, uncertain how Darcy Egerton's revelation would impact their relationship. At the same time, Marianne resolved to focus solely on his tenth book and delay her contemplation of the author.

"Without Elizabeth, I'd still be in hell. Now, I'm a prisoner seeking liberation. But does everyone assume that breaking free is simple? Confronting the world outside is terrifying."

He wished to explain to Elizabeth why he'd left her, although she probably already suspected.

"I need time…"

The sincerity in his declaration diffused the tension in the room. Darcy Egerton was, after all, just a man. Darcy Egerton existed. Marianne now felt assured. "We've got time to adjust," she said, suddenly eager to learn about his plans.

Her torment did not calm but, with every second, became something else—that incredible blissfulness every publisher feels when faced with the achievement of a lifetime.

"I hope so. But we must keep the secret for the foreseeable future," he said.

Marianne looked to Elizabeth for confirmation. "Yes, I've agreed to certain conditions. Rowan will submit his tenth novel to us, and he'll reveal his identity in July at Warminster."

Marianne nearly choked, and once again, Rowan—or rather Darcy Egerton—smiled her way.

"You're going to give us your tenth novel?" she asked, her incredulity quickly vanquished by an immense joy as overwhelming excitement flooded her.

"Yes," he responded. "Can you think of another solution to this situation between Collister's director and myself?" A hint of sarcasm laced his words, grounding them in that reality beyond the walls of the house.

"I'm not sure. Did she force you?" Marianne asked, wondering how she could jest at such a moment.

"Yes!" he exclaimed as Elizabeth looked at him sternly.

"Do you wish to start a new legend about the ruthless publisher who forced Darcy Egerton to surrender his new book?" Elizabeth asked.

"Yes, that's a fine idea. She truly is ruthless," he remarked, glancing at Marianne.

Yet Elizabeth intervened with a firm gesture—she was the head of Collister, determined to secure the most extraordinary contract for her company. "Only we and Olivia, who already knows, will be privy to our plans. And, of course, Arthur, but he's the most reliable of all of us."

"But where do we go from here?" Marianne asked, her uncertainty palpable as she alternated her gaze between the two, unsure who held the decision-making power.

"I'll give you the novel for editing in April. Elizabeth decided in your place that you will be the editor—"

"It's an honour!" Marianne murmured and turned white while Elizabeth's heart warmed with pleasure.

"We'll follow the same protocol as every year,"

Elizabeth explained.

"You know how I proceeded every year?" Rowan asked Elizabeth, shocked.

"Of course I do. Every publisher does. The fortunate editor announces the title at noon, and by 5 PM, the book is available in the shops. All in one day, leaving the other publishers—who'd hoped for a year—sighing, '*maybe next year*'," Elizabeth jested, only to discover Rowan looked embarrassed.

"You're not amused, my love?" she asked tenderly, reverting to her role as a woman in love.

"I only observed the events from my perspective. I wasn't aware of the buzz it caused in the publishing world."

"How's that possible?"

Elizabeth remembered her father's disappointment and frustration, even though he held fragile hopes each year. "*You* initiated this crazy model."

"At first, it wasn't a deliberate choice. I discussed the idea of remaining hidden for a year with the first publishers. Then, the interest that followed inspired me to extend the mystery…and then, I don't know—it seemed easier to continue this way, and the public appeared to enjoy it. After all this time, it's hard to pinpoint exactly how or why. But initially, it wasn't a deliberate plan."

"Fascinating," Marianne remarked. "Alright, then. We'll announce that we'll publish your tenth novel, hold a press conference—preferably in London for greater impact—and release the book in shops at five o'clock. Is that alright, Elizabeth?"

Elizabeth nodded, but she was obviously pondering. "Organising such an event without involving the marketing department might be challenging."

"I'll contribute to the promotion as I have every year," the earl interjected.

"I know, but if Marianne is the expert when it comes to your novel, the promotion is entirely done in the marketing department, and this year, Anna is overseeing the entire project. I cannot give you an answer now. I am not ready to make a definitive plan. We can delve into this matter after you submit the manuscript. I need to think."

"At that press conference, will Darcy Egerton also be revealed?" Marianne asked.

"No, we're planning two separate events," Elizabeth said to the surprise of both Marianne and Rowan. "We'll reveal his identity at the end—at nine."

"Why nine?" Rowan asked.

"Because sunset on the 14th of July is at twelve minutes past nine, and we need darkness for the fireworks."

Marianne knew Elizabeth well, but Rowan was caught off guard, realising that the woman he loved was the manager who had the last word in Darcy Egerton's project.

"The visible fireworks, in the sky over Pemberley. Darcy Egerton's tenth book is the fireworks we've been seeking…desperately. Only Dad knew it would happen," Elizabeth mused, imagining Thomas Collister there in that room, looking at them with his sarcastic yet loving eyes which said, '*I told you so*'.

"Fireworks?" Rowan asked, his eyes fixing Elizabeth with a glimmer of curiosity.

"When we hired Anna Wilson, she told us that we had a good plan but not an outstanding one. We needed a fireworks-like event to crown our achievement."

"But that's not true. You've had at least two displays of fireworks so far," Rowan said. "The conference in Oxford was outstanding, while the train event…well, it was unexpected and gripping."

"You stalked me?" A grumpy Elizabeth asked Rowan, her lover.

"Stalked you? That's what you call looking into some events that interested me?" They forgot about the presence of Marianne, who smiled as she needed that conversation to understand that Darcy Egerton, *her* author, was, eventually, a real person she couldn't lose as long as he loved Elizabeth Collister.

"Sorry, Marianne," Elizabeth said. "Yes, all we plan to do is original and gripping, but the book will be the fireworks. While Darcy Egerton coming forward, that'll be something else. We have to release his book first, and then at Pemberley, we'll announce who he is."

"A solid plan," Darcy concurred. "Though, of course, it depends greatly on the subject of the novel."

Elizabeth's suspicion was reignited. She loved the man deeply, yet her trust in the writer—whom she held responsible for her months of agony—remained tenuous. "What do you mean, Mr Egerton?" she probed.

"Perhaps the subject of my novel will force us to have another separation," he said cautiously, seeming not yet ready to reveal his plans. "I can't say for certain at the moment."

"Alright, then," Elizabeth responded with unexpected ease, suddenly more concerned about his well-being, sensing his fragile state of mind. She had pushed him from the first moment, unaware of how daunting it was for him to transition from an enigma to a reality. "We can resume that discussion at the end of April and determine the next steps."

Marianne closed her eyes, attempting to calm her bubbling excitement. "I'm overwhelmed and embarrassed for not having trusted Thomas. He asked me to believe in him, but I couldn't. I didn't."

"No one did, Marianne. Overwhelmed by Dad's obsession, we couldn't fathom that he might truly find Darcy Egerton," Elizabeth reassured her, recalling Darcy Egerton's often irritating presence in her life during recent years. But her earl had nothing to do with her father's madness.

"You'll have to do the editing here in this building. I've got an office on the first floor."

"Did you do the same every year?" Elizabeth asked, realising they were far from knowing all the secrets surrounding Darcy Egerton.

"Yes. I rented a flat every year for the editor. But of course, we communicated only through email and by phone."

"You will find a computer there, everything that you need," Rowan directed.

"Of course, I'll do whatever you want," Marianne eagerly agreed, relieved that such details were already being discussed. Still, a lingering fear remained that something might emerge between the earl and Elizabeth, threatening her plans.

"And I'd like to go back to Warminster and work there," he added, his gaze fixed on Elizabeth.

Elizabeth chuckled, seeing the expression on his face as if he were a child pleading for a trip to Disneyland. "I had no idea you had such affection for the place. I might consider it," she teased.

"I wrote most of my novels there. I find myself needing to write there from time to time."

"Even with all the noise and distractions?" Elizabeth questioned.

"Yes."

"Then, for now, we seem to have most things settled," Elizabeth concluded.

"It's surreal discussing my plans with you in person rather than in my own mind, as I've done for so many years. There'll be no communication via phone or email about this. We'll address any problems here or in the office," he continued.

"Yes," Marianne agreed.

"You're welcome to voice your opinions or objections to his decisions," Elizabeth prompted Marianne, re-establishing a sense of equilibrium in the room.

"No, if he asked me to go to the South Pole to fetch ice

for his whisky, I'd be on my way," Marianne quipped, indifferent to Elizabeth's words. For her, all that mattered was his novel.

And only then did Elizabeth realise what Darcy Egerton meant to the editor-in-chief of Collister. Caught up in Thomas's obsession, Darcy Egerton had ceased to be a real person. As she said, he was more the Holy Grail, the unreachable dream. Amidst her feelings for the earl, she didn't grasp the whole significance of the moment. There wouldn't be fireworks in July, but a supernova exploding in the sky over Pemberley.

Rowan popped open a bottle of champagne, and they clinked glasses.

"Who's proposing a toast?" Marianne enquired, gazing at them.

"I will. To you, Dad, wherever you are!"

"To Thomas!" Marianne said, and then her attention turned to Elizabeth's hand. "You're wearing a lovely ring, Miss Collister."

"It's not what you might think. Last night, Miss Collister turned down my proposal."

"Of course you did, Miss Bennet!" Marianne laughed for the first time that morning, more at ease.

"Yes. *Pride and Prejudice* lives on. Jane Austen couldn't have foreseen how enduring her work would be. Poor Darcy is still met with rebuffs and sharp words two centuries later. A fitting start for a Jane Austen novel."

"So, you've decided to use Jane Austen's framework for your novel?" Marianne enquired, quickly adding, "Of course, you're free to write whatever you wish. Not that it matters, as long as Collister publishes it—"

"Now, hold on, Marianne," Elizabeth interrupted. "You're undermining my negotiations. He's already agreed to write on this subject. As Dad decided!"

Chapter 36

Olivia arrived shortly after Marianne had left. No longer shocked as she'd had the time to reflect and analyse, she felt a mixture of awe and shyness that she'd rarely experienced before.

"It feels as though I already know you," Rowan remarked warmly, wearing an open and smiling expression.

"I could say the same, but it's so different in my case. I know every word of your novels. I'm familiar with Darcy Egerton, but I hardly know Rowan Stafford."

"You can easily get to know me. I have an income of £10,000 a year in Regency pounds, a house in London, and an estate renamed the new Pemberley," he joked.

"Let me remind you that I am Mrs Gardiner, not Mrs Bennet, sir!" Olivia responded in the same tone. They liked each other, and Elizabeth beamed with joy beside them.

"Dear aunt, I'm not Elizabeth Bennet, so I'm interested in his money. And, if I marry him, it'll be for his tenth novel."

"Dear niece, no one said that Elizabeth Bennet didn't relish marrying the owner of Pemberley."

"Olivia, this is sacrilege! You're dismantling two hundred years of marrying for love."

"No, I'm only saying that none of Jane Austen's

characters are flawless. I believe she's still read today because she portrays real people. Elizabeth Bennet has faults like everyone else, but finding pleasure in the prospect of a life of leisure isn't a fault."

"Mrs Johnson's right," Rowan approved.

"Olivia, please call me Olivia, and I need to hear the whole story before any Jane Austen debate."

"Shall I serve lunch, madam?" a voice suddenly interjected, and Olivia turned to see Rowan's butler addressing Elizabeth.

"Yes, Soames, thank you. Soames is our butler, and this is my aunt, Mrs Johnson."

Elizabeth made the introductions, and the man bowed slightly with a smile. "I'm honoured to meet you, madam!"

"He promised not to speak to me until *madam* was back in this room," Rowan quipped to the two ladies.

Elizabeth smiled, touched by the man's affection for her earl. "An exceptional man," she declared.

"And did he keep his promise?" Olivia asked, delighted by the earl's openness and the love he radiated for Elizabeth every time he looked at her.

"Yes, of course. Aside from the usual household discussions, he just listened. It was quite a punishment, as he was the only person I could freely converse with during those years."

"Soames knows?" Elizabeth asked, surprised.

"He knows. He was my sole genuine connection to the real world, and my secret relied on his discretion. Yadira also knew, but she was too far away for me to use her to alleviate my solitude."

"Remarkable!" Olivia exclaimed, referring to Soames. "In this world of deceit and media power, such loyalty is rare."

"He's part of a fading tradition that stretches back to when gentlemen were knights and had a loyal henchman ready to lay down his life for him."

However, as Soames returned with lunch, the conversation shifted to the hot topic of Darcy Egerton.

"I've never had lunch as Darcy Egerton," Rowan said. "It is hard to grasp—frightening and exciting at the same time."

"For me, it's only excitement," Olivia chimed in. "The profile was eerily accurate," she told Elizabeth.

"What profile?" Rowan enquired.

Finally, Elizabeth decided to reveal *most* of the truth to him. She still had reservations about their actions concerning the contest, but the rest could be said.

"Well, Mr Egerton, we also have a story to share," Olivia said. "But first—was it truly a game between you and Thomas?"

"Why does everyone ask me that?"

"Because you might not live a life like Darcy Egerton's, but you played a huge part in ours. We were continually exasperated by Dad's obsession with you. We doubted him so many times."

"And we were anxious about his investigative methods," Olivia added for Elizabeth, then she paused. She also thought Thomas's 'unconventional' activities should remain undisclosed, buried forever.

"Don't worry, Aunt, there were dubious activities on both sides. He's at my mercy."

"I certainly am not, madam!" Rowan protested, yet Olivia could sense how much he enjoyed being at her mercy and arguing with her at the same time. In a way, she envied Marianne; she could appreciate the literary moment in its pure form. The publication of Darcy Egerton was a lifetime achievement, but for her, that joy came second after Elizabeth's happiness. She looked at the beautiful ring on her finger and admired it.

"Stop staring at the ring," Elizabeth joked. "It's not what you're imagining."

"Miss Elizabeth rejected your proposal?" Olivia asked

Rowan, who nodded. "It's the same old plot. I suppose you're not particularly fond of her family, sir."

"I like you. But I fear Kath, and I might not be able to resolve her predicament as Darcy did with Lydia. Her Wickham was far worse than the archetype."

"Well, that's true, but neither is Kath like Lydia. Kath's IQ is 140, and I have a hunch that her Wickham didn't realise the formidable adversary he left behind. She's also the daughter of Thomas, the man who tracked you for eight years. She's got a photographic memory and has spent the last two days at Scotland Yard with her handbags, shoes, and car, convinced that he left a trace. Kath's changed, and I'm overjoyed to have my other niece back."

"I'm happy for her and for you," Rowan said. "Still, our secret will be kept between your husband and us, but he's the one I'm least worried about."

"Because he's a man and knows how to keep a secret!" Elizabeth chuckled.

"Yes, darling!" the earl responded serenely. Olivia didn't quite follow the conversation, delighted by the earl who didn't hide his love. *They will often be in different positions, but this man will stay near her all his life*, Olivia thought affectionately. Thomas knew who Darcy Egerton was, of course. Yet, he wanted Elizabeth to discover him, not just for Collister but for herself. He'd sensed that the earl was the man Elizabeth needed. Ultimately, she'd been far more important than his obsession or games. As she watched them, how happy they were, her heart warmed.

Ultimately, Thomas had played with Darcy Egerton, and Elizabeth's potential happiness had been his reward. On the border between life and death, he had that incredible intuition that Darcy Egerton was the man Elizabeth needed, and perhaps, just before dying, he had seen their beautiful love story in a future he wouldn't know.

But then he knew Elizabeth well enough to be sure she remained Collister's strong leader even in the most thrilling moments. He never doubted that Darcy Egerton would craft a remarkable novel for Collister and her.

"I answered Collister's advertisement for Pemberley. Now I realise that Thomas was asking for a house that mirrored the one in my novel—the rooms, vast lawns, a ballroom, huge parlour, beautiful library, everything Warminster had. I can't fathom how I didn't realise that he knew exactly what he was looking for. I walked right into the trap. After years of suspicion and concealment, I let my guard down right before him, the one who'd relentlessly tracked me."

"Obsessively," Elizabeth interjected.

"Yes, perhaps, but he was also remarkably shrewd and composed. Not at all the maniac you all depict. He came to Warminster, examined the place, and then studied me as if I were an insect under a microscope. It didn't even occur to me that he knew the truth. It wasn't until last night that I finally understood…" He grinned, not at all vexed by this revelation. "He's the father I would have wished for. I'm sorry to say it, but my father never played a role in my life."

"And you're the son he would have wished for," Olivia asserted confidently, as she knew her late brother-in-law very well.

"He could still have me," Rowan said, "if this lady would only say yes—"

"No," Elizabeth replied, shaking her head with the same gesture Olivia remembered from when she was a little girl and resisted entering a dark room.

"Why not?" Olivia asked, although she knew it was a game between them.

"I don't trust him. I want to see the novel, and I want the family jewels."

This prompted laughter from everyone. "I think the family jewels were sold long ago, or if there are any left, you'll have to contend with the other countess for them. Don't expect me to intervene!"

"So, Thomas went to Warminster…" Olivia said impatiently, eager to uncover more about Thomas. It was a glimpse into his character they'd never hoped to attain.

"We liked each other from the first moment. I can't quite explain it. Maybe I'd been too isolated and needed someone to talk to, but no matter the circumstances, we would have liked each other. He was sarcastic and intelligent—"

"A Mr Bennet?"

"Not quite, or a Mr Bennet who would have resolved the entail and turned Longbourn into a thriving business. Thomas was both a manager and a negotiator. Yet, he also appreciated my library as Mr Bennet would have. And I'm certain he would have turned my tenth book into a spectacular event."

"I can do that, but not in these conditions where we're left alone to prepare everything," Elizabeth said. "Don't tell me you'd have come out differently with Dad still alive."

"We'll never know. Initially, I was frightened that he knew. In March, I didn't have a concrete plan for my tenth novel. I knew I had to reveal myself, and I liked the idea of publishing with Collister, but it was only an idea. I enjoyed the contest—"

"You enjoyed the idea of participating in the contest?" Olivia questioned, somewhat surprised.

"Yes, what better way to test Collister Publishing than to return after nine years and submit a novel. That's what Thomas suggested, and naively, I believed him while he continued to search for me." Rowan smiled.

"Don't judge Dad when it was you who deleted our manuscript archive," Elizabeth quipped.

"I did not delete your archive, Miss Collister. Or at least you can't prove I did."

"As I told you, he isn't Rowan the honest earl, so I'm not afraid of any revelations about Dad."

"When I saw the advertisement for Pemberley, I realised that the competition wasn't the solution for us any longer.

It was a better game, just between the two of us. I didn't anticipate falling into his trap. I imagined *me* telling him the truth…and a jubilant ending."

"You didn't suspect that Thomas still had the first version of your novel," Olivia stated, and Rowan nodded. "Thomas would've found your house even if you hadn't responded to the advertisement. He was prepared to search all of southwest England for the estate described in your book. He had a list! I assure you he would've shown up at your door sooner or later."

"Yes, I get it now. In March, I thought I'd play a bit with the man who'd been following me for many years. Then, I completely forgot everything and simply enjoyed his company. He really cherished this Jane Austen celebration, and his plans were intriguing. I saw what you did in Oxford."

"Then you mustn't have seen my press conference!" she said, looking at him, and his eyes recognised that he didn't remember a word but her—vibrant, elegant, and sexy. Almost too sexy for his liking; he would have preferred her in a grey suit with a long skirt to conceal her breathtaking body.

"I might have seen it," he replied hastily, shifting back to the subject of Thomas. "We met several times, and even then, I never suspected anything. His generosity surprised me but knowing that Warminster would regain some of its former grandeur was comforting. From that point on, my house became Pemberley—Thomas's Pemberley. It was his vision, and I didn't object. It was marvellous.

"Then…" Rowan paused for a while, uncertain whether to continue.

"Then you learned about Dad's illness."

"Yes, it was a tremendous shock. We met in London, and he told me how serious his condition was. Initially, I thought I was devastated because my plans had been shattered. But I soon realised I grieved for him, my friend

Thomas Collister. I didn't care about my plans. I was ready to tell the truth and show him my ideas for a novel. But he never returned. I wrote to him desperately pleading for a last meeting, but he replied that I was to continue my plans with his daughter, Elizabeth.

"My goodness! Only now I understand! He said I was to continue all *my* plans with Elizabeth…*my* plans, not his, not ours."

He fell silent, gazing at Elizabeth, then kissed her hand, and they all mourned for Thomas.

"Thomas left each of us a message…how to go on with a project he'd initiated, yet he wouldn't see its deployment or end."

"What was your message?" Rowan asked Elizabeth.

"To read everything he gave me. Obviously, he pushed us into each other's arms."

"Yes, he knew who I was, but how did he know we'd end up together?"

"Who knows? Maybe one's last wish before death is fulfilled by God," Olivia said.

"Or you have to know who to ask. My adored dad was an opportunist. He prayed to all the gods—Zeus and Aton, Jesus, Allah, or Lord Shiva, the destroyer of worlds—to give me Darcy Egerton…only I thought he was speaking about the writer."

Chapter 37

"I'm really happy for you, Lizzy!" Kath exclaimed in her usual enthusiastic manner.

Elizabeth met her with intense embarrassment after deciding not to reveal the truth about Darcy Egerton.

Thankfully, Kath was so engrossed in her own matters at Scotland Yard that she noticed nothing beyond her sister's happiness.

Elizabeth and Rowan hadn't crossed paths by coincidence at the concert on New Year's Eve. There'd been a scheme behind her back. When Elizabeth had made up her mind to attend the concert, Kath had asked Clarice to tell the earl about it, as they often spoke on different matters.

"Did he find you after the concert?" Kath asked, certain that seeing her that night with Kaiden, seemingly close, had made the earl jealous enough to reconsider his decision.

"Yes," Elizabeth replied, hoping she sounded composed. She didn't like lying, even in that situation.

"Good. Whatever his reason, it wasn't because he didn't love you."

"Perhaps he'll tell me one day."

"Yes." Kath nodded, giving her sister a look that made Elizabeth feel even guiltier. After all, Kath had every right to know, but she wasn't sure whether her sister could or would want to keep such a secret.

"Your earl's been a great help in this mess with Adam, though confessing my story to the police was quite embarrassing. You acted so swiftly that I didn't have time to think. I'm not sure I would've gone the next day. What's worse than admitting you've been duped by a swindler?"

They quietly sipped wine from that part of the cellar that contained their father's finest bottles.

"Do you think Dad would be angry with me?" Kath asked, sounding like a small girl.

"Dad was sad because he thought you were wasting your life, not his money. Bless him!" Elizabeth said with affection. "He was full of advice, often annoying, but he was right. When I was around twelve, I organised a picnic for my class. It was a school project, and we all had to contribute equally. I took charge of the event and put in all the money upfront, only to lose almost half of it. Furious, I went to Dad, thinking I could sue those who hadn't paid or had paid less. Obviously, nothing could be done. They were all kids. But he told me something like, 'You didn't lose money—you paid for a lesson.' Then he made me list the mistakes I'd made while organising the picnic."

"That's so Dad!" Kath chuckled. "Well, my lesson cost me a part of the inheritance he left me. It was a bit too expensive for a lesson."

"I don't know. The price matched the importance of the lesson."

"You paid a hundred pounds for a lesson in management—"

"And you paid an undisclosed sum in millions for a life lesson which might change your life for the better."

"You sound just like Dad."

"I am Dad. Half my DNA is his. I want to find my own path, but I also want him to be proud of me at every stage."

"That's what I want too," Kath murmured, and for the

first time, Elizabeth was confident something had shifted in how her sister approached life.

"Dad made me promise I'd change and start enjoying life like everyone else, and I was so angry he made me promise that on his deathbed. But then, after a while, while partying one Monday in Singapore, I realised I was furious because he was gone, and his words had affected me so profoundly that I couldn't enjoy my lifestyle anymore. I looked at the people around me and saw how empty it all was, and I was one of them. Shopping and visiting clubs and beaches around the world lose the charm when you do it nearly every day. I flew to Monte Carlo that night... You know the rest."

"It's not Adam making you think about change, but Dad."

"Yes, but then Adam came along, confirming that it was the right thing to do. Get married, live a good life with a man I love, and occasionally fly to Dubai or Monte Carlo for a weekend of partying with you, him, and some friends."

"You can't go back to Dubai for another year," Elizabeth quipped, more a joke than a reprimand.

"Wrong. I renegotiated, and I'm free to return. I promised to open an office in Dubai."

"That's a great idea," Elizabeth said.

"I spoke to Mum. Arthur told her what happened," Kath said.

"Good. I feel bad for keeping her somewhat distant from my life."

"Yes, we need to do something about that, but"—Kath laughed—"our mother didn't say, 'Don't worry, Kath, I'm here to take care of you, my money is your money.'"

Elizabeth joined in the laughter. "The earl and I need to arrange a time for our mothers to meet—a one-time event with everybody. God help us!"

∞∞∞

"No," Rowan protested that evening. "I'm not ready for a meeting like that."

"Olivia and Arthur will be there too."

"No, I need peace to focus on my writing."

"Are you going to play the part of the poor artist and cast me as the horrible woman who disrupts his creative space whenever I ask something unpleasant?"

"Why not? Can a person write a good novel with chaos all around them?"

"You did it nine times with all your relatives at Warminster."

"That was different. I rarely saw them."

"It's just for one night."

"What if your mother expects me to attend her dinners, parties, or charity events?"

"We'll politely decline."

"You'll owe me for this," he warned.

"I won't pay you to see my mother. That's absurd. And remember, I'll have to meet your mother too."

"Then compensate me for something else. Like disappearing with that singer into his dressing room and the fuss he made over your supposed friendship."

Elizabeth studied him with playful eyes. They were having dinner at his apartment, where they'd decided to live temporarily.

"No, I don't feel guilty. I was a free woman then because the love of my life had dumped me."

"I'm the love of your life?" he asked, forgetting everything else.

"Yes, why are you so surprised?"

"Because it's the first time you've made such a declaration, whereas I—"

"I was right not to declare my feelings earlier. You left

me."

He returned her gaze with a teasing look. "And you didn't waste much time replacing me, madam."

"Jesus," she murmured, "you're so much like Dad. Even in the most delightful moments, he could be sarcastic."

"Aren't all of us men a Mr Bennet in some way?" he asked, engrossed in looking at her with love, tenderness, and sarcasm, knowing he had to win her over differently every time.

"Yes, I suppose you're Mr Bennet, Mr Austen, and all those gentlemen Jane depicted in her novels. As Olivia says, we don't pay enough attention to Jane Austen's men, focusing only on the women. Yet, without them, the story, or history, wouldn't make sense."

Suddenly, his gaze shifted in a way she couldn't decipher. "What?" she asked, somewhat puzzled.

"You're a genius," he declared, sweeping her off her chair and into his arms to dance while Soames turned on his heel and left the room. There would probably be a delay in serving the next meal, but that was unimportant.

Rowan led her to the bedroom and made love to her without uttering a word. She let herself drown in the immense pleasure he gave her while holding onto the memory of his look, eager to uncover all his secrets one by one.

"I never anticipated this," he said, kissing her breasts, eliciting those familiar moans.

"What?" she breathed, finally more interested in his words.

"That I'd find a woman who'd delve deep into my mind, where my creativity originates."

"What are you saying?" she asked, trying to wriggle out of his grasp, eager to hear what he had to say.

"It's a secret."

"No, I won't accept any secrets between us. I won't make love to you until you—"

"Really?" he whispered in her ear, winning her over despite her resistance, which soon transformed into the rhythm of love.

"Please tell me," she finally pleaded, her voice irresistible.

"You just gave me the subject for the novel—you and Olivia. Can we meet her…tomorrow?"

"Tomorrow's Saturday," Elizabeth pointed out.

"And?"

"They go fishing on Saturdays."

"It's winter, my love. Who goes fishing in winter? Don't look so annoyed. I've never been fishing."

Discovering things the earl had never done was quite delightful. "The coarse fishing season runs from June the sixteenth to March the fourteenth," she informed him, her tone resembling that of a well-informed child about an activity cherished by her family.

"Oh my, how do you know that?"

"Because we spent our childhood at my uncle's house, swimming, fishing, and roaming the woods picking mushrooms. Maybe it's time to do that again."

"I need to see Olivia tomorrow if you still want a novel for July. Normally, I'd have a year to prepare."

"You'll manage," she said, using the tone she reserved for her department managers who complained about time or budget constraints.

"Then ask Olivia to come here in the morning, and we can go fishing afterwards."

Elizabeth regarded him sceptically. "Is this a trap?"

"No, a trap is when I hold you in my arms and prevent you from going to the office in the morning. This is a friendly offer to spend time with your family."

Chapter 38

Olivia was pleased to have been invited for breakfast at Darcy's apartment, even at an hour when she was usually enjoying a Saturday morning lie in. Surprised by Elizabeth's call, she suspected that Darcy had invited her, which meant it was about the book.

"Darcy," she said instead of saying good morning as she entered the apartment.

"Every time you call me Darcy, I look around, startled. The secret's so deeply ingrained in me that it'll take a while until I get used to hearing it spoken aloud."

"I need to make sure that it's true because it feels like a dream when I get home. But even calling you Darcy isn't enough, as she's called Elizabeth," she said, gesturing towards her niece. "We're in a novel!"

"Then call me Egerton," Rowan said. "I have to get used to it. People will eventually call me Darcy Egerton, and I'll just look blankly at them. Do writers usually go by their pen names?"

Olivia laughed, in a good mood. "Yes, your readers will call you Darcy Egerton."

They ate quickly, as Rowan was eager to talk to Olivia. When they finally sat down to work, he smiled and said, "I have the perfect subject for the novel, but it's actually yours."

Olivia observed him curiously, finding a different man from the one she had met a day ago. Excited and impatient, she could almost sense the ideas swirling around him; his desire to start the novel was so strong that it enveloped all of them in a delightful frenzy.

"It's overwhelming," she said honestly, feeling like she was fully participating in the unique process of creation.

"The 2017 celebration centres around Jane Austen's gentlemen. That's what you said. That should also be the focus of my novel if you're willing to grant me the rights to your idea."

Olivia laughed. "I don't have any rights to the idea."

"Of course you do. At least moral rights."

"Then you can use the idea as you wish—" She paused, looking at Elizabeth.

"I don't even have moral rights. Thomas does."

Elizabeth nodded, remembering the brainstorming session at Pemberley.

"Dad told you about the duchess dedicating her diary to all the men who had supported their ladies through time…you said this story…"

"Yes…yes, but Thomas told me more, as if he wanted me to understand his idea wholly.

"One of the last times I saw him, he told me that he was proud and at peace with you becoming the head of Collister. Then he whispered, word for word, *'Maybe it's time, and it's fair to speak about us, the gentlemen—'*"

"No!" Elizabeth exclaimed. "Are you sure?"

"I'm very sure, but I was so sad and troubled by his departure that the idea only fleetingly crossed my mind—"

"Yet enough to flourish into this amazing idea," Rowan said as new ideas flowed into his mind.

"I can give you everything I wrote for the conference," Olivia murmured, still shocked by her revelation.

"Would you?"

"Absolutely. You can use all my ideas…it seems they're not entirely mine. As always, Thomas had the final say." She smiled, remembering her friend whom she admired deeply.

"That would be really helpful. I usually do extensive research for a book, which takes a long time—time I don't have right now. But luckily, the subject is already taking shape! In 1922, Elizabeth Austen, who was already the Duchess of Lancashire, published her diary. She recounted her love story with the future duke in that tumultuous year of 1917, a hundred years after Jane Austen's death."

"*Elizabeth's Diary* was a huge success for Collister," Elizabeth added.

"Indeed, mostly because it was groundbreaking. The duchess's book focuses on women and their destinies one hundred years after Austen. How she influenced women's fight for their rights—"

"*Elizabeth's Diary*," Elizabeth repeated, and they could see she was thinking deeply.

"A woman's perspective on the events of a century," Darcy continued. "But in 2017, I want to reveal the male perspective on the past two hundred years. Your father's a crucial figure in our love story. Thomas Collister serves as the reason for my coming forward. And other men, including that Adam, who portrayed Wickham's role so convincingly. Each of us superimposed on Jane Austen's gentlemen. And then it's about Warminster, which ultimately becomes Pemberley."

They sat in silence for a long while, overwhelmed by the intensity of his words.

"*Darcy's Diary*," Elizabeth whispered, and he looked at her as if she were a miracle.

"This woman is a genius…and she's mine. The novel will also explore Darcy Egerton. My road from the first novel to the moment I met Thomas…and then Elizabeth.

"What do you think?" he asked Olivia.

Olivia exhaled, overcome with emotion in a way she

rarely felt, as she was seldom surprised by an idea.

"I think it's wonderful. Challenging but wonderful. You're all such strong gentlemen. Thomas, like a recurring theme—"

"He'd be the central figure in my novel. Ultimately, the man who pursued Darcy Egerton for his art finds a son. The quintessential gentleman…"

"Yes, you're so right," Olivia replied in haste. "Two centuries after Jane Austen, we still discuss women. Their right to work, to love freely, and to have an independent life akin to what men have always enjoyed. Jane Austen created the modern woman through her intelligent and independent characters. Many women in our world are her descendants who fulfilled her ideals—"

"But Austen, in her pure geniality, envisioned a gentleman to support, understand, and love the leading lady. She depicted gentlemen for Elizabeth Bennet in *Pride and Prejudice*, Anne Elliot in *Persuasion*, and Elinor Dashwood in *Sense and Sensibility*. We've followed the destiny of the ladies, but did anyone ever consider what happened to the men?"

"Yes! Exactly what I've been thinking!" Olivia exclaimed, elated. "She created that gentleman. Not a blueprint for all novels, but many—ranging from the wealthy, audacious, arrogant aristocrat in *Pride and Prejudice* to the reserved Edward Ferrars, who's ready to sacrifice love for duty. For each of her inspired women, she painted a corresponding man."

"Don't stop. I need much more…every key lady she portrayed finally finds a man," Rowan said, captivated by her words.

And Olivia continued. "All six of Jane Austen's novels culminate in weddings. *Sense and Sensibility* closes with a double wedding—Elinor and Edward are married '*in Barton church early in the autumn*', while Marianne starts a new life '*in a new home*' with Colonel Brandon. In *Pride and Prejudice*, Mrs

Bennet gets '*rid of her two most deserving daughters*' on the same day. The last page of *Northanger Abbey* witnesses Henry and Catherine's marriage, the bells ringing, and everyone smiling. *Mansfield Park* concludes with Fanny and Edmund's wedding, their happiness '*as secure as earthly happiness can be*'. In Emma, the protagonist and Mr Knightley marry with '*no taste for finery or show*' but with '*perfect happiness*' in their union. Anne Elliot, who is '*tenderness itself*', weds Captain Wentworth in the final chapter of *Persuasion*."

"I'm taking notes," Rowan murmured, and Olivia smiled, giving her consent with a grand gesture.

"Legend has it that once, Pope Julius II handed Michelangelo the brush he had dropped from the scaffolding while working on the Sistine Chapel's ceiling. When Michelangelo wondered at this incredible gesture, the pope said, 'Posterity will only remember me for giving you this brush.'"

"You're exaggerating, distinguished lady, still in shock at discovering Darcy Egerton," Elizabeth said, and Rowan nodded.

"Not at all. I'll be remembered by my students and specialists who appreciate my interpretation of certain literary works. But now I am participating in this incredible act of creation that is taking place miraculously in front of us," she said, pointing to Rowan as if she was still asking herself if he were real.

Darcy smiled and bowed. "I'm greatly flattered by your words and the confidence you place in me, madam!"

"Then learn to never interrupt a woman, or she'll lose her train of thought." Olivia laughed.

"Please, by all means, continue."

"We have the superficial men—the scoundrels like Wickham, womanisers and gamblers. John Willoughby who might be unfaithful, but I believe he loves Marianne in his own way. Austen even describes him as '*a man resembling the hero of a favourite story*'. He might also be a victim of a society where a man of his status had to marry for money. We consider this acceptable in the case of women, but we deny men this right and brand them scoundrels. Even the amiable Colonel Fitzwilliam, Darcy's cousin, is in this situation—the second son of an earl with no fortune of his own. He explicitly tells Elizabeth that he must marry for wealth."

"My second son will inherit the distillery in Scotland," Elizabeth quipped.

"So you do plan on marrying me and having my children?" Rowan asked, playfully merging the novel and their real-life situation.

"No, absolutely not. And please, don't interrupt Olivia with your concerns. Let's get to work! You have a novel to deliver to Collister by April. Olivia?"

"We won't forget the real Thomas Langlois Lefroy, the young man Jane Austen loved but couldn't marry—again, because they were *both* poor. And it seems she didn't forget him, as a possible mention of Lefroy appears in *Emma*. In chapter 9, Emma Woodhouse and Harriet Smith discuss a poem. Austen might have hidden the word 'tolmeyfor,' an anagram of 'Tom Lefroy', in the poem.[6]

"Then there's Mr Collins. That incipient modern woman is subtly projected in interactions with this character. By rejecting this obsequious and pompous man, Elizabeth and Jane demonstrated that progress was taking root in the Bennet family. The Bennet sisters could choose their husbands, even in dire financial situations."

"I need a list of all the men in the novels," Rowan requested, and Elizabeth rolled her eyes.

"A list? Are we going back to making lists?"

"Be quiet, Elizabeth," both Olivia and Rowan said at the same time, and she merely smiled.

"Then?" he prompted.

"Next, we mustn't overlook the tradesmen and businessmen, the early agents of the industrial revolution.

These gentlemen also held slightly different aspirations from their fathers or grandfathers, and their vision and courage facilitated progress.

"Austen believed women possessed reason and common sense just as men did, and their role in society should be significantly different from the early 19th century. They needed a solid education, and the ideal marriage should be between two people who loved and respected each other. Fitzwilliam Darcy—"

"No, please, give me another man, someone less well-known than Darcy."

"Alright, let's discuss *Mansfield Park*, her third published novel, released in 1814 by Thomas Egerton."

"Yes, that makes sense."

"*Mansfield Park*, initially ignored by critics, became a great success with the public. The first printing in 1814 sold out in six months. The second in 1816 did the same."

"Wow!" Elizabeth remarked. "Mr Darcy Egerton, I have high hopes for you too."

"Thank you, madam." Rowan was in a rare state of happiness. He enjoyed writing and researching his novels, but he had never imagined his heart could be so full of love. He had tried to plan the unveiling of his identity, but what was happening now was the best possible scenario. Olivia occasionally let them bask in their love, as being in his home and life gave her insights that few critics had into a writer.

"Speak, Olivia," Elizabeth said, her gaze fixed deeply on Rowan's eyes, sensing the significance of that morning for Darcy Egerton.

"So, *Mansfield Park*. By the end of the last century, it had become Austen's most controversial novel. In 1974, American literary critic Joel Weinsheimer described *Mansfield Park* as perhaps her most profound and problematic work. Margaret Kirkham, a former lecturer at Bristol Polytechnic, sees *Mansfield Park* as a critique of Jean-Jacques Rousseau's popular 1762 work, *Emile*, or *On*

Education, which depicted the ideal woman as delicate, submissive, and physically inferior to men. Many critics found Fanny Price passive, naive, and difficult to like. 'Priggish' is the commonly accepted term, but that may hold true only in the first part of the novel. The second part reveals a significant transformation in the heroine, shaping Fanny Price into the most intricate character in Jane Austen's repertoire.

"From the outset, Elizabeth Bennet possesses all her admirable qualities. She emerges as a true heroine from the opening pages of *Pride and Prejudice*. We could say that she plays a decisive role in Fitzwilliam Darcy's evolution—"

"Much like our case," Elizabeth interjected with a touch of humour.

However, to their surprise, Rowan turned to her and spoke with undeniable emotion, "Yes, my love, that's absolutely true!"

"I'm thrilled for you," Olivia murmured. "And for myself as well. I have the rare privilege of witnessing the birth of a novel from its nascent ideas and emotions."

"Fanny isn't Elizabeth Bennet," Rowan eagerly pointed out.

"Indeed. Fanny Price undergoes a seamless and remarkable evolution throughout the novel. This transformation holds far more weight than portraying a character like Elizabeth Bennet who begins the novel as a progressive and independent woman for her time. Fanny learns by herself to place reason above compliance, and ultimately, love triumphs over duty. Fanny's refusal to yield to Sir Thomas's desire for her to marry Henry Crawford is now seen as one of the earliest explicit acts of women's rebellion. Her victory is built upon her virtues—integrity and compassion—but also on reason and good judgment. That challenges the prevailing notions of femininity and propriety in Regency England. And speaking of gentlemen, Edmund Bertram, Sir Thomas's second son, takes the role of the lead male character. He aspires to become a clergyman and falls for Mary Crawford, who continually tests his calling. Edmund proceeds with his ordination and, by the end of the novel, unexpectedly marries Fanny Price, appreciating the woman she's become.

"Recent literary criticism suggests that Fanny and Mary Crawford could symbolise conflicting facets of Austen's personality. Fanny represents her seriousness, objective observations, and sensitivity, while Mary embodies her wit, charm, and wicked irony. Despite *Pride and Prejudice* being the most beloved and renowned of Austen's works, I contend that *Mansfield Park* stands as her most mature and comprehensive achievement. The novel's scope remains confined to a single estate, yet its subtle references extend globally, touching India, China, and the Caribbean. In her non-confrontational yet potent manner, Austen addresses numerous problems in their society—references to slavery, matters of property and morality, and the decline of religion. Juliet McMaster has argued that Austen often employs understatement, with her characters masking powerful emotions beneath seemingly mundane behaviours and conversations."[7]

Olivia paused, studying Darcy's reaction.

"Your conclusion is that in each of Austen's novels, we encounter gentlemen who admire or love independent heroines who dare to voice opinions and challenge social conventions. This is evidence that Jane Austen encountered men who viewed women as equals and who would eventually contribute to their emancipation."

"Absolutely!" Olivia exclaimed.

"We've never truly contemplated how Austen's male characters perceived women's liberation," Darcy remarked.

"Because liberation wasn't yet a goal—not even a distant dream. Women's liberation began at Somerville College and Lady Margaret Hall in 1879," Olivia continued.

"No, Olivia, no! Darcy is so right." Elizabeth addressed

him as Darcy, for that morning he was Darcy Egerton. "It began much earlier, with those witty, educated women of the 1800s resembling Jane Austen—and with the men who recognised women as their equals."

Rowan nodded enthusiastically, reading from his notes. "The first concrete victory happened in 1918 when the Representation of the People Act was passed in Parliament, granting voting rights to women over thirty who met specific property criteria.

"But—a significant 'but'—that act was passed by men, indicating that at that time, men like the Darcys and Mr Bennets outnumbered those who opposed the change."

Darcy Egerton was already writing his novel mentally, a fact evident to both women.

"Stay at home and write," Elizabeth whispered, excited by his visible turmoil.

"No, I need some fishing to clear my mind. I need a few days before I can write, and we can discuss Jane Austen anywhere. Just spare me the title 'Darcy'," he jested, offering a smile to the two lovely women who were willing to do anything to help him craft his novel. "I see three key moments in the evolution of gentlemen. Darcy and Mr Bennet serve as prototypes for men who embraced the budding concept of women's liberation, though confined to the domestic sphere. They treated their daughters, mothers, and wives differently within the family, considering them partners. Then, in 1900, men voted for those initial women's rights. However, there remained a long journey to true equality. And now, in our era, I include myself as one of those men who entrust their futures to women, much like Thomas did when he named Elizabeth his successor. But let's go fishing now," the earl invited the ladies, who seemed reluctant to leave their seats.

With a hint of sorrow, they rose to leave, as the car was already waiting.

"You're on the right track already. It's brilliant," Olivia

commented.

"It might be best to prepare me for fishing now. Do I get a fishing rod?"

"Of course, my love," Elizabeth replied, still struggling to comprehend that he had never been fishing before.

"My upbringing was different from what you experienced," he admitted as he climbed into the car.

Rowan held her hand, delighted by that unusual day. "It's strange for me to have family in London, but I could get used to it."

Elizabeth beamed with delight at his words. Considering Olivia and Arthur his family was the most precious gift he could offer her.

"Did you tell the people in Tangiers about leaving me?"

"Are you crazy? Yadira would've killed me. She made it clear when we left that I needed to set a wedding date, as they wanted to come to England. But then I didn't leave you for good."

"No?" she questioned irritably. "Because it seemed pretty clear to me that you were quite determined, and you certainly didn't mention *pausing* our relationship, if such a thing really exists or if it's a bloody writer's invention."

Chapter 39

Arthur hesitated before meeting the earl. Rowan was Elizabeth's lover, but at that moment, Darcy Egerton was Collister's most valuable asset, and he feared those young people who had loved each other one day and broken each other the next. *This relationship has to last*, he thought with a shiver, as Collister's future now depended on that fragile thing called love.

He had reviewed Thomas's estimates on the print runs of Darcy Egerton's book and prepared a budget for the massive printing that would definitely happen in July, relieved to be part of their secret and financially prepared for the event.

Rosa was also waiting for them, eager to see *her girl's* fiancé yet secretly excited to meet an earl. Having forgiven him for making her sad, she only wanted to know when they intended to marry.

"I'm not sure," Arthur told her just before their arrival. "But please, let's not discuss that."

"Should I curtsey?" Rosa asked upon hearing the car stop outside the house. "I've never been so close to an earl before."

Arthur smiled, aware that Rosa would likely curtsey no

matter what he said. He even suspected that Rosa's dream of serving in a noble family was now coming true with *her girl* allegedly becoming a countess.

∞∞∞

Arthur and Rowan shook hands and observed each other with unhidden intensity. Elizabeth and her uncle shared common family traits, instantly making Rowan like him.

"Have you eaten?" Arthur asked as they entered the dining room where Rosa was waiting for them, deeply excited.

The presentation went quite well on both sides; Rowan was delighted by the suddenly shy woman he already knew from Elizabeth's stories, while Rosa almost fainted under his eyes and then whispered to Olivia, "He's a gentleman!"

As they sat down for a second breakfast, Kath joined them in her pyjamas. She seemed surprised by the gathering and then kissed her sister. After a moment's hesitation, she also kissed Rowan, who didn't seem surprised. "My little girl doesn't talk much in the morning," Rosa said to the earl. "But she's much friendlier after her coffee."

Laughter followed as the little girl was already eating, seemingly indifferent to the others.

"They have a club nearby, about a ten-minute drive." Kath finally explained her presence. "Henry took me."

Thankfully, her sleepiness and hunger prevented her from noticing the excitement at the table.

"I have a proposal," Olivia said, knowing that Elizabeth and Rowan were both highly anxious about their mothers meeting each other. "How about we invite Lady Warminster and Cybil to an informal dinner here tonight?"

Rowan didn't reply immediately. He looked at Elizabeth, but soon they exchanged smiles like mischievous children about to play a prank.

"Alright with me," he said, while Elizabeth nodded, and they both left the room to call their mothers.

"Well," Arthur complained with his natural humour, "there goes my quiet weekend." Yet he was somehow concerned that the meeting could end in disaster, even if he doubted that Elizabeth and Rowan would care much. He relied on Olivia to rein in the two equally difficult ladies.

"What are your plans?" he asked Kath.

"Are you joking? I wouldn't miss the first meeting between the Countess of Warminster and Mrs Cybil Collister."

Only Rosa was terrified. Hosting an earl and a countess at her table was something she'd never even dreamt of.

"I can't do that," she whispered, but Kath hugged her and laughed. "Just make them pozole and tacos—"

"What on earth are you saying, girl!" Rosa exclaimed, horrified. "I have a countess at the table. Those dishes are for peasants."

"Stop," Olivia intervened. "Just order dinner and have your usual assistants come tonight to help you." Rosa relaxed; she had done this many times for Olivia's guests.

"My mother's coming," Rowan announced quite calmly, as his mother knew well how to handle their relationship in public.

"Cybil's also coming," Elizabeth added, taking his arm. "In this atmosphere, they'll behave, you'll see."

"My mother wanted to come with her sisters." Rowan sighed.

Elizabeth laughed. "Don't worry. Rosa will shoo them out once dinner's over."

They didn't end up going fishing that Saturday. Instead, they strolled along the riverbank, enjoying the day and each other's company. Arthur showed Rowan his fishing spots, and they decided to do that on one of the upcoming weekends. Walking ahead of the ladies, they seemed to be getting along fine, and Olivia had her two nieces by her side again.

They had sandwiches for lunch and plenty to drink as Kath recounted her adventures at Scotland Yard.

"He won't escape this time," she said, referring to Adam. "No matter how long it takes, the agent is optimistic they'll find him. I remembered everything he might have touched. They took fingerprints, a few hairs, and some other pieces of evidence," she said mysteriously.

"Come on, tell us everything," Elizabeth pleaded. "After all, it's not every day we're on the trail of a criminal."

"Alright, my curious sister! Luckily, we don't have the countess and Mum at our table yet." Kath laughed before continuing. "We were in my car, and I…gave him a…*hand job*—"

"Kath!" her uncle exclaimed, more amused than shocked, as they were never prudish, and the girls were already grown.

"You wanted to know!" Kath said, continuing unabated. "He had taken my car out just before leaving under some pretext, and we found out he'd taken it to the valeting place. He was so attentive to every detail."

"Oh my!" Elizabeth exclaimed.

"A professional job. He did everything meticulously, making sure not to leave any traces. We never went to my house, and when we used my car, he drove so that he only touched the steering wheel and a few buttons. Well, he wasn't so cautious with me when…" This time, she hesitated.

"Yes, we know when." Elizabeth laughed.

"I wiped my hand on a tissue and put it in my coat pocket."

"Ugh!" Olivia exclaimed.

"Yeah, 'ugh', but that 'ugh' might just catch him. I remembered that…incident and went back to Scotland

Yard with the coat."

"And you told them the whole story?" Elizabeth asked, laughing, imagining her uninhibited sister speaking to detectives at Scotland Yard like a scene from *Basic Instinct*. "I hope you at least had your underwear on."

"I can't remember," Kath jested. "But I had already taken my handbags and shoes to Scotland Yard, just in case he'd touched them."

"Shoes?" Elizabeth asked, almost naively.

Rowan kissed her hand and said, "Hush, honey, I'll show you what she meant." Laughter erupted around the table.

"And they took the tissue from your Burberry coat pocket?"

"Gaultier, and yes, yesterday morning. They promised to keep me updated."

"But what can they do if his DNA isn't in any database?"

"The national police forces can access vast DNA databases," Rowan explained. "Not just for criminals but also containing DNA from genealogists and research projects. Suppose Adam is unlucky enough to have a distant cousin in that database. In that case, he's doomed, as the police could trace him through his family."

"Exactly. That's what they're hoping for. And in Adam's case, the database is extensive. He operated in at least seven countries. His criminal profile suggests he's from the US. They might find his fingerprints somewhere on my belongings, but DNA is more definitive."

"Speaking of DNA, the Duchess of Lancashire was Jane Austen's great-great-grandniece," Kath said.

"Yes, absolutely," Olivia agreed.

"I wonder if they have descendants."

"They do, and Dad told the Duke and Duchess of Lancashire about our plans. We'll send them an invitation to Pemberley in July," Elizabeth said.

"Your estate has lost his name and become Pemberley. How does it feel?" Olivia asked.

"Natural," Rowan answered. "Thomas had this power to manipulate people, but in my case, it was brainwashing. But I'm happy about everything he did. Finally, my estate has a purpose and a future."

"Jane Austen and Thomas, let us be fair," Olivia said. "So, Rowan, is the man from 2017 upset about losing the power he held for so many centuries?" Olivia asked, after considering how to phrase the question in a way that made it seem like a casual lunch conversation.

"I don't think so. The change took nearly two hundred years. It happened gradually, sometimes imperceptibly. A new way of life and behaviour developed across generations. I'm ready to take care of our children while my wife goes to work," he said, looking at Elizabeth.

"You don't have a wife, dear earl," Elizabeth answered.

"True, but I hope to have one, and I want children."

"No, that's absolutely out of the question. I'm not even thirty-three yet."

"You're getting on a bit for having kids." Rowan laughed.

"What are you saying? Dad had me when he was forty-one."

"Yes, dear, but your father was a man. Your mother was twenty-five," Arthur chimed in.

"Well, Olivia, there's your answer. You asked Rowan if they've evolved. The answer is no, they still think the same way they did in 1800. Meanwhile, we're here, voting and running companies." Kath laughed.

Chapter 40

They retired for a few hours after lunch. Rowan walked around Elizabeth's room in wonder. Untouched since she had been an adolescent, he could imagine her at sixteen on her princess canopy bed with white lace, dreaming of her future.

"I did not dream about my future," Elizabeth said.

"I want to make love to you in this virginal bed."

"Pervert!" she said while she undressed under his incredulous eyes.

"Impudent," he answered, still dressed, taking her naked into his arms. "I hope you won't express yourself like you do in my bedroom. We can be heard here."

"And? Everybody in this house knows what's happening in this virginal room. By the way, what did your mother say when you invited her?" Elizabeth asked.

"She deemed it entirely inappropriate to make such an invitation on the day of the dinner, but then I mentioned that Mrs Collister would also be coming, and she agreed. She's probably out shopping for an extravagant outfit for our informal dinner."

"Did you *inform* her that we're near the river at my uncle's country house?"

"Yes, but she didn't grasp the concept," he said and

laughed.

"Almost the same thing happened with Cybil. I *informed* her that she would meet the Countess of Warminster. From that point on, she didn't hear anything else. I think that when Dad was alive, her secret aspiration was to attain a noble title. She was quite knowledgeable about the process. She already knew you were the 15th Earl of Warminster," she said, and Rowan smiled.

"Did she Google me?"

"Probably. And she was exceedingly impressed."

"Speaking about making love," he said while he caressed her naked body.

"We weren't speaking about love," she said while trying to undress him.

"We are now. I was quite impressed by your sister's abilities in the matter. Does that run in the family? Will the future countess give me a blow job in my car?" he asked while helping her undress him.

"My God!" Elizabeth laughed. "Imagine the headlines if they caught us—Elizabeth Collister, head of Collister Publishing, sucks off the secretive novelist."

And she continued laughing while he took her to the bed where she had slept as an innocent girl. He covered her mouth with his hand, knowing what she could do when he loved her, but then forgot as feeling her depth was the ultimate aphrodisiac.

∞∞∞

Cybil was the first to arrive, nearly half an hour before seven o'clock. Surprisingly, she was dressed in trousers and a stylish jacket. Only her jewellery demonstrated her desire to impress the countess.

"Shoot me," Kath whispered in Elizabeth's ear. "Mother is truly excited to meet the earl and countess."

The earl gallantly kissed Cybil's hand, and she responded with a smile. He regarded her kindly, as Elizabeth strongly resembled her. He pictured Elizabeth thirty years later, and that thought filled him with joy. And remarkably, Cybil Collister took a liking to him as well.

"Did you tell her that he's your lover?" Kath whispered in her sister's ear, making Olivia look at them as if they were still two mischievous children.

"Why? Do you think she's searching for a new husband with a title?" Elizabeth replied, struggling to suppress her laughter, as Rowan escorted their mother into the dining room in a scene reminiscent of a Jane Austen novel.

His mother arrived when Big Ben presumably struck seven o'clock, leading to a brief commotion during the introductions. Elizabeth felt the urge to curtsey to the countess, who responded with a reserved smile yet tried to be graceful. If Rowan had been impressed by Elizabeth's resemblance to her mother, Elizabeth was astounded by how much her lover resembled the beautiful sixty-four-year-old countess. The two mothers ended up standing next to each other, a well-planned move that turned initial politeness into a conversation about the finest spa in London, mutual friends, and plans for joint charitable galas.

"Perhaps I've misjudged her in recent years," Rowan whispered in Elizabeth's ear, his concern fading away as a friendly rapport developed between the two women, and when they joined the general conversation, they were gracious, bordering on warm.

"I'm delighted that Rowan's leased our beloved Warminster to such a lovely family," she remarked. "I was somewhat anxious about the transformation, but I think the old house desperately needed renovation."

"It's no longer called Warminster," Rowan interjected. "As long as it's rented to the Collisters, it's known as Pemberley." His teasing was accompanied by a smile, and his mother responded with a radiant grin.

"Of course, it's a wonderful name. I'm pleased that our home's contributing to your celebration."

The countess had done her homework and bestowed her approval as if it were essential. She refrained from probing about their relationship and conversed with Elizabeth only on neutral subjects. Ultimately, an evening initially slated to last a maximum of two hours stretched until midnight, and it was deemed a success. Rosa received all the accolades for the dinner she had ordered in town, yet she handled her responsibilities admirably.

"Are you not staying the night?" Olivia asked Elizabeth.

Rowan answered for her. "Thank you for a wonderful day, but we've interrupted your fishing weekend long enough."

"We're heading to Pemberley in the morning," Elizabeth responded, and with that, they left, leaving the Johnsons tired but content.

∞∞∞

"I'm so pleased with how today went," Arthur remarked. "Seeing the girls laughing together like in the old days and Cybil almost behaving well—it's a double miracle."

"And his mother's tolerable," Olivia added. "The countess isn't among my favourite people. Still, she conducted herself graciously and will likely encounter Cybil again in the future. This is good for Elizabeth and Rowan."

"Is he writing?"

"Yes, I think the novel will turn out splendidly, and it's a gratifying feeling to have contributed to his work, even in this small way."

"It's not insignificant, my dear. If he weren't Elizabeth's man, I would have demanded a tidy sum for selling him the rights to your idea," Arthur said, and Olivia wondered if he was joking.

She rested her head on his shoulder, and he embraced her tightly.

"Believe it or not, it wasn't my idea…it was Thomas's. Why do I sense that he orchestrated everything and led us to follow his plans?"

"Because that's exactly what happened. He told me to be prepared to bolster the budget of *Books*, and I did so long before learning about Darcy. Because I trusted him!"

In the warmth of their living room, they both shuddered, feeling Thomas's presence and, in some enigmatic way, his contentment.

"I think, my dear," Olivia said, "that the dreadful year of 2016 has ended, and from now on, we'll see brighter days. And please, let's not discuss *him*. After what happened with Adam, we should take Rowan's insistence on secrecy seriously."

Chapter 41

In unanimity, the Collister Commission officially declared Laura Maclean as the winner of the Collister Fiction Prize in February.

After a brief discussion, Olivia and Marianne agreed that her novel was the finest.

"Goodness me, Olivia! Thomas was truly remarkable," Marianne commented with affection and sadness.

"Don't tell me he had designated Laura as the winner."

"Yes, that's precisely what happened. He secretly confided in me that he thought Laura's novel was the strongest in the competition. He even speculated that Laura might be Darcy Egerton."

They both laughed, and Olivia recounted how Thomas had inspired her to develop the ideas about Jane Austen's male characters.

"The closeness to death granted him some unique insights, but he didn't jot down a plan or his ideas. Instead, he instilled them in us, making them even more potent. Then, devising Elizabeth's journey to the earl was a brilliant move," Olivia commented.

"I still don't get why Thomas kept pushing us to uncover Darcy Egerton when he knew who he was by April," Marianne said, pointing out the only part of Thomas's legacy that was still unclear. "Could he have been unsure?"

"No, he was certain. But he didn't want us to figure out who Darcy Egerton was before Elizabeth did. We were so fixated on those three men that we completely overlooked Pemberley and the earl. Yet Thomas's plan suffered a setback when Elizabeth didn't read the manuscript before going to Pemberley. But in the end, it couldn't have gone wrong as Rowan had decided to give her his novel anyway. It was only a matter of days before he revealed the truth to her."

"So he had written something?"

"He was rather vague when I asked him. I think he'd had some ideas. He'd written something, but he wasn't satisfied with what he had," Olivia said. "All's well that ends well."

"And Laura's novel truly is exceptional. I foresee a brilliant career ahead," Marianne mused. Yet, her thoughts were not solely in the room; they also resided in Thomas's office, where they had deliberated together over past winners—some of the most remarkable moments of her editorial career.

∞∞∞

Laura signed the contract, and her book was scheduled for release at the end of June, marking the final Collister event before Pemberley.

Laura Maclean's gothic novel was eerie and romantic at the same time. In a posthumous encounter, Jane Austen engaged with her main characters, allowing them to express their discontent or admiration for their portrayals.

On the morning the novel was chosen, Rowan received it from Marianne. He enjoyed it so much that he read some excerpts to Elizabeth when she returned from the office.

"You do wear glasses," she said, surprised. She had seen him wearing them before but hadn't paid attention.

"I'm getting old," he replied, gazing at her.

"Ah!" she exclaimed. "That usually means you urgently need something from me as old age comes knocking."

"Yes, I want to get married. I want children."

"And I won't stop you from having that," Elizabeth responded, looking at him. "There are plenty of young women eager to become a *Contessa*."

"You're cruel. I spend the entire day waiting for you, and when you return home, your bath is drawn, and dinner awaits you—"

"Thank you, Soames," she jokingly called out, even though he wasn't in the house.

"Why don't we marry then?"

"Because I don't want to marry an obsession."

"That's the harshest thing you could say. You'd be marrying Rowan Stafford, not an obsession."

"No, I want to marry Rowan Stafford, who writes under the pen name Darcy Egerton. Please read."

"It's a way to nudge or blackmail me into coming forward. I said I will."

"It's a way to help you lead a normal life. Read, or I'll fall asleep. I had an eight-hour meeting."

And that evening, he ended up reading far more than he had intended. They both relished the engaging story that unfolded at a brisk pace, witty dialogues, and insightful excerpts about Austen's prose.

"This is truly excellent," Elizabeth commented later that night. Secretly, she thanked divine forces that Darcy hadn't entered the contest.

"The competition was fierce," he said, as if reading her mind. "Had I entered, it would have been challenging."

She looked at him and nodded, imagining the inferno they would have faced if he had entered, and another writer had emerged as the victor.

"What would your novel have been about…if…?"

"Back in January, when I started, it was hazy, distant,

unfocused. I'd planned to write about Jane Austen writing her novels while living her life. A bio of a writer."

"Wow, that sounds fascinating!" she exclaimed, ready to declare that she would marry him as she began to also love that damned Darcy Egerton.

"I've got an idea. I need to discuss it with the ladies," he said. The following day, he invited Olivia and Marianne to dinner for a conversation.

∞∞∞

They arrived, their curiosity piqued, as each meeting was a delightful intellectual exercise for them in his laboratory. However, Rowan began by saying, "This isn't about me."

Both of them turned to Elizabeth, wondering if she had made a decision about marriage—an event they anticipated with equal excitement.

"No, it's not about me either," Elizabeth confirmed.

"It pertains to Laura's novel," Darcy said. "Have you decided on the play to be performed at Pemberley?"

Elizabeth shook her head. It was one of the few outstanding issues. Rehearsals were to begin in March, yet they hadn't found a suitable play to match Pemberley's ambience.

"I might have an idea," he said. "I read passages from Laura's novel to Elizabeth last night. Reading it aloud, I was struck by its dramatic potential. The dialogue is already excellent."

Olivia exchanged a glance with Marianne. "He might be onto something. The dialogue is indeed strong. Do you have it here?"

Darcy proceeded to read from the book for about half an hour. Ultimately, both ladies declared their satisfaction in finding the play.

"Rowan is right. It lends itself well to dramatization,"

Marianne remarked.

"I'm not giving him anything for his consultancy," Elizabeth quipped, and they all laughed.

"It's a splendid idea. I'll talk to the stage director," Marianne declared, with Olivia nodding in agreement.

Just before going to bed that night, Rowan approached with a notebook.

"I've jotted down what you owe me for consulting—"

"As I said, I'm not paying you anything. It's too much of a struggle to contend with Arthur for a budget," she replied with a smile before taking the note from him. "Fourteen blowjobs? Are you joking?" she exclaimed. "You want children, yet you're acting like a hormone-fuelled teenager!"

"In that case, I'll put on my old man reading glasses and read by your side…every evening."

"Really?" Elizabeth asked and pulled off the blanket to reveal her naked body.

Chapter 42

Even the weather seemed sunnier than usual at the end of April.

Because I am in love, Elizabeth thought each time she gazed out of the window of their bedroom at Pemberley, observing the park as it took shape. Shrubs, conifers, and unfamiliar bushes appeared in an elegant display that didn't crowd the lawns but gave them personality.

Rowan joined her, pointing out the changes that were taking place.

"The scene will be set there, where the future countess touched down in her helicopter."

"I never promised to marry you," she protested, a familiar refrain whenever he broached the topic of their marriage. "Let's finish Pemberley and your book first, and then we'll see. And then I want everybody to know who Darcy Egerton is…not for Collister but for you, my love."

The work continued at a rapid pace, the progress observable from week to week.

To everybody's surprise, in the second-floor bedrooms, they discovered incredible frescoes hidden under previous paintings done in haste and in total disregard for the works of art beneath.

With each day, Pemberley looked better both inside and

out.

Rowan worked at Pemberley and in London, trying to be with Elizabeth almost every evening and night.

"Remember, I'll need to work ten hours a day," he had cautioned her back in January, anxious about her reaction.

But Elizabeth nodded and assured him, "I understand, and I won't disturb you."

"No, let's not exaggerate. I do need some distractions. Sometimes, my inspiration is drawn from you. And I certainly won't reject a hand job that doesn't really interrupt my work."

"The earl likes to have his offspring in a napkin?" she joked. Despite adoring his body as much as he loved hers, ready to give him satisfaction in any possible way, she was fighting him in an endless game with no losers, only winners.

"No. I prefer my DNA inside you, mixed with yours."

∞∞∞

But then it turned out that a napkin was also a valuable asset. In late April, just a few days after Rowan submitted his novel for editing to Marianne, Kath arrived at their home in London unusually excited. Elizabeth recalled her own reaction from the night she'd discovered Darcy Egerton's true identity.

Kath wanted a drink. Her face radiated excitement, so they allowed her time to calm down, aware that the news was bound to be sensational.

"They've caught him!" she eventually exclaimed.

"Adam?" Elizabeth asked incredulously.

"Yes, Adam! Or Boris Miller from Junction, Kimble County, Texas, USA."

"Incredible!" Rowan chimed in.

"And was it all because of that napkin?" Elizabeth asked with a smile.

"Yes, this story has a moral. A small stone in the road can overturn a massive cart. He orchestrated everything so meticulously that he succeeded to an almost incalculable degree for fifteen years. When they pieced together all the data, they estimated he'd swindled women and men out of around sixty million dollars."

"Sixty million, wow!"

"Perhaps even more. They tracked his movements during those fifteen years, following the victims who reported the theft. But there were periods when nothing happened, and the police suspected many more victims never reported being conned."

"Most likely married women or some overly proud individuals who couldn't admit they'd been duped. Do you know how they caught him?"

"Yes, and it's brilliant. Just as you said, my hand played a starring role!" Kath laughed while Elizabeth earned a playful, reproachful look from Rowan, as she'd refused his similar request.

"Boris is forty-two, and he has got a mother he spoke to, who was undoubtedly his accomplice, but they couldn't pin anything on her, so she's free. Clever Boris had an intricate plan each time. He relied on the shock of his victims, assuming they'd be too distressed to take quick action that might find traces that had evaded his careful cleaning. But he miscalculated. He's got an estimated IQ of around 120—"

"While yours is 140," Elizabeth proudly interjected.

"Yes, his first mistake was underestimating my intelligence. That was a glaring oversight in his plan. But he met me in Monte Carlo at the roulette table after finding out that I was an heiress, and that was all he needed to strike. Then, on that night with the *napkin*, I don't know, but I felt that he genuinely liked me. Another mistake. He wasn't nimble enough to catch the napkin.

"He made another blunder at what's now considered to be the start of his career as a con artist. He had an affair with a maid called Octavia Casales, who worked for the woman he conned."

Elizabeth couldn't fully concentrate on her sister's tale, captivated by Rowan's interest.

"It's not clear how Octavia told him about the child, as she vanished shortly after giving birth."

"Good Lord," Rowan remarked. "He killed her! He's a ruthless murderer."

"Yes, he probably did kill her. Then, he thought he was safe. Wrong again. He couldn't harm the baby. Little Roberta was raised by a wonderful family who received substantial sums from an untraceable account. He never anticipated that even though she lived with a good Christian family, the girl was restless, much as he probably had been. A year ago, fourteen-year-old Roberta ordered DNA testing kits for herself and secretly for her parents. And, surprise, she discovered she was adopted despite her birth certificate's claims. The astute girl began searching for her biological family. Her results were added to a global database, and…her DNA combined with my napkin did the magic! The police reconstructed the whole story in no time—the missing biological mother, her mistress who had been conned by a man fifteen years ago—finally, not so difficult to track him down."

"What a blunder! He maintained some form of connection with that family," Rowan observed.

"Exactly. So intricate, so aligned with his style that he thought he was safe from repercussions. But he wasn't. I suspect the police didn't share the entire truth with me. I deduced Octavia's disappearance myself. They were so determined to catch him that they formed an international task force, and eventually, the FBI traced him to Texas…and arrested him because of me and Roberta."

"You could write a novel out of this," Elizabeth commented, glancing at Rowan and only afterwards realising what she'd said. She was unsure whether it was best to let the words go unnoticed or to elaborate, but to their immense surprise, Kath burst into laughter.

"You two poor kids made the same mistake as Adam Boris from Junction, Texas. Although it's quite unacceptable in Elizabeth's case, considering you've lived with me for the last 30 years. I know who you are, Rowan!" she declared, still laughing and sipping her drink.

Rowan shot Elizabeth a reproachful look, but she shook her head. "No, how could you think I told her?"

"She didn't have to. Besides, thank you, sis, for having faith in me."

"Really?" Elizabeth questioned. "If you were in my shoes, would you trust yourself?"

Kath didn't respond immediately, then murmured, "I might have been a loose cannon, but Darcy Egerton was Dad's dream. Do you honestly believe I'd jeopardise Dad's plan in any way?"

"Thomas's plan?" Rowan queried.

"Yes, I suspected he'd found you out when he decided to rent your rundown castle." She laughed again. "Sorry, Rowan, but that's the way it was."

"Are you saying you've known that Rowan was Darcy ever since Dad rented Warminster?" Elizabeth asked, stunned.

"I had a suspicion, but when he left you and then returned, your behaviour, Rowan, was so stupid that it confirmed my suspicions. Then everybody else—it's like Marianne's on cocaine, even Olivia acts strangely around him. I was somewhat hurt, but as you said, it takes time to build trust."

"Thank you, dear sister," Rowan said, approaching Kath to kiss her hand. "You're amazing, and despite what other family members might think, I have faith in you. And I'm a bit afraid of you too."

"Well, dear Earl of Warminster, AKA Darcy Egerton, I've concocted a brilliant promotional plan, waiting for you to confess the truth."

Elizabeth breathed a sigh of relief, knowing that the promotional plan was the only downside so far of Darcy Egerton's campaign.

"Let's get drunk, Darcy Egerton, along with your simpleton future wife," Kath suggested.

"Wait, will you be getting your money back?" Elizabeth asked.

"It's uncertain. They haven't told me yet, but I have my doubts. Anyway, that's our lawyers' problem from now on. And as Dad said, I paid for a meaningful lesson…but it was also quite fun!"

Chapter 43

A few weeks later, upon returning home from work, Elizabeth discovered an exquisite gold and glass box on the table. With trembling hands, she extracted a book printed on Oxford India Paper, much like *Elizabeth's Diary* a century ago.

"*Darcy's Diary*," she read aloud, gazing into his eyes to convey the depth of her feelings for that priceless gift. "It's marvellous!"

"Read it first," he urged, his anxiety impossible to conceal.

The book was his story as Darcy Egerton. The book was their love story. The book was about Thomas's constant search for the writer he'd lost years ago. From that strange beginning when he attempted to publish his book at Collister to the moment when Elizabeth learned his true identity.

While some aspects remained private, his ten-year journey, Thomas's constant search, and their love were unequivocally portrayed. He worried she'd be embarrassed by the exposure or that his Elizabeth wouldn't like how he'd told their story. Her opinion mattered above all else. He felt the same nervous anticipation he'd experienced ten years earlier while awaiting Collister's judgment on his debut novel. Life was indeed full of peculiar twists.

"This is the book I promised Thomas. It's also the book I pledged to you for your Jane Austen celebration. But at the same time, it's the book I needed to write for my readers who patiently allowed me to remain hidden for all these years. They deserved to know the truth of my journey and how I managed to safeguard my secret."

Elizabeth's eyes pleaded for more explanations, suddenly scared about all she'd find in his book yet tremendously proud and eager. "No honey," he jested. "Not a single word about our *covert* exploits. It's a work of fiction, after all."

"But it reads like a diary."

"True, but everyone interprets reality differently."

"For Thomas," she read aloud from the first page, her eyes glistening with tears as she looked at him. After all, everything that had happened was her father's victory.

"I hope Dad's here, reading along with me!" Elizabeth said, settling onto the sofa. She didn't allow him to join her. "Go away, do something else—cook, do some washing, give me the space to savour my reading!"

Yet, he couldn't leave the room. Holding a tablet in his hand, he sat across from her, following his story reflected on her face during the long hours she read, watching the range of emotions as she immersed herself in his novel. She laughed, cried, spoke to herself, seemingly oblivious to his presence. A blush crept onto her cheeks when he delved into their love story. "Ah, the bastard, he's got no shame," she mumbled. "How will I face people after this?" Yet their love was so beautifully portrayed that, as the pages turned, she became lost in the story she knew only from her heart. She conceded that he had kept many moments between them concealed.

Darcy's Diary was the duchess's one-hundred-year anniversary book seen through a magic mirror that transformed the background, letting Jane Austen shine with the same intensity two hundred years after her departure.

If *Elizabeth's Diary* was rooted in Jane Austen's portrayal of women and their burgeoning awareness of an elusive freedom, Rowan's story concentrated on Darcys of the twenty-first century, who took immense pride in their love of all kinds for the descendants of Elizabeth Bennet.

He discussed the Darcys across each epoch. The original Fitzwilliam Darcy, still grappling with his emotions for Elizabeth in 1800, yet finally revealing his incipient opposition against prejudices and the social customs concerning women. Marrying Elizabeth Bennet stood as the ultimate testament to his personal evolution. Moving to 1917, Darcy Lancashire nearly lost Elizabeth due to his difficulty in fully embracing her pursuit of emancipation. Yet, in the end, the Duke of Lancashire had been among those advocating for women's rights in 1918. Lastly, the story shifted to individuals like Thomas Collister and Darcy Egerton, alongside the men of their time, who regarded their exceptional ladies as equal partners in love and life.

The thread connecting the Darcys wasn't one of bloodline, but a shared bond founded upon respect, love, and admiration for their mothers, daughters, sisters, or wives.

If Fitzwilliam Darcy hardly kissed his Elizabeth in the pages of *Pride and Prejudice* and, in opposition, the duchess had created a scandal with her explicit love story, the earl chose to depict their love in a charming mist that at the same time hid and revealed their feelings and their path towards blissfulness.

Long after completing the story, Elizabeth remained silent, clutching the closed book in her hands, leaving him to doubt his words with mounting despair. Her expression remained serene, but it was impossible to gauge her true feelings.

"You didn't like it," he blurted, his fears exploding in his soul. Only then did Elizabeth glance at him as if momentarily forgetting his presence in the room.

"You exist, Darcy Egerton," she said as though surprised by this realisation. "You truly exist, and you are my earl." Still enveloped in the ambience of the novel, she understood his turmoil.

"Say something, Elizabeth, you're killing me!"

She gazed at him, and suddenly, it was Rowan Stafford on the sofa instead of Darcy Egerton.

"I'm bewildered," she murmured. "I don't know who I love now—my earl or the writer. Dad would have adored your book. Thank you!"

She'd cried a lot when she'd read about her father. Rowan had painted a vivid portrait of the strong, intelligent, playful man who'd relinquished his lifelong ambition of finding Darcy Egerton for Elizabeth's happiness. Thomas Collister had not only found Darcy Egerton before his death, but he had also liberated him, offering Rowan a life brimming with light and joy.

Then Thomas Collister had entrusted his legacy to Elizabeth, confident that she was the natural continuation of the dynasty of men who had built Collister. He believed that 21st-century Collister needed a woman to forge ahead.

"Both you and your father embody Jane Austen's unspoken dreams," he whispered, looking at her.

"I often doubted my ability to fulfil Dad's dream. Strangely, your book restores my self-assurance, as if—"

"As if Thomas guided my words."

"Yes," Elizabeth whispered. "At times, I forgot that the book was yours. It felt like it held my father's words."

"That's true. Throughout these intense months, I sensed his presence, overseeing my writing and inspiring me as a friend and father. I've never finished a book in four months before. I wasn't sure about how good my book was, but I was never concerned about deviating from Thomas's wishes. It was you I feared!"

With the book clutched against her chest, she settled

onto his lap. "Good heavens, Darcy, it was astonishing. I can't believe how wonderful and powerful it is. I want to live with you. I want to marry you."

Rowan kissed her, refraining from his usual gestures. "Then marry me tomorrow."

But Elizabeth shook her head. "No, not you, earl. I want to marry Darcy Egerton."

"And how do you propose to do that, you wild woman?" he quizzed.

"I want to read the book again."

"Not now, my love. Now, I want to feel you in my arms," he said, and for her, he became Darcy Egerton, who had never loved a woman before, hidden away for so many years.

And there, in that bed, the man who loved her and the one who had written about her became one—her future husband, the 15th Earl of Warminster.

"I have a porno version only for your eyes, my love," he said much later, still holding her in his arms.

"I want to read it!" She grinned in the darkness, envisioning their passion described in words. "It's good to have your own writer."

"Let me act out some excerpts with you," he tempted her.

"Your novel's marvellous," she murmured. "I can't say enough how grateful I am. I cherished every word."

"You're hardly an impartial critic," he teased.

"That's right, I'm not impartial in this bed. But reading you is different even if the novel is still you, in words—such a strange and exciting sensation."

"So you do love me, Elizabeth Collister."

"Who is this *me*? I certainly love Darcy Egerton—"

"I am Darcy Egerton, my love," he whispered.

"Yes…sometimes."

"Then marry both of us."

"Are you mad? I can't be bigamous!"

"Then who do you want to marry?" he asked.

"I need to decide. Let me read the novel again!"

Chapter 44

"I've been following Darcy Egerton's bets for this year," Kath said during a meeting with Olivia and Marianne in the earl's apartment in June. "Everyone thinks you're going to write a romance."

"That's logical. It's a genre I've hardly explored before," Rowan responded.

"And your romance turned out brilliantly." Marianne was more devoted than ever to supporting her writer who had given her a masterpiece.

"I wanted my book to sound like *Elizabeth's Diary*. To capture its essence."

"And it did, with a masculine touch emerging from Mr Bennet and Thomas's sarcasm," Olivia chimed in. She relished every conversation they had. While Marianne focused only on *her* novel published by Collister, Olivia saw things from a different angle. She was the critic fortunate enough to be part of a novel's creation, getting insights from the author's private process.

"Lately, I've come across so much misinterpretation of Jane Austen's male characters that I believe my book restores their image. In fact, *our images* of men in love with Elizabeth, in any era," Rowan said, aware that Olivia strongly opposed applying modern psychological analyses to old works.

Olivia nodded. "I've made an effort to counter notions like Darcy suffering from 'chronic depression, dwelling on the past and unable to take responsibility for his own actions.'[8] They're trying to diagnose a man from two centuries ago using contemporary psychiatry.

"It's hard to grasp that the man in the 19th century was at the pinnacle of society, empowered by centuries of privilege. He held absolute control over all aspects of life and society in ways unimaginable today. Jane Austen would've been appalled to see her male characters dissected and criticised in that absurd way two hundred years later.

"Ultimately, as you've said, this book's a restoration. The familiar figures like Fitzwilliam Darcy, Mr Bennet, Colonel Brandon, and even the tormented Mr Bingley represent the epitome of the evolved man in Jane Austen's era. Edward Ferrars, who loves Elinor Dashwood but is willing to forsake his love for duty, Henry Tilney from *Northanger Abbey*, a remarkably considerate and articulate man, John Knightley from *Emma*, Captain Frederick Wentworth from *Persuasion*, Edmund Bertram, the classic Austen leading man—all these extraordinary gentlemen transcended the constraints that weighed on women, paving the way for women to assume new roles in their lives. Jane Austen envisioned the nascent modern woman aspiring to independence and freedom, helped by the nascent modern man who embraced, respected, and loved this lady. This is the legacy we admire today."

Olivia paused and looked around the table at her companions. She smiled and said, "Forgive me. Don't let me lecture you."

"No," Kath interjected. "We adore you and hang on your every word."

"Well, most of my words are from Darcy's book."

"For me, having a chronicle before the novel's publication is a privilege," Rowan said. "Of course, they'll accuse you of bias," he continued, addressing Olivia.

"Let them do so," Kath responded, imagining a literary battle that would only intensify interest in the book.

"It's amazing how well you capture those three instances of progress in gentlemen's attitudes," Marianne commented.

Elizabeth smiled, remembering about other parts of the book. Initially, she'd had reservations about the candid depiction of their love. But it was just a story; even if their feelings were genuine, the words created a separate realm where only characters existed. He wrote about an Elizabeth and a Darcy living in the twenty-first century—a continuation of Jane Austen's characters, two centuries later. He blended humour and documentation, ultimately presenting a couple of lovers traversing time.

The narrative also focused on her father. A precious account of his final weeks, as seen through Rowan's eyes. And then, as he'd promised, Rowan revealed Darcy Egerton's secret and presented the truth to the readers, while his game with Thomas was an essential moment of the book. Necessary for his decision to end the mystery around Darcy Egerton.

"Now, we must discuss the promotional strategy and devise a plan. We need to make significant changes, considering the subject," Kath announced.

They all turned their attention to her, acknowledging her as the mastermind behind that critical endeavour.

"As you're aware, there are already rumours that Darcy Egerton will publish with Collister," Kath began.

"There have been rumours like this every year involving at least five publishers," Rowan interjected.

"Yes, but the odds are most in our favour this time. That hasn't happened in the past."

"My readers tend to be romantic. They might view my work as a cyclical journey that starts and ends at the same point. And then there's Thomas's death…"

"Or perhaps I've *helped* the bookmakers with their odds." Kath chuckled in her light-hearted manner.

They'd discussed using rumours to build anticipation, as experts closely followed the odds set by betting houses.

"Are we not undermining the element of surprise by encouraging rumours about his Collister publication?" Marianne questioned, concerned that prematurely spreading this news would diminish the impact of the official announcement.

"No, it's a diversion for the bigger surprise we're preparing, which is his public reveal," Kath explained. "And Rowan had another brilliant idea in this regard. You know how much he enjoyed Laura's book—"

"Gripping," he praised the book he'd genuinely enjoyed. "So, I'm more than willing to write a commendatory note for Laura's book—"

"What?" Marianne exclaimed, surprised. She wasn't entirely sure if this was a good move, but Kath had already accepted the idea.

"Alright, I don't want to interfere with your decisions," Marianne continued. "Still, if Laura's book comes out two weeks before his launch, everyone will assume we have the author."

"They might suspect it, but they won't be sure. And that's exactly what we want—to create a stir, anticipation, and speculation, but not certainty. Let them be preoccupied with this rather than beginning a debate about him coming forward, which must be a colossal surprise for everybody," Kath emphasised.

"I think if he writes that note, it will be certain that he's publishing with Collister," Olivia said. "Marianne might have a point."

"The news is already in the air. We'll announce the Fiction Prize two weeks before the Pemberley event on the fourteenth of July. That'll trigger a frenzy of media enquiries during those two weeks."

"But if we launch Darcy's book immediately after Laura's, won't it overshadow her novel?" Marianne queried.

"No, because Darcy's endorsement of her book is a substantial promotion, and she'll have two weeks to boost sales. Then, the play will add to the buzz. I watched it yesterday, and it's exceptional."

"Did the conceited aristocrat agree to all this?" Elizabeth spoke as if he wasn't present, causing him to jokingly toss a napkin in her direction.

"Did anyone inform him that I hold a black belt in karate and was trained by a Japanese master?" she retorted.

"Are you eager to endanger your star author, Miss Collister?" he responded, while Kath rolled her eyes in mock exasperation.

"May I remind you all that we have less than a month until the Pemberley event and a lot of work ahead of us?"

Despite the work ahead, everyone enjoyed the relaxed atmosphere in the earl's splendid residence, into which Elizabeth had already infused some artistic transformation. The once austere decor was now enlivened by art nouveau accents—Lalique crystal sculptures and two paintings by her favourite artist, Franz Marc—gifts from her father.

"Let's wrap this up," Kath decided. "The press conference is already set for the morning of the fourteenth of July at one o'clock in London, ostensibly focused on the launch of Pemberley's celebrations. Instead, we'll unveil Darcy Egerton's tenth book by revealing the cover. Simultaneously, the most prominent screens in the UK, Canada, Australia, and the USA will go live with the book trailer an hour later. Our four magazines will hit the shelves and the internet at noon, featuring the cover, a blurb, and Marianne's interview with him. Our Pemberley event begins at eight o'clock in the evening, when the book will be in the shops and the e-book available for download."

"Hold on a moment, please," Rowan interjected, intrigued. "What trailer are we talking about? Did we discuss a book trailer?"

"Alright," Kath replied, unruffled by his concerned tone. "Take a deep breath and watch this."

She turned on the TV, where she usually presented her plans. For exactly sixty seconds, they were treated to a captivating and glamorous presentation of the book. It started with a helicopter landing on Pemberley's lawn, just like in reality, with the actor playing Rowan standing in the middle of the muddy ground, meeting Elizabeth.

They exchanged glances in the room, torn between enjoying the trailer and being angry with Kath. But then Thomas appeared in the library, and Elizabeth's eyes welled with tears. The library was filled by Jane Austen's characters, surrounding Thomas like in a dance. The trailer showcased Pemberley and the Collister HQ in beautiful images, and it concluded with the two actors laughing on the wet lawn, with him holding her in his arms.

"Beautiful," Olivia sighed. "Absolutely beautiful!"

"Yes, it is," Marianne said.

But Kath was looking at Elizabeth and Rowan. They remained silent but exchanged a smile. She breathed a sigh of relief; they liked her trailer.

"It's unexpected, but yes, Marianne's got a point. It's beautiful," Rowan agreed, oddly invigorated by seeing his life and novel come to life on screen.

"He's right, Kath, but where on earth did you find such gorgeous actors? How did you pull it off? And how many people know about this?"

"Let me answer one question at a time. I didn't tell you because I wanted you to see the finished product, not just an idea. The actors are from a West End theatre— incredibly talented and dedicated."

"But you had to tell them—"

"No, nobody knows. I wrote the script. Since it was filmed at Pemberley, I told them it was for Pemberley's promotions. Then I had those recordings of Dad that were secretly made by your earl!"

"Secretly?" Rowan exclaimed, amused. "I gave you those recordings, and I assure you Thomas loved the idea of being filmed in Pemberley's library."

"It's certainly beautiful, and it captures the energy of the book," Elizabeth finally agreed.

"OK, thank you," Kath said. At that moment, everyone in the room saw the young woman who had finally found her calling and wholeheartedly embraced her new role.

"At seven forty-five, we start the show at Pemberley. Elizabeth's speech will be followed by a fifteen-minute presentation of our 150 years of achievements on four large screens as a fast-paced spectacle prepared by Henry. Then, Laura's play. Everything at Pemberley will be coordinated with the events in London and worldwide."

Kath grinned, proud that her plan had unfolded so seamlessly.

"Having Darcy Egerton return to Collister will be presented as my father's remarkable success. Darcy Egerton was won over by Dad, who finally redeemed his 'mistake'—"

"It wasn't a mistake, Kath," Marianne intervened, staunchly defending Thomas, as always. To her, Thomas remained a legendary figure, akin to King Arthur or Superman, on a quest for his own grail.

"I've still got two very delicate problems to solve," Elizabeth began. "First—how do we break the news to our colleagues?"

"That's also covered, thanks to Rowan's contribution," Kath assured her. "They'll arrive at Pemberley on Friday morning. Rowan can ensure complete digital isolation for the mansion. No one will be able to make calls or send emails outside. They'll have access solely to the Collister intranet. The department managers will be updated with information regarding Darcy Egerton's book."

Elizabeth looked at him, surprised. "Really? Can you do

that?"

"Yes, I can."

"But isn't that potentially illegal?"

"No, it's my property, my rules. It's a measure to ensure the secrecy of our intentions."

"And the second problem—" Elizabeth hesitated to name it as it deeply worried her.

"We still haven't figured out how to present Darcy Egerton," Kath said. "But you know what? This project has had a life of its own from the start, sometimes dictating its course to us. I'm confident that the final act—Darcy's public appearance—will come to us as an epiphany when the time is right."

"I will not step onto the stage," Rowan said, looking at them, almost pleading.

"No, that never crossed my mind," Elizabeth murmured, and Kath agreed.

"But I've got an idea," Kath announced, and they trusted her as she had led the whole campaign in a rigorous yet spectacular deployment to the final fireworks.

Chapter 45

Very early on the day of the celebration, they had a frugal breakfast at Pemberley with Yadira and her husband, Driss, who'd arrived in London a few days ago.

"I'm so happy to find Warminster looking so beautiful," Yadira said, tears in her eyes. "I never thought I'd see this place restored to its former glory."

"The gardens are stunning," Driss said with nostalgia. During their time in Warminster, he'd also tended to the gardens. Still, his efforts couldn't compare to what a team of gardeners had accomplished recently.

Yadira nodded. "They certainly are, but the house is absolutely breathtaking. Every room, every hallway…the staircase. It took me a whole day to see and admire everything!"

"Thank you, Yadira," Elizabeth said. "Pemberley was Dad's idea and his last wish."

"Your father, my dear, was a visionary. I'm grateful you convinced Rowan to live a normal life after many years."

"It's also because of him that I didn't lose my mind," Rowan said, his voice filled with deep emotion.

"Now, let's put the past behind us and look to the future. When's your wedding scheduled?" Yadira asked.

Rowan gave Elizabeth a reproachful look. "This lady

doesn't seem to want to marry me."

"Nonsense, you haven't asked her properly!" Yadira exclaimed.

"I wrote her a book! And I gave her a beautiful ring. What more can a man do?"

"Choose a wedding date?" Yadira suggested. She glanced at her phone and asked Elizabeth, "How about getting married at the end of August with the reception here at Pemberley? Say, the twenty-sixth of August?"

Elizabeth nodded, her expression as serene as that of a wise child. "Yes."

"And what about me?" Rowan interjected. "Doesn't anyone care about my opinion?"

"Quiet, Rowan!" Yadira retorted without even looking at him, a gesture she'd likely repeated countless times when he was still her little boy. Then she embraced Elizabeth, whispering, "Thank you."

"Now, Soames," Yadira continued. "How can we help you?"

It was useless to dissuade Yadira from being involved. Warminster was her home, and she viewed the Collister event as the most important work she had ever done. For her, it celebrated the moment when her *boy* had finally emerged from the shadows that had enveloped him for so long.

They followed Soames, the master of the festivities.

∞∞∞

Elizabeth and Rowan returned to their apartment to change. At breakfast, they had worn the djellabas Yadira had brought them, similar to the one Elizabeth had admired back in Tangiers.

"We don't have much time," Elizabeth murmured in Rowan's arms.

"We have enough time for me to say I love you."

"You've never said that before, not in reality or in the book."

"Have you?"

Elizabeth met his teasing gaze. "I love you," she declared, her eyes locked onto his. "And I want to marry you at the end of August."

"In that case, my love, let's kiss, and then you can head down and face the Collister management team's wrath."

∞∞∞

The limousines carrying the top management team arrived at seven o'clock. Elizabeth and Rowan welcomed a group of excited children, captivated by the journey, the luxurious limousines, and the prospect of those memorable days that marked the culmination of a year of hard work and their entire professional endeavour.

Laughter and jokes filled the air, even Elizabeth's voice failing to dampen their high spirits. She glanced at Rowan since they didn't have much time, but he offered a reassuring smile and a comforting caress on her back before stepping away.

"My dears, I assure you that you'll have time to play, but not now. We're on a tight schedule. The press conference begins in less than six hours."

Her concerned tone contrasted with their buoyant mood. They followed her to the same room where they had brainstormed, now transformed to resemble a parlour from the 1800s, albeit with a modern screen from 2017.

"Could you all please be quiet for a moment?" Elizabeth asked. "I have something rather dramatic to confess." She paused to gauge their reactions, and their previously jubilant expressions turned serious in response to her words.

"Kath advised me to tell you first that you've all been

fired. So the relief of knowing you're not fired will precede the actual news…but I'm gentler than she is. So, Henry, if you would."

On the screen, the emblem of the Pemberley event materialised—a fusion of the silhouette of Louis Collister, the founder of the publishing house, and the shadow of Jane Austen's portrait by her sister Cassandra.

Waiters entered, as they had months ago, but they bore only champagne glasses this time.

"We haven't eaten, boss," some protested.

"Drink up, ask for refills. Trust me, you'll need it, and it's better to be a bit tipsy!" she instructed, pointing their attention to the screen coming to life.

Everyone turned towards the screen, glasses in hand. Thomas was shown in his office, the familiar movement from their campaign, pacing in front of the bookshelves. He halted, uncorking a bottle of Taittinger, his preferred champagne, which they also had. With a glass in hand, he appeared poised to toast with everyone in the room.

Then he spoke. "My dear colleagues, despite your constant jests and mockery, the tenth Darcy Egerton book is now published by us, Collister Publishing! Let's rejoice and celebrate, for this is our triumph."

And the *Darcy's Diary* cover appeared on the screen.

Several glasses dropped onto the parquet floor, and a profound silence followed. No one could utter a word, stunned beyond belief, almost pained by the astonishment they felt.

"Impossible!" someone finally exclaimed, echoing the collective sentiment. At Collister, Darcy Egerton had been a nightmare turned obsession. Now, they were told it was a happy dream come true. Their gaze shifted from the screen to Elizabeth, their disbelief evident. Despite the cover displayed before them, they struggled to accept that the news was confirmed, delivered by their former boss, who had passed away nearly a year prior.

"Let's not ruin the floor," Elizabeth quipped as the waiters hurriedly cleared the broken glass.

"We don't have time for an extensive explanation before the press conference each of you have to prepare for. You're the only ones in your department who know this news, so devise a plan amongst yourselves. After twelve o'clock, you'll brief your respective departments. You won't be able to send external emails, and your phones won't work until the press conference begins. This is part of the contract with Darcy Egerton. I trust you to manage the workload quickly and be prepared."

Elizabeth scanned the faces of her team. Andrew appeared shocked and slightly affronted, while others seemed to oscillate between surprise and euphoria that was otherwise hard to discern. Darcy Egerton was their culmination, and ending their project this way was incredible.

"Incredible," murmurs rippled through the room, and they came forward to congratulate Elizabeth. Grabbing more glasses, they raised them in a toast.

"You'll have to make do with sandwiches." Elizabeth smiled and let out a relieved sigh. Suddenly, applause erupted throughout the room. They saw Thomas's confident smile on the screen, content that his announcement had the desired impact.

"It's monumental!" Andrew finally declared, his happiness evident as he enveloped Elizabeth in a heartfelt hug. Then, turning to his colleagues, he exclaimed, "Let's get to work!"

"A room's been set up for those who've got work to do. I'll stay here with those participating in the press conference. You'll find folders with all the necessary information," Elizabeth said.

She paused, her gaze returning to her father's image on the screen. "Dad did it, after all!" Tears streamed down her face, shared by everyone in the room, their emotions intertwining.

"I'm sorry for keeping you in the dark, but, as you can imagine, it was because of the contract we signed with Darcy Egerton."

"So he exists!" someone said.

"Yes, and Dad found him," Elizabeth said.

$$\infty\infty\infty$$

"You're all unharmed," Kath joked on the screen. She had been keeping track of the events at Pemberley from London, with Anna, who was also smiling.

"Almost. There was so much tension in the room that I felt sick for a moment," Elizabeth said.

"It's strange how big achievements can be hard to process and celebrate," Kath remarked. She was right. Elizabeth felt the same way. After years of wanting Darcy Egerton to become a reality, the goal seemed to fade and become almost unreal.

Still in shock, they didn't ask questions. But surely, her colleagues had many.

Elizabeth found Rowan in the library. He'd witnessed the events in the parlour and was ready to comfort her. "I've known about everything for six months now, but it only feels completely real now," she whispered.

"Do you think Henry knew from the beginning about the novel?" Rowan asked.

"I'm not sure. I think Dad recorded many messages for all sorts of situations."

"I don't think he recorded that many. He was confident that I'd publish with Collister even before I'd made up my mind. Then, from beyond the grave, he sent me his 'trojan horse'."

Elizabeth laughed. "I've never been called that before."

"Well, maybe it wasn't exactly a horse, but when Miss

Collister undressed in my bedroom, the game was over."

"Let me remind you that it was you who made a move on me."

"I remember that you were just as bold. That afternoon was the best of my life."

"Mine too," Elizabeth said.

"No, there'll be many best things in my life…that was just the beginning."

∞∞∞

The press conference was organised to unfold similarly to the announcement at Pemberley. While the journalists accepted glasses of Taittinger champagne more cautiously, everyone eventually took one.

Then Thomas Collister made the same announcement that silenced the room. However, unlike at Pemberley, the silence lasted only a moment. The eruption of exclamations was quickly followed by a barrage of questions.

Finally, Kath and Anna restored order, allowing Elizabeth to speak from Pemberley.

"The book will be in shops and online at eight o'clock. This will also mark the start of our celebration here at Pemberley."

"The shops close at five," Elizabeth said.

"Not that night," Kath answered, proving she thought at every aspect. The shops that matter will be open."

"Will you have copies of the book at Pemberley?" someone enquired.

"Of course. They'll be available for all our guests and members of the press," Elizabeth answered.

She stepped back, letting others field the questions. She found Olivia and her uncle waiting for her in the library. They embraced in silence for a long time, overwhelmed by the events of the day and saddened by Thomas's absence.

"We'll take care of your mother and the countess when they arrive. You don't need to worry about them," Arthur assured her. She looked at them with gratitude. From that moment on, she had a million things to attend to.

"Thank you. Clarice is already with Rowan, waiting for me."

Three further people at Collister knew about Darcy Egerton. Henry had to be brought into the secret to prepare the presentations, although he likely already suspected or knew.

"What did you promise him?" Rowan had asked, intrigued by the young man they had seen often with Kath over the past weeks.

"Nothing. It was Kath."

"What?" he questioned, curious.

"She agreed to marry him."

Elizabeth smiled, watching Rowan nearly choke on his coffee.

"What?" he exclaimed. "You Collister girls are ready to sell yourselves for the company." He laughed, coughing, and speaking at the same time.

"I didn't exactly sell myself," Elizabeth replied.

"No, but you were prepared to," he teased.

"Getting involved with any Darcy Egerton for the sake of a novel...yes, absolutely," she quipped, and he reached for her.

"But is she actually going to marry the poor man?" he asked, pulling her into his arms.

"Yes, of course. He's not a fool. Besides, they've been in love since they were seven."

Then there was Clarice, who'd walked into Elizabeth's office about six weeks before the event and hesitantly said, "Elizabeth, I know about...Rowan...Darcy."

Elizabeth wasn't surprised. She nodded and simply said, "Thank you."

Her trust in Clarice was unshakeable for good reason, yet she said nothing to Rowan or the others for a time. Only Kath knew and was pleased, as Clarice could be crucial in the final days leading up to the events.

"I think I owe you a blank cheque at—" Elizabeth laughed.

"Hermès," Clarice finished for her in the same jesting tone.

Elizabeth and Kath wouldn't have been able to accomplish the work of the past few weeks without Clarice's help.

And the last to find out had been Anna Wilson.

Elizabeth had seen right—Anna Wilson was invaluable, a rare lady who had proven her worth and earned their trust. Kath had confided in Anna two weeks earlier, considering it both a reward for her exceptional work over the past months and a valuable aid in the challenging days to come.

∞∞∞

Finally, a day before the event, they'd settled on how to reveal Darcy Egerton.

During the last 'secret' meeting in the Pemberley library, Kath presented her plan to everyone aware of Darcy Egerton's identity, including Soames, who was prepared to pop open the champagne.

Kath spoke with her usual emotion when it concerned her father. "Dad urged me to change my life. I was so petrified by pain and anger that I only recently remembered something else he told me. When I realised that all of you had received an insight about the project, I was disconcerted to be the only one to have received a scolding instead of a message. But no! Dad believed in me."

They listened with emotion and nostalgia. Thomas's legacy had been essential to plan and undertake this vast project. With his waning strength, he'd outlined the plan to his closest collaborators, family, and friends in a few cryptic phrases.

"Dad told me that *essential secrets aren't meant to be fully revealed*. It was only in the last few days I understood—that was the approach to take with Darcy Egerton's unveiling. Suddenly, his idea became so clear, as if he had spoken to me at length—as if Thomas Collister were here with us."

"He is with us in so many ways," Olivia remarked, looking at Rowan and Elizabeth.

Rowan nodded. "He told me to continue with *my* plans with his daughter—"

"He told me to read all the documents he left," Elizabeth said. "And I didn't follow his advice."

"He provided each of us with a key idea to follow, outlining a plan that will culminate tomorrow," Olivia continued.

"What have you decided?" Marianne asked Kath, confident they would all support her plan, which Thomas had directly inspired.

Kath turned to Darcy and spoke only to him. "The incredible secret you kept for a decade must be revealed like a curtain drawn back just a bit. Tomorrow, your book will be the only direct revealing of Darcy Egerton's identity. We won't say a single word about you or present you as our trophy. This will be the ultimate game between Darcy Egerton and each of his readers, who will discover you as a personal prize by reading your novel."

They stood silently for a long while, Kath's words carrying immense weight. As she'd anticipated, they all agreed, waiting for Darcy to respond.

"It makes sense," Darcy said, and they all could see the relief on his face. "Thank you, Kath! Thank you, Marianne, for your excellent work. I don't remember ever liking this editing work so profoundly. And then thank you, Olivia, for giving me this fabulous idea."

"Thomas is to blame for that too—"

"He wanted to be glorified," Elizabeth jested with tears in her eyes.

"And he was," Arthur said.

They drank their champagne in silence, imagining Thomas as they knew him—intelligent, sarcastic, generous, creative.

"This end doesn't mean you're exempt from all the duties of a writer." Elizabeth finally spoke, and everybody laughed. "So, little sister, enlighten the man on what he needs to do."

"Lady Warminster, Mum, and Rowan will greet the VIPs and sit in the front row next to their Royal Highnesses, the Cambridges and the Duke and Duchess of Lancashire. Also, Marianne and Olivia will be there to help them. No one will be able to approach the front row because of the security.

"The novel will be in the library by the time our celebration ends at Pemberley, and obviously, in a short time, the press will figure out who Rowan is.

"But by that time, it'll be too late for any ambush, as the front row will be empty. Rowan will leave with his VIP guests and will have to face only them. You will have to announce your identity to them."

"Marianne and Olivia will do that," Rowan said.

"Yes, that's what I thought too. There'll be no commotion, perhaps a bit of polite surprise. But from tomorrow onwards, I hope you've hired enough bodyguards. And from Monday on, you'll begin your new life as a regular Collister writer," she quipped, looking at Rowan.

Then they'd raised their glasses and talked long into the night, remembering each moment of that year and, most importantly, celebrating Thomas, who had succeeded in all his plans and schemes.

"And no one got arrested. Quite the success!" Elizabeth

whispered to Olivia and Marianne, prompting laughter from them.

Chapter 46

"This life will end in an hour," Rowan whispered, gazing out from a balcony at the people assembling in front of the scene set in Pemberley's gardens.

Elizabeth embraced him, deeply touched by his inner turmoil. He'd had six months to prepare for this moment, but overcoming years of secrecy was difficult.

"It wasn't an exceptionally joyous life, but it was very—" he started.

"Peaceful," Kath finished his sentence as she joined them on the balcony.

"Yes, peaceful. I'm not sure I'll behave properly in a crowd who know who I am."

"They won't immediately understand that the earl is Darcy Egerton, and you'll be away from the bustling crowd when that happens," Kath reassured him.

"They'll pursue me, unsatisfied with our decision," Rowan replied, his voice suddenly tinged with sadness.

"On Monday, dear future brother-in-law!" Kath laughed.

"It's unjust to be sad tonight," Elizabeth declared, wanting to dispel the sorrow. "We're all happy."

"I'm not sad," he said. "I'm uncertain in this new life. In a way, Darcy Egerton never truly existed."

"It's time for him to come into existence, my love," Elizabeth said firmly. "Let him embrace the role he holds in your life. He's neither a dream nor a myth. He's you." She looked down at the crowd, not with fear but with anticipation.

He spotted Olivia and Marianne waving; memories of the intense months spent working on his tenth book flooded his mind. This book had a different genesis compared to his previous nine. He remembered Elizabeth's smiles and tears as she read the novel, a connection he'd never felt before—the incredible bond with his readers. Then Thomas came to mind, the one who'd searched for him obsessively for years. When he eventually found Darcy Egerton, he allowed Elizabeth to uncover the truth—not for Collister's glory but to find love.

"You called me Darcy the first time we met. I was alarmed, thinking you knew who I was—"

"I called you Darcy as in Elizabeth Bennet's beloved."

"I know, but from then on, I realised I was Darcy Egerton as much as I was Rowan Stafford. The first crack in the ice of my personal Antarctica. I'm more scared than sad. I mostly fear the press intruding into our…our life."

"They'll hound you for a while, but what truly matters are your readers," Kath said. "And your readers will love Darcy Egerton, even more so when they learn the whole story. Being completely sincere is an incredibly fair way to approach this and end the ten years of secrecy."

"And I love all of you." Elizabeth smiled at him. "Rowan, whom I met covered in mud, and the Earl of Warminster, who might make me a countess—"

"Does it matter?"

"Of course it does. They'll have to address me as Lady Something and your ladyship. And you, Darcy Egerton, have substantial payments from Collister awaiting you to buy extravagant jewellery for your future wife."

Finally, a smile graced his face.

"But…" Elizabeth began and hesitated.

"But?" he asked, curious and in better spirits in the presence of her beauty and love.

"But truthfully, you are my man. I don't care what your name is, as long as I see this love in your eyes every day—"

"And night," he finished, bursting into laughter at last.

"You are horrible!" Kath smiled as she left them.

∞∞∞

An hour and a half later, on the stage, Elizabeth gazed at the audience and grinned. The project presentation and the play had been a remarkable success, punctuated by applause and laughter, putting everyone in a buoyant mood.

When the central screen illuminated, Elizabeth received the message that the book was in the library. Then Thomas Collister appeared, and silence enveloped the audience. He nodded slightly and his image froze, displaying the familiar smile Elizabeth knew so well—love and just enough sarcasm to avoid taking life for granted.

And Elizabeth began her speech.

"Your Royal Highnesses, Your Graces, esteemed guests, readers, colleagues, and members of the press, earlier today we announced that Collister has the honour of publishing Darcy Egerton's tenth novel. The volume has been on shelves for a few minutes now, and I'm certain readers worldwide have it in their hands or on their screens. It's now time to receive your own copy."

As she spoke, students dressed as Jane Austen's characters and led by Olivia appeared, pushing trolleys with books for the audience. At the same time, Kath, Clarice, and Anna distributed books to the first row, with Kath later joining Elizabeth on stage.

"This was how Dad intended to conclude this celebration, and we're proud that everything unfolded according to his vision," Kath declared. She glanced at her father, seeking approval in his eyes.

"Not too long ago," Elizabeth continued, "I was called upon to reveal something I hold secretly dear, among the rights and liberties a woman possesses in this, the 21st century."

She paused, her gaze fixed on the earl in the front row, as excited as she was.

"It is *my* right to love. Finally, men and women are equal in the realm of love.

"While there's no doubt that we enjoy fundamental rights and freedoms in our time, the freedom to love is personal to me. Not a political matter like voting, nor a familial matter like working eight hours for a wage. It's pure pleasure and self-determination. Dear Jane Austen, we— the Elizabeths, Emmas, Elinors, Mariannes, Fannys, and Catherines of this world—we are finally free to love and choose what we do with our bodies without state, man, church, or society interference. For that, we are grateful."

Applause erupted after her words, temporarily drowned out by commotion from the journalists' section.

As anticipated, the press had discovered Darcy Egerton's identity from those who'd already purchased the book.

"It's beginning," Kath noted, indicating a man and a woman making their way towards the stage.

She gestured for them to approach. "Lucas Jackson from The Sunday Times and Annabel Wild from the BBC," she whispered to her sister, recognising the man from the Oxford press conference as the first candidate for Darcy Egerton.

"Ms Collister, it seems we now not only have the book but also the identity of Darcy Egerton."

A collective gasp spread throughout the audience, everyone reacting to that incredible news.

Kath had foreseen this scenario when planning the

evening. In the stir created by that colossal news, Rowan had invited all his VIP guests to enter Pemberley, and in that commotion, nobody had seen them walking towards the house; all attention had concentrated on Elizabeth.

Elizabeth waited patiently for the buzz to subside. The dedication page and the second cover appeared on the screen, featuring a beautiful image of Warminster.

Only then did she speak. "Indeed, Darcy Egerton has chosen to step forward with this book. It's our privilege not only to present Darcy Egerton's tenth novel but also to introduce him to his readers. But in his habitual style, he's decided to make a full confession," she said, and both sisters laughed.

"Is what we learned from the book true?" Annabel Wild nearly shouted.

"Ms Wild, this isn't a press conference," Kath calmly stated, quieting the audience. All eyes were fixed on Elizabeth and Kath, eager to hear their words.

"Please be seated," Kath said in the same decisive yet friendly tone, as the *Darcy's Diary* trailer played on the screen.

When it concluded, it was Elizabeth's turn to speak. She turned towards the Warminster terrace, where Rowan and their mothers had led the VIP guests. "Your Royal Highnesses, Your Graces, esteemed guests, Darcy Egerton remained a deep enigma for a decade. My father, Thomas Collister, who envisioned this celebration in incredible detail, told us just before leaving us that true secrets aren't meant to be entirely exposed. He urged us to reveal Darcy Egerton's identity in a different way. There's only one way to truly know writers—by reading their books. The novel you hold tells the entire story, reveals all secrets, and finally introduces Darcy Egerton to you. Once you've experienced his story, Darcy Egerton will embark on his journey in the world. He'll initiate his digital presence on Facebook, Instagram, and Twitter in exactly twelve hours, ready to meet you, his readers, for the first time."

An odd yet amusing occurrence transpired as everyone opened the book while Thomas Collister smiled from the screen. Elizabeth was almost sure that when he'd filmed that video nearly a year ago, he already knew what would transpire at Pemberley that night.

"Who's Darcy Egerton?" voices resonated from the audience, though everyone already knew who he was.

At that moment, the screens illuminated again, displaying a photo taken in Pemberley's library, depicting Thomas and Rowan standing together.

"After a decade of silence and concealed existence, we bring you Darcy Egerton," Kath announced, gesturing towards the screen, but as planned, still not saying who he was, as they let the readers discover that for themselves.

At that instant, all the lights dimmed, and magnificent fireworks lit up the sky. Simultaneously, Darcy Egerton said from the screens, "I now declare the Jane Austen ball at Pemberley open!"

[1] Darcy Egerton is a combination of Fitzwilliam *Darcy*, the main character of Jane Austen's novel *Pride and Prejudice* and Thomas *Egerton* who published *Sense and Sensibility*, which, like all of Austen's novels except *Pride and Prejudice*, was published 'on commission'—that is, at the author's own financial risk.

[2] The first volume of the current series, *E&D 1900*, is centred around the *Austen Integral,* published by Oxford University Press in 1917. Darcy Lancashire and Elizabeth Austen meet when they are invited to write together a presentation on the *Austen Integral*. Then, in 1922, the duchess publishes her famous book, *Elizabeth's Diary, with Collister,* which narrates her love story with the future duke. *Elizabeth's Diary* is, in fact, the first volume of this series, as they contain the same account.

[3] *Elizabeth's Diary* contains the story that the reader can find in the first volume of this series, *E&D 1900*.

[4] A reference to the characters and the plot of *Elizabeth & Darcy 1900*, the first volume of the current series.

[5] Fitzwilliam Darcy's annoying aunt in *Pride and Prejudice*.

[6] Sheehan, Colleen A. (25 November 2021). "https://www.wsj.com/articles/jane-austen-tom-lefroy-kipling-emma-persuasion-love-decoding-pride-prejudice-11637794443". Wall Street Journal. ISSN 0099-9660. Retrieved 4 December 2021.

[7] https://en.wikipedia.org/wiki/Mansfield_Park

[8] http://thesecretunderstandingofthehearts.blogspot.com/2011/05/sebastian-faulks-on-mr-darcy.html

Made in the USA
Thornton, CO
03/01/24 16:47:47

6ea83189-500d-42c6-b5b4-70d3f48d5339R01